D0937650

ROYALLY WILD

A Crazy Royal Love Romantic Comedy, Book 2

MELANIE SUMMERS

Copyright © 2020 Gretz Corp.

All rights reserved.

Published by Gretz Corp.

First edition

EBOOK ISBN: 978-1-988891-31-6

Paperback ISBN: 978-1-988891-32-3

No part of this book may be used or reproduced in any manner whatsoever without the prior written permission of the publisher, except in the case of brief quotations embodied in reviews.

This is a work of fiction. Names, characters, businesses, places, events, and incidents are either the products of the author's imagination or used in a fictitious manner. Any resemblance to actual persons, living or dead, or actual events is purely coincidental.

Cover by Victoria Cooper.

Edited by Kristi Yanta, Melissa Martin, and Brooke Sperfslage of Show Me Edits.

Proofread by Nevia Brudnicki, Laura Albert, Audrey Borst, Karen Boehle-Johnson, and Kellie Porth-Bagne.

 Created with Vellum

Praise for Melanie Summers

A fun, often humorous, escapist tale that will have readers blushing, laughing and rooting for its characters. ~ *Kirkus Reviews*

…Perfect for someone that needs a break from this world and wants to delve into a modern-day fairy tale that will keep them laughing and rooting for the main characters throughout the story. ~ *ChickLit Café*

I have to HIGHLY HIGHLY HIGHLY RECOMMEND *The Royal Treatment* to EVERYONE!
~ *Jennifer, The Power of Three Readers*

Very rarely does a book make me literally hold my breath or has me feeling that actual ache in my heart for a character, but I did both." ~ *Three Chicks Review for Net galley*

Also Available

ROMANTIC COMEDIES by Melanie Summers
The Crown Jewels Series

The Royal Treatment

The Royal Wedding

The Royal Delivery

Paradise Bay Series

The Honeymooner

Whisked Away

The Suite Life

Resting Beach Face (Coming Soon)

Crazy Royal Love Series

Royally Crushed

Royally Tied (Coming Soon)

WOMEN'S FICTION by Melanie Summers

The After Wife

The Deep End (Coming Soon)

Dedication

For My Mom on Her 70th Birthday…

To the lady who knows me better than anyone, who loves me no matter what, who laughs with me, cries with me, and listens to me, who comes over to our house to try to make order out of the chaos that is our life, who quietly tackles the mountain of laundry and knows where to find everything when the rest of us have no freaking clue. I am so incredibly lucky I got you for a mom.

Thank you.

With all my love,
Melanie

A Letter From The Author

Dear Lovely Reader,

Writing this book has been interesting, to say the least. In a nutshell, the last several months have included the big pandemic, which, in our case has led to having our three kiddos at home 24-7 for the better part of a year (with about another year to go), one dog who had to have her *only* eye removed (my sweet Lucy, who is doing beautifully with the whole thing, by the way), and a leaky roof which led to an entire house renovation (and me thinking I could serve as the general contractor—insert maniacal laughter here).

So, even though the pressure of a looming publishing deadline has been, at moments, a teensy bit more than I can handle, joining my dear friends in Avonia is never a chore. This book has been a welcome escape for me, and my sincerest wish is that it will be for you as well. May their crazy antics make you chuckle, smile, and fall a little bit in love...

All the very best in life to you and yours,
Melanie

I'm Shagging on a Jet Plane... Don't Know When I'll be Shagged Again...

Will Banks

On Royal One Private Jet Somewhere over the Atlantic

"ARE YOU NERVOUS?" Arabella, my beautiful girlfriend, props herself up on one elbow and rests her other hand on my bare chest.

"About what?" I ask, lifting my head off the pillow and giving her a quick peck on the lips.

We're snuggled into the massive bed on her family's private jet for our overnight flight from my home on Santa Valentina Island in the Caribbean to her home—the kingdom of Avonia (a tiny island just north of Belgium and slightly to the east of England). Her father is the king which makes her a princess (obviously), but trust me, she's not the dainty, stuffy kind. She's more of the elegant, well-spoken, compassionate, kick-arse-when-needed type of princess.

We fell in love while filming a nature docu-series/survival show a few months back and have been inseparable ever since. Just to give you an example of exactly what a renegade she is—she had to sneak out of the palace *in the boot of a car* so she could escape to Zamunda for the show because there was no way her family would have let her go. See? Daring *and* determined. And did I mention how beautiful she is? Oh, I think I did.

She's literally the best person I know. Just staring at her right now fills my entire being with a sense of happiness and contentment I've never experienced in all my thirty years. She's it for me. She's my one and only. (Which is a little insane because if you had asked me six months ago if I'd ever fall in love, I would have said 'not likely.' And if you'd asked me if I'd ever want to build a life with a princess, I would have laughed out loud.)

Anyway, we'll be spending the next two months in Avonia promoting our upcoming television show. *Our* show. That's odd to say. The whole 'we' thing is totally new for me. It's something I never thought I'd have, and I'm shocked at how quickly I've grown accustomed to it. *We* just spent a few shag-o-delic weeks together sailing around the South Pacific. *We* prefer sunrises to sunsets. *We're* planning on spending the rest of our lives together.

Well, I'm pretty sure we are, anyway. I haven't asked her yet, but that's only because we've been together twenty-four seven, which hasn't exactly left me any time for ring shopping and planning the perfect proposal. One simply does not ask for a princess's hand in marriage without finding the most romantic of settings possible and a spectacular ring—like Hope Diamond-spectacular.

The woman bought me a yacht, for God's sake. And that was only a 'we should give this relationship a go' gift. So, there's a wee bit of pressure on the proposal front, especially for someone without a Hope Diamond budget.

She's giving me that skeptical look she's mastered, with one of her perfectly shaped eyebrows raised while she waits for me to figure out why I should, in fact, be nervous right now. "Oh, I don't know," she says. "Maybe because in exactly six days, the show is going to air and it could be a giant flop, thus ending your career."

Shrugging, I say, "It won't." *I hope.*

Narrowing her eyes, Arabella says, "How about facing the Avonian media as the utterly unsuitable boyfriend of the king's only daughter?"

"The press loves me, and they love you, which means they're going to love us together almost as much as I do." I reach up and tuck a lock of her blonde hair behind her ear. "And if they don't, I really couldn't care less."

She gives me a conciliatory nod. "How about meeting my disapproving family for the first time? Surely that must make you feel the slightest bit squeamish."

My stomach flips, but I ignore it. "Are you kidding? Give me ten minutes with them, and they'll be eating out of the palm of my hand. Figuratively speaking, of course. I wouldn't want people eating off my palms. That would be a little gross, really."

"Not to mention slightly demeaning for them."

"Exactly."

Arabella pauses for a second and tilts her head. "But you're really not *at all* worried about meeting my father—a well-known nasty monarch—or my brother, who could ruin you with one phone call? I can count on one hand the number of people he actually likes in this world."

"I thought your brother was a huge fan of mine."

"That was *before* you started shagging his little sister. Now, not so much, I'm afraid."

Oh, bollocks. That's not good. "He'll get over it when he sees how happy I make you."

I let my lips hover over hers for a second, then give her a slow kiss in hopes of putting an end to her line of questioning, because truth be told, some of this bravado is indeed on the false side. I'm actually more nervous than I've ever been, but since part of my charm is this whole confident, adventurous, nothing-bothers-me thing I've got going, I can't exactly tell her that, now can I?

I've made my career as a professional adventurer/nature show host, meaning I managed to convince the Avonian Broadcast Network (ABN) to pay me to do all the insane stunt stuff I love in the most remote places on the planet. And Arabella is a princess who has had one of the most sheltered, dull upbringings of all time. But you know what they say about opposites attracting each other...

"You're always so confident. It must be so nice to be you," she says, trailing her finger down my abs.

I give her a naughty grin. "At the moment, it is very nice to be me."

Her smile widens, then she gives me a thoughtful look. "No, but seriously, nothing ever rattles you. How do you do it?"

I pretend. "It's simple, really. I only do what I like, and since worrying is absolutely no fun, I don't do it." I lean over and kiss her again, trying to loosen the knot in my stomach. The truth is, there's about a ninety-percent chance her family is going to hate me on spec, and about a two-hundred-percent chance they'll hate me when they find out Arabella wants to go Megxit so we can have a life of adventure.

"I wish I could do that. *Everything* worries me."

"Hmm, I think I can help you with that," I say. "Did I ever tell you I have a superpower?"

"Other than that thing you do with your tongue?" she says, her smile returning.

"I'm pleased you enjoy that so much. Very gratifying. And yes, I have one other superpower. You tell me what you're worried about and I'll make you forget all about whatever it is."

"You're just going to do that thing with your tongue, aren't you?"

"Maybe. But you have to admit, it'll work for a few minutes anyway." I brush my lips against hers. "But in all seriousness, tell me what's on your mind."

Her eyebrows knit together, and I know whatever it is must be big. "I'm scared the show might come between us."

She means because I used to host a one-man show with me as the star, and now I'm sharing the limelight. In fact, they've renamed it *Princess in the Wild* from its former title *The Wild World* which frankly did sting at first, but now that I'm a man in love, I *want* to put her out front and centre so everyone will know how incredible she really is. I'm about to reassure her I'm fine, but she continues talking so, like the good boyfriend I am, I zip it.

"I know you're fine with the new title and all, but I can't help worrying about how they'll spin things we said and take them out of context to make us sound bad," she says. "I mean, two people getting along nicely isn't exactly compelling television."

"Well, I'm sure there'll be a bit of that. Especially the first couple of days out in the jungle."

"And that giant fight near the end..."

"That too," I say. "But none of it really matters, does it? You and I know what we've got together, and we know exactly how we got here. Nothing they do or say can get in between us. Not if we stick together."

"Which we will," she says firmly.

"Of course we will." I cup her cheek with one hand. "This is *us*, Belle. You and me. Think of everything we've been through together in such a short time. When things went horribly wrong out there in the jungle, we took care of each other. And that was life and death. This is just..." I shrug. "... a 2D-rendering of what we've already lived through."

She nods. "You're right. We know the truth of what happened, even if they try to make it out to be something it wasn't."

"Exactly. It's five one-hour episodes—a tiny fraction of our actual time together. I'm actually looking forward to reliving it all with you."

She smiles. "I'm a bit excited to see me being a total badass."

"Me too. Tell you what, let's watch every episode together, just you and me. In bed."

Wincing, she says, "I already told my family we'd watch the premiere together. You're invited too, of course."

My gut flips at the thought. "Oh, well, brilliant. Just as good. Give them a chance to observe me in my element."

"That's what I was thinking. You can impress them straight out of the gate." Arabella smiles, then, after a second, bites her lip. "It'll be all right, won't it?"

"Yes, it will. We've already *more than* proved our love to each other. And now we can prove it to the world."

Nodding, she says, "Yes. Five episodes, then onto bigger and better things."

"Speaking of which..." I say, leaning in and letting my lips brush along the nape of her neck.

Arabella makes a little moaning sound, indicating that round three is about to begin. She murmurs, "We should be sleeping but we also need to make the most of the time we have left."

"You say that as if these are our final moments together forever."

"Well, not *forever*, obviously. But things are about to get considerably more difficult." Kiss. "I'm going to miss having you in my bed every night." Kiss. "Although I imagine I'll get a lot more sleep." She nips at my bottom lip.

I freeze in place. "What do you mean you won't have me in your bed every night?"

"Well, we're not married, so it's not like you can stay over at the palace or I can stay with you. Not without causing a scandal."

It's not? "Would it really be such a scandal? I mean, you're almost thirty, for God's sake."

"Not for another five months, thank you very much," she says in a warning tone.

"Sorry. I didn't mean to imply you're old," I say, then narrow my eyes. "When is your birthday, anyway?"

"March third." Her expression screams, 'we barely know each other.'

"We do so." Lifting myself up, I flip us, so I'm now on top of her.

"What?"

"We do so know each other. *Very* well."

Chuckling, Arabella says, "You *did* know what I was thinking just now, didn't you?"

"Yes, so stop worrying. We'll be fine." I kiss her again, but the thought of us being apart for the next several weeks has me pausing. "You know, sex before marriage is widely regarded as acceptable these days."

"Premarital sex is acceptable for everyone *other* than the royal family, I'm afraid."

Pulling back, I give her a confused look.

"The general consensus among the taxpayers is that if they're paying for our lives—which they aren't—we must conduct ourselves in a manner befitting the ultimate role models for society. I'm quoting the senior advisors there."

"Doesn't that seem rather silly?"

"Oh, yes, it's absolutely ridiculous and leads to all sorts of pretending." She lifts her head and kisses me hard on the mouth. "But with great privilege comes... a great deal of hypocrisy."

I roll off of her and lay back, my mind racing to figure out where I'm going to stay when we land. Like an idiot, I assumed we would stay together, obviously at her family's massive palace where there are probably a hundred empty bedrooms.

She turns on her side, her face filled with concern. "I'm sorry, I thought you knew."

"I suppose I should have. I guess I didn't think it through."

"Now I've totally killed the mood when my intention was to drink in every last drop of our alone time together."

"No, it's totally fine." I shake my head and smile. "Obviously, I can't stay with you, but it's all good. It'll be fun, actually. We'll have to sneak around. It'll add a sense of danger to the whole thing that an all-access pass doesn't have."

Arabella grins at me and raises and lowers her eyebrows. "Oh, I like the sound of that."

I go straight for her earlobe and do that thing that makes her make that noise.

Ah, there it is—victory.

And now she's kissing me again in that way that tells me she's had enough chitchat. And I couldn't agree more.

Overbearing Older Brothers, Accomplished Older Women, and Princesses Acting Like Ostriches...

Arabella

"WELL, THAT WAS RUDE," I say as I slide across the backseat of the limo. My older brother Arthur, the heir apparent who *apparently* thinks he can run my life, sent his driver into the airport to get me and told him to refuse to give poor Will a ride under the pretence of me needing to be back at the palace immediately on urgent family business. "You couldn't even be bothered to get out of the car and say hello to Will."

Arthur leans forward and takes a bottle of water out of the fridge. He offers it to me, but I shake it off, even though I am quite parched. Shrugging, he opens it for himself and has a long swig before he answers. "Sorry about that, but I'm in a bit of a hurry, what with trying to help run an entire kingdom whilst being a hands-on dad to my children and a loving husband."

"Which is why you shouldn't have bothered coming to get me," I say, opening the fridge and getting my own water.

"Knew you were thirsty."

Rolling my eyes, I say, "What's going on?"

"By any chance, did you and Adventure Boy happen to see the ads for your little show?"

"Don't call him that, and no, we didn't," I say, feeling my heart speed up. A tiny smile flits across my lips. "We were rather busy."

"Gross." He picks up his tablet and hands it to me. "You'll want to see this because as soon as we arrive at home, you've got some explaining to do."

My gut tightens as I press play. Delicate classical music starts up, paired with footage of me in a blue evening gown walking into a hotel. I almost smile when I realize that was the night I met Will. The scene cuts, and I'm now dressed in a flowy light pink dress at a garden party, nibbling on a scone. The music stops, and a man's voice says, "This dainty, beautiful princess has no idea what's in store for her. She's about to spend ten days out here."

Footage of the jungle flashes on the screen at the same time as African drums begin to beat. "...with Will Banks, Avonia's answer to Bear Grylls. They'll have only each other and their wits to get them out alive."

The drums pick up pace while a montage of moments from our time in the jungle plays out. "Starting Thursday, September seventeenth, watch as Princess Arabella transforms from this..." An image of me in the blue gown appears again. "To this." And now the shot of me covered in mud, dragging Will behind me and shoving Dylan in the face plays out.

The drums die down and an eerie violin solo begins. "But even more shocking than her transformation, are the secrets she spills. Lust. Divided loyalties. Betrayal. Survival. One thing is certain, lives will be forever changed. Tune in Thursday at 8 p.m. to ABN's *Princess in the Wild* and be part of history in the making."

The ad finally ends, and I press pause as my body breaks out into a cold sweat. Swallowing hard, I do my best to put on a nonchalant expression as I hand back the tablet.

"What secrets, Arabella?" Arthur asks.

Shrugging, I say, "Nothing. They're clearly trying to make it seem scandalous to get ratings."

"Nothing? Based on this, there must be something. Think hard. What did you tell him?"

I take a long sip of my water, my mind racing at what they might have got on film. Sex. That's the shocking secret to which they're referring. My face heats up a bit and I stare out the window, avoiding eye contact with him. "It's probably because we... really got to *know* each other while we were out there."

Arthur sighs and rubs the bridge of his nose, something he does when he's trying to stay calm. "Are you saying you may have accidentally made a sex tape?"

"No!" I snap. "God, no. I'm not a complete idiot. We were very careful about shutting off the cameras before... anything happened." At least, I'm pretty sure we were. "You know, this is more than a little insulting, Arthur. You show up at the airport unannounced, refuse to give Will a ride, stranding the poor man at the terminal, then you confront me about this stupid ad. Honestly, it's a rather shit homecoming, if you ask me."

"First of all, if Will can't find his way out of an airport terminal, he probably shouldn't have his own survival show. Second, don't get snippy with me. While you've been off traipsing around on a yacht with Adventure Boy—"

"Don't call him that."

"—I've been dealing with a very concerned team of lawyers and advisors who—since this ridiculous ad started airing—are up in arms about putting a stop to whatever's about to happen. I'm trying to help you because, in a few minutes, you'll be facing a dozen suits, all of whom are waiting for an explanation from you."

Bugger, I hope it's just the sex. "Are you serious? All because of a silly ad? I mean really, Arthur, they're obviously misleading the public. I can't believe you, of all people, would fall for that."

He scoffs and shakes his head. "I haven't fallen for anything, but as your big brother, it's my duty to protect you. And if there's any truth to it, we need to get out in front of this thing."

I instantly see red at the whole 'duty to protect' thing and I purse my lips together. "First, I don't need protecting—something I more than proved when I was out in the jungle. Second, as I already said, there's no secret. No scandal. Nothing other than the fact that we fell in love out there. That's what they're referring to when they say lives will be forever changed. That's it. Therefore, there's absolutely no need for a big fuss."

"You better hope you're right because we've had the legal team approach ABN for an advanced screening, but they've refused. And they can do it, too, because you signed one hell of an iron-clad contract." He sighs, disappointment radiating from him.

My shoulders drop, and I turn my gaze to the window to avoid eye contact with Arthur. What could they possibly have? Nothing, right?

"Don't hold out on me, Arabella. I can't help you if I don't know what we're up against."

The car slows and turns left toward the bridge that crosses the Langdon River. On the other side is home—the sprawling one-hundred-acre palace grounds complete with a forest, private grave-yard, a lake, and my cozy, warm bed that I am desperate to dive into so I can hide from whatever is about to happen. Actually, I'd much rather grab Will, get back on the jet and go to Paradise Bay because I have a terrible feeling that I am, in fact, about to be embroiled in a horrific scandal, but my brain is far too sleepy to recall all the potential things I did and said four months ago. Did we have sex without shutting off the cameras? I mean, we had *a lot* of sex out there, so it's entirely possible. But we wouldn't have had the GoPros pointed at us, so it would only be... sounds. Urgh. I cannot tell my brother that there is even a remote possibility that the world is going to hear his sister in the throes of passion.

Arthur stares at me, knowing how much I hate awkward silences. He thinks I'll crack.

Dammit. He's right.

"Look, Arthur, if I *did* say something on camera, it can't have been important because I have no recollection of it. Honestly, if I had spilled some big secret, I'd remember, and I'd certainly fess up to it now, but it didn't happen."

"So there's nothing to worry about?" he asks, running his tongue over his teeth.

"*Nada.* Everything is absolutely fine."

I hope.

Why did I come home? This has been the worst day I've had in years. As soon as we arrived, I was made to change into dress clothes and attend a horrific emergency meeting with all the suits grilling me about what happened in Zamunda. It was awful—even one of the junior suits took a run at me. I spent the entire time reassuring them that nothing of consequence occurred, other than my relationship with Will, that is. But they wouldn't let up no matter what I said. Finally, I resorted to my default way of getting out of situations like this—and I'm *not* proud of myself, okay? So please don't judge me. In fact, I hate myself for what I did next.

I cried.

Yes. That's right. Arabella, Warrior Princess, who dragged a grown man out of the jungle, just turned on the water works to end a meeting. I suck. I really thought I was better than that but, apparently, no.

As soon as that horror show ended, I was rushed into my office by my assistant, Mrs. Chapman, who sat me down in front of a pile of overdue correspondence so high, I could barely reach the top. Okay, I'm being a bit dramatic about that, but it will take me days to catch up and there is no way I can cry my way out of anything with Mrs. Tight Bun No Nonsense.

I'm still working on it now, even though I'm physically exhausted and emotionally drained. We only slept for about two hours the entire night on account of being so busy storing up shags that we won't be able to fit in over the next few weeks. My eyes close and I'm almost immediately asleep, sitting up when my phone buzzes.

When I swipe the screen, I see a text from Will. *How is it possible that I miss you this much already? #patheticmaninlove.*

Me: *That works out well because I literally felt the life being drained from my body the moment we parted ways. #stupidarchaicrulesforprincesses*

I smile at the screen for a moment, then dig around in my handbag for the shell Will gave me on our last day on the yacht. I was feeling particularly sad that the most relaxing, carefree, incredible time of my entire life was about to end, so while I was having a shower before supper, he dove into the ocean and found a tiny, perfect, pink and ivory conch shell. At supper that night, he gave it to me and told me to keep it with me always so that no matter where I was or what was happening, I could come right back to our time on the yacht and know how much I am loved.

Plucking it out of my bag, I hold it in my palm and run my fingertips over its smooth surface. I am loved. Aaahhh…

We really are perfect for each other. And I know everyone *thinks* theirs is the greatest love of all time, but in our case, it's true. His gorgeous face when we said goodbye pops into my mind— the dimples that appeared when he smiled at me, his chiseled jaw that lets you know he's the manliest of men, and his coffee-coloured eyes shining at me. Oh, those eyes.

Eyes.

Eyelids.

Good God, my eyelids are heavy.

Nope. Must stay awake.

Mrs. Chapman knocks at the door, then enters my office with a trolley of tea and biscuits. "You're going to need some energy for your first teleconference with the Equal Everywhere Campaign Director. It starts in exactly twelve minutes."

I busy myself writing the birthday card for the chairperson of the Avonian Introverts Society (of which I am a patron) while she pours my tea. I can feel her staring before she finally comes out with it. "Is that too much bronzer or have you actually allowed your skin to tan?"

"The second one," I say, without looking up. "It's very difficult to be out on the open water for that many weeks without tanning, even if you are careful." Which I wasn't. I grin to myself a little, thinking of how shocked Mrs. Chapman would be to discover I don't have any tan lines.

Yes, I'm a very scandalous princess these days, with a crazy hot manly boyfriend and my own adventure show that's about to air on international television. Nothing dull about this lady anymore. She's wild and fiercely… fierce. And too tired to think of a good way to describe herself. And stuck at her stupid desk with a pile of stupid mail.

———

Exactly eleven minutes later, I have sucked down two mugs of tea with extra sugar, my office has been staged, complete with a bouquet of fresh flowers, and I am seated at my desk waiting for the host to let me into our Zoom meeting room. I finally see Malika Jelani, the director of the Equal Everywhere Campaign, on the screen. She's smiling brightly and speaking, but there's no sound so I wave and say, "Hello. I can't hear you. Can you hear me?"

She shakes her head and mouths what I'm sure is 'I can't hear you,' then the two of us spend the next couple of minutes fiddling with the settings and trying to talk with neither of us figuring out the magic combination. Frustration builds as I tap at the microphone button for the one-hundredth time and mutter, "I'm too tired for this shit today. How is this any better than using the bloody telephone?!"

Malika's face falls. "The sound seems to be fixed."

"Brilliant." Crap on a stick. *That* she heard? I smile brightly, hoping it makes up for my foul language.

"If you'd rather reschedule, I have an opening next Tuesday."

I laugh and shake my head. "Oh no, I didn't mean I'm too tired for the *meeting*. I was talking about technology. I'm afraid it's not my strong suit."

Her face softens. "Mine either."

Thank God she bought it. "No, I'm absolutely beyond thrilled to be the Avonian ambassador for the campaign."

Malika smiles, the skin around her eyes crinkling as she does. To look at her, you'd think she's a warm grandmotherly type who bakes cookies and knits baby blankets all day, but with her resume, I doubt she's had time to do either of those things even once. She's a professor at the prestigious University of Cape Town with PhDs in both International Law and Political Science. She was one of the first women to receive the World Science and Health Forum's Heroes Award for her tireless efforts to raise awareness of the AIDS epidemic back in the eighties. She also won the Indira Gandhi Peace Prize and has made the list of the "100 Leading Global Thinkers" by Foreign Policy magazine four years in a row.

All that to say, I'm out of my league here. "I cannot think of more important work and am looking forward to throwing myself into it with everything I've got."

"Excellent," she says. "Someone with your impeccable reputation and passion for philanthropy is always a welcome addition. But before we get started, I do need to ask about your upcoming reality television series. It's... unusual for one of our ambassadors to take part in such a ... thing."

Flashes of Will and me doing it all over the jungle pop into my mind and I feel my face heating up. "Oh, yes, it was quite out of character for me as well, but I needed to do it, Malika. I had to test my mettle, you know?"

"Right, of course," she says, scratching her head. "But um... is there anything we ought to be aware of before we announce you?"

"Nothing I can think of." I shake my head with confidence, my mind flashing to me screaming strings of curse words as I drop from my helicopter. Oh, and screaming in ecstasy as well. So, generally lots of rather undignified screaming. "Really all pretty routine, I'd say, as far as jungle adventures go."

Malika is giving me a hard look through the screen and based on the way her mouth is set tight, I'm pretty sure she's already seen that footage of me shoving the showrunner, Dylan Sinclair, in the face and knocking her onto her arse in the mud as we crossed the finish line. I'm sure that little moment played on the news every hour for at least a week straight.

I clear my throat, a little too hot under my Smythe Duchess wool blazer. "It's not a reality show, per se. It's more of a nature documentary/adventure survivalist show. We were able to showcase some of the Congo's vulnerable species such as the bonobos and... river otters." They're not vulnerable at all, to be honest. Turns out river otters are quite a rapey bunch, but I couldn't come up with another example.

Hmph. She doesn't look convinced. "Yes, but it would seem as though the network is billing it more on the tabloid television-side of things."

I chuckle as though that's the craziest thing I've heard, even though there is a very good chance that's exactly what they've turned it into. "Oh my, no. Mr. Banks and I were utter professionals the entire time. If anything, I hope my performance in the jungle will be inspirational to women everywhere who believe themselves to be too weak to accomplish difficult, gritty tasks. Especially the last twenty-four hours where I had to overcome not only my fears, but was forced to stretch my physical capabilities to their limits in order to bring Mr. Banks to safety." Ooh! That sounds good. I'll have to remember that line for the press junket.

Malika stares at me for a moment, tapping her fingers on the table. "So, no reason for us to hold off on announcing you until after the show airs?"

I should just tell her the truth, which is that I'm really quite wild now and have no idea how bad they're going to make me look. None whatsoever. But I *really* don't want to lose this opportunity. It's literally the most important thing I'll ever do in my life. Smiling sweetly, I say, "None that I can think of."

"Well, excellent. Now that that's sorted, let's get down to business. You'll find being a UN ambassador is likely going to be one of the greatest joys of your life. It's vital work and also will afford you opportunities to travel to places you otherwise may not have seen and meet groups of women who are incredibly inspirational. We work at a fast pace and although it's a significant time commitment, I don't believe you'll find it overwhelming, given your usual schedule. We'll be holding a small conference in two weeks' time in Vienna. From the twenty-fifth to the twenty-ninth. Do you think you can make it?"

Oh, yes! That sounds very important, doesn't it? Attending a *UN* Conference. I do my best not to look too thrilled. "I may have to move a few things around, but I'll be there."

The meeting goes on for another forty minutes. The entire time I oscillate between trying to focus on what she's saying (and staying awake so as not to insult her) and wishing we weren't on a video call so I could rest my eyes, just for a few quick seconds. It would feel so… floaty. Floating on a fluffy cloud in the warmth of the sun…

"Your Highness?! Are you asleep?"

I sit up straight in my chair, my eyes flying open. "No. Totally awake. I was … I've got something in my right eye, like a bit of dust. I was… trying to blink it out."

"And the snoring sound?" she asks, glaring at me.

"Allergies."

Shit.

3

Life with Chicken Little

Will

"Dwight, old buddy. How's the world's greatest agent?" I'm standing in front of the brick townhouse belonging to my extremely anxious manager, Dwight Anderson. His front garden is as neat as a pin, with not even one errant leaf on the perfectly trimmed grass. It's a chilly autumn morning with crisp air telling me to get back on a plane and go straight home to the Caribbean.

"Not so good, Will. Not good at all. Where are you? I need to see you as soon as possible."

"How about thirty seconds from now? Or however long it takes you to open your front door…"

"What?"

"I came straight from the airport." Well, that's not *exactly* true because I did stop at my cameraman Tosh's place first, to see if I could stay with him, but it turns out he and my sound guy, Mac, are in Guadalajara right now filming *Death in Paradise*. Since they'll be gone for months, he sublet his apartment, and Mac gave up his completely, which brings me here. "I stopped at Starbucks and got your favourite matcha green tea latte. You should let me in before it gets cold."

"All right, what's going on?" Dwight asks, his alarmist tendencies on high alert.

"Nothing. Everything's fine. I have a small favour to ask. Well, maybe not a *favour* so much as a win-win situation. I'd like to offer you the rare opportunity to know where I am at all times over the next few weeks."

Doesn't that sound better than saying I'm desperately seeking somewhere to crash? There's no way in hell he is going to want me to stay with him, by the way. This is also the last place I want to be, to be honest. I once rode in his car and wasn't allowed to get in until he fitted some plastic down on the seat and I put little booties on over my shoes.

He opens the door and pockets his mobile phone. He's already dressed in his suit, clearly ready to head out to work (which is perfect because I need a good nap). Crossing his arms, he says, "You figured you'd be staying at the palace and only just found out she's not allowed overnight guests, didn't you?"

"Yup."

"And you've already been to Tosh and Mac's only to discover they're away."

"Yes, but only because they both live closer to the airport," I say, giving him a bright smile while gently tilting his latte side-to-side in what I hope will be a very enticing way.

Scowling, he says, "I'm not big on houseguests."

"I figured as much based on that time I rode in your car. But I promise I'll be a very neat and tidy guest. You'll hardly notice I'm here."

He sighs and steps aside to let me in.

Yes!

———

Or no.

Because that's the word I've heard most in the last ten minutes, as in, "No leaving your clothes on the floor, no lying all over the top of the bedspread. Just get into bed when the time comes and make it as soon as you get up. No sleeping in the nude unless you want to replace the sheets."

"Okaaay," I say, peeking my head into the stark spare bedroom which has only a bed with all-white bedding, and a single nightstand (white, obviously) with a small old-fashioned alarm clock ticking away on top of it.

"No eating unless you're in the kitchen—and I mean it. Not in the living room, not the bathroom—"

"Gross. Why would I eat in the bathroom?"

"Why would you have that disgusting beard?"

"Arabella likes it."

"That's because she's probably not educated on what lives in beards. Now, can we continue? Because we're only a third of the way through my house rules and I really must get to the office."

"Sorry, go on."

"No eating in the bedroom."

"Obviously."

We walk down the hall, and he points to his bedroom. "Off limits."

"Why? Is that where you keep the bodies?"

"You're welcome to stay somewhere else, you know," he says, turning around and taking me back to the living room/kitchen combination where the waft of bleach hits my nostrils again. "No answering the phone, especially if my mother calls."

"Are you avoiding her?"

"No, but I'm pretty sure she thinks I'm gay, and having a man living here would only confirm her suspicions."

"Really?"

"She grew up in a small village. The only tidy man she knew was also the only gay man in town."

"Does it really matter if she thinks you're gay?" I ask.

"Yes, because she keeps trying to set me up with other men which is not only awkward, it's unfair to them when they find out the truth."

"I see. So, no answering the phone and pretending we're snuggled up having a lazy Sunday lie-in."

Dwight gives me a deadpan expression. "There are plenty of Airbnbs in town."

"I was only trying to lighten the mood. I promise I won't answer the phone."

"Excellent." He sets to work checking his fanny pack for his essentials—keys, hand sanitizer, wipes, and Tums (which, if I had to guess, I'd say he keeps an entire closet-full in his bedroom). He pauses for a moment. "Why do you want to stay here, anyway? Surely, you can afford a hotel room."

"I'm saving up for a ring," I say, feeling slightly sheepish admitting it out loud.

He looks up at me with a small grin. "So, she's the one then? The woman who beat you into submission?"

"No, she's the woman who opened my eyes to love."

"Same thing."

"Some day you'll understand," I say, giving him a purposefully condescending look.

He busies himself clipping on his fanny pack and pulling on his suit jacket. "Now, I must run. You look like shit, so get some sleep. The press junket starts Thursday, so you'll need to be camera-ready by then." He gestures to my chin. "Best go to a barber to get that mess off your face. I don't want any beard shavings in my drain. You're obviously overdue for a haircut as well."

I give him a wide grin. "Yes, well, I ran out of time when I was off sailing the South Pacific and having an unbelievable amount of sex, so…"

Dwight rolls his eyes. "When you're out shopping for a ring, go buy a few new suits. You'll need to be well-dressed for your television appearances."

"Righto. Excellent point."

He purses his lips for a second. "You're also going to want to watch the promos for the show. It's got a very different… feel to it than the previous seasons." He walks over to the front door and puts his hand on the knob. "I'll be sending you a list of questions to help you get prepared for the interviews. We can go over them tonight when I get back."

"I'll be fine. This isn't my first rodeo."

"It's your first one with the entire kingdom watching and wondering exactly what kind of man is trying to join the royal family."

Urgh. That made my balls shrink up to the size of macadamia nuts. Too much info? Probably. Sorry about that. "You've forgotten I've handled much scarier situations—with ease, I might add."

"I don't think you understand what's at stake here. Your entire career is on the line, obviously. But it's so much more than that because your future wife's reputation could also suffer irreparable harm, depending on what happened out there and what ABN decides to show."

Now, they're the size of raisins. My apologies. I can't seem to stop talking about my balls. "Well, on that note, I think I'll curl up in the fetal position until you get home."

"Just don't do it on the rug. I don't want the oils from your skin getting into the fibers."

"Now all I want to do is lie around naked on your rug." I hold up one hand and add, "Obviously I'm kidding. What do you want for supper tonight, sweetie? Should I call your mum and find out what your favourite dishes are?"

Narrowing his eyes, he says, "No cooking. In fact, I'd prefer it if you went out to eat when I'm not here."

"Sounds reasonable," I mutter. Then raising my voice, I say, "Dwight, thank you. I really appreciate you letting me stay here. If I can ever repay you, just ask."

"Oh, you're going to repay me all right," he says, opening the door. "I'll give you a bill at the end of each week to offset the extra water, power, and food you consume."

Welcome home…

4

Pajamas, Portion Control, and Having it All...

Arabella

"WELCOME TO MARGARITAS AND MAN-BASH MONDAY," I say as I step aside to let Tessa (the world's greatest sister-in-law) and Nikki (her bestie and now one of mine) into my apartment. Tessa has her blonde hair up in a ponytail and she's dressed in her Sponge Bob pyjamas, while Nikki, who is a hairdresser (sporting bright pink-to-purple ombre locks today) is in Juicy sweats and a tee. They walk in, and as I'm closing the door, I realize Bellford, my faithful bodyguard, heard me. I poke my head out into the hall and say, "Not you, obviously."

"Of course, Your Highness," he replies with a slight nod. Bellford is the best. He's been my bodyguard since I was a teenager. He's like a calming presence in my life and always allows me just enough space to give me the illusion of being independent whilst keeping me completely safe.

I shut the door and turn. "Let the games begin!"

"Yes, let's! Four months without man-bash Mondays is way too long," Nikki says, setting down two large paper bags on the dining table.

"Did you get me the kung pao chicken with the sauce on the side?" Tessa asks as she unpacks our dinner.

"Yes, Your Majesty," Nikki says, bowing at the waist.

I gasp, then realize Nikki's trying to wind us up by calling Tessa by a title reserved solely for the ruling monarch.

"Oh, good. You remembered the steamed rice." Tessa has been trying to lose the last twenty pounds of baby weight for over two years without much success. Poor thing can never quite be as glam as Impossibly Perfect Kate (as we call her), which really bothers her. Tessa's only got one manny (who works days) and twins, neither of whom are what you'd call 'good sleepers,' meaning she's up with one or the other every night only to wake early to a full itinerary. As she's explained to me several times, this causes her to have uncontrollable sugar cravings due to reduced serotonin. She also has a serious addiction to crisps and freshly baked scones (which are basically unavoidable when you live in a palace), but we don't talk about that.

The three of us start lifting lids off the containers and plating the food, Tessa careful to only take the steamed vegetables and the plain chicken and broccoli with a tiny dollop of sauce on the side. When we're done, Nikki shakes her head at Tessa's plate. "What a sad little dinner."

"Agreed," Tessa says, staring longingly at Nikki's heap of saucy colourful goodness. "But it's T-minus one-month until we go to England where I'll be forced into another official couples photo with Princess Perfect and two sexy crown princes."

I'm about to pour her a margarita, but she covers the glass with her hand. "None for me, thanks. This is a DEFCON 1 situation here. Xavier's got me down to 1200 calories a day, and I already went over at lunch when Flora didn't finish her alphabet pasta. Did you know there are over a hundred calories in only three tablespoons of that stuff?"

"I can't say I did." I walk over to the liquor cart and lift a bottle of Skinny Bitch Vodka, holding it up to Tessa. "Sixty calories okay?"

"Dear God, yes, but promise to stop me at one," Tessa says. Scraping two spoonfuls of steamed rice back into the container, she says, "Maybe two."

She means four.

When I return to the table, I set her drink down in front of her and take a seat. I'm about to take a bite when Nikki says, "So, tell us everything. How was sailing around the South Pacific with Will Banks, the hottie hot hot adventure man? How's the sex? Fantastic, right? I bet he's amazing, what with all those climbing and agility skills he's got going on."

I grin, my cheeks heating up as I nod. "It was wonderful. The water was just so *blue* and warm. I've never been as relaxed in my entire life."

Nikki and Tessa both give me the 'quit holding out on us' look.

"And he's incredible in bed."

"I knew it," Nikki says, rolling her eyes. "He's probably quite acrobatic, like those Ukrainian dancer men."

"Oooh, yes!" Tessa says. "I'd never have thought of that, but with all that crouching and kicking, I imagine that does translate quite well in the bedroom."

I grin at them. "Based on my… *ahem*… research, I can safely say physical prowess is rather helpful when it comes to more… intimate pursuits."

"Lucky bitch," Nikki says, shaking her head. "Both of you, really. It's a wonder I love you bitches as much as I do."

"It's because we're rather loveable," I say with a wry grin.

"True," Tessa adds, nodding at me. "We're absolutely delightful."

"That's because you royals have all the fun," Nikki says, wiping bright-red sauce off her bottom lip. "You two seriously need to find me my own prince already. I've had it up to here with being a commoner."

"God no. No princes," I say, ripping off a small bite of onion cake and popping it in my mouth. "The last thing you want is to end up with some dreadfully dull royal."

Tessa holds up her glass. "Arthur is *anything* but boring, thank you very much." Looking over at Nikki, she says, "I promise I'll continue the hunt for the perfect man for you."

"Thanks, sweetie. Honestly, he doesn't even have to be royal. I'll take super hot and crazy rich, even if he's new money."

"Obviously," Tessa answers. Turning to me, she says, "Now, back to you and your man. Have you two discussed how you'll handle the fallout from the show?"

I shrug. "Won't be a problem. We know how the whole reality telly thing works—they'll take everything we said and did out of context to try to create a scandal. It may result in a few unflattering headlines and some nasty Reddit threads for a couple weeks, but things'll die down, and we'll go back to normal by November."

Tessa sits back in her chair and tilts her head. "Hmmm… I don't know. I'm worried you may be underestimating Dylan's ability to be evil."

Stopping myself just short of rolling my eyes, I say, "And if you'll remember, I *do* know how to handle her." I suck back as much of my margarita as I can without risking brain freeze, then set the glass down. "Besides, Will and I know what *really* went on out there. No amount of editing can change reality—or our feelings for each other."

"Are you sure?" Tessa asks. "Arthur and I went through hell with the whole 'Brooke is better' thing. It really got in my head and it almost ended us."

Tessa comes from a 'normal family,' so there were some people in our upper crust crowd who weren't exactly thrilled when Arthur announced their engagement. They started a whole campaign to have him dump her and marry Lady Brooke Beddingfield, an awful snatch who had the 'right' upbringing. Thank God it didn't work because there is no way in hell Brooke and I would be sitting around in our jammies getting tipsy together.

"That's true. She was a total mess, Arabella. Trust me," Nikki adds. "And you've got those 'Will's Wild Girls' who would love to see your head on a spike."

"Thanks for that image," I say, wrinkling up my nose. "They're not going to be a problem. Honestly. I'm sure they're a bunch of tweens sitting in bedrooms that have been freshly decorated with unicorn everything. Besides, not only have I learned a lot from watching what you and Arthur went through, but Will and I have already made it through some crazy shit together. Literal life and death stuff. And when push came to shove, we chose each other." I pick up a spring roll with one hand, dip it in the plum sauce, and take an enormous bite. When I'm done chewing, I say, "The truth is, though, I need some advice from you, Tess. But not about the show. I need to help him ease into royal life."

Tessa tilts her head and stares at me for a second. "I thought you and Will were going Megxit."

"Not *full* Megxit," I say, my stomach tightening at the idea of giving up my entire life for the unknown. "I mean, I considered it briefly, but it's all so much more complicated than it seemed at first, what with the need for a security detail and letting all my charities down and—"

"Having to pay for everything yourself..." Nikki adds.

"That too," I answer. "Also, I've got the UN gig now, which is something I've always dreamed of. I can't really abandon ship now, can I?"

Tessa sips her vodka. "I suppose not. How does Will feel about joining the royal ranks?"

I push my chicken ball around on my plate with my fork so as to avoid eye contact with her. "Um, I'm sure he'll be fine with it. I mean, once he gets to know everyone and gets a glimpse at all the perks."

"Have you two *not* talked about this?" Tessa asks.

Clearing my throat, I say, "Not as such. The truth is, we've only gotten as far as knowing with absolute certainty that we *do* want a life together. I mean, that bit alone takes a while. But, now that we're here, we'll sort it out. Right?" I ask, glancing back and forth between them.

Tessa makes a clicking sound and sucks some air in through her teeth. "I don't know, this would be a complete lifestyle overhaul for a man like Will. It's not exactly footloose and fancy-free."

"You could build him a gigantic jungle gym in the meadow," Nikki offers.

"He's not a *monkey*," I say. "Surely, Will and I can find a way for him to meet his need for adventure whilst allowing me to continue on with my family and charitable obligations. It can't be *that hard*, can it?"

"Maybe." Nikki rips open a packet of plum sauce and squeezes some onto her plate. "Especially if you two keep filming survival shows even after you're married."

"Well, I'll be quite busy as a UN ambassador, but he can certainly continue on doing a show or two a year," I say. "The whole thing will fit in quite nicely with whatever charities he wants to take on actually."

"Why do I get the feeling you're trying to come up with a way to sell this to him?" Tessa asks.

"Because I am," I admit, feeling a pang of guilt. "The thing is, as soon as I got back here, I realized how much I missed my life. Well, aspects of it anyway, like you two, and Gran, and the twins and well, frankly, living in a palace isn't all that bad either. And now that I'm finally doing something *meaningful*, I don't want to give that up, and honestly, I don't think Will would ever ask me to. He's not that kind of man."

Risking a glance at Tessa, I can instantly tell I won't like what she's got to say. I quickly continue before she can impart her happily-married-woman wisdom. "I'm not about to make any major decisions without him, and if this life made him terribly miserable, we'd figure something else out. I was hoping you may have some ideas as to how I could help him find *his own version* of this life."

Tessa sighs. "I'm not sure how many versions of this life are possible. It's kind of a full-on lifestyle, and once you're in it, you get sucked in all the way."

"Which I would happily welcome," Nikki adds. "No more scrubbing scalps for a living."

I pour myself another margarita, then top up Nikki's. "So, you'd be happy to give up your career for this life?"

"In a heartbeat," Nikki says, taking a long pull of her drink. "But I'm not sure I have the same feelings about my career that your man does. I pretty much became a hair stylist for the gossip."

I chuckle, then my heart drops when I think of Will. "He really does adore his job." I sigh and look at Tessa. "You had to leave the journalism world for Arthur. Do you ever regret it?"

She sets her fork down. "Yes and no. I mean, when I realized I had to quit working as a reporter, it was a bit of a shock in a way, as stupid as that sounds. But I had to ask myself what I *really* wanted to get out of reporting the news. Clearly, it wasn't the money because I never made much at it. It was respect, which is something I have now."

"Do you?" Nikki asks, wrinkling up her nose.

We all laugh, then Tessa says, "For the most part, I'd say so. Well, among my family anyway." Holding up one finger, she says, "Now that I'm doing so much charity work and I'm momming, they see me as slightly less of a failure than they used to. It's nice, really."

"Okay, good. That's good," I say. "I'm sure Will wants respect, too, and we can make that happen, no?"

"Maybe, but men are different." Tessa stands and drops some ice into her glass, then free-pours more vodka, apparently deciding to stretch her 'two-drinks' as far as possible. "Arthur would never agree to live off of me, if I were the one with the cash."

"Well, that's *Arthur*," I say, my hackles going up slightly. "Will and Arthur are about as different as two people can get."

"Tessa might be right," Nikki says. "It's harder for a man to join a royal family than a woman. Think of Prince Phillip. He did not adjust well *at all* to being the consort to the queen."

Urgh. "So say the writers of *The Crown*. Whatever. The truth is, I'm not going to be the reigning monarch, ever—thanks for that, by the way, Tessa." I wink at her. "And I've already begun to forge the path for us to have a much more… liberated existence than most royals. I'm sure we can find a way for him to go do all his wild man stuff while I'm busy with my causes." I nod confidently, even though there's a niggling feeling in my stomach. "Besides, Will is the most confident man I've ever met. There's no way he'd let a little thing like money bother him."

"Then you two should be just fine," Tessa says, even though I can see uncertainty written all over her face.

"Absolutely," I say, tipping back my drink to wash away my worry. "I'm sure with a little finesse, we can have it all."

Lifting her margarita, Nikki says, "Here's to having it all."

We click glasses together and toast, "To having it all." Then, we each down our drinks.

"And, if for some reason, it doesn't work out and Will can't handle being married to a princess," Nikki says, "I could totally go gay for you. You're gorgeous, and I promise I'd have no problem whatsoever living off your family's money." She raises and lowers her eyebrows at me. "Oh! We could get married and get ourselves some hot guy—or *guys*—to share."

Chuckling, I say, "Thanks for the offer, Nikki. I'll keep that in mind."

"But in the meantime, please continue looking for a hot, rich guy just for me."

"Obviously," I answer with a quick nod.

———

Three hours later, Tessa and Nikki weave their way to the door of my apartment. We exchange tipsy goodbye hugs and promises to text each other tomorrow. Tessa gives me a concerned look. "You may want to tell Will you're not going full Megxit sooner than later."

"Righto. Probably a good idea."

"I'd say so. The last thing you'd want is for him to feel like you've tried to trap him into a life he won't want."

"Good point," I say, my head spinning a little. "I'll make sure to sit down with him and tell him the truth about how I feel and see where he's at with all of it, just as soon as possible."

"I don't know," Nikki says. "You two are going to have enough to deal with when the show airs. Maybe focus on getting through the next couple of months, then sort out the long-term stuff after."

I nod. "She brings up an excellent point."

Tessa gives me another goodbye hug and says, "Just don't wait too long."

"I won't."

5

The Part Where the Princess Has to Eat Crow (and a Bunch of Other Disgusting Things)

Arabella

Four Days Later

"YOU CLEAN UP NICELY, MR. BANKS," I say, letting my eyes sweep over my smartly dressed, freshly shaved boyfriend. He's in a dashing navy suit jacket, a crisp white shirt, and dark jeans for that 'I have to dress up, but you can't tame me' look. See? He can totally fit in with my life without having to lose who he is.

Will crosses the room and pulls me into his arms. "That's funny, I like you best when you're very dirty."

"Opposites attract," I murmur while he nips at my earlobe.

We're in the green room at the ABN studios where, in a few minutes, we'll be filming a live pre-show show. Did I mention it's live? I've been increasingly nervous as this day has drawn nearer, but somehow, at the moment, I can't even remember what I was so worried about because the man I love is looking at me like I'm the only woman who has ever walked the earth. And when he does that, the rest of the world melts away, and I forget everything I'm meant to be worrying about. Quite dangerous, really.

"I missed you," he says, lifting one hand to my cheek and smiling at me. "I can't believe we've gone so long without seeing each other."

"It's been awful," I say, leaning in so our bodies are as close as possible while fully dressed. "I wish we could lock the door and just throw down right here."

"Don't tempt me. There's no way ten minutes will be enough to make up for so many hours apart," he says, kissing me on the neck. "But maybe we can sneak back in here when the show's over."

"You wickedly smart man," I murmur.

"I figured we could get reacquainted on that couch over there."

A knock at the door has us both quickly jumping back as we call "Come in!" to whoever it is.

As it turns out, Dylan Sinclair, evil showrunner/PR witch/Red Bull addict is the one doing the knocking. She rushes across the room with an open-mouthed smile. "Princess Arabella!" she calls in her sing-songy way. "*Gorgeous* as always. Love your dress. *Love* it. Sophisticated yet simple. Flattering yet modest. Professional yet friendly. You must have gotten my e-mail with suggestions because this is spot-on."

I'm in a light moss sheath dress with three-quarter-length bell sleeves, my usual boring beige pumps, and delicate pearl drop earrings to finish the look. I nod and smile, surprised that she doesn't seem to be holding a grudge about the whole me-using-her-face-to-push-her-to-the-ground thing. Huh. Remarkable, really. I'd still be super pissed. "How are you, Dylan?"

"Never better," she says, pulling a can of Red Bull out of her suit jacket pocket. She cracks it open. "This is going to be the single greatest week of all of our lives. *The. Greatest!*"

Will puts his arm around my shoulder while she tips back the can. "We're really excited to see the final product."

"It's incredible, if I do say so myself," she says. "It very well may be the most spectacular television show ever made, so I suppose one could say I nailed it first try."

"I'm sure you did," I answer, resisting the urge to roll my eyes. "I want to apologize again about shoving—"

Dylan holds up one hand. "Nope. Don't even. That little move was the cherry on the top of the 'transformation of a princess to a kickass warrior' sundae."

"But still, it was most unbecoming of me and beyond rude."

"Which makes for superb ratings," she answers, looking at her watch. "Okay, I have to run next door and make sure we're all set up for you. You are going to absolutely die when you find out what the format is of tonight's show. It's going to be wildly fun. Think *The Newlywed Game* meets *Fear Factor* meets *Entertainment Tonight*. You'll be answering questions while you complete challenges."

"Wow, that is… not what I was expecting," I say.

"*Right?* Sometimes I scare myself with my big ideas. I was out running a couple of weeks ago while I was brainstorming interview questions, and it popped into my head—'Dylan, a plain old interview has been done to death. You need to make it harder, better, faster, stronger.'"

Will nods, keeping a poker face. "Were you listening to Kanye West at the time?"

"How did you know?" Dylan asks. She turns to me. "Scary that he knew that. Okay, so rules for today—*try everything*. Just really go for it, no matter what we throw at you. The more into this you are, the more excitement we can generate for the show." She tips back her can and takes a few gulps. "And guess who the host is?"

She's going to say it's her, isn't she?

"Me!" she announces.

"I was racking my brain for the right host—someone exciting with that certain *je ne sais quoi* who we could quickly bring up to speed on what we're trying to achieve here, and I thought, 'Dylan! You're all those things!' Plus, I'm semi-famous as that woman Princess Arabella shoved into the mud, so it adds that whole 'is she going to be nasty to the princess' tension!" Dylan grins at me. "Spoiler alert—she's not. Seriously, we're fine."

"Brilliant," I say, even though I cannot imagine that any of that is true.

"Oh, and speaking of spoilers—we don't want any! Not one. The world has already figured out you're a couple, so we can't go 'will they or won't they.' No biggie because we pivot and highlight the mystery of how this happened. That is what will have butts in chairs every Thursday night for the next five weeks."

"Well, that and our ability to survive in the Congo whilst making our way to civilization under the most dire of circumstances," Will says, sounding slightly put out.

"That too," Dylan agrees before sucking back the rest of her drink. "Okay, I better go make sure the lighting is going to flatter me. It gets harder to light women over a certain age. Remember you're thrilled about the show, your relationship, and your future together. Give specific yet vague answers. Be friendly and open yet maintain an air of mystery."

"Sure, no problem," Will says as Dylan hurries out the door.

Once the door is closed, I look up at him, "Be honest yet deceitful."

He grins down at me. "Distant yet close."

"Stymied but also victorious," I add.

"Exactly."

————

"Welcome to *Princess in the Wild - The Pre-show*!" Dylan shouts into the camera. "I'm your host, Dylan Sinclair, and tonight we begin the epic, sexy adventure that is *Princess in the Wild*! In just a moment, I'll welcome Princess Arabella herself and wild man Will Banks to our stage where they will be subjected to various tests of faith, disgusting challenges, and daring feats. But that's not all, folks, because we are going to have a little fun with the new couple as well in our segment called, 'How Well Do You Know Each Other?'

"*Princess in the Wild* which debuts this Thursday at 8 p.m. here on ABN, is already being touted as the most adventurous, sexiest series on the telly."

"By whom?" Will whispers in my ear.

"Dylan, obviously," I murmur back to him, and we both silently chuckle.

We're standing behind a curtain just off the stage, waiting for our cue, and to be honest, I'm perspiring a little due to the hot studio lights and an absolute fear of the unknown. Will seems positively giddy with anticipation while I pretty much feel like vomiting. Did I mention this is being filmed live? Oh, yes, I did. But, there's also a live studio audience. Why do people say a live audience? As opposed to a dead one? When has that ever happened? *"This show was filmed before a dead studio audience."*

Dammit, Arabella, focus, already!

Dylan walks across the stage while she says, "Now, if you haven't been living under a rock for the past few months, you already know that ABN has a very special nature documentary series coming your way starring the gorgeous and talented Princess Arabella herself and, of course, Will Banks, one of the world's greatest *and hottest* outdoor enthusiasts. We whisked them off to the Congo and dropped them into the jungle where they were forced to make their way out with nothing but their wits and each other."

Dramatic pause and hair flip. "And let me tell you folks, things got pretty steamy out there in the jungle, if you get my drift." She aims an open-mouthed wink into the camera. "So, without further ado, let's get them out here, shall we?"

The audience bursts into applause. Will takes my hand and we walk out onto the stage together. I smile brightly while I tighten my grip and pray he won't let go.

"Welcome, Your Highness and Will!" Dylan says, with her arms open. When we reach her, Will lets go of my hand, and Dylan gives me a kiss on each cheek, then does the same for him.

Now that we're out on the stage, I can get the lay of the land, and at first glance, I don't like it even a bit. There's a cheesy red heart-shaped love seat and matching chair where I'm assuming we'll conduct the interview portion of things. There are two wooden posts ominously set up on the far side, which have me more than a little concerned because I know they're not there to dress up the stage since they're under a large sign that reads "Posts of Defeat." My eyes land on a counter bearing a sign that says, "Gross Out Kitchen." There are several plates covered with silver domes which cause the hair on the back of my neck to stand up. What in the bloody hell is crawling around under those shiny domes? Oh bugger, why did I agree to do this?

"Now, you two are probably wondering what is about to happen to you. I know I'd be curious," Dylan says. "So, I'll let you in on what we'll be doing tonight. A normal celebrity interview would be way too dull for the world's most adventurous couple, so we've come up with what might be the most exciting interview format ever. Think *Truth or Dare* meets *Survivor* meets *The Newlywed Game!*"

Will glances at me excitedly, and I mirror his expression while I order my legs not to run out the emergency exit. Oh, they want to run so very, very badly.

Dylan gestures over to the seating area and we follow her over like… two rubes about to be humiliated on national television. We're all sitting now. There's a light blinding me, and I squint as she says, "So, it's no secret that the two of you have been an item for a few months now. Never before has there been a case of two more polar opposites who end up finding love with each other. Will, orphaned at age seven, grew up sailing, surfing, exploring deserted islands in the Caribbean, while the princess grew up in a lush palace with hundreds of servants catering to her every whim. I don't want to use the word *pampered*, but if the glass slipper fits… am I right?"

The audience seems to find this less insulting than I do. Instead of booing her as I hoped they would, they break into laughter while Dylan throws them a wink. Oh, how I wish I could sink into this tacky crimson couch and disappear forever. Actually, no. I wish I had my brother's ability to snap back with some cutting yet witty remark. Instead, I continue smiling like a very vapid princess. Oh, excuse me, a vapid, pampered princess.

Will covers my hand with his. Oh, that's nice and warm and comforting right when I need it. God, I love him.

"That's what I thought at first too, Dylan," he says.

Wait. What?

I'm about to give him the raised eyebrow when he continues. "But it's really an unfair characterization of Arabella. Her life hasn't exactly been all roses. I never realized how much pressure there must be on royal children, what with being hounded relentlessly by the media and being judged for every little thing they do. And like me, she lost a parent at a very young age, which I know from experience makes things quite difficult, but she's a person who rallies when the chips are down. And I can tell you this is one princess who's made of pure steel."

Dylan wrinkles her nose slightly. "Well, we'll all have to tune in each week to find out if you're right. On that note, shall we get on with the games?"

The audience cheers, and Will sits forward a little. "Can't wait."

I can. I can definitely wait.

Oh God, she's giving instructions and I'm not hearing a word she's saying. I'm watching her mouth move, but her words aren't making any sense.

"…For every wrong answer, you'll have to eat one of the food items (and I use the term food loosely) from our Gross Out Kitchen!"

Will is picking up two stacks of large white cards and two Sharpie pens. He's handing me a set and keeping one for himself.

What am I meant to do with these? What are the rules? Why is it so hot up here?

"Lower the No Cheating Wall!"

No Cheating Wall? What the shit is going on? I glance up as a large white divider slowly moves toward us from the high ceiling. Will scoots away from me to give room between us, and I have to say, it feels a bit ironic that something is *literally* separating two people who only moments earlier promised each other we wouldn't let anything come between us. The only bit of the man I love that is visible to me now are the tips of his dress shoes. Shit. Now I can't copy off him, and I have no idea what we're meant to be doing to avoid eating bugs… or worse.

Dylan holds up some cue cards. "Remember, write down your answers, but don't say anything or give each other any hints! We'll start off with something easy. Question one: Arabella, what would Will say is your most attractive attribute? Will, write down the answer, and Your Highness, please write down what you *think* he's going to say."

Bollocks. How is *that* the easy question? It's obviously my naughty bits, but I can't exactly write that down, now can I? Breathe. You can answer this. He'll write something gentlemanly because he won't want to embarrass me. Lips? No, still sounds dirty. Eyes? He'd never write down anything that lame. Sense of humour? No, I'm not very funny now that I think about it. Dammit. Why can't I be funny?

"Oh, Princess Arabella is having some trouble with this one. Will was quick to write down his answer, but she is really struggling with this one."

Shut up. I'm trying to guess what Will wrote down. Sense of style? No. Sense of justice? Yes. That's it. I take the lid off my Sharpie and get writing. When I finish, I place the card behind the others and look up at Dylan.

"Finally thought of something, did you?"

I chuckle gaily, even though I want to strangle her skinny neck. "I'm afraid the pressure is on. I'm a bit concerned about what's under those silver domes."

"As you should be. We've gone to great lengths to find the most disgusting things possible to feed you," she says. "Now, question number two is a tough one. Arabella, what is Will's most annoying habit? And Will, write down *what you think* bothers Princess Arabella about you the most."

Fuckity fuck. He's obviously rather cocky, and at times, he can be a bit of a know-it-all, but I can't exactly write either of those down, can I? But I don't want to eat anything that's still moving. Or raw cow's tongue. I stare at the dome, trying desperately to think of something that won't hurt his feelings. He flosses his teeth in bed. Drives me nuts, but that's not an option since we're pretending I'm a virgin for all the elderly royal fans out there. Okay what will *he* say I find most annoying about him…

"Five seconds!"

Shit. I scrawl my answer down, feeling a bead of sweat trickle down my back.

"Question three: if Arabella were on *Who Wants to Be a Millionaire*, who would her phone-a-friend be?" She pauses and grins back and forth between us.

Arthur. Done.

"Question four is a two-parter: What's the best gift you've given each other. And what's the best gift you've received?"

Yacht. A shell.

"Question five should make for an interesting drive home: how many children do you want? Write your true answer down and if they don't match, we'll lift the lid off another dome."

Two.

"Question six: who won the last argument the two of you had and what was it about?"

Oh God, what was it? *Titanic*! Yes. And I won. Bill Paxton, not Bill Pullman, starred in *Titanic*.

"Okay! Time's up! Let's lift the wall!" Dylan announces.

The audience breaks into applause, and I grin nervously at Will as he comes into view. I lean in and whisper, "I love you."

"I love you too," he says, taking my hand in his and giving it a squeeze.

"Okay," Dylan says. "Let's reveal the answer to question one: what would Will say is Princess Arabella's most attractive attribute?"

We hold up our cards while craning our necks to see each other's answers. Laughter fills the studio, and my face flushes as I read his answer: *Her smile.*

When I look at him, he says, "I thought it was a physical attribute, but you're right, sweetheart, it really is your sense of justice that draws me to you."

"More than her smile?" Dylan sneers.

"Well, she does have the most beautiful smile of any woman on the planet, so you can hardly blame me, right?"

I grin up at him. "Excellent save, Mr. Banks."

"But not good enough!" Dylan says.

A producer rushes over with a platter. He holds it in front of us and lifts the lid with a flourish. Oh, that doesn't look so bad. It's two tiny peppers.

"Are those...?" Will starts but trails off.

"Carolina reapers? No! We'd never do that to you," Dylan says as though that's the craziest idea ever. "They're ghost peppers! Dig in!"

Trying to seem brave, I nod and pick mine up. "Bon appetite!"

I take a dainty bite, chewing as quickly as possible. Oh, well that's not so...

BAD! IT'S VERY, VERY BAD.

MY ENTIRE FACE IS ON FIRE.

Chew. Chew. Chew.

Swallow.

You can do this. You are not going to DIE!

Yes, I am. I am going to die right here on this stage! Death by ghost pepper at the tender age of twenty-nine!

Snot pools in my nostrils, and my eyes shut involuntarily while I swallow and cover the lower half of my face with one hand. Every pore in my head opens up to let out the heat in the form of sweat. Suddenly, a cool glass is thrust into my hand. I open one eye, but just barely since it wants to clamp shut again, but before it does, I see it's milk.

I suck it back in long, huge gulps, not caring that it's pouring down the sides of my mouth onto my dress. It's either humiliate myself or wind up with third degree mouth burns.

When I finally recover enough for my eyes to open up, I glance at Will who doesn't seem even the slightest bit affected by the pepper. He does however look very concerned, and if I'm not mistaken, the tiniest bit horrified. It's the snot, isn't it?

"You okay?"

I nod quickly, reaching for the tissue box and snagging out several whilst keeping my other hand over my face. I blow my nose, some-thing I've *never* done in front of anyone other than my nannies when I was a wee girl.

Dylan shouts, "We'll take a quick commercial break and give Princess Arabella a chance to recover. Stay tuned for question number two!"

The lights dim down a bit, and Dylan leans forward. "Are you all right? That one really got you."

"Yes, absolutely fine." I blow my nose again as a makeup artist comes rushing toward me, brushes in hand. I blink and sniffle repeatedly while she sets to work on my face, her hands a flurry of action while my mouth continues to burn. Dylan and Will, meanwhile, fill the two minutes with some witty banter about how experienced they are at eating spicy food. Apparently, they've both been to India and dined on some of the hottest dishes on the planet with ease. If my eyes weren't still stinging, I'd be rolling them right about now.

"Ten seconds!" the director shouts. The makeup artist abandons me, and the lights come back up.

"Welcome back to *Princess in the Wild - The Preshow*! For those of you just joining us, I'm your host, Dylan Sinclair. Will and Princess Arabella got question one wrong, so they've faced the first food challenge—one of the hottest peppers on the planet, cultivated right here in the U.K.," Dylan says. "Your Highness, are you ready for question two or do you need some more milk?"

"Let's just keep going," I say, my words coming out raspy.

"Let's!" she calls. "Question two: what is Will's most annoying habit?"

I wince as I hold up my card. His face falls as he reads what I wrote: *Know-it-all*. Guilt thwacks me on the head when I read his: *Guessing the ending of movies*.

I look into his eyes. Obviously, they're dark-brown pools of pain. "Sorry, darling," I murmur. "I'm afraid I froze up… and I thought you'd write that since that was my biggest pet peeve when we first met. You're not really a know-it-all. But you do have a great deal of knowledge about a myriad of topics."

He nods and raises his eyebrow. "Sure, yeah. I figured you'd say the thing about the movies since we were just joking about it the other night when we were watching *Parasite*."

"Uh-oh! Trouble in paradise?" Dylan asks gleefully.

"Not at all," Will says. "I think we just interpreted the question very differently."

"Indeed," she says. "Next dome!"

I close my eyes, afraid to see what's under it. The audience groans, and "ewww" can be heard around the room. Opening one eye, I see some beetle larvae crawling around on the silver platter. My knees go weak at the same time that my mouth waters in that way it does right before I vomit.

Dylan chimes in with, "Now, Princess Arabella, you couldn't eat these in the jungle. Can you do it now?"

Will picks his up, twists its head off, presses on its body to empty the digestive tract, then pops it in his mouth. He picks up the next one, does the first two steps again, and hands it to me. "Pretend it's a gummy worm."

"Bring out the Bucket of Shame!" Dylan shouts.

Bucket of Shame. Oh, what I'd give to flip her the bird right now —with *both* middle fingers. But I really should be angry with myself. Know-it-all. Why would I think he would write that? I *deserve* to eat this putrid larva after writing something so awful about Will. I gingerly take it and put it in my mouth, chewing and gagging intermittently until it's gone.

Dylan, who herself is looking a little pale, says, "Let's hope you got question three right."

6

Unintentional Insults, Arguments Made Public, and Wildly Unpopular Canadian Cuisine...

Will

"OKAY, QUESTION THREE..." Dylan gives us a wide-eyed grin. "If Arabella were on *Who Wants to Be a Millionaire,* who would her phone-a-friend be?"

I smile back, holding up my card. *Me.*

Then, I glance at Arabella's and see *Arthur* written in black ink. Huh. I was not expecting that. I keep my smile plastered on while I set my card down, feeling like a total fool.

"Oh dear," she says. "You're zero for three. Bad luck."

"Your brother? Not me, the know-it-all?" I ask with a playful bump on her arm.

Arabella blanches. "I'm *awful* at this. Of course you would be my phone-a-friend."

Dylan tilts her head. "Then why'd you write down your brother's name?"

"Can't you have more than one phone-a-friend?" Arabella's voice is so quiet, it's nearly a whisper. "I mean, depending on the question?"

"I'm afraid not," Dylan says, giving her a mock-sorry look. "For our purposes, it's just the one and you chose your brother."

Arabella turns to face me, her eyes filled with guilt. "If I could choose two, you would absolutely be my phone-a-friend. Especially if the question had to do with surfing or survival stuff or nature or filming a television show. No one knows more than you about those things."

"Or so Will thinks, according to you," Dylan adds, salting the wound some more.

"I only wrote down Arthur because I was thinking of questions related to foreign affairs, history, politics, or the like…" Her voice trails off and she gives me a sheepish look. "Sorry."

"That's fine, really." I nod and wink at her to cover up the sting of knowing she thinks her brother is smarter than me in almost every way.

The producer appears with a domed plate. When he lifts the lid, there's a small white tented card on it that reads: *Posts of Defeat: you will now complete the rest of the interview while standing on a post with one foot in the air.*

"Brilliant," Arabella says, as we both stand and follow Dylan across the stage where two wooden posts await us. They're each set three feet off the ground but are only about four inches in diameter.

Arabella looks down at her heels and bites her bottom lip. "We're in it now, aren't we?"

"Yup," I say, watching as she daintily removes her shoes.

I hold out one hand and help her get up onto her pole. Once she seems steady, I step up onto mine, using my left leg to balance since my right ankle is still a little weak from breaking it while we were filming the show.

"All set?" Dylan asks.

We both answer in the affirmative so she fires the next dreaded question at us. "Remember, question four is a two-parter: What's the best gift you've ever given each other. And what's the best gift you've received?"

Flipping my card over, I let the world in on the financial dynamics of our relationship. You know, so I can feel extra shitty. My card says, *A shell, a Yacht.*

I look at Arabella's and it says, 'a yacht, a shell.'

"Yes! We got it!" she shouts. "Well done, us!"

I grin through my humiliation while balancing myself. Is it too much to hope that there won't be any follow-up questions to that?

"So, you can't write that type of answer without expecting some follow-up questions," Dylan says.

Of course.

"So, Arabella, you bought Will a yacht, and he gave you... a shell?"

Arabella wobbles a bit and holds her arms out, trying to maintain her balance. "Yes, well, there's so much more to it than it sounds. The yacht was because I felt awful about—"

A loud horn sounds, startling everyone in the audience, then red lights flash while a canned voice repeats: "Spoiler Alert. Spoiler Alert."

Dylan smiles. "I'm sorry, Arabella, you can't answer that question without giving away what happened in the jungle."

Brilliant. Let's just let that answer hang out in the wind until it reeks up our relationship.

Arabella glances at me, the word sorry written all across her face. I give her a thumbs-up. "We got one right at least."

She tips back and forth, managing to regain her balance.

"Moving onto question five," Dylan says. "How many children do you want?"

Arabella has given the safe answer of 'two,' while I have written 'five.'

"Five?" she says, falling backwards and landing on the stage floor.

The audience bursts into laughter. Dylan looks positively gleeful at this revelation. "Well, that's certainly surprising news for the princess."

Quickly recovering, Arabella says, "Two, five. Basically the same."

"Tell that to your lady bits," Dylan mutters.

"You don't really want five children, do you?" she whispers.

I shrug. "I love kids."

"I also love children, but not necessarily in large groupings."

"Oh dear," Dylan says. "It looks like these two have a lot to talk about when we're through here. But first, you'll need to eat the next item from our Gross Out Kitchen since yet again, your answers didn't match."

Arabella tucks her card under her arm and carefully climbs back up onto the post. When she stands, she's got that determined look on her face that I've grown to love.

The dome is lifted and a pungent stench of rotting fish hits my nostrils. My head snaps back and I cover my nose instinctively while Arabella reaches out and plucks a piece off the tray, popping it in her mouth before Dylan can even tell us what it is. She chews furiously, swallows it, gags twice, then says, "Your turn."

"This is a delicacy from French Polynesia called farfaru," Dylan says. "It's fish that has been sunbaked and fermented. Apparently, Princess Arabella is a big fan."

"Not really. I'd just really like to get down and go home now."

I pick mine up and toss it in my mouth, swallowing it whole. Here come the fish burps. Blech.

"Well, Princess Arabella may soon get her wish. Last question! And it should be a fun answer. Who won the last argument the two of you had, and what was it about?"

I flip my card over, knowing we're sunk before I even look at hers. My answer: *We haven't had an argument since we became a couple.*

Hers: *Me. Bill Paxton, not Bill Pullman, starred in Titanic.*

She looks at me. "You can't lie in your answers and expect us to win."

"Sorry if I wanted to protect our relationship. Besides, you didn't win that argument."

"Yes, I did."

"No, you thought Bill *Pullman* was in Titanic. *I'm* the one who knew it was Bill Paxton."

Arabella scoffs, then steadies herself. "Sorry, darling, but you said it was Pullman, remember? You said, 'the guy from the one with Sandra Bullock about the woman who works in the subway toll booth?'"

"I was mixed up about which Bill was in *While You Were Sleeping*, but I knew who I meant. I meant Paxton."

"Well, just because you meant Bill Paxton, doesn't mean that's who you said."

"Oh, to have that conversation recorded," Dylan says. "Or the one when you leave here tonight!"

Arabella turns to her and asks in a very formal tone. "May we climb down now?"

"Yes, of course," Dylan says. "Now, because you missed yet another question, we have one last thing for you to eat."

"I don't think so. I'm done," Arabella says.

"What?" Dylan asks, her face falling for the first time this hour.

"I don't wish to eat anything else. I'm full. And I'm afraid I'll become ill, which doesn't make for very good television."

Dylan tilts her head and scrunches up her nose as if she's very sorry to be giving bad news. "If you're full, Will is going to have to eat two because the game isn't over."

"Come now, we've been good sports and all," Arabella answers. "We've answered your questions and done the challenges, and now we should move on to the next segment. I'm sure the audience has grown tired of watching us choke down disgusting things."

Turning to the audience, Dylan yells, "Are you tired of seeing them eat things from our Gross Out Kitchen?"

A resounding *NO!* comes from the crowd. Of course.

The dome is lifted, and on it are two large brown jiggly blobs. "These have been flown in all the way from Canada. It's called jellied moose nose and yes, it's exactly what you think it is. They cut off the nose, spice it, add onions, boil it, remove the hair, boil it again, then cover it in a broth that turns to jelly."

"Oh, wow," Arabella says, turning her face away from the plate.

"At least it isn't a sour toe cocktail," I say.

She looks up at me. "Tell me that's not really a thing."

I nod. "Up in the Yukon, when someone loses a toe to frostbite, they—"

Arabella holds up one hand, looking slightly green.

"I'll tell you the rest later," I say.

"Or not at all," she answers, staring at the jiggly brown blobs.

"And we wonder why Canadian cuisine hasn't caught on around the world…"

I pick up mine and pop it into my mouth, letting it slide down my throat in lieu of chewing first.

Wow, that was super putrid.

Arabella, beyond caring about seeming rude, clamps her nose with a finger and her thumb. She chews quickly, then gags out, "They missed a hair." Pulling the hair out of her mouth, she finally manages to swallow it, but as soon as she gets it down, she retches. The producer makes it to her in time with the Bucket of Shame and she lets it all go. Repeatedly.

Compassion pushes away my hurt feelings and I rush over, shielding her from the camera as best I can while I hold back her hair. "It's okay," I say, knowing it's anything but okay for a princess to puke on national television.

When she's done, she whispers to me, "I have to leave now."

"All right," I say, putting my arm around her back like a body-guard rushing a celebrity through a mob of fans.

We exit the stage while Dylan informs the audience that it's time for a commercial break, but we'll be back with more in just a couple of minutes. One of the producers descends upon us with a squad of minions. She talks quickly, trying to pep us up whilst Arabella is ushered to a sink backstage and handed a toothbrush, toothpaste, and mouthwash. She sets to work brushing the moose nose vomit out of her teeth.

The director calls, "Thirty seconds!"

"Okay, you two. The hard part is over. When you get back out there, we'll have some fans in the audience lob some softball questions at you. No more food challenges tonight."

"No, we're done," I say to her.

"No, you're not. We've got another twelve minutes of air-time to fill and you're under contract, so you will both be heading back out on the stage."

"Or what?" I ask.

Arabella rinses and spits, then puts one hand on my arm. "It's fine, Will. I'm fine. Let's just get this over with."

I look down at her, my heart lurching at the sight of her pale skin. "Are you sure?"

She nods. "I signed up for this, right?"

I sigh heavily as I follow her onto the stage.

———

"How exactly were those softball questions?" Arabella asks as soon as we settle ourselves into the backseat of her limo. "I mean *really*? How?"

"Yeah, I honestly don't know if I've ever felt so… wiped out," I say, blinking slowly. "The first question was okay—the one about our favourite moment in the jungle, but then everything… just turned."

It turned all right. Instead of answering easy questions about the upcoming show, we were repeatedly peppered about our relationship until the time ran out.

Now we're safely tucked in behind tinted windows while her driver, Norm, pulls out of the ABN parking lot and onto the street. My phone is buzzing away in my suit jacket pocket with Google alerts, which means the show has made quite a splash. Great for my career. Horrible for my relationship. "And did you notice who was in the audience?" she asks, throwing her hands up in the air and continuing before I can answer. "It was clearly packed with women in their child-bearing years, who, let's face it, do not want to see us work. Did Dylan do that on purpose?"

"I don't—"

"I bet she did. That would be such a Dylan thing to do. Bringing on that nasty Will's Wild Girls blogger." Arabella pulls a sour face and imitates the woman who claims to be my biggest fan. "*It's a well-known fact that media attention creates tension in even the best of couples. With the two of you clearly coming from two different worlds and barely knowing each other, do you really expect your relationship to survive?'* Umm, yes, bitch. Actually, I do."

"Yeah, I'm really sorry about her."

"It's not *your* fault," Arabella says. "I mean, other than being stupidly handsome and daring—which you probably can't help anyway—you've done nothing wrong."

"Thanks." I think.

Arabella groans loudly. "And I was a disaster. I basically proved to the world that I'm not up for the challenge of so much as a simple interview."

"You were not a disaster. You were incredible," I say, leaning over and giving her a kiss on the temple.

She rests her head against the seatback. "Liar. I was a sweating, snotting, vomiting, insulting disaster."

"Oh, come on, it wasn't *that* bad."

She looks at me from under her eyebrows. "You needn't coddle me. Especially not after how I insulted you out there."

The sting of her answers comes flooding back, but I dam it off, wanting to concentrate on how I can use this situation to bring us together instead of tear us apart. "Listen, that was a highly pressurized environment—one in which we won't find ourselves again, so there's no use in overanalyzing it. I say we move on to bigger and better things."

I lift her hand and kiss her knuckles, hoping to show it's all right.

But it doesn't work. Arabella shakes her head and purses her lips, clearly on the verge of tears. "I called you a know-it-all and led the world to believe I think my brother to be smarter than you." She sighs. "Not to mention the stupid yacht/shell thing. That can't feel very good. Why did I write that down?"

"Because you wanted to win. I wrote it down too, in case you forgot," I say.

"And we both made you look like… I don't know what."

"A cheapskate?"

"I was going to say poor, but yes, I suppose it does both."

Ouch. She must be able to see through my smile because tears are pooling in her eyes now.

"So what? I'm on the edge of having my career bust wide open, Belle," I say, shifting in my seat so I'm facing her. "This is it for me. I can feel it. Besides, when people see the show, they'll realize why you bought me the yacht. I can hold out until then knowing the world thinks you're my sugar momma."

Arabella lets a tiny grin escape her lips, then she shuts it down and goes back to grimacing. "I can't. I want them all to know how amazing you are and how lucky *I* am to have *you*."

"Isn't it more important that the two of us know how lucky you are to have me?"

That worked. She snort-laughs. "I suppose so, but I still want the world to know what you had to do to get that shell for me."

Shrugging, I say, "In a way it's nice to have our little secret about why the shell means so much, isn't it? It's like having a piece of our story that no one can touch." I kiss her again, gently at first, then with enough passion to let her know we're okay. Tonight was hard, but it was also a step forward for me career-wise.

After a few minutes of snogging each other senseless, the car comes to a stop. I look out the window and see we've arrived at Dwight's. "Come in for a while so I can show you how hot your sense of justice is."

She laughs, then her face falls. "I want to, like, with every bit of my sense of justice, but I really can't. I have to go do damage control with the advisors. They'll be holding an emergency meeting right about now, and if I don't show up, they'll make decisions neither of us will like."

Well, that's the worst thing I've heard all day, which is saying something. I give her a nod and smile. "After the meeting? Maybe I could sneak into the palace for some alone time?"

She gives me a skeptical look.

"I heard it too, yeah. A palace probably isn't the easiest place to sneak into, is it?"

"Not really, but sneaking out isn't all that hard."

"Really?"

"Really. I have some serious apologizing to do."

"I promise to accept. Over and over and over…"

7

Welcome to the Promotional Circuit. It's Everything You Dreamed It Would Be...

Will

"WAKE UP. Will, it's time to get up," Dwight says, his voice muffled by the door.

I open one eye and look at the alarm clock. 5:30 a.m. "Go away. I had a late night."

"Yes, I'm aware of that. I could hear everything, so thanks for that."

I wince and pull my pillow over my face, then, realizing I need to apologize like a man, I get up and cross the small room to the door. When I open it, Dwight takes a few steps back, clearly put off by the sight of me in only my underwear. I give him a sheepish look. "Everything?"

"Enough."

"Sorry, mate, it's just that she was so upset when we left the studio, and I was really hoping to make her feel better about how the interview went."

"Oh, you made her feel better all right." Dwight, who is already dressed in his suit, taps on his wristwatch. "Now, you've got to hustle over to KLAM for their morning show. Your segment starts in forty-five minutes."

"Right. I forgot about that."

"Not all that surprising, really. Now, make sure you look presentable because as soon as you finish there, you have to hightail it over to VTV for the *Mona in the Morning Show*. You're going to be teaching the audience how to tie knots or something."

"Okay," I say, rubbing my eyes.

Dwight starts to walk away, then turns back. "Oh, I don't know if you've ever listened to KLAM, but they're in the shock jock business, so they're going to do their best to piss you off. The worst thing you can do is lose your temper because they'll make you look like a complete jackass. Laugh it off, promote the show, and get the hell off as fast as possible."

"Got it. Stay calm. Keep it light."

"Exactly," he says, pivoting and heading toward the kitchen. When he's part way down the hall, he calls over his shoulder, "And don't forget to strip the sheets and burn them."

———

"Welcome to K-L-A-M radio in the morning. I'm your host, Bowser."

"And I'm Candace the Cutie. And with us as always is Dopey Dan."

"That's right, I'm the dumb one."

Sound effect of an audience making an *awww* sound plays.

Yuck. This is way too much energy for six a.m. My eyes aren't even fully open yet. I have a sip of the stale coffee they offered me when I got here and watch as the three hosts, all dressed in sweatpants and hoodies, pretend they're crazy-excited to be here.

Candace yawns and continues, sounding surprisingly peppy. "It's Friday, so you know what that means!"

A recording of an audience shouting, "No Knickers Day!" plays.

"That's right! It's No Knickers Day, and I, for one, am extra excited because at this very moment, I am looking at none other than Avonia's sexiest man, the fellow all the guys want to be and all the ladies want to be with—Will Banks of the highly anticipated new show, *Princess in the Wild*."

"I was hoping it would be *Princess in the Buff*," Bowser says, hitting the button for an old-timey car horn sound to play.

I set my jaw, then tell myself to relax because the worst thing I can do is get angry. That's what they want, but I have news for them. I'm not going to play their game.

"Tell us the truth, Will," Candace says. "Are you wearing underwear? I'm asking for a friend."

Okay, could I feel any cheaper right now? I laugh off the question without answering while I dream of a day when I don't have to step foot in a radio station again.

"I bet every day is No Knickers Day for Will," Dan says. "He looks like a total free-baller, doesn't he, Bowser?"

"You know it, Dan. Free Willie!" Bowser says, prompting them all to laugh while I sit and wait for an actual question.

Bowser looks at me. "Willie, what about your girlfriend? Does she wear knickers? And if so, what kind?"

Time to change the game. I sit back in my seat and take off the headphones, which garners an immediate reaction from all three of them. They start shaking their heads, and Bowser covers his mic with one hand and says, "Okay, okay. Don't leave."

I give him a long glare until Candace says, "That was offside, Bowser."

"Yes, you went *way* over the line," Dan says. "Don't mind him, Willie. He ate a lot of paint chips as a kid. But seriously. Let's talk about the show because that's what you're here to do."

"Thank you," I say, putting the headphones back on and leaning toward the mic. "The show airs every Thursday night on ABN, and it's a wild ride right from the second we're dropped from a helicopter into the Congo."

"Sounds cool," Bowser says. "I'll be tuning in for sure. Any hard feeling toward Princess Arabella? I mean, here you had a terrific show, *The Wild World*, a total testosterone fest—man vs. nature at its best— and then she prances in and takes over. That's got to feel like a hair up your arse, no?"

"Definitely not. I'm more than happy to share the limelight—"

"—Oh, wait a minute folks, the bullspit metre is climbing!" Candace says. "It's at a level six and still moving up."

Canned laughter.

"Seriously, Will, tell us what happened last night after you two love birds left the studio after your disastrous interview," Bowser says, scratching his shaggy grey beard. "For those of you who missed the show last night—and based on the ratings released by ABN this morning, it was almost nobody in the entire kingdom—you and your new leading lady were on ABN for a pre-show game show of sorts to get people all hyped up to watch your boring nature documentary—"

"Come on, now," Candace interjects. "Anything with a man this hot could never be called boring."

"Thanks, Candace," I say before I realize what exactly I'm thanking her for.

Candace continues. "I stayed up way past my bedtime to watch, and I gotta be honest, Will. You two don't seem to see eye to eye on *anything*. You only got, like, one question right the entire time. Ouch."

"Yeah, Will," Dan says. "What was that car ride like on the way home?"

"Honestly, it was—"

"Oh snap!" Bowser says. "He's going to pretend it was fine, but we all know the truth, don't we? There is *no way* they are in a good place right now."

"I don't know," Dopey Dan says. "I'd let a woman that hot get away with insulting me on national television too."

"Of course you would," Bowser says. "But that's only because you wouldn't have understood what she was saying."

Audience laughter and irritating car horn again.

"Okay, okay, you two," Candace the Cutie says. "We need to let the man talk. Willie, did you guys have lots of makeup sex last night or what?"

"Well, since I'm a gentleman…"

"Snap! They totally did!"

Dan and Bowser high-five each other.

"You totally got it made, mate. I mean, here you are, hooking up with a beautiful princess who is not only a major career boost for you, but she's so rich, she bought you a yacht."

"Yeah, tell us about the yacht. What did you have to do to score a gift like that?" Bowser asks. "Because I gotta tell you, I'd be up for anything if that was the payday."

Stay calm. Don't let them win. "I can't really get into specifics because—"

"Her dad made you sign an NDA?" Dan asks.

"You don't want your girlfriend to cut you off?" Bowser adds.

"Hey, don't give him a hard time," Candace says. "I'd want to keep them happy too if I was him. He never has to work again. Isn't that right, Will? If you keep the princess happy, you can live off of her daddy from now on."

Oh, this sucks big hairy balls. "Well, obviously I have no intention of—"

"Sure you do," Bowser says, laughing. "I know I would."

Bugger. They're going to make me look like a giant arse, aren't they? "Well, when you have self-respect and you love what you do for a living as much as I do—"

"*Nobody* loves their job," Bowser says. "That's why they have to pay you to do it,"

I raise my voice and talk over him. "—Then you definitely wouldn't want to give that up for anything. Luckily for me, Princess Arabella doesn't expect me to."

Bowser raises his voice over mine. "Oh, sure, that's what she says now, but once you get that ring on her finger, ooohhheee!"

"Speaking of rings on fingers, are you going to make an honest woman of her or what?" Candace asks.

"Well, that's a rather old-fashioned way of thinking about—"

"Yeah, baby! They're doing it all right." Inappropriate moaning sound.

Annnddd… I'm done. "All right. That's about enough. I came here to talk about our upcoming show," I say. "But clearly your goal is to have a go at me, which I don't mind, but you're also having a go at Princess Arabella, and that's where I draw the line."

"Look at you taking charge of the interview," Candace says. "Mummy likey!"

"Great," I say. "Anyway, the show airs for the next five weeks starting this Thursday at 8 p.m. on ABN. I'm really proud of the work we did and how Princess Arabella rose to the challenge. We were dropped into the Congo and we had to make our way out of the jungle with only each other and a small supply of survival gear. No food, no water, not even a proper first-aid kit, which would've been helpful because we faced some potentially fatal situations out there."

"Our audience is probably more interested in the *positions* you found yourselves in rather than the deadly situations," Dan says before squeezing the car horn again. *Uh-ROO-Gah!*

"Okay, very funny. We all get it, but I would remind you that the princess is deserving of respect as both a member of the royal family and as a woman." Now I sound like the principal at a stuffy private school, so I guess they win, but sod it. I really don't care at this point.

"Somebody's getting defensive!" Candace says. "As a woman, I have to say I really wouldn't mind talking about having sex with you. In fact, if you want to head down into the break room with me, I'd be happy to come back and tell everybody all about it."

Moaning sound.

"Well, that's all the time I have," I snap. "I have a very busy day ahead so thank you for having me, and I wish all your listeners a wonderful day."

"Oh, he's standing up and walking out, folks. Looks like we've managed to upset the unflappable Mr. Adventure Pants."

"Oh, he's gone. He's a bit of a sensitive Sally, isn't he?"

"He's a whiny Wilma."

"I'd still do him."

"So would I."

8

Trolls Be Trollin'...

Arabella

WILL's Wild Fangirls Blog Post Entry #912
September 16th Edition

Hey fellow fangirls,

I finally did it. I finally met my future husband in-person. That's right! Last night, yours truly had the thrill of a lifetime as an audience member at the ABN studios for the season three pre-show of The Wild World (I'm still calling it that because I REFUSE to give her top billing). In a surprisingly smart move by the network, they invited all the applicants for the co-host position to be in the audience so we could meet Will live and in-person.

And I have to say, he is every bit as delicious in-person as he is on screen— even more so. He radiates a masculine energy that is like catnip or chocolate or like Pierce Brosnan for my mum.

The only problem was that she *had to be there (and we all know who I'm talking about, so don't make me use her name). Oh well, what the hell? Let's give her a name, shall we? Princess Useless Face?*

Princess Pukes-A-Lot?

You decide. I'll post a poll at the bottom and the one with the most votes becomes her new moniker here on WillsWildFangirls.com.

Anyway, SHE was there messing the entire thing up for poor Will, who had to eat all kinds of disgusting things just because she couldn't seem to get any answers right. I mean, honestly, does she not know him at all? Clearly a man like him would want more than two children (which was her stupid answer). And he SHOULD have more than two. In the event of an apocalypse, he should be solely responsible for repopulating the planet with his perfect genes.

But I digress because I was talking about the disaster that is Princess Pukes-A-Lot. (That one's growing on me).

IMHO, last night was definitely the beginning of the end for them. Not only is she horrible under pressure, but she also made so many disparaging remarks about Will, I wouldn't be surprised if they broke up before they left the building. My favourite part was the bit when she called him a know-it-all who actually knows very little. I'm basing that last bit on her not picking him as her phone-a-friend. Can you believe it? She'd pick Prince Arthur, that total wanker, over WILL FREAKING BANKS?

Seriously stupid.

Anyway, onto me and Will's moment together when I was selected to ask him a question during the Q&A at the end of the show. The way his eyes locked on mine when I was questioning their relationship—there was DEFINITELY something between us. It's like the entire world disappeared and it was the two of us alone and he just knew that I'm the one who truly gets him. Sigh.

That was the single greatest moment of my young life. It was the beginning for us. I know it was.

He'll dump her sorry arse so we can be together forever. There's no way someone who grew up so spoiled and sheltered could ever be the right girl for him.

And to my darling Will, I say this:

It's fine if you want to have your fling with the pretty princess. I don't mind, really. Because soon you'll grow bored of her pathetic, weak-stomached, boring self, and you'll be ready for a real adventure girl—and that's where I come in. I'll be waiting right here for you, Will. Always. Knowing my chance with you is right around the corner,

The future Mrs. Will Banks

. . .

COMMENTS:

WillGirl25: Get in line. I was there last night too, and I didn't notice any spark between the two of you. But truth be told, there was no spark between the two of them either, so I guess there's hope for the rest of us. Princess Pukes-A-Lot all the way for me.

Reply: FutureMrsBanks: You're clearly blind if you didn't see what was going on between us. Blind, I say!

ChickPea411: She was awful last night. A total disaster. I can't believe how quickly she sold him down the river after everything he's tried to do for her. And honestly, how much dramatic vomiting can one person do? And the gagging? Pulease! She should just go back to her daddy's house and live out the rest of her days cross-stitching and sipping tea. My vote is for Princess Useless Face.

Reply: FutureMrsBanks: Right??! Seriously! She might as well have called him stupid to his face. And she bought him a yacht? How desperate does a woman have to be to buy a guy a yacht? Like for reals.

RealHouseWivesRock: LOL! You nailed it. I've never seen two people worse for each other in my life. I give it a week, tops. Also, I vote for Princess Pukeface. It has a better ring to it.
Reply by FutureMrsBanks: Haha! That's a good one too. I'll throw it in the poll.
WillGirl25: A week? I'm sure it's already over, based on their body language when they were walking out to the limo. He couldn't even look at her. Whatever they're pretending to have is solely for ratings.

. . .

ChickPea411: But what about their yacht trip? You really believe they'd spend all that time floating around the ocean together if they weren't really an item?

WillGirl25: As if they even got on a yacht together. FAKE NEWS!

———

Text from Arthur to Me: *Do yourself a favour and don't go online for a while. Reading the comments about your interview will not do you any favours.*

Me: *Too late. Just reading what Will's Wild Fangirls have to say about me.*

Arthur: *Close the page immediately! Do NOT torture yourself with the words of the jealous and sad. And whatever you do, do NOT respond to any of it! Take it from me, you'll only get sucked into an unwinnable negativity vortex.*

Me: *Don't worry. I'm not a complete idiot. (No offence.)*

Arthur: *Some taken.*

Me: *Your ego is large enough to survive that little jab.*

Arthur: *You're welcome for looking out for you.*

Me: *Thank you.*

9

How to Lose Friends and Upset People...

Will

"I NEED YOUR HELP," I say into the speakerphone.

"Trying to figure out how to end things with Arabella after that disastrous interview?" Emma asks.

"Ha. I'm serious, Emma."

"So am I. It was awful, and as your big sister, it's incumbent upon me to let you know when I see some red flags in my baby brother's relationship. Two kids versus five? That's a pretty big difference. Plus, she didn't even pick you as her phone-a-friend."

"We're fine. She's just not good under pressure. Now listen, I need to talk to Pierce if he's around."

"He's right here listening. We're still in bed."

Pierce is a famous author from Avonia who happens to have grown up with Prince Arthur and his crowd so he's the perfect guy to go to for advice.

"Hi, Pierce."

"Hi, Will. Don't listen to Emma. The interview wasn't *that* bad," Pierce says.

"Thanks. I'm glad I have one ally. Listen, I'm going to meet the family and I need to know what to wear."

"Ooh! Meeting the family," Emma says. "That *is* a big step. You only get one chance to make a first impression."

"And that's why I need your help. I have no idea how to dress or what to say or what to bring. I mean, what kind of gift do you give a king?"

"Generally speaking, they love paintings of themselves commissioned by famous artists," Pierce says. "Or quasi-meaningful bronze statues."

"Well, since that's not exactly in my budget or my time frame, we may have to think outside the box."

"Right. When's the big meet?"

"I'm heading over there in two hours."

"In that case, stop at Porter's Fine Liquors and pick up the most expensive bottle of cognac they've got."

"Okay, good. I can probably swing that. King Winston likes cognac?"

"No idea, but it's a classy drink," Pierce says. "To be honest, it'll likely get passed on to a servant at Christmastime, but the effort will at least count for something."

"Ooh! What about something for the babies?" Emma says. "People love that when you spoil their children."

"Good. Okay," I say, jotting down 'baby gifts' on a scrap of paper I found in Dwight's recycle bin. "But what would you get for toddlers?"

"Let me text Libby," Emma answers. "She'll have loads of ideas."

"Thanks, I appreciate that. So what should I wear, Pierce?"

"Depends on what the invite said."

"Verbal invitation from Arabella."

"Any clue what you'll be doing?" Pierce asks.

"Obviously they're watching the premiere of *Princess in The Wild* together..." Emma says in a 'you should've known that' tone.

"Righto. Congratulations on that, by the way," Pierce says. "I hope it's a massive hit."

"Pierce is going to tweet about it later," Emma says.

"I am?" Pierce asks.

"Of course you are. Because you want my baby brother to succeed so he doesn't end up living in our guest room, right?"

"Excellent point. We've already had to suffer through my brother living with us. I don't know if I can handle yours."

"Thanks for that," I say, pretending to be offended. "Now what do you hoity-toities wear when you're heading over to watch telly with the royal family?"

"I'd go sports event casual, myself," Pierce says.

"Could you be more specific? I seem to have forgotten my chart of appropriate attire for visiting the upper crust."

"Huge mistake. You should probably laminate it and tether it to your suitcase from now on," Pierce answers. "Sports event casual includes a sports jacket, obviously, in a casual colour such as navy or light brown. No black. Button up shirt by either House of Bijan or Brioni, preferably in a light blue. Starched and ironed."

"Obviously," I say, scrawling notes as quickly as possible with a shaky hand. "And what? A nice pair of dark jeans?"

"God, no. The most casual I would go would be chinos in light tan, starched and ironed with a crease down the front at dead centre, and matching socks. Add a pair of brown leather dress shoes in matte, not shiny—shiny's too dressy—and you should be good to go."

"Tell him what kind of belt to wear," Emma adds.

"Oh right. A belt. I almost forgot," I say. "Should it match my shoes or what?"

"That would be a safe choice," he says. "You *do* sound nervous. What time is it there?"

"5:42."

"Hmm, that really doesn't give you much time. Tell you what, Boccino's Men's Wear will still be open for another eighteen minutes. I'll ring them up and have them stay open late for you. It won't be cheap, but they'll make sure you're royalty-ready."

"Thanks, Pierce. I really appreciate it. I need everything to go perfectly tonight."

"Will, this sounds serious," Emma teases. "I've never heard you like this before. 'What gifts should I bring? What belt should I wear?' You might just love this woman."

"That's the problem. Anything from Libby yet?"

"Yes, she wrote back with three options: Brio's My First Railway, Fisher-Price Bounce and Spin Puppy, or a Radio Flyer 3-in-1 wagon with canopy. Whatever you do, don't get anything that plays Baby Shark. They'll hate you forever."

"No Baby Shark," I mutter as I flip the paper over and write that down.

Emma starts humming the tune, then says, "Oh for...! Now I've got it in my head. It'll be there for days. Thanks a lot, Libby."

Pierce laughs and sings, "Mommy shark! Do-do-do-do-do-do..."

"Pierce! That is not funny!"

"Okay, thank you guys so much. I better run if I'm going to make it to the fancy liquor store, the clothes shop, and the toy store. Crap. I forgot I should pick up something for the Princess Dowager as well. What do you get a woman in her eighties?"

"That one I know—she's a big gin drinker," Pierce says. "Grab a bottle of Spring Gin Gentlemen's Cut if you can or Ferdinand's, but only if they have Goldcap."

"I should probably have started this yesterday," I say.

"No," Emma says. "A few weeks ago is more like it."

"Thanks for that very helpful bit of hindsight," I say.

"You're welcome," she says. "Text us to let us know how it goes."

"I probably won't, but that doesn't mean I don't appreciate your help."

———

"How long until you're here?" Arabella asks.

"I'm just crossing the bridge now. I can see your family's shack from here." I shift into low gear, wishing I had rented a Jaguar. As reliable as this Volkswagen is, it's not exactly going to fit in parked in front of a palace.

"Excellent," she says, sounding as excited as I feel nervous. "I'll head to the front entrance and meet you there."

"Can't wait." Well, that's not strictly true. I'm not sure any man throughout history has ever been giddy with anticipation when he's about to meet his future in-laws. (Well, hopefully they'll be my in-laws. And in my case, multiply the feelings of dread tenfold because I'm sure there's no way any of them will approve of me. I'm not exactly what most fathers would want for their daughters, let alone a king.

Well-educated? No.

But, he must have a stable job, at least? Oh wait, no, he doesn't.

Surely he has a nice home that they can share? Nope. Tiny two-room villa in the staff quarters at his family's resort.

Oh, but if they own a resort, he must come from money, no?

Nope. They barely get by.

My gut tightens as the looming four-storey stone palace grows nearer. The sun has set already and the grounds are lit up in a way that some would likely find inviting, but to me, it all looks rather shadowy and sinister. If we could have met under *any* other circumstances, I'm sure it would've been better than the situation I'm about to walk into—watching the first episode of our reality TV show together. I'm sure Dylan included any and all disparaging remarks I made about Arabella that first day, likely on repeat before and after every commercial break. Urgh.

They're going to hate me, aren't they? I'd hate me if I showed up to date my daughter. Oh, that sounded wrong. Dammit. I hope I don't say anything that stupid in front of them. *Baby shark! Do-do-do-do-do-do...*

Bloody hell, that song really does get stuck in your head.

When I reach the tall wrought iron gates, I'm stopped by a man in full dress uniform who steps out of the guardhouse and holds up one gloved hand, palm out, facing me. I roll down the window and smile, wondering if he'll recognize me. "Good evening."

"Name."

Apparently not. "William Banks. I'm a guest of Princess Arabella."

He gives me a hard look, then says, "Oh, yes. I do recall seeing your name on the list. I'm going to need you to step out of the car and open the trunk, sir."

I do as he says and find myself being patted down from my neck to my ankles, including a quick check for weapons in my new tan socks by the surly guard while his partner, who seems to have appeared out of nowhere, goes through the gift bags in the trunk. "Sven, it looks like we're going to be getting cognac for Christmas."

"Hennessey Limited Edition?"

"Nope. The cheap stuff."

Cheap? That was close to two-hundred dollars!

Sven rolls his eyes and finishes patting me down while the cognac critic continues looking through my things. He unzips my duffle bag and digs around, lifting out my toothbrush. "Are you planning on staying the night?"

"Only if you think the princess will respect me in the morning," I say.

Clearing his throat, he drops the toothbrush back in the bag and glares at me. "We're on heightened security alert at the moment, so you'll either give a straight answer, or we'll happily turn you around here."

"Honestly, it's fine, mate. I'm Arabella's boyfriend. I'm no threat to anyone, unless you had your eye on her, that is." I offer him an easy smile, but he doesn't accept it. "Okay, I'll just shut up and let you finish your job."

"Thank you."

———

"There you are," Arabella says, rushing down the stone steps to greet me. "I was worried you got a flat or something."

I walk around the car and hold my arms out, suddenly feeling overdressed. She's in a pair of grey jogging pants and a long-sleeved black T-shirt. And I'm in the most expensive outfit I've ever owned. "The guards were quite thorough in checking me over. You may have to tell them I'm a friendly."

She reaches up and puts her arms around my neck, then gives me a quick kiss on the lips. "Mm, you certainly are." When she pulls back, she looks me up and down. "I thought we said it was a casual evening."

"What? This?" I ask. "I threw on the first thing I saw in my closet."

"Liar. You clearly went all out at a high-end men's wear shop." Taking my hand, she tugs me toward the stairs. "Come on. I can't wait for you to meet everyone."

"One sec," I say, letting go of her. "I come bearing gifts."

"Really?"

I pop open the boot. "Well, I only get one chance to impress the family of the woman I love."

"That's so sweet of you." She glances at the massive boxes for the kids. "Oh wow, Will, you may have gone a bit overboard."

"Too much?" I ask, staring at the Bounce and Spin Puppy and the wagon that fill almost the entire space. "I was hoping I could at least win over your niece and nephew."

"They'll be asleep by now, but that is so thoughtful of you, really. They are going to love these."

I stack the puppy box on top of the wagon box while Arabella picks up the gift bags. She peeks into the bag for her father. "Ooh, Chateau de Montifaud. Father adores this brand."

"Now, you're the one who's lying."

"He'll appreciate the thought."

I hand her the bag with the gin. "This one is for your gran."

"*This* one will be a big hit."

A footman appears out of nowhere and holds out his arms. "I can take those for you, sir."

"No, thanks, mate, but if you could shut the boot for me, that would be terrific."

We hurry up the steps and two young pages open the massive wooden doors to an enormous hall with marble floors. I fall a little behind Arabella because I'm too busy staring up at the murals on the ceiling to remember to walk. "Wow," I mutter.

"Oh, yes, the front hall is quite grand, but I promise when you get to the apartment, it's very much like a normal house," Arabella says, looking a little embarrassed. "Anyway, we're going to Arthur and

Tessa's. The babies—well, they're toddlers really, but I can't seem to stop calling them babies—should be asleep by now, and since they don't have a night nanny, we need to go to their place if we want to see them in the evenings."

"Brilliant. Who else will be there?"

"Don't worry. Just Gran and Father. I didn't want to overwhelm you with too many of us at once."

We start down a long, wide hallway lined with enormous paintings of people who I assume are Arabella's ancestors. On the right, we pass by a library (obviously, because who doesn't have a library in their very normal house?), next comes a room that I imagine is called a conservatory or something. The other doors are closed, and when we get to the end of the hall, we stop and Arabella pushes an elevator button. "Now, there's no reason to be nervous. Everyone is going to love you."

"Sure, right," I say as the elevator doors slide open. Am I sweating? I am. These boxes are surprisingly heavy and this stupid wool sports jacket is insanely warm.

"No, seriously," she says, stepping on and pushing the three. "You're thoroughly impressive. As soon as the show starts, they'll get a chance to see you in action. Quite an advantage for a man meeting his girlfriend's family for the first time, really."

I highly doubt that.

A few minutes later, we've finally reached the tall white doors that serve as the entrance to her brother's 'apartment.' Two guards stand on either side, dressed in black suits and matching deadpan expressions. I give them each a nod and say hello but neither responds.

Arabella knocks, then opens it without waiting for a response. When we walk inside, we enter a foyer with tall ceilings that leads to the main living area, which is riddled with toys. Huh, that is kind of normal. There's a large blue velvet sofa with a matching love seat, an enormous ornate fireplace with a huge flat screen television hanging above it, and a large grey pig walking towards us.

Arabella sets the bags down on the floor and crouches down when the pig stops in front of her. "This is Dexter. He loves everyone."

She scratches him on the chin. "Who's a good boy? You are, Dexter. You're a very good pig."

He steps closer to Arabella and rubs his head against her leg.

"Hello, you must be Will," a woman on an exercise bike behind the love seat says with a wave. "I'm Tessa. Lovely to meet you. I can't stop pedaling though. According to *The Weekly World News* and a bunch of other media asshats, I'm too fat."

Arabella stands. "You are not! You're lovely." Turning to me, she asks, "Isn't she lovely, Will?"

Okay, this is awkward. "Yes, very. It's wonderful to meet you, Your Highness."

Tessa sips from the water bottle in her hand. "Nope. Just Tessa, okay? Are those for the children?!" she asks, gesturing to the boxes I'm carrying. "Oh! They're going to love those! The Bounce and Spin Puppy especially."

I set the boxes down against the wall and stand, just in time for Dexter, the pig, to mosey over to me. He sniffs my new shoes, then works his way up to my crotch.

"Dexter, don't bug," Tessa says.

"That pig is a total ball-sniffer."

I turn to find the source of this shocking comment, only to see a tiny, old woman in a purple tracksuit. She shakes her head at Dexter while she walks toward me, looking surprisingly spry for someone so wrinkled. "Jesus, he looks like he's going hunting for truffles. Dexter, stop that!"

Yes, I do wish he'd stop that. Being aggressively crotch-sniffed by an enormous pig doesn't exactly make it easy to focus on the conversation.

When she reaches me, she holds out one hand. "I'm Arabella's grandmother."

"Princess Florence, it's an honour to meet you," I say, bowing a little as I shake her hand. Was I supposed to kiss her hand? Bowing and shaking seems wrong somehow. Why didn't I ask Pierce about that? "Arabella's told me so much about you, I feel like I already know you," I add, trying to dislodge the enormous snout from my inner thighs.

The Princess Dowager offers me a wry smile. "Well, the only thing she's told me about you is you're great in the sack."

"Gran!" Arabella says, turning bright pink. "I told you no such thing."

"You should have though, because I can tell by looking that he is," she says, giving me a wink.

Oh, God. Can I go home now?

"Will's brought you your favourite gin," Arabella says, handing the gift bag to her gran.

"Ooh!" Princess Florence says. "Let's crack that shit open, shall we?"

She walks over to the bar area, yanking the bottle from the bag.

"Will, make yourself at home, please," Tessa says. "I'm sorry to be so rude. Normally, I'd offer you a drink, but if I get off this stupid bike before the ride ends, my trainer/manny is going to call me and nag the shit out of me." She pants. "He really is insufferable sometimes."

"It's fine. I'll get him something," Arabella says. She turns to me. "Beer, okay?"

"That would be great." Although, I could use something stronger.

Thankfully, Dexter abandons his search of my nether regions in favour of having a noisy drink of water from a huge porcelain bowl on the floor next to the window. I join Arabella at the bar and wait as she takes two beers out of the fridge, handing one to me. She gestures toward the couch, and when I turn to head in that direction, I'm met by Dexter's snout again, only this time it's freezing cold and soaked as he crams it against my crotch. "Oh, Jesus!" I mutter, shrinking back from him only to spill beer on my four-hundred-dollar shirt. "Bugger."

"Dexter, no!" Tessa shouts from her perch. He backs up, seemingly shocked into submission by her tone, but it's too late. I already look like I pissed myself. Lovely.

Arabella hurries behind the bar to grab a towel while the Princess Dowager glances at my pants while she holds up a crystal glass. "Welcome to the family."

"Thanks," I say, trying to sound agreeable whilst trying to blot my crotch as discreetly as possible.

She tips back her gin and downs it in one go, then sets the glass down and looks past me. "Are they asleep?"

I turn to see who she's talking to. It's Prince Arthur, dressed in sweats and a white T-shirt. Great. So she really *did* mean casual. I tug at the collar on my shirt, wishing I hadn't said full starch.

Arthur rubs his eyes. "Yes, they've been asleep for a while. I nodded off in there. It's just so dark and soothing." He gives me a once-over, eying my wet shirt and pants. Raising one brow, his expression says, 'disaster' as he extends his right hand. "You must be Will."

One firm pump and he's done. "Nice to meet you. I enjoyed your show before you started shagging my little sister."

What do you say to that? My face falls, and I stare after him while he passes by me and goes straight for the bar.

"Arthur! That was terribly rude," Arabella says.

"Honesty's the best policy," he answers, getting himself a beer. He gestures to me with his bottle. "Speaking of which, it seems you've soiled your pants. And your shirt, inexplicably."

Wow. This is just... exactly how I hoped the evening would play out. At least it can't get worse, right?

"You know bloody well Dexter did that," Arabella snaps.

Arthur wrinkles up his nose. "Do I?"

Smug bastard.

"Of course you do," Tessa says. "Now, Will, being the extremely thoughtful person he is, has brought gifts for the kids." She points to the boxes, her legs pumping away on the bike.

Arthur looks at them, then says, "Excellent. They love their Bounce and Spin Puppy, so now we'll have one if theirs breaks."

Shit. Of course they have it already. "I can exchange them," I say, feeling my skin heat up even more.

"Arthur!" Tessa whisper-yells. Then she mouths, "That's enough," to him.

I'm about to say it's fine and I'm happy to take it back when there's a knock on the door. King Winston strides in, dressed in grey slacks and a sweatshirt with a Valcourt United football team logo covering his round stomach. The ensemble looks very out of place on someone who carries himself with such a dignified air.

"Nice shirt, Dad," Arthur says. "Scotch?"

"God, yes. I feel positively ridiculous in this getup." He turns to Arabella, clearly not noticing me yet. "Is this casual enough to make your young man feel welcome?"

She points to me. "Why don't you ask him?"

"Oh, my apologies," he says with a little bow of his head. "William. Pleasure to meet you."

He gives me the same intimidating once-over his son gave me, only he has the decency to say, "Dexter got you, hey?"

A wave of relief comes over me. If there's one person in the room I want to win over, it's him. We shake hands, then he turns to his daughter. *"He's not dressed like a complete wanker."*

"I wouldn't say that," Arthur mutters, before walking over to a fish bowl on the cabinet that contains a single Betta fish. He picks up the food container but before he can open it, Tessa barks, "Nope! You do not get to feed the fish."

Yikes, controlling much?

"But Walter looks hungry. We can't just let him swim around being hungry all the time."

"That's what fish do, and he already ate today," Tessa says. "James fed him."

"You let the *babies* feed him but not me?"

Tessa nods. "They already have a better grasp on proper fish care."

Arabella leans in to me. "Arthur killed Tessa's first fish, Chester, by overfeeding him."

"Did not," Arthur says.

"Did too," Arabella answers. "And then he got his assistant to run around town in the middle of the night to find a replacement, thinking she wouldn't notice."

"Like I don't know my own fish," Tessa tells me, panting a little and rolling her eyes.

I am so tempted to burst out laughing only I don't think I should. Not if I don't want Arthur to hate me forever. But damn, if this isn't awkward as hell because I have to react with just enough delight to show I'm siding with Tessa and Arabella. I settle for a wide-eyed smile in her direction and a laugh that comes out like a cough or some sort of creepy giggle. Why didn't I fake a broken limb so I could get out of this? Or actually break a real limb?

"Thank you ever so much for bringing that up again, Arabella," Arthur says. "Much appreciated."

"So, William," King Winston says. "Arabella tells me your family owns a resort in the Benaventes."

I turn to him with a smile. He might not hate me. Sweet! "Yes, my brother and his wife run it, and my sister is the head chef at one of the restaurants."

"Hmph," he says, before walking over to the bar.

Okkaayyy. I guess the small talk portion of the evening is over.

"Oh, the show's about to start!" Arabella says. "Arthur, turn it on."

She walks over to the telly and faces everyone. "Before we watch the big premiere, I want to thank everyone for coming together. This isn't just a TV show, it's the start of a new life for me, one filled with courage." She pauses and glances at me, "And love."

"Aww, adorable," Arthur says sarcastically. "Now, sit down already so we can make fun of you."

Rolling her eyes, Arabella adds, "Anyway, I hope this will be the first of many nights spent like this, together as a family, watching Will and me fall for each other while we navigate our way through the treacherous jungle. It's a rare opportunity for you to really get to know the man I love, to see him in action, and to see just how tough yours truly can be. By the end of the season, my hope is you'll love Will as much as I do and that maybe you'll even be a bit scared of me."

"Doubtful on both counts," Arthur mutters.

"I think I already do fancy him as much as you," Princess Florence says, giving me the side-eye.

Oh, God, she's like Rosy on steroids.

"Splendid speech, Arabella," Tessa pants. "Really lovely."

King Winston merely nods and offers the smallest hint of a smile.

Everyone settles themselves in the living room, King Winston choosing the armchair, Arthur and Gran on the couch, and Arabella and me on the love seat with Tessa directly behind me spinning away and breathing hard at my back. I suddenly don't know how to sit. I start out with one hand on each knee, back perfectly straight, but then realize I need to look relaxed, except I don't remember how to do that at the moment. Arabella tucks her hand under mine on my knee, but I flinch and move over slightly, making a space between us. I lift both our hands and place them very chastely on the seat cushion. There. That's better.

Video footage begins of Arabella set to classical music, showing her in various dresses, getting out of limos, waving from a carriage, and standing next to her brother and Tessa on the steps of a church at their wedding. Just when I'm starting to think I'm not going to actually be on the program at all, they finally show a picture of me (hmm, no shirt on) while African drums take over the classical music. The words *"One Princess, One Bad Boy, Ten Days Alone in the Jungle..."* flash across the screen, followed by *"What ever will these two get up to out there?*

There's a thin line between lust and hate...

And we're going to find out exactly what it takes to cross that line on...

PRINCESS IN THE WILD"

King Winston clears his throat and stands, then strolls over to the bar and pours himself a scotch that is at least three fingers deep.

Oh, bugger. This is going to be just awful, isn't it?

———

Yes, yes, it is. In fact, it is so much worse than I could have imagined. We've just come to the bit when Dylan blindsides me by announcing Arabella as my co-host, and we all sat here watching in silence as I take Dylan aside and say this little gem, "She's going to be utterly useless out there. No, that's inaccurate. She'll be *worse* than useless because I'm going to have to *literally* carry her through the jungle," to which Dylan says, "It'll give you a chance to test yourself in new ways —not just surviving but also keeping someone else alive." I glare at her and say, "To what end? So she can go on using up oxygen that real people need?"

Arabella's hand slid away at that point, and I can feel four sets of eyes on me. I laugh nervously. "I don't even remember saying that. That is... I'm so sorry... not my finest..."

75

Fuck.

———

We're now thirty-two minutes into the special ninety-minute premiere, and I have never wanted to jump out of a window so badly in my entire life. It's only three storeys up, so a broken leg at best, a snapped neck at worst? Either would be preferable to sitting through another hour of this hell. So far, the show has Arabella painted as the sympathetic heroine, with me cast as the total dickhead who wants the poor thing out of *his jungle*. They seem to have cut any moments of kindness that I showed on day one of our time in the jungle and I know there were at least a few.

Weren't there?

The only bit that anyone in this room found the slightest bit funny was when Arabella rappelled out of the helicopter swearing the entire way down, and only her gran found it amusing. Her father was clearly very irked, Tessa was horrified on her behalf, and Arthur seemed to be filled with disdain when he shook his head and said, "Can't wait to deal with that one tomorrow."

"Sorry," Arabella squeaked.

"Why?" Princess Florence asked. "You showed some spine for once. Good on you."

"Yes, because that's what the people want," Arthur said. "A foul-mouthed princess who shows some spine."

10

So This is Why Most of the Couples from The Bachelor Break Up...

Arabella

WHY THE HELL did I think watching this with my family was a good way to introduce them to Will? Like seriously? WHY? *Why?*

This is the most awkward, awful first impression ever made in the history of first impressions. Will definitely lost any potential allies in the room with his 'oxygen' comment. And even though I really don't remember what I said on our first day, I have a sick feeling it was really nasty. Now that I'm watching us out there, all of the hate I had for him on day one has come rushing back to me. To be honest—and I'm loathe to admit this about the love of my life—he is kind of, sort of, definitely coming off as arrogant.

"Now, Princess Arabella and I are lucky because we have a machete. With this handy device, not only can I cut a path through the dense vegetation, I can also turn stalks of bamboo into a torch, a fishing spear, a fresh water source, as well as an effective weapon."

I roll my eyes in a most unladylike fashion. "I had no idea I was out in the wild with MacGyver. By any chance, can you teach me how to make a bomb out of some seeds and a chewing gum wrapper?"

"If the seeds contain palm oil, sure," he says, getting the best of me. "Now

that it's starting to get dark, we both need to keep our wits about us and watch for anything that could be a threat. This jungle is home to a variety of snakes, the black button spider, not to mention some large wildcats that might be feeling hungry right about now. Most of the animals out here feed at dusk and dawn, which makes this the most dangerous time of day."

I make a squeaking noise and Will turns to me. "What was that?"

"I didn't say anything," I say, raising my eyebrows at him as though he's losing his mind. "For someone who says he's in such a hurry, you certainly stop a lot to make videos."

"It's part of the job," he answers, narrowing his eyes at me. "Oh, right. Sorry. A job is something people do to make money. You see, they have to perform certain tasks as laid out by their employer. If they complete the tasks, they get paid so they can afford things like food and rent."

"Are you still standing there talking?" I say, then start walking again.

Will rushes to get in front of me and says, "I know it's not royal protocol but out here, you walk a few steps behind me."

"Right. I'm happy to let you go first," I say.

Oh, shit. Please cut the scene here.

"If that's what it takes to make you feel like a big man…"

Nope. Of course not.

He turns to me again. "Oh, I'm sorry. Earlier I forgot to explain what rent was. You probably don't know."

"I suddenly understand why you love it so much in the wilderness," I say in a facetious tone. "It's the only place big enough for your giant ego."

"I do not have a giant ego."

"You most certainly do," I say. "You're by far the most arrogant, smug man I've ever met. And I know Kanye West."

"Really? Of the two of us, you think I'm the one with an attitude?" Will lets out a frustrated chuckle. "That's rich coming from someone who's probably never even seen a washing machine."

"You know what?" I ask, clearly looking flustered. "Shut up!"

"Great comeback, Arabella," Arthur says, oozing sarcasm. "You really showed him."

On screen, I continue yelling. *"…I can't bear another word of your self-satisfied, know-it-all commentary about the jungle and survival and… and… me! You don't know the first thing about my life, so just shut up already."*

"Let's get one thing straight. This is my show." He stabs himself in the chest with his thumb. *"Mine. And in case you hadn't noticed, you need me, and not the other way around, so don't tell me to shut up or to do anything else for that matter. Because if you do, I'll happily leave you here to get eaten by leopards."*

My father turns from the screen and just glares in Will's direction. Fuck me, this is the worst idea I've ever had.

"Oh really?!"

"Really!"

"You think that's going to scare me?" I scoff. *"I'd actually rather be torn apart by a pack of hungry leopards than have to suffer through another minute of listening to you drone on and on with that smug smile on your stupid face."*

"For your information," Will says, *"Leopards rarely travel in groups, and if they do, it's either called a leap or a prowl. Not a pack!"*

"She's not wrong about the know-it-all thing, is she?" Father asks Arthur.

"Not a bit."

Will turns and storms off with me stomping along behind him, imitating his voice. "I'm sorry. You probably don't know what rent is. Oh, that's rich coming from someone who's never seen a washing machine." Now, I'm holding up both middle fingers and scowling at his back. "I've seen washing machines, thank you very much. I own a television."

I sink down into the couch while Gran hoots with laughter. "This is the greatest thing I've ever seen! You made a complete arse of yourself, child."

Onscreen, Will is telling me we have to rappel down a cliff to get to the place we're going to camp for the night.

"I'll go first so I can help you if you run into any trouble. Unless you want to go first? I don't want to be sexist about it."

"Just go."

"Gladly. If you could just lean over the edge and film me while I make my descent, that would be very helpful."

Shaky footage by me shows him confidently rappelling down the cliff while I mutter, "Show off."

"Okay, your turn. I'll film you and you go," he calls.

"Perfect," I murmur. *"Make sure you get lots of footage of my sweaty arse in these baggy pants while I slam into the side of the cliff repeatedly. Or better yet,*

when my arms give out and I fall, killing us both. At this point, I'd welcome death so long as I take you out with me." More footage of the ground while I grope around for a vine and say, "You don't want to be sexist. Sure you do, BLEEP-BLEEP. Everything out here can kill you. Don't touch anything and don't drink anything and don't eat anything except these putrid larvae. Oh, and don't be here because I don't want you here."

I turn to Will with a sheepish grin, and he winks at me. "Don't worry about it. I had it coming."

My father decides now is a good time to chime in with, "I should say you did."

Lovely. Thanks, Dad.

The footage switches to Will's camera and he can be heard muttering, "Don't fall and break your neck, Your Highness. It would be such a tragedy to rid myself of your royal uselessness."

Brilliant.

————

Finally, the show is over. Dylan Sinclair appears on the screen and smiles into the camera. "Keep it here to join everyone's favourite feisty fashion critic, Nigel Woods, and me as we do a post-show wrap-up."

Arthur turns to us. "Perhaps we don't watch that bit?"

"I think that would be for the best," I say, my voice barely coming out as a squeak.

He shuts off the telly as soon as the end credits start to roll, putting us out of our misery.

The room is deadly silent for an uncomfortably long time, until finally Tessa says, "Well, I hate to be rude, but I should shower." She slides off her Peloton and grunts out, "Lovely to meet you, Will."

"Yes, I should go too," my father says, standing and making a beeline for the door.

Gran gets up too. "Poker night. I better run."

"Right," I say, unable to move or think or do anything of any value whatsoever.

Arthur glances over his shoulder to make sure Tessa's gone, then he walks over to Walter to feed him. "Well, I imagine you two... need to talk."

He turns to us, finding us both still shell-shocked on the love seat. "Thanks for stopping by, Will. It's been... interesting. Arabella, you'll need to be in the large conference room at about half past seven for whatever emergency meeting the advisors call. I doubt I need to lecture you on the shitshow you've begun."

"No, I'm pretty sure I get it," I say with a nod, feeling tears prick the backs of my eyes.

———

As soon as the elevator doors close, we both let out a long sigh. We're careful to avoid eye contact as we stand against the back wall. Bellford stands at the front of the elevator, and I love him for the fact that he's trying to make himself as small as possible (which is not very small for someone of his stature).

"Listen, Belle, I'm so..."

"Oh, you don't have to," I say, shaking my head. "I feel every bit as bad as you must. Even worse, really. I was horribly unkind."

"No. You were just scared and out of your element, but honestly, I'm not taking any of that personally."

"Oh, thank goodness. And believe me, I'm *absolutely* not taking anything you said personally either. Not even the bit about me being a waste of oxygen. All in good fun, really."

"Good, good," Will says, nodding. "Oh, and when you were imitating me—hilarious. You were spot-on, really. Well done, you."

We both glance at each other and nod, then turn back to the doors as they open. Bellford gets off and steps aside, turns, and keeps his eyes trained down the hall.

"I probably shouldn't stay over, though," Will says, glancing at Bellford as he gets off. "Not because I'm upset or anything. Because I'm definitely *not upset*. But you have to get up really early and... and it's probably best for us each to have a little bit of time to shake this off."

"Absolutely," I answer, nodding as I step off the elevator and head toward the Grande Hall. "If anything, I need some time to get over what *I* said because I feel so guilty."

"Same here," Will says. "I really didn't mean a word of that."

"Oh, I know you didn't."

"Brilliant. Well, that's settled. Maybe we could have dinner tomorrow night?"

"Yes, absolutely," I say. "Let's set something up for tomorrow evening."

We walk in silence until we reach the front door, and a page, who must have been watching the show on his phone based on his inability to make eye contact with either of us, opens the door with a small bow.

"Thanks, mate," Will says, his voice completely devoid of any of his usual charisma.

I step outside with him, only to have two more pages and several guards glance up at us, then stare at their shoes. Will leans in and gives me the lightest peck on the lips possible. "Sleep well."

"You, too."

He turns and jogs down the steps as though his feet can't carry him away from here fast enough, but to be honest, I can't blame him after what has just happened. We've both been caught behaving very badly, *and* they've exposed it to the world which I must say is absolutely shitty. And he's definitely dug himself a giant hole when it comes to my father and Arthur, and truth be told, once those two decide to hate someone, it takes an act of God to get them to change their minds.

I stand for a moment and watch him back out from his spot and make a sharp turn, spitting up gravel with his back tires as he goes.

Oh, Arabella, you idiot, what have you done?

11

Princesses Under Pressure, Scuba Masks, and Ill-Timed Ships Coming In...

Will

I LIE IN BED, trying to ignore the strange brushing sounds and the scent of bleach wafting in from under the door. It's a little after seven and I could use another couple of hours of sleep, having tossed and turned until well after two in the morning. Plucking my phone off the nightstand, I check to see if Arabella has tried to reach me. Huh, she hasn't, but there are several unread messages from my family on our group text.

Emma: *Umm, are you still saving up for that ring? Because if so, after that show, I'm thinking you need to go two-carat minimum. Ouch!*

Libby: *It wasn't THAT bad. How are you and Arabella doing? Everything all right? Did you unwind with a glass of wine after? Maybe managed to laugh it off?*

Harrison: *Oh, it was bad, all right. I'm guessing awkward goodbye as soon as the show ended and you haven't heard from her since.*

Pierce: *Sorry, Libby, I'm with Harrison and Emma on this one. Yikes. Waste of oxygen? I don't even know if it's possible to erase that little gem from their minds. BTW, how'd the cognac go over? And the gin?*

Libby: *Don't listen to them, Will. You two will be just fine. Every couple has their challenges.*

Rosy: *Cuddle Bear, come home where you've got lots of people who love you. (Assuming you broke up already. You did, didn't you?)*

Ugh, I hope we didn't. Sighing, I send Arabella a quick text: *Are you up yet?*

Arabella: *Yup. Already finished ballet, showered, ate, and am now heading into an emergency meeting with the advisors.*

Me*: Wow. Productive princess. I'm still in bed. Do you have a minute to talk?*

My phone rings, and I swipe to answer it when I see Arabella's face light up the screen. "Good morning," she says. "I just want to say how bad I feel about the show. I'm sick about it."

"Me too. I barely slept last night," I say, feeling utterly deflated. "I didn't mean any of those things I said."

"Oh, I know that," she says with a forced chuckle. "I mean, really, you don't think I meant any of the things I said, do you? It would hardly be fair of me to hold you to what you said that day either. It was a horribly stressful and unusual situation for both of us."

"Glad we agree. The last thing I want is for some silly TV show to come between us."

"It won't. You and I are going to be fine," Arabella says.

"Definitely." I turn over in bed and prop myself up on one elbow. "I wish you were here with me right now."

"Me too."

"This whole thing is hard enough without us having to spend our nights apart," I say. "I miss you so much."

I hear a voice in the background, then Arabella covers the mouthpiece of her phone and I hear her murmur something. When she comes back on the line, she says, "Darling, I really must run. The meeting's about to begin."

That thought makes my gut churn. "God, I hate like hell that you have to face that alone. I should really be there."

"Oh, no, I'm afraid that wouldn't make it easier, to be honest," she says. "But never mind. I can handle myself."

There's something about her tone that sounds slightly defensive. "I know you can, Belle. Of all the princesses I've dated, you're the toughest."

She chuckles a little, and the sound makes me feel approximately one percent better about what has happened. "God, I love you."

"I love you too, sweetheart," I answer, not wanting to say goodbye. "Listen, I know you've got a tough day ahead, but I want to take you to MacGillivray Bluff for a picnic tonight. It's supposed to be a warm evening and it's super secluded. Just the two of us. I'll plan everything and pack us some supper. All you have to do is come along."

"That sounds like the very thing we need—some time to be truly alone," Arabella says.

She's the best, isn't she? "Perfect. I'll pick you up around six this evening?"

"I'll be waiting."

"I hope the meeting goes well."

"It won't, but at least we'll be together soon."

With that, she rings off, and I lie back down, worry clouding over the warmth of the last bit of our conversation. If this is how badly the next five weeks are going to be, she and I will have to work extra hard to make this work. I am most definitely going to have to pull off a magical evening that will remind her exactly why we're so perfect together.

Getting up, I throw on a T-shirt and make my way down the hall to the washroom, only to find Dwight standing in the shower, wearing shorts, a T-shirt, water shoes, and a snorkeling mask. He's holding a toothbrush in one hand and a small glass container filled with what I know is bleach in the other. I watch him for a moment while he dips the toothbrush into the liquid, then begins to vigorously scrub the grout between the gleaming white tiles.

"A little early morning cleaning?" I ask him.

He turns to me, his eyes bulging out from behind the lens of his rubber mask. "You take rather long showers, so I'm concerned about mildew forming on the grout. Prevention is key to maintaining a clean home."

"Want me to take a turn?"

He wrinkles up his nose and shakes his head. "Thank you, but I have a system."

Of course he does. He told me the same thing when I offered to load the dishwasher. "Okay, but if you think of something I can do to help around here, please let me know."

"My new favourite client doesn't have to help out at all," he says, dipping the toothbrush and getting back to work.

"Favourite? I take it the ratings were decent last night?"

Grinning over his shoulder, he says, "Better than decent. You knocked *Newlyweds in the Wild* right off their pedestal. ABN hasn't had ratings that good… well, ever, now that I think of it."

A slow smile spreads across my face.

"This is it, William. Your ship has come in, my friend. You are going to be huge—bigger than huge. And I never say that to any of my clients."

"You told me that the first day we met."

"Oh, did I?" he asks. "I was just blowing sunshine up your arse, but this time I actually mean it." He gets distracted by an invisible mould spore and repeatedly scrubs the same spot. "In about twelve minutes, you're going to get a call from Kenneth Abernathy, the CEO of Abernathy & Co. Mountaineering Equipment. They're looking for a spokesman for an all-new line of carabiner clips they're launching."

"Are you serious?" I ask, my heart rate picking up.

"I would never kid about anything like this. He wants you to fly to London to have dinner with his team tonight."

"Tonight?" My stomach drops. "Is there any way we can put it off by a day? I promised I'd take Arabella out for a much-needed escape from reality."

Dwight slowly turns to me. "Will, the CEO of Abernathy & Co. Mountaineering Equipment wants to meet you, and you want me to tell him that you have a date?"

"Obviously not. We could come up with some other reason, couldn't we?"

"No, we can't. I'm sure Princess Arabella will understand, and if she doesn't, you have bigger issues to deal with than some hurt feelings about last night's show."

"Obviously she'll understand," I say, feeling slightly defensive. "It's just that at this very moment, she's being raked over the coals by the royal advisors and I promised I'd make it up to her."

Dwight pauses for a moment and stares up at the ceiling. "How about this? You make the most of this unbelievably rare opportunity that's being offered to you so that you can become fabulously rich. Then she won't have to worry about what anyone thinks anymore because you'll be able to buy your very own palace and spend the rest of your lives playing by your own rules."

I stare at him for a long moment, considering his words. "When you put it that way…"

12

Know-it-all Mannies and Very Disappointed Lady Bits...

Arabella

WELL, I don't want to bore you with all the details but suffice it to say it has been an absolutely crap day. My 7:30 a.m. emergency PR meeting lasted until well after lunchtime with me sitting saying things like, "yes, but—" and "I really don't think—" without finishing a single sentence the entire time. But I didn't cry, so I suppose that's a mini-victory for someone as truly pathetic as I am. Yay, me.

After wasting over five hours listening to the three lawyers covering the same ground in circles, I got back to my office only to find messages from six of my charities, all needing to speak with me urgently regarding my comportment out in the jungle. I spent the rest of the day trying to laugh off what happened and saying things like, "Honestly, Peter, I think it may be a form of Tourette's that only shows itself when leaping from helicopters."

(Incidentally, that one didn't go over well. Who knew his sister has Tourette's?)

Anyway, I'm filled with relief that this day is over so I can let Will help me forget all about it with a whole lot of make-up sex. Not that we need to make up. It's not like we had a fight or something. It'll be more like regular sex—fabulous, passionate, sexy sex with the man I love. Yes, that's precisely what I need. I hurry down the hall toward my apartment to shower and get ready for my date. Will must be crazily excited too because he has texted me at least a dozen times today, asking me to call him about tonight. He even left an old-timey message on my voicemail.

I dial his number, not breaking my stride.

"Hello?"

There's his sexy voice. Mmm.

"Hello yourself. Somebody's excited about tonight," I say in a flirty voice before realizing Bellford can hear me.

"There you are. I've been trying to reach you all day."

Huh, he doesn't sound at all sexy and excited.

"Yes, sorry I couldn't call you back. It's been one horrible meeting and phone call after another all day. To be honest, the only thing that has gotten me through it is the thought of our romantic evening. I cannot wait to see what you have planned."

In the background, I hear a man's voice over a loudspeaker: *Flight number 1082 to London, England, now boarding at gate 56.*

My heart drops to my knees. "Are you at the airport?"

"Yeah, that's why I was trying to reach you. I'm so sorry, Arabella, but I got a call from Kenneth Abernathy. Do you know him?"

"No," I say, stopping in front of the elevator doors and stomping my foot. I won't push the button yet because I lose reception between the second and third floors.

"Oh, I wondered if you might run in the same circles. Anyway, he's the owner and CEO of Abernathy & Co. Seems like a nice enough chap."

"Okkkkayyy…" *Please don't say our date is off. Please don't say our date is off.*

"God, I feel so terrible about this. Kenneth wants to offer me a sponsorship deal and he's asked me to fly to London for dinner tonight."

"Tonight?"

"Unfortunately, yeah. I tried to postpone, but this is the only night he could meet me. I felt just sick about it all day, knowing I was going to have to disappoint you."

"Oh, goodness, don't worry about that," I say, masking my hurt. I push the button, hoping the elevator arrives soon so I can get off this call. "This is a huge opportunity for you. Of course you have to take it."

"It's a huge opportunity for *us*, sweetheart," Will says. "The more my career takes off, the better chance I can build a really great life for us."

"Flight number 1082, now boarding passengers seated in rows five through thirteen."

"Shit, that's me," he says, sounding concerned. (As he should be). "Are you sure you're okay with me missing our big date?"

"I'm absolutely fine with it. In fact, I need time to get myself prepared for my Equal Everywhere Conference next week, so I'll do that this evening."

"You're such a trooper, Belle. I still feel awful about it though. It's just that Dwight says I need to strike while the iron's hot, and I have a feeling he's right. The ratings last night were through the roof, and if I don't make the most of this opportunity —"

I step on the elevator, avoiding eye contact with Bellford, who knows exactly what I'm doing. I push the number three while Will blathers on about making hay while the sun shines. Finally, the phone starts to crackle.

"Will, I'm probably going to lose you. I just got on the lift. Have a lovely time in London."

"Thanks, hon. You're the best. I promise to make it up to you tomorr—"

The call disconnects, and I shove my phone roughly into my suit jacket pocket. The doors open and I grumble as I stalk down the corridor. Bellford, who has obviously heard the entire thing, keeps a polite distance behind me. "You'll make it up to me tomorrow night," I mutter under my breath. "Maybe *I'll* be busy tomorrow night. Who knows? Maybe the head of Nike is going to call and beg me to model sports bras."

"I'm sorry, what was that, Miss?" Bellford asks.

"Nothing, just… being immature."

"Ah, yes, of course."

As soon as I step into my empty apartment, I'm overcome by loneliness and a horrible restlessness. It's suddenly too quiet in here. And too… sterile. I long to be back in the jungle or swimming in the warm Caribbean with Will, even if he is a total date-breaker.

I glance at my desk, seeing the folder of Equal Everywhere notes waiting for me. Nope. There's no way I can go from the tingly anticipation of an incredibly romantic evening to *that*. I walk over to the window and stare out at the meadow behind the palace and the forest in the back. The autumn sun is setting behind the forest, and I spot Tessa jogging whilst the twins ride tricycles in front of her. Her musclebound manny/trainer, Xavier, is strolling along beside her while she huffs and puffs along the pea gravel path.

Tessa—that's who I need right now. I quickly hurry to my room to get changed.

———

"What are you still doing here?" Tessa asks, panting between words. "Shouldn't you be on your date by now?"

"I got stood up, so I thought I would join you for a little fresh air," I say, falling into step with her.

Flora and James both turn their heads to see who's behind them, still furiously pumping their short, chubby legs. Their little faces squeeze my heart, suddenly making me feel slightly better about being thrown over for a business opportunity.

"Hi, Auntie!" James shouts. "Me gots a Tyronnanon." He holds up a tiny dinosaur, causing his trike to make a sharp turn. He quickly puts his hand back on the handlebar and corrects himself while his sister, Flora, an extremely early talker, corrects him. "Tynannosaurus Rex."

I grin at their little exchange.

James ignores his sister and says, "He be named Rex."

"Lovely to meet you, Rex," I say, nodding at the small plastic toy now gripped between his fingers and the handlebar.

"Princess Tessa, you're going to need to bring your pace up a bit," Xavier says to her. "Your heart rate is falling under one hundred."

Tessa turns to me and rolls her eyes. "Okay, thanks, Xavier." Covering her mouth with one hand, she mutters, "I actually think I'd prefer the Shock Jogger at this point."

"I heard that," Xavier says with a little grin. "Don't get discouraged now, Your Highness. It's only two more weeks until the big trip. You *will* lose the rest of that baby weight!"

"Yes, you've already told me that," Tessa says. Lowering her voice again, she pants out, "Good God, my legs are like jelly."

"That's why you better keep running," Xavier says. "Faster, kids! Don't let Mummy catch you!"

"This is slightly humiliating, no?" I ask her, feeling my heartbeat pick up. "We're being outpaced by preschoolers."

"Those tricycles have special wheels or something…" Pant, pant. "…that make them unbelievably fast. Now, back things up to the moment before James interrupted you." Pant, pant. "The bit about how you got stood up."

"Yes, Will got a better offer," I say, then quickly realize how bad that sounds. "He has a chance to rep some company that makes mountain climbing equipment. He's flying to London as we speak to meet up with the CEO."

"Ah, his star is on the rise," Tessa says with a firm nod.

"So it would seem," I say, starting to pant. I hate running. "I'm happy for him, I really am."

"But?"

"But we needed to have an evening together alone."

"I take it things ended on a sour note last night?" Tessa asks as we make a left turn and follow the path toward the river.

"Time!" Xavier shouts suddenly, causing both Tessa and me to jump.

I stop running thinking that he means her workout is over. Tessa stops running as well, but she quickly hops over to the grass and starts doing burpees while her kids skid to a halt and count them out with Xavier's help. I stand there, slack-jawed, as I watch her jump in the air, then crouch down, plant her hands on the ground, flailing her legs out behind her into a plank position, then jump back up. When she gets to ten, her kids cheer for her and she nods at them, giving them an exhausted-looking thumbs-up before getting back on the path. "We get to walk for thirty seconds now," she says with a tired smile.

"Thank God," I answer. "Where were we?"

"Sour note," Tessa says, sucking in some air.

"Righto. I wouldn't say it was so much sour as extremely awkward. I mean, I'm not mad at him, *at all*. And he's totally cool with what I said, too. If anything, I needed to come to terms with how poorly *I* had behaved."

"How mature of you," she says sarcastically.

"Okay, between you and me, hearing myself described as a waste of air wasn't exactly a welcome experience. But he really didn't know me at the time, and it's not like I had very positive feelings for him when we first met."

"True, it was pretty much even as far as nasty insults went."

I let out a long sigh. "I wish we'd never filmed that show."

"If you hadn't, you wouldn't have fallen in love."

"Good point."

Tessa stops walking and turns to me. "Listen, this whole thing is going to be a challenge for you to get through, but if you can do it, you two'll be golden."

"Keep it moving, Your Highness," Xavier says.

Tessa drops to the ground. "Just need to tie my—"

"I'm not buying the shoelace thing again."

"Damn," she says, straightening up and picking up the pace.

"It's all so complicated, you know? I mean, trying to make it work with such different backgrounds and lifestyles. And it's not like he's going to get Father's blessing. Or Arthur's, for that matter. He was completely pissed at him last night and that was *before* the show aired."

"Listen, if Arthur and I could make it work, anyone can. Just think of all the horrible things I wrote about him and, well, the entire family, really. We've all gotten past that long ago."

"Yes, we have," I say, even though her awful words pop into my mind without my permission. *Inbred leeches. Useless drains on society.* "What you wrote about us was far worse than what Will said."

"Exactly. And if you managed to forgive me and found it in your heart to welcome me into the family, your father and Arthur can do the same with Will. It'll just take some time."

"Yes, you're probably right," I say, even though she's completely wrong. It's one thing for me to have forgiven Tessa, but I'm a total softie, whereas Arthur is like a stone wall when it comes to anyone hurting his family. Will would have to do something monumental to win him over.

"Be patient. Let the show wrap up, then we can get everyone together again for a do-over," she says. "But in the meantime, I'll be sure to distract Arthur every Thursday night."

"Brilliant, thank you," I say, feeling briefly grateful before I go right back to feeling like an idiot. "Honestly, why did I think watching the show together would be a good idea?"

"Not sure, really," Tessa answers.

"It's because you're proud of Will," Xavier says, strolling along beside us. "And you love him, which caused you to forget all about how much you two hated each other when you first met."

And I thought Will was a know-it-all. He's got nothing on the manny. Although, now that I let his words sink in a bit, I realize he's right, and I actually do feel slightly less stupid about the whole thing. "Thanks, Xav."

"No problem, Your Highness," he says. "Now, pick up the pace, you two. We're heading into a ninety-second burst at level eight exertion. That's where the real fat burning happens."

Tessa's shoulders drop as she starts to run faster. "I should just pretend I'm sick and make Arthur go on his own to England."

"Or you should realize you're absolutely beautiful the way you are," I say.

"Nope, both bad options," Xavier says. "You set a goal, Princess Tessa. Don't fail yourself now. Not when you're so close."

"I hate him sometimes," she mutters to me.

Xavier interjects with, "No you don't. You just hate being held accountable to yourself."

"Do you have to be right *all the time?*" she pants as she kicks it into high gear.

Instead of answering, he zips ahead of us to grab James, who has gone off the path and is now heading in the direction of the river. Tessa and I immediately stop running, both of us bending at the waist with our hands on our knees.

"Well, I suppose when he does stuff like that, it's worth having him around," I say.

"Just barely," she answers.

13

Liar, Liar, Chanel Skirt on Fire...

Arabella

"YOU'RE IN ITALY?" I ask, sitting back down on my bed. It's early morning and I woke to a text from Will telling me to call him as soon as I got up. "So I guess we're not going out tonight?" I ask, unable to come up with anything intelligent to say.

"I'm *so* sorry. Supper with Kenneth went so much better than I could have expected. We got to talking about the best places in the world to climb—he's a real climber too—and it turns out neither of us have been to the Dolomites, which is crazy when you really think about it because it's in the top five climbing spots on the planet. Honestly, it's right up there with Kalymnos and El Capitan. So he just said, 'Let's go, we can film the commercial while we're there,' and we hopped on his jet and here we are," he says, sounding far too enthusiastic for this hour of the day. "Kenneth's so cool. You'll love him. He even called Bear Grylls a total hack. Can you believe it? He also said I'm the real deal, which is why he wanted so badly to meet me. It's actually kind of flattering."

"Sounds like it," I say, aiming for a supportive girlfriend tone but missing badly.

He doesn't seem to notice. He just keeps rambling. "Anyway, I didn't want to call from the plane in case I'd wake you. I hope you're not upset. We'll only be a couple of days, and to be honest, it's going to be really great for the show, because we'll be live-streaming our climbs. But I'd hate it if you were mad about this."

"Mad?" I ask. Hell yeah I'm mad. Who goes to Italy on a whim without bothering to tell his girlfriend he's leaving? I get up, tucking my mobile between my ear and shoulder, then pull on my ivory silk robe. "Of course I'm not upset. This is huge for your career."

"Thank God, because the entire time we were flying, I was so worried that you're going to be really upset or that you'd feel like I'm basically abandoning you when things aren't necessarily going well."

"Not going well? Between us?" I ask, my heart speeding up in my chest as I stare out the window at the meadow.

"No. God, no. I meant with your family and the whole first episode and all that."

The way he says it is casual and detached, as though it has nothing to do with him. It's as if the fact that my family completely disapproves of him is utterly irrelevant to him. Or maybe he's just excited and I'm reading something into it that isn't there. "Do you know when you'll be back?"

"Kenneth thinks we should be in and out of there in three days. He knows I'm expected back in Avonia by Tuesday. Dwight booked me a breakfast television guest slot teaching people how to make bannock or something like that. I'm not really sure. Anyway, I'm hoping to see you Sunday night, but Monday at the very latest, depending on the weather. Either way, I promise I'll make our date extra incredible."

"Brilliant, yeah. It'll be all the more wonderful for the anticipation." There, did that sound sufficiently supportive? I turn from the window and walk toward my en suite, my bare feet slapping against the cold marble floor.

"Have I told you lately how lucky I am that you're my girl?" he asks, melting my chilly heart a little. "Honestly, Belle, you're the best. A lot of women would be annoyed when something like this pops up without any notice, but not you. It's one of the things that makes us such an amazing couple—we both understand what it's like to have to rise up to these types of obligations."

"Well, in your case, it's rising up by way of belaying." I chuckle a little to soften what started out as a supremely sarcastic comment.

"You are upset, aren't you?"

Apparently my chuckling didn't quite cover my true feelings. "If I were, would you get on a plane and rush back home?"

"See, when you say something like that, it makes me think you're actually not happy."

"Honestly, my feelings on the matter are irrelevant to the outcome. You're already there, and it's a wonderful opportunity for you, which I would never want to take away. And so, we pivot and press on."

"Is that your family motto?"

"No, our motto is *neque oblivisci nec ignoscetis*. Neither forget nor forgive."

(That's not really our motto. It's actually *officium potissimum*, which is Latin for duty above all, but scaring him a wee bit isn't necessarily a bad thing, is it?) "Now, I really must run because I have a full day ahead of me. Have a marvelous time. Be safe and I will see you in a couple days for our incredible incredibly romantic date."

"Yes, you will. And yes, it will be."

"Love you."

"I love you too."

———

Two days later

ABN Entertainment News Weekly

"I'm Veronica Platt. Welcome to Entertainment News Weekly. Tonight's top story—trouble in paradise for a certain princess? That's what the entire kingdom's been buzzing about since Princess Arabella's new beau, Will Banks, her co-host on *Princess in the Wild*, has gone MIA—to Italy of all places. Giles Bigly joins us live in-studio from the unscripted television headquarters of the ABN Studios."

Giles is seen standing in front of the glass doors that read 'Unscripted' in white lettering. He's looking off to the left speaking with someone. "This is ridiculous. I can literally see the studio door from where I'm standing. Is it really necessary to have me out here in the hallway when I could be—"

He stops speaking and turns the camera. "Good evening, Veronica. We've got quite the story on our hands today as the producers of *Princess in the Wild* have been scrambling to find a replacement for several promotional events that Will Banks was meant to take on this week as part of his contractual obligations."

"Yes, yes, that's very interesting," Veronica says. "But I think our viewers may be more concerned about what's happening between Princess Arabella and Will, relationship-wise. And why would he disappear to one of the world's most romantic places without the woman he claims to be the love of his life?"

Giles narrows his eyes, his shoulders slumping slightly. "Yes, I suppose that is what people are interested in, isn't it? Now that the lines between reality TV and actual news seem to be crisscrossed so badly, no one can untangle them. It's like a spool of thread that's been left with a litter of unsupervised kittens all afternoon."

"And apparently we're mixing a little poetry in now to top it all off," Veronica says, letting out a hearty laugh. Her face grows serious again. "Joining me in the studio is Hannah Gable, owner of the website and blog, Will's Wild Fangirls, to discuss these recent events. Hannah, you call yourself the quintessential expert on all things Will Banks. Thank you for joining us."

Giles' voice can be heard over the audio of Veronica. "*She* gets to sit at the desk? That tweenage stalker who's obsessed with Will Banks' abs? Have you seen her site? It's just shirtless—"

"Oh, the producer seems to have forgotten to shut off Giles' mic. Darrell, can we cut him, please?" Veronica stares intently at the camera. "Much better. Sorry about that, folks." Turning to Hannah, she smiles. "So, you have a theory as to exactly what's happening between Princess Arabella and Will. Would you like to share that with us?"

"Love to. I'll tell you exactly what's going on between them—

absolutely nothing. It's a ruse, Veronica. One of these Hollywood set-ups for publicity."

"How can you be so sure? If it is a ruse, they've definitely gone to extraordinary lengths to make it appear as though they're a couple. They've been photographed together in places as far as the Cook Islands, the Benaventes, and of course here in Avonia."

Hannah purses her lips and shakes her head knowingly. "Have you ever heard of a green screen, Veronica?"

"I definitely have, having spent the better part of my adult life in the film and television industry. Have you got any proof that they're not a real couple?"

"Does anyone have proof that they are a couple?" Hannah asks. "Listen, I've been studying Will for over three years now. I know his every habit. I've watched every second of every piece of footage that's ever been shot of him. I know his favourite food. I know his favourite band. And I know that someone as dull as dishwater like Princess Arabella simply could not hold his interest for more than a few hours. Is she pretty?" Hannah shrugs. "I suppose in a conventional sense, yes. But does she have staying power to keep a man like him interested?" Shaking her head, she says," Absolutely not. I mean, look, the first chance he got, he took off to Italy, which, in case you don't know, is on the other side of Europe. It's like *really* far. When I found out he was over there, I tried to book a trip to follow him, only I don't have enough flyer miles to go. But trust me, if it is a real relationship, he's looking for a way out."

"Well," Veronica says, tilting her head thoughtfully. "I do have to say, when they were on the pre-show, they didn't seem to know each other all that well. They got less than thirty percent of the answers right. He wants five kids and she wrote two?"

"Right?" Hannah nods. "I mean, she didn't even pick him as her phone-a-friend."

"There you have it, folks. A man on the run, a princess left behind. And only her brother to be her phone-a-friend."

"Oh, for fuck's sake." I shut the TV off and pour myself a tall glass of gin, top it up with a splash of orange juice, and a couple of ice cubes. Well, this is just great. First, Will takes off without even bothering to tell me he's going, and now I've got these yahoos talking about how dreadfully dull I am.

Am I dull?

Maybe I am. I catch sight of myself in the mirror. My hair is still in the tight bun from this morning, and my barely there, very dignified makeup is still in place. Huh, that woman staring back at me *does* look dull. And uptight actually. And much older than twenty-nine.

I have a sip of my drink then shake my head. No, I'm fun and Will knows it. His trip is just a business opportunity. I'm fine. I'm going to treat myself to a nice bath and a face mask. And I won't give that stupid gossip show another thought. I refuse to let the likes of Hannah Gable get in my head. Honestly, other than to ask him one question from thirty feet away, she's never even met Will and yet she calls herself an expert on him? Pu-lease.

————

Two gins later, I am now working on a list that I shall burn as soon as I commit it to memory.

How to Keep a Man Like Will

- *Be accomplished and impressive at all times.*
- *Be interesting. Find tidbits from the news (especially topics that interest him) and bring them up should there ever be a lull in the conversation.*
- *Be funny.*
- *Quickly become totally athletic.*
- *Be sexy no matter what time of day or what's happening.*
- *Be amazing in the following areas: baking, cooking, sex (ie. be a total sex cat).*

A loud knock at my door interrupts my list-making. The knocking grows more insistent, and I hear Tessa's voice. "Hey, it's me. Whatcha doing girl?"

I quickly stick the list in a coffee-table book about coffees from around the world and hurry to the door, only to find her standing in front of me with a Scrabble box.

"If you've come to distract me from watching the news or reading anything on the internet, it's too late. I already saw it." I walk back toward the living room, holding up my gin in my right hand. "Unless you've come by to drink and commiserate, there's really no point."

"Damn. I had to wait until Arthur got back from that dinner he was at before I could sneak over. I was worried I'd be too late."

"You are. Gin?"

"Sorry, love," Tessa says, following me into the living room. "I met my caloric maximum for the day. Well, truth be told, I'm already over by three-hundred cals. Somebody brought Krispy Kreme doughnuts to a meeting for the Female Sheep Ranchers Society this afternoon, and I went a little nuts." She flops down onto the couch and pats the spot next to hers.

"Wait, are they ranchers who only raise female sheep or females who are sheep ranchers?"

"The second one," she says, settling herself on my couch. "Confusing name, right?"

"Very." I sit down and let myself slouch for once. "This sucks. I mean, I knew it would be hard, and so did Will. But I didn't realize it would be *this* hard. The level of humiliation is something I've never experienced before."

"Take it from the Queen of Humiliation, it'll pass, I promise. The important thing is not to let them get in your head, no matter what they say or how many beautiful supermodels he's travelling with."

"Oh, don't worry about her," I say, having a sip of my drink. "She's there with the owner of the company. Apparently, she's his girlfriend."

"Excellent," Tessa says, looking slightly relieved before catching herself. "Not that I was worried Will wouldn't be faithful or something. He seems like a great guy. It's just that these sorts of situations can get in a girl's head and do some nasty things."

"I'm fine with the beautiful women," I say. "It's the nasty ones that bother me."

"You mean that Hateful Hannah Stalker Face?" Tessa asks.

Nodding, I say, "I know I shouldn't let the likes of her get to me. It's just…"

"It's just that she's getting to you."

"Yes." I chew on my bottom lip for a second. "I know she's merely a symptom of the trouble with being a royal, but it still stings to have strangers questioning your relationship."

"So long as you and Will aren't questioning it, it really won't matter," Tessa says. "But trust me, I completely know where you're at. If it were me, I'd be upset too."

I lean my head back against the couch, glad to have someone who understands.

"Yes, if it were me, I might even be doing something as silly as writing up a list of how to keep a man like Will interested which would be totally counterproductive."

My gaze follows hers and I realize the top of my stupid list is poking out of the coffee-table book. When I look up at her, Tessa's got one eyebrow raised.

I make a groaning sound. "Can you blame me?"

"No, I can't. But, I also don't want you to go down that rabbit hole," she says, leaning forward and sliding the list out of the book. She holds it up. "This type of thing will cause nothing but trouble."

"Oh, don't—" I start, but realize it's too late because she's already reading it.

Tessa snorts. "Be a total sex cat. How many drinks have you had, anyway?"

"This is my second."

"Maybe stop there."

"Good idea."

She rips up the paper, then tucks the pieces in her pocket. "You are enough, exactly the way you are. And Will loves you. It was very clear when I met him that he was desperate to make a good first impression, which is not something a man does when he's casual about the woman he's seeing."

Nodding, I say, "Right. Yes. I have no doubt that he loves me."

"Good. But, about that advice I gave you the other day—about not waiting too long to have 'the talk' about your future…"

"Yes?"

"If you haven't done it yet, I think you're right to wait. This shit is enough for you two to muddle through for now." She tucks her leg under her bottom and turns to face me on the couch. "Unless you've already had the talk, in which case, ignore me completely."

Shaking my head, I say, "We've only managed a couple of very short phone calls and some texts, and that's a topic that requires us to be in the same room. Or the same country, at least."

Tessa pats me on my knee in a way I imagine a mum would. "It'll be all right. Just be patient and have faith in what you two have. And seriously stop watching that shite."

"Okay, I will."

"Promise?"

"Promise."

"I'm going to hold you to that, Arabella."

And I'm going to fail miserably.

14

Loads of Strings Attached...

Will

San Candido, Italy - Early Tuesday Morning

TEXT FROM DWIGHT: *I managed to re-book your Breakfast Television Slot for Friday. They aren't pleased, but who cares? You're making quite the splash with these live-streams, so if Kenneth wants to keep doing them, I say stick with the climbing for now. Just sent back the contract to his team with the amendments. Please don't do something so spur of the moment again. Terrible move to go before the papers are signed. It all looks good though, and you should have enough for that ring you want (and then some). (On a side-note, if you don't nip the stories about you and that model in the bud, you may not have use for an engagement ring.)*

Text from Rosy: *What the hell are you doing in Italy? There are some amazing places to climb here! You could come home to make your commercials and give the resort some free publicity at the same time. Also, who's the ho you're with? I don't like it.*

. . .

Text from Arabella: *Got your messages. Sorry I missed you. I was on that conference call all afternoon with the Equal Everywhere Campaign committee. We have much to do before the big conference next week. Sorry to hear about the rain delay and the problem with the camera angle. Can't believe you have to reshoot the entire thing. You must be exhausted, what with climbing all day and partying all night. ;) BTW, apparently the entire world thinks we broke up or were never a real couple to begin with. Urgh. Fingers crossed that you and I can curl up and watch episode two together Thursday night. The rest of my family seems to have begged off, so I'll be alone at Arthur and Tessa's babysitting the twins while the show airs. A and T have a state dinner they forgot about. Father decided not to watch any more episodes on account of all the implied sex, and Gran has a hot date. If you do come, I'll whip us up a batch of my award-winning brownies. I'm off to bed. Championing women's rights around the globe is tiring work. Good night, darling!*

Text from Emma: *Dude, are you and Arabella okay? I keep seeing stuff online that you broke up. Is that true? Are you really in Thailand with some hottie climbing woman?*

Text from Kenneth: *Will, get down to the restaurant already. Lara just came up with an amazing plan for the commercial. We need a quick meeting to discuss the change of plans.*

"Shit." I roll out of bed and stand, unable to fully appreciate the mountain view from my hotel suite on account of my pounding head and my quivering gut. Between my hangover and the fact that I need to get back to Valcourt stat to fix my relationship, I'm a bit of a mess.

My phone rings. Harrison's name flashes across the screen.

I sigh, then answer it. "Hey, buddy, what's up?"

"Just wanted to give you a heads-up not to answer if Emma or Rosy call. They're totally freaking out that you're cheating on Arabella."

I sigh and scratch the stubble on my chin. "That's a little insulting."

"Agreed. I told them you'd never do that." He pauses, clearly waiting for me to elaborate.

"The mystery woman is the new girlfriend of Kenneth Abernathy. She's a model."

"Obviously."

"He's putting her in the commercials to keep her happy. She can't even climb."

"Ah, that all makes sense now," he says, then quickly adds. "Of course I knew there was some simple explanation, but you know how Rosy and Emma can get."

"I'm glad I could clear that up for them," I answer, putting extra emphasis on the them so he knows that I know he also thinks I could be a cheater.

"Brilliant," he says in a slightly sheepish tone. "How are things going there?"

"Good and bad," I say, tugging on a pair of shorts. "Kenneth's got the ability to really make my career. He's even been talking about giving me my own line of outdoor gear."

"Seriously? That's incredible, Will."

"Yeah, it's pretty crazy. The timing is nuts. Season three just started, and it's like a whole new world is opening up—one with money for a change."

"Wouldn't that be nice?"

"It would," I say, making my way to the bathroom to put tooth-paste on my brush.

"What's the bad bit?" Harrison asks.

"I promised Belle I'd be back last night at the latest, but we got rained out, then yesterday's filming had to be scrapped because the lighting was off. When I left, things were on a bit of an… awkward note, I guess you could say. I really need to get back there to smooth everything over."

My phone buzzes and I see Kenneth's name. "I got to go, Harri-son. I'm late getting downstairs for a breakfast meeting and my sort-of boss is calling."

"Okay, hang in there," he says. "Get it? Cause you're climbing?"

"Got it. Bye."

"Bye."

———

"There's the man!" Kenneth shouts as I cross the restaurant with a plate of toast and packets of jelly in one hand and a large glass of freshly squeezed orange juice in the other.

I smile and give him a nod, even though my spinning head would much prefer if I were to lie very still for another couple of hours. How is it possible that he doesn't look in the slightest bit hung over? After all the shots he did last night? His 6-foot supermodel girlfriend hangs off his arm at the shiny round wooden table. She's got oversized sunglasses on, and, based on what I can see of her face, she feels about as good as I do. Kenneth, however, having dedicated his life to the pursuit of optimal health, is a 42-year-old man with the stamina of a steam engine. He just keeps going and going. But to be fair, he doesn't spend the entire day climbing. He goes up once, then hangs around at the bottom waiting while the commercial is being filmed.

"That's not all you're going to eat, is it?" He asks, eyeing my plate as I set it down. "Oh, don't tell me you're hung-over!" he says, laughing far too loud for this hour in the morning.

"Only a little," I say, sliding into my chair.

"Well, no worries. We won't leave for the climb until three. The light should be perfect by then." He kisses Lara on the top of her head. "And this one should be feeling up to shooting by then, too."

Three? Son of a bitch. I sit down and do my best to sound indifferent. "Oh, I thought we were going right after breakfast so we could fly back tonight."

Kenneth takes a massive bite of scrambled eggs, then has a sip of some kind of disgusting green drink before answering. "Change of plans. Lara had a terrific idea. We should go for a multidimensional commercial so that our customers can imagine themselves using our products in *more* than one place."

"Yes," Lara says, nodding slightly. "As beautiful as it is here, it's really expensive in the alps. We should try to incorporate places that are more accessible to the average person."

"She's so smart, isn't she?" Kenneth asks.

"Yes, very," I say. "But, back to this other location idea. Are we talking in the near future because I do have to get back to—"

"Yes," Kenneth says. "The best thing is to keep the momentum we've got right now. Besides, Giorgio is available for the next week so we should take advantage."

Giorgio is the director. He's from Trieste, and Kenneth has him shoot all of his commercials, and the fact that he's available isn't actually a positive as far as I'm concerned. Kenneth calls him 'a true artist,' and if by that he means total ball-buster, I'm in agreement. It's like he thinks we're making an arthouse film that'll be up for a cinematography Oscar instead of a commercial for carabiner clips that'll play while people are waiting for their YouTube videos to start. He's the reason we ended up here for an extra day so the last thing I want to do is go to a second location with him.

My heart drops to the tile floor as I try to think of a way out of this.

Lara picks at the fruit on her plate, then sets her fork down. "We're thinking Moonlight Buttress in Zion National Park, Utah."

Kenneth gives me a 'how about it?' smile.

"Utah?" I say, quickly calculating my flight time in my head. Well, not that I can actually come up with it, but I'm assuming it's really fucking long. "Sure, but could we stop in Avonia on our way, perhaps?"

It's not on the way at all, but I have to try.

"You seem really intent on getting back there, Will."

Nodding, I say, "Truth be told, I am a little concerned about Arabella. Things have not exactly been easy since the first episode aired, and I definitely should be there to support her."

"Why don't you invite her to come along?" Kenneth asks, leaning back in his chair and wrapping his arm around Lara's shoulder. "Whisk her away from her worries."

"Ooh, yes!" Lara says, suddenly perking up a bit. "It'll be fun— kind of like a wild several-day double date. She could climb too. Then I won't look like the worst one out there."

I hold back the defensive retort on the tip of my tongue and exchange it for a clearing of my throat. "Well, I can ask her, but she's getting ready for a United Nations Conference next week so I can't see her being able to drop everything to join us."

"Invite her, and either way, we'll carry on," Kenneth says. "At least if you've extended the invitation, she can't be mad at you for not coming back when ordered."

"Oh, hey," I say, holding up my palms. "She didn't *order* me to come back. In fact, she's been extremely supportive of what we're doing. It's just that with the show and all, she could use a friendly face, even if I'm only there for two days, maybe?"

He gives me that 'you better play ball look' he gets once in a while when I'm not necessarily on board with his latest idea. It's the kind of thing a guy like him gets to do because he holds all the cards. And since he's pretty much the only person waving huge wads of cash in my face, I should grab my glove and get in the game.

"What about Germany?" I ask, offering him a location that's closer to Avonia. "We could head over to Devil's Crack. Amazing scenery, totally different than what we've got here, and they've got some terrific short climbs that would be perfect for all three of us, really." I offer an amiable smile to Lara, who wrinkles up her nose.

Kenneth shakes his head, "Been there, done that, you know. Ooh! What about Railay Beach in Thailand? It's supposed to be amazing, and that long flight will give us ample time to hash out some ideas for your new outdoor gear line."

Oh, shit. How do I turn that down? It is literally my best chance at giving Arabella the life she deserves, and, based on what I've seen of her family so far, she desperately needs out. I nod, even though I know that in the short term, this is a very bad idea. "Sounds perfect."

———

Thailand - Friday Morning Indochina Time

"Christ, I've missed your voice," I say to Arabella, who has finally picked up the phone after the sixth attempt on my part. I'm sitting on the bed in my hotel room, staring out at the unbelievably beautiful

Andaman Sea, but instead of enjoying the view, I'm miserable. "Actually, I've missed all of you. How's my favourite girl?"

"Fine," she says, in a slightly formal tone. "Doing really well despite everything."

Uh-oh. "That doesn't sound good. What's going on?"

Arabella lets out a long sigh. "Nothing worth talking about. How's life in Railay Beach? Hot and fabulous?"

Shit. She's mad. And she has every right to be. Twice now, I've promised to come back, and both times, I broke it. When I told her we were boarding a flight to Thailand, there was a pause on the line that was so long, I checked my phone to make sure we weren't disconnected. "Honestly, it's kind of tiring, even for me. Kenneth's like an animal. I don't know how the guy never runs out of energy. He literally does not need to sleep."

"Cocaine?" she suggests.

I bust out laughing, and she joins me. After a moment, I say, "God, it feels good to laugh with you. I wish you were here."

"Me, too," Arabella says. "But you'll be back soon enough. No sense in dwelling on it."

"Pivot and press on, right?" I ask.

"Right."

I lie back on the bed and stare up at the slowly spinning fan above my head. "Did you find anyone to watch the show with you tonight?"

"Dexter," she says, trying to sound upbeat about it.

"I'm sorry, sweetie, I wish I could be there."

"Oh, it's not all bad. I'll crack open some wine and a bag of crisps and curl up on the couch with my other favourite pig."

"Hey, was that a shot?"

"If you have to ask, it means I missed."

"Ha! Good one." I glance at the bedside clock, then immediately wish I hadn't because it means I have to hang up. "Listen sweetheart, I have to run. I'm hoping today is the last day of filming, but Giorgio is such a perfectionist, I honestly don't know if we can get it wrapped up."

"Sounds awful," she says, sounding less than sincere.

"I want you to know that if this wasn't so important for my career, I would never want to be away from you for this long."

"I know."

"I feel terrible about it, but these types of opportunities don't come along very often."

"Don't worry about it. I understand."

"That's why you're the best." I close my eyes for a second, hating like hell that I have to ring off. "Okay, I better get going. Love you."

"You too."

Bugger. She always says *I love you too*, but that time she went with 'you too' which tells me I have to get my arse back to Avonia as soon as humanly possible.

15

If You're Going to Jump, It Might as Well Be to Conclusions...

Arabella

Episode Two

"Good evening, I'm Dylan Sinclair, your host of ABN's hit show, Princess in the Wild!" Dylan fans her arm out to point to a large screen behind her, displaying the show's thumbnail shot. "Tonight, the ugliness continues as Will Banks and Princess Arabella show just how different they are. We'll also hear some shocking revelations about royal life from the very lips of Princess Arabella herself, and see what happens on their first night together in the jungle. Will they or won't they?" she asks, grinning into the camera.

"But first, a recap of last week's show."

"Oh, great," I say to Dexter, who is lying beside me on Arthur and Tessa's couch, his head resting on my leg. "Like I really need to see that again."

Flashes of me in those short shorts start up, then Will calling me 'useless' and demanding that I be left behind, now me rappelling from the helicopter complete with bleeping. Now, I'm clomping behind him and holding my middle fingers in the air. And it all wraps up with him suggesting it wouldn't be a tragedy if I break my neck.

Dylan comes back on and says, "And a quick preview of what's in store for you tonight…"

Cut to me sobbing loudly and yelling, "I've had to use the loo for hours now and I'm afraid to ask how that even works because I hate you so much and I just know it's going to be horrifyingly embarrassing and likely you'll have to stand guard while I squat somewhere only to end up wiping my arse with some sort of plant that will cause a horrible rash!"

"Perfect. Just perfect," I say, as the commercial break starts. I sigh, glancing at my phone, even though I know Will is busy filming his commercial and won't likely be texting me for hours. I look down at my date, who is slobbering on my sweatpants. This is a new low, even for me. "You want some crisps, buddy?"

Dexter lifts his head and slides his huge grey body off the couch.

"You know what that means, don't you?" I ask, getting up. "Almost makes me want to stop eating bacon."

He follows me to the kitchen and parks himself directly in front of the cupboard where the junk food is kept. I open it, trying not to think about how pathetic I am, spending my last night before I go to Vienna alone, babysitting. Oh well, at least I'll also be torturing myself with footage of me having a total meltdown. That should add some fun to the evening.

A couple of minutes later, Dexter and I are back in the living room munching on classic salt-flavoured crisps out of my brother's best china.

The show starts up again and Dylan leads in with, "We'll pick up where the unlikely pair left off last week. They were just about to set up camp for the night. As you'll see, the first day of hiking proved to be too much for our royal co-host. She's about to fall apart in a huge way…"

Footage of me gingerly rappelling down what I now see is a rather short cliff starts up. When I reach the bottom, Will says, "Hey, that was pretty good. You didn't shout any curse words that time."

I glare at him. "That's because I've lost my will to live. At this point, between being faced with the prospect of spending another few days out here with you or just ending it all quickly, the second option sounds far more appealing to me."

"Ooh, that was offside, wasn't it, Dex? Now, I'm kind of glad Will isn't here."

"The first day is always the worst," Will says.

"Oh, is it?" I quip.

I clomp over to the stream and crouch down, plunging my hands into the water, but Will's voice stops me. "Oh, don't do that. We need to boil that first."

"Obviously I wasn't about to drink it. I only meant to splash some on my face."

"That's a total lie. I was definitely going to drink it," I say, popping a crisp in my mouth.

"Don't do that either," Will says. "You could get a parasite in your nose or mouth, and it'll be game over."

I stand and shake my hands off, scowling.

"God, I look like a total brat, don't I?" Glancing down at Dexter, I add, "Don't answer that."

"I can have our camp set up in about fifteen minutes, but it'll be a good two to three hours until we can eat."

"No. That can't be right." I take my backpack off and drop it, then crouch, unzip it, and start taking everything out. "We must have some protein bars or something. They wouldn't have sent us out here to starve."

"We're not going to starve. We're going to survive. Did you not understand the premise of the show?"

"Yeah, I got it, thank you," I snap, scowling at him. "I'm just a bit hangry right now is all."

"Well, the good news is we're surrounded by vegetation and protein sources. Since the rhino beetles weren't your thing, I'll catch us some fish and dig up some wild yam tubers. In about three hours, we'll be nice and full."

I slump down onto a fallen log and let my body go limp. Tears fill my eyes and I shake my head. "Okay, forget it. I'm not meant for this. I give up. Just call the helicopter and have them come get me. I don't want to do this anymore. I thought I wanted a great adventure, but this is not what I had in mind. You win. My brother wins. My father wins."

I let one arm flail out to the side. "The entire staff at the palace—they all win. I am just a sheltered, spoiled, soft princess who has no business being out here whatsoever. I'm sorry I wasted your time and the time of the network, and I sincerely apologize to the People for Animals Society for losing the funding, but please, I must leave now."

He holds his hand out to me and barks, "Get off that log. You're about to be attacked by a colony of bullet ants."

"Ouch! BEEP!"

I jump up, screaming, "Get them off me! Get them off me!!!!" while I run to Will.

He stops me with both hands, then brushes the ant off me while I continue to scream.

"It's okay. It's gone now."

"No, it's not okay," I say, shaking my head wildly. "Just call them. Call them and get me out of here now! This is over. You were right. I was wrong. I can admit it, okay. I'll go home and go back to giving tours to those hateful nonagenarians. It's not that bad."

"This is the worst moment. I promise it gets better from here."

"No, it won't," I sob loudly. "I thought this was like Survivor—*if something goes wrong, they always have people nearby to rescue them."*

*"*Survivor's *a game show. Have you not watched* The Wild World?"

"I assumed you didn't show the safety people," I say, sniffling in a most undignified way.

"That's because there aren't any safety people," he says, shaking his head. "What did you think the danger bonus was for?"

"I don't know, to make the whole thing more dramatic?"

"No, no, no, no, no, no, no!" I plead to the screen, sitting up so suddenly, I startle Dex. I watch, utterly helpless as on the telly, I'm clicking my hiking boots together at the heels, saying, "There's no place like home. There's no place like home."

"Why?! Why couldn't she have cut that out?" I shut my eyes tight and cover them with my hands as I hear myself go into a total nuclear meltdown.

"I'm sorry I did this. I never should've applied. I think maybe I'm having some sort of quarter-life crisis or something. I've just turned twenty-nine... which would mean I'm planning to live to be almost one-hundred and twenty. Maybe it's a third-life crisis. Is that a thing?"

"Not sure," Will says. "But the math sounds solid."

He's the voice of reason to my hysterical nut job.

"...I'm under a tremendous amount of pressure to find a husband before I turn thirty. Only all the men I know are complete wankers and I could never be attracted to any of them. They want to set me up with the future Earl of Wimberly, and do you know what his nickname is? Hal, as in halitosis! Yeah, imagine kissing that until death do us part. No, thank you."

"Oh my God," I whisper, my stomach churning. "Why couldn't they have cut that out? Why did I have to say that?"

"Then I drank too much champagne at your sister's stupid wedding. Who has a champagne fountain? I mean really! How irresponsible can you be?! After my third glass, I met you and I thought, 'Yes!'"

I look up at Will. "No, not like that. I don't want to marry you. God, no. You're a total BEEP. I wanted your life for a while. The way you were bragging about it, you made it sound so free and easy and wonderful—all lies, by the way— but I thought to myself, 'If I could just be him, even for a few short days, it would all be okay.'"

"Oh, wow, they're showing the entire thing. Every last stupid word. The bastards." I consider shutting it off, but I can't bring myself to do it. For one thing, the remote is all the way over on the far side of the coffee table and my entire body is frozen with shock and guilt and humiliation. For another, I probably should know exactly what kind of trouble I'm going to be in tomorrow morning. Am I still yelling? Yes, yes, I am. "Shut up, you idiot," I tell myself.

"...Yeah, no garlic! And I'm not allowed to wear heels taller than two inches or miniskirts. In fact, I can't even wear anything that cuts off above the knee, as if my bare knees are so scandalous. I've had to dress like I'm some woman in late menopause since I was... wel ... born, I guess. And honestly, that makes it really hard to attract a man."

I step closer to him and put my hands on his upper arms. "You know when I got to wear those shorts earlier? That is probably the most free I've felt in my entire life. But then you said I had to change, and it was over, like that." I snap my fingers in his face. "And now, here we are. I'm in my baggy, ugly communist-chic outfit, and I'm going to get us both killed. I am, Will. We are going to die out here. Possibly today, maybe tomorrow, but most certainly before the end of the week. I'm not going to see my niece and nephew grow up. I mean, they're so cute and cuddly, and they adore their Auntie Arabella".

"Oh, God. Could this possibly get any worse?" I ask, suddenly feeling sick. I give Dexter my bowl of crisps to finish. "It's like I blocked all of this horribly embarrassing stuff out of my mind as soon as it was over, but now, it's right out in the open for the world to see."

I burst into uncontrollable sobs until tears are pouring down my cheeks. The camera angle tilts down and now Will's GoPro is filming the top of my head and back. You can see his arms are wrapped around me and hear him shushing me.

"And I've had to use the loo for hours now and I'm afraid to ask how that even works because I hate you so much and I just know it's going to be horrifyingly embarrassing and likely you'll have to stand guard while I squat somewhere only to end up wiping my arse with some sort of plant that will cause a horrible rash!" I sob into his shirt. "An itchy, painful rash. And I'm not allowed to scratch anything, let alone my bottom. It's going to be excruciating!"

"Oh, wow," Will says. "When you fall apart, you really go for it."

Yes. Yes, I do. And now I'm doing it for the entire world to see...

"I'm not allowed to fall apart!" I wail.

"Okay, Arabella," he says. "Let's deal with one problem at a time. Using the loo is pretty simple, really. I'll find some moss for you, then dig a little hole near a log—one without bullet ants—then I'll walk away to give you some privacy. You do what you need to do, then you cover the hole and we don't ever have to talk about it again."

I nod and sniffle. "That sounds dreadful."

"It's not all bad. Once we've dealt with that, I'll set up the camp and feed you. I promise, you'll feel a thousand times better once we do those things, okay?"

I sniff again and nod. "Okay."

Wiping my cheeks, I stare at the ground. "Sorry. I don't normally fall apart like that."

"Can I tell you something?" he asks.

I nod and dab daintily at my eyes.

"The first night is always the worst. I promise. And it really will get better from here."

"Not if we die."

"We're not going to die. I won't let that happen."

"Shit," I whisper, watching as Will places both hands on my shoulders. "I didn't think it was possible, but episode one was actually far less awful than this."

Dylan's face fills the screen again. "What a man, what a man, what a mighty good man," she says. "Look at how he calmed her down just there. He should be called the Princess Whisperer. Stay tuned to see the incredible meal he whips up and to hear Will's own shocking revelation of his first time out in the woods."

Will appears onscreen again. "I cried the first time I spent the night out in the wilderness."

"Oh for God's sake," I mutter. "He was only seven years old at the time. Dylan is such a C-word."

Twenty minutes later, I watch as we eat some fish and yams, and then Will checks my feet for infection and makes a salve for my sore ankles. I sigh wistfully, remembering the feeling of his strong hands on me as he took care of me. "Why can't my family be watching this bit? They'd totally love him. I'm pretty sure that was the moment I fell for him," I tell Dexter, who is snoring away now, having gone into a crisp coma.

Will looks into the camera. "You can see the consistency of the salve is a nice thick liquid so it'll glide on smoothly. We'll let it cool for a while before I apply it, but in the interest of allowing my co-host some privacy, I shall now bid you good night and turn off the cameras until morning so the batteries can charge up while we charge our own batteries." The video feed shuts off, there's a click, then audio recording picks up Will's voice. "That was cheesy."

"Just a bit. There. Much better."

"Yes, we're alone now."

"Children behave, that's what they'll say when we're together," I say.

"Wait a minute. He said he shut the camera off," I mutter, my heart pounding a little in my chest. A minute later, I can hear myself belting out a Tiffany song completely off-key. I let out a gasp. "Dear God, no."

I grab my phone and dial Dylan's number, tapping my foot on the carpet while I wait for her to pick up. I get her voicemail and hang up, then call one of the VP's of Unscripted at ABN, Kira Taylor. No answer.

In the background, I can hear myself admitting to having yucky feet. "Why is this being filmed?"

I dial Will's number, knowing it's useless. I wait until the beep and leave a message, "Hey, babe, listen. Slight problem with the show. I guess you forgot to shut the audio off because I just heard us singing 'I

Think We're Alone Now,' which happened *after* you said you were shutting the camera off. Call me," I say, trying to sound breezy.

"I'm not ready to sleep just yet. I want to stare at this until I know I'll never forget it."

"It's amazing, isn't it?" he asks. *"People go their whole lives without seeing the earth and the sky for what they really are. They just stay stuck in their boxes from the moment they are born until they die."*

"I've spent my entire life in a box. A very grand, luxurious, safe box," I say.

"Is that why you came, Arabella? Because you can't stand being confined anymore?"

"I needed to get out. I felt like... I might..."

"Die if you didn't?"

"I know it sounds horribly ungrateful. For someone like me to feel any sort of discontentment when my life is one of incredible privilege."

"Not to me, it doesn't. To me, your life sounds really sad."

"I don't know if it's sad," I say. *"But it comes with a list of dos and don'ts that could fill up that whole night sky."*

"How did you convince them to let you do this?"

"I didn't. I approached Kira Taylor in private, then I had to sneak out of the palace without my security following me."

"Are you serious?"

"My grandmother plays poker once a month with the guys who work in the garage. One of them was into her for a lot of money, so I was able to offer him a nice wad of cash to hide me in the boot of his car and take me straight to the airport."

"Okay, can I just say how impressed I am?"

"You may," I say in a regal tone.

Oh no, why the regal tone again? People are going to think I'm serious.

Dylan comes back on. "You may," she says, imitating me. "Must be nice to have handsome men offer to wash your feet. Clearly, based on her tone, she's grown to expect that kind of service. Anyway, that's it for our show tonight. Stay tuned as Nigel Woods and Hannah Gable, of Will's Wild Fangirls fame, join me on the couch to dissect tonight's episode. And there is a lot to talk about!"

Text to Will: *Call me please. Issue with the editing or something. I need to talk to you now.*

I stand and start pacing the room, then walk over to the bar and pour myself a glass of red wine. "He wouldn't have secretly filmed me, right Dex?"

I down the drink and pace some more, my mind racing. I'm about to help myself to another drink when the door opens. Arthur and Tessa walk in, her in a lovely black gown and him in a tux.

Arthur looks at my drink. "You do know you're babysitting the future queen?"

Tessa glares at him. "And her brother."

I ignore the exchange and launch into an incoherent explanation of what happened, right from the start of the episode to Will taking such good care of me to our horrible singing. The words spill out non-stop and I don't even take a breath until after I ask, "It must have been an accident, right? I mean, if he did secretly video me, he really should have told me by now, shouldn't he have?"

In the background, Nigel Wood is saying, "And is it me, or did that conversation sound a lot like Arabella was trying to get Will to feel sorry for her? I mean, the whole bit about living in a luxury box? Come on, people!"

Tessa hurries to the television and shuts it off.

Arthur, who poured himself a scotch while I was yammering on, sighs. "He obviously did it on purpose. He's clearly using you to get ahead."

"You don't know that, Arthur," Tessa says.

"Sure I do. He *left her* to deal with the fallout from the show," he says. "And do you really think it's a coincidence that he's gone at the exact moment she's discovering he secretly recorded her every word?"

I chew on my thumbnail. "I mean, it could have been a mistake, right? Maybe he just did it the one time and didn't even know he did?"

Arthur rolls his eyes. "Give me a break. You don't think he knows how to work a GoPro?"

"No," Tessa says, shaking her head. "You're wrong. He invited Arabella to meet him in Thailand. If she were there, he'd have to face her in person."

"But I wouldn't be watching," I say, my heart pounding in my ears.

"What?" she asks.

"I'd be out climbing right now and I'd have missed the entire episode."

"But other people you know would fill you in on it," Tessa says. "My mum, for example. She's definitely glued to her telly right now."

Arthur walks over and puts his hand on my shoulder. "I'm sorry, Arabella, but it's too convenient. He leaves the audio on, gets you to admit to hating your life, makes you sound like a total idiot, and makes himself sound like the ultimate boyfriend material. I know you have strong feelings for him, but it's time you put your guard up before you get hurt. He's not to be trusted."

"Arthur!" Tessa starts, but the look on my face stops her.

"He may be right," I say, forcing out the words, even though I hate myself for thinking them. "I mean, it all seemed so real, but it's true. He did leave, didn't he?"

Tears prick my eyes, but I blink them back inside.

"Oh, sweetie," Tessa says, rushing over to me.

I hold up one hand, not wanting to fall apart in front of my brother. "Thanks, but I'm fine. I'll go back to my place so I can try to get a hold of Will."

"Good. Give him a piece of your mind," Arthur says. "And then hand him over to me. I'll go up one side and down the other. He's going to wish he never met you."

"Or," Tessa says, giving Arthur an urgent look, "You calmly ask him if he knows how this may have happened. You need to leave room for the possibility that this isn't his fault."

"Do I?" I ask, turning toward the door.

"No," Arthur says at the same time Tessa says, "Yes."

When the door shuts behind me, I close my eyes and let out a long breath. The shitstorm I've unleashed is going to be unbearable and it looks like I'll have to face it alone.

16

Impatient Directors, Starving Supermodels, and Phone Calls You Never Want to Get...

Will

"Okay, Will, stop there and go back down," Giorgio, the director, calls into the megaphone. "We're going to need you to do that again so we can get the drone to circle counter-clockwise this time."

Seriously? I just had to redo the entire climb so the drone could go clockwise, and to be honest, I'm getting more than a little annoyed at this point. It's about a thousand degrees out, I've been up and down this cliff-face more times than I can count on both hands (mainly because my fingers are cramping up too badly to use them for counting), and I'm thirsty as hell. Oh, and Giorgio insisted I climb without a shirt which is inadvisable for several reasons including, but not limited to, scraping the bejeezus out of your skin and/or risk of sunburn. The worst bit is that, directly under me, the calm, crystal blue sea beckons me with the promise of refreshment, only I can't let go and jump in on account of all the recording equipment strapped to me. "The whole thing or just the last twenty feet?" I ask, glad that I'm mic'd up so I don't have to shout.

"*Un secondo*," he says.

Sure. No problem. I'll just hang out here against this cliff in the blistering sun while you review the footage.

I glance down at Lara and Kenneth, who seem totally oblivious to what's going on. They came along for the fun on the first ascent, then spent an hour or so canoodling in the water and are now sipping cold drinks under the pop-up tent for the crew. And I know, I'm getting paid for this, and I am grateful—really, I am. But I'm also tired and worried because of how I left things with Arabella. Even though she's been supportive of me taking this opportunity, I'm pretty sure Kenneth and I are stretching her patience with this second stop on our globe-hopping commercial shoot. And I have a niggling feeling that the longer I'm gone, the worse it'll be for our relationship. The truth is, I let her down, even if I did do it for the right reasons. And that's the very last thing I ever wanted to do.

Finally, Giorgio makes a decision. "Come down halfway and we'll see if we can do it from there in one shot. And can you do it faster this time?"

"Faster." Jesus, I'd like to see him do it *at all*, let alone do it faster. Giorgio works up a sweat walking from his car to his director's chair. Giving him a thumbs-up, I say, "You bet."

Lara walks over to him and he puts his megaphone down while the two of them have a brief conversation. Oh, for shit's sake. Why don't we just get everyone in a two-mile radius to make suggestions?

He lifts the megaphone to his mouth and says, "Forget it. Come all the way down."

"For the day or for a few minutes?" I say. "If I have to come back up, I'd rather finish it up now."

Lara, who, along with everyone else on the set is wearing head-phones, takes the bullhorn from Giorgio. "You'll want to come down, Will. There seems to be some sort of emergency and …. uh… *someone* is desperately trying to reach you."

I start loosening the slack and rappel down. My heart pounds extra hard because I'm sure it's Arabella, based on the fact that Lara didn't want to give away who it was. Bugger. I bet this has something to do with Dylan. When I reach the sand and unclip myself, Lara hands me my phone. "Sorry, I didn't read her messages, but your phone kept buzzing and dinging, so I figured you'd want to know."

"Thanks, yeah," I say, wiping the sweat off my forehead with the back of my arm (which is also sweaty, so I'm basically smearing more sweat everywhere).

Crap. Eight missed calls and fourteen text messages, all from Arabella.

Call me immediately. It's about the show.

Where are you?

Seriously—this is bad.

Will, for real. I need to talk to you.

I look at Giorgio. "I'm going to need a couple of minutes and some water before we do the last shot."

Without waiting for permission, I turn and walk down the beach, away from the crew, while a feeling of dread takes over. I dial and wait for Arabella to answer.

"Finally, "she says, in place of hello. "I've been trying to reach you for *two hours*."

"Sorry, Belle," I say, turning my back on everyone and facing the ocean. "We're shooting that commercial this morning, remember?"

"Yes, I'm fully aware of that," she snaps. "But while you're off living the dream, my life is pretty much falling apart."

Giorgio walks over and leans his head down so he can get in my face. He gives me the twirly finger 'hurry up and finish the call' gesture.

I wave him off and turn away. "What happened?"

"The show happened, which means the entire world has heard me complain about my shit life and now I look like the most ungrateful, tone-deaf, overprivileged, hateful brat on the planet," she says, her voice shaking slightly. "The on-line backlash has already started, and it is *ugly*, Will. Ugly."

"Wait a minute, hang on," I say, my stomach churning. "What are you talking about?"

"I just need to know one thing, Will," Arabella says, her voice suddenly angry instead of emotional. "Did you do it on purpose?"

"Do what?" I walk farther away from the crew and find a boulder in the shade to sit down on.

"On our first night in the jungle, did you *mean* to leave the camera on?" she asks. "If you did, I could almost understand because we got off on the wrong foot, but on the other hand, you *really* should've told me, if not when we started seeing each other, *definitely* before this aired."

"Slow down, Belle," I say. "I'm having trouble understanding what you're talking about."

"Our first night in Zamunda. At the campfire. We sang Tiffany and I admitted to you that I hate my life. You told me you shut the cameras off, but you recorded it," she says. "Do you know how hard it's going to be for me to come back from this? I mean, I'm a *princess*, for God's sake, complaining about my horrible existence when there are literally millions of people around the world who are starving and homeless!"

I rake my hand through my soaked hair, trying to figure out what the hell happened. "Hold on. There's footage of you after I shut off the GoPros? "

"Yes, there's footage! All of it. Remember when you put that salve on my ankles and I asked you to turn off the cameras because I was embarrassed about my sores and you said you shut them off? And then we were singing—horribly offkey, by the way. I had no idea what an awful singer I was." Her words spill out fast and filled with bitterness. "And I told you how I live my entire life in a luxurious little box and it's such hell for me. You recorded the entire thing!"

My heartbeat picks up again in my chest and my mind races to catch up with what's happening, only I'm slightly dizzy from the heat and exertion, and none of this is making any sense to me. "They have video of it?"

"Audio only," she answers. "So, you're saying it was an accident?"

"Of course it was. Why would I...?" I stop for a second and suddenly it all becomes clear. And I don't like it one bit. "Wait...you actually believe I secretly recorded you, then said nothing about it?"

"No, well, maybe... I don't know. I'm just so upset and confused." Her voice goes up two octaves. "The first chance you got, you took off and now it seems like you're not going to come back even though I need you here. Also, you were the one running the cameras so I thought..." Her voice trails off, leaving me to fill in the blanks.

"—You thought I would secretly record you, not bother to mention it, then conveniently leave the country so I wouldn't have to be around for the fallout?"

"When you put it that way, it sounds silly," she says.

"Doesn't it?" I ask with a biting tone I wish wasn't there.

"It's just that Arthur said—"

"Said what? That I did it on purpose to humiliate you?"

"Yes," she says, sounding slightly sheepish now, which she should if you ask me.

I glance over my shoulder to see if anyone can hear me, only to realize that the assistant director is standing directly behind me, holding out a Gatorade. She gives me a sympathetic wince, hands me the drink, and mouths "sorry" before walking away.

Giorgio, clearly not interested in my personal drama, yells into the megaphone, "We're losing the light, Will."

Ignoring him, I say, "Listen, I'm *really* sorry that this happened, and I promise you I have *no clue* how any of that would've been recorded. And I hate that you're having a rough go of things right now. Honestly, I *hate* it." I take a breath and try to calm down, but her accusations have rocked me to my core. "But, for you to think I would do something like that on purpose? And then take off so I wouldn't have to face you when you found out? Do you even know me at all?" Nope, can't manage to sound calm. "We're *building a life* together. At least I thought we were, but if you actually believe I could do something like this—"

"I don't," she says, her voice breaking. "I just had to ask."

"No. You really didn't."

"Will, you don't understand," she says. "When you're in my position, it's extremely difficult to know who you can trust."

"Come on." I let out a frustrated chuckle. "You should know I'm in that category by now, shouldn't you?"

Her tone comes out stronger now. "It's just that Arthur thought it was highly suspicious that as soon as you got me back here, you left me to deal with everything—"

Arthur again. For fuck's sake. "Oh, well, if *Phone-a-Friend Arthur* thinks I'm using you, he must be right, since he's so smart. I guess that makes me what? A giant prick?"

"No, Will," Arabella answers. "But you've got admit, with that awful recording and you disappearing, it just…" she stops herself, probably before she insults me again.

"Just what, Belle?" I spit out. "It's just that I get an amazing career opportunity, and the minute I'm gone, you start doubting me?" I stand up and start pacing the sand. "I can't believe you actually think I would betray you like that."

"I'm sorry. I never should've said anything," she whispers.

I feel a tap on my shoulder and I turn to see Giorgio standing in front of me. "*Mi scusi*, but you're really going to have to wrap this up. Those clouds moving in are going to ruin the shot if we don't get it right away."

I nod at him and hold up one finger. "Listen, I have to—"

"—I heard it. Just go." She sounds defeated, but I'm too upset to worry about her feelings at the moment.

Letting out a loud sigh, I say, "I'll be back there as soon as I can. In the meantime, if you wouldn't mind *not* discussing our relationship with your brother, I'd really appreciate it."

With that, I hang up the phone and shove it in the pocket of my shorts. I open the Gatorade and suck down the entire bottle in one go, then stride back to the ropes to hook up, humiliation and frustration building in me as sand fills my climbing shoes.

Kenneth and Lara walk over to me. He scratches his chin and says, "Rough go with these princesses, eh? Maybe you should try supermodels instead. They're not nearly as high-maintenance."

I give him a questioning look, then he says, "Your mic was on."
Brilliant.

"Are you okay?" Lara asks. "You need a minute?"

Yes, yes, I do. What I really need is to jump into that ocean right there and go for a long swim until I burn off all this anger, but that's not an option, is it? And since I've already been embarrassed enough for one day, I need to man up and act like my career is riding on what I do next—because it is. Giving her an easy smile, I say, "I'm totally fine. Never better. Ready to race to the top."

———

I'm currently on my third beer with no plans to stop until I'm blotto. I'm sitting oceanside at a table on the hotel's restaurant patio, watching the sun sink down into the sea. Thankfully, for the first time in days, I'm alone with some time to think, which may or may not be a good thing. I stare down at my phone on the teak tabletop, and reread Arabella's last text. *Will, I'm so sorry about everything. I'm leaving for Vienna around six tomorrow morning, so I'm afraid it will be a few more days before we can talk this out in person. Call me if you want so I can grovel and tell you how much I love you. I'll be back on Wednesday. I hope you'll be there when I arrive home. If I've thrown away what we have together, I will never forgive myself.*

I chew on my lip, my head swirling with everything that's happened since we left the Caribbean. Honestly, nothing has gone right between us since we got off that plane. It's like the entire world is trying to pull us apart.

As hurt as I am, I also don't know if it's one hundred percent her fault. Arthur pretty much talked her into believing the worst of me, and since he's been her biggest influence her entire life and I've only known her for five months, it's not a difficult leap for her to trust him over me. The problem is, the longer I'm gone, the more his voice will fill her head. Not to mention the fact that I *did* take off the first chance I got, I *didn't* come back when I said I would, and I *have* left her to deal with the fallout from the show.

"There he is," Kenneth calls from across the patio.

"Shit," I mutter before turning and doing my best to look happy to see him. Honestly, I have no desire to be around anyone who was witness to my budding dysfunctional relationship.

He takes a seat at my table and stretches out his legs, eyeing the bottles of Phuket Lager lined up in front of me. "Party for one?"

"More like an evening of self-reflection."

Is there any chance he'll take the hint? I don't think so either.

"Women, eh?" he says, flagging down the waitress, pointing at my drink and holding up four fingers.

"Nah, she's not like that," I say. "Anyone would crumble under the pressure."

"That's very charitable of you."

"Where's Lara?" I ask, hoping to steer the conversation away from my girlfriend to his.

"Back at the room. Her mum called. They'll be yakking for a good hour."

I nod as though I have the first clue what it's like to take a call from your mum or have a girlfriend who has a mum, for that matter.

"Listen, I've got something that might cheer you up," he says with a grin. "I talked to my head of development, and he thinks it's possible to move up production on the outdoor gear line. So, rather than heading back to Valcourt for a battle royale, what would you say to spending the next few weeks with our design team in London?"

The waitress brings the beers, and he waits while she sets them on the table. I thank her while he has a swig. "Our branding department is already working on the perfect logo for you. I told the team about your idea for making the world's lightest backpack, and they *loved it*. And I don't want you to feel like this is just something you're stuck slapping your name on. I want you to be *excited*, Will. You pick the colours, you pick the fabrics. If we work fast, we could be ready to roll out next spring."

He leans back and smiles at me before tipping his bottle back again.

I open my mouth, then close it, not sure whether to be thrilled or filled with dread. I am definitely at a crossroads with Arabella, and the decision I make at this moment will most certainly determine so much more than my financial status. "Well, Kenneth, that is an incredible offer."

"It's the offer of a lifetime," he says, narrowing his eyes a little. "But I can tell by your expression that you're preoccupied by that business this afternoon. Don't worry about it, okay? The entire crew is under strict orders not to say a word to anyone. No one will be airing your dirty laundry, or they'll answer to me."

My face burns with humiliation. "I appreciate that."

"I mean, obviously there's going to be a bit of attention coming your way when the world finds out you two broke up, but you know what they say about publicity…"

"Right, the thing is, we're not going to break up," I say. "At least I hope not. She was wrong about what happened, but she's right that I did abandon her at a bad time, which doesn't exactly make me good boyfriend material."

He cocks his head to the side. "Seriously, mate?"

"I know it sounded bad, and it was, but she's a wonderful person when her life isn't falling apart."

He sets his beer down. "Will, I'm a few years older than you, and I've been through my share of relationships with high-maintenance women. They're *all* wonderful people when things are going their way, but the thing is, that can't always be the case. Trust me, you'll be much better off with someone who doesn't expect quite so much. You don't have to put up with shit from anyone—not with how rich and famous you're about to become."

"Kenneth, as much as I appreciate your advice, trust me when I say Arabella is worth the trouble. Not that there's trouble usually. Can we just say it's a very stressful time for both of us and leave it at that?"

"Suit yourself, but I was serious earlier about supermodels. I don't know whether it's all the starving they do or what, but generally speaking, they're surprisingly low-maintenance. Lara has dozens of friends in the industry who I'm sure would be thrilled to date a guy like you."

"Thanks, I'll keep that in mind."

"No, you won't," he says with a sly grin. "You're going to stay with this woman no matter what. I can tell."

"Yes, I am," I say with a small smile.

"How about this, then? Let's go to London tomorrow to meet with the team. Give her a few weeks to worry. We get started on the product line, and when you get back, she knows she can't treat you like that again."

I consider his words, wishing like hell that this offer wasn't coming at this exact moment in my life. My gut hardens. "You have no idea how badly I want to say yes right now."

"Then do," he answers. "It would be the smartest decision you'll ever make."

Shaking my head, I say, "I know it would, but the thing is, I can't keep breaking promises to her, especially when I'm a big part of the reason her whole world is falling apart. But if your team could give me a bit of time, I'll get to London as soon as possible."

He breathes out hard through his nose and I know he's not happy. "When? A day? Two days?"

I almost say yes, but deep down, I know a couple of days won't cut it—not when things aren't going to get easier for her until after the final episode of the show. "Realistically, it would be more like a few weeks, possibly a month. She and I promised each other to stick together while the show airs, so I can't very well say, 'good luck with that, see you when it's over.'"

"Seriously?" he asks, looking quite annoyed. "I'm offering you the chance to have your name on the world's best outdoor gear and you want to hold up my entire team so you can go hold your girlfriend's hand for a month? I'm about to make you wildly rich, Will—beyond what you ever dreamed. All you have to do is say yes."

This is it—a chance for steady money for the first time in my life, which would make me far more acceptable in the eyes of Arabella's family, and in my own, for that matter. I could give her *all* the things— stability, an amazing lifestyle, freedom, a home worthy of her. But if I say yes, at this moment, when things are falling apart between us, there's almost no chance of sharing any of it with her.

I blow out a long puff of air and rub one hand over my scruffy chin. "Believe me, Kenneth, I know this is the greatest offer I'll likely ever get and that turning it down is one of those things I will quite possibly look back on and deeply regret, but the thing is, all the money in the world is worth nothing if I don't have her to share it with."

Kenneth stares at me for a moment, then says, "I'm serious, Will. I'm not going to make this offer twice. I have a corporation to run, and if you don't want in, I've got to move on."

My gut flips and my heart drops down to my knees. "No, I want in, believe me. And I get that you're the kind of guy who moves fast. In fact, I admire you for that." *Don't say it. Don't turn him down. Take the money.* "But as grateful as I am for the opportunity, I can't say yes. Not right now."

"Is she really worth giving it all up for?"

"Yes, Kenneth, she is."

When You Sink So Low, Even You Can't Stand Yourself...

Arabella

Princess Arabella Allowed Out of Her Luxury Prison to Attend UN Conference in Vienna

Written by: Uma Yung, Royal News Correspondent, The Daily Times

AVONIANS THE NATION *over are finding themselves utterly irritated with fourth in line for the throne, Princess Arabella, after comments she made about the trials and tribulations of royal life were made public last night. A generally quiet, and for the most part respectable member of the royal family, Her Highness has been making waves over the last six months, including sneaking away to film a reality TV show,* Princess in the Wild, *with professional survival expert Will Banks, with whom she is currently romantically involved.*

The patron of dozens of charities throughout the kingdom, Princess Arabella has been a steadfast source of grace for the oft-troubled family. But last night's comments shocked and horrified even her most fervent fans. Several royal bloggers took to their computers last night to express their disdain for her complaints about royal life. Granted, during the audio recording of her confession, she did make mention of the fact that complaining about her privileged and luxurious life was not something she should do openly.

The palace clearly agrees that this is a total blunder, having put out the following statement only one hour after the show aired:

> *"Princess Arabella's comments were made at a moment of weakness during her difficult time in the harsh jungle environment, after a long day of hiking through treacherous terrain. At the time she made them, she was suffering from exhaustion, dehydration, and severe epidermal injuries to both ankles.*
>
> *"The show's producers chose to take advantage of her in this weak state and it must be stressed that she believed this was a private conversation between herself and Mr. Banks, and at no time was she informed that their conversation was recorded, neither before, nor after, filming.*
>
> *"Always a reliable champion of her many causes, Princess Arabella has a generous nature, an open heart, and is overwhelmingly grateful for the blessings she has received in her life. We ask that Avonians take those comments with a grain of salt and a full understanding of the context in which they were made."*

Whether or not Her Royal Highness meant the comments, they have certainly proved themselves to be wildly unpopular, earning her the nickname Princess Precious by one particularly popular royal blogger who goes by the name of King-Slayer99. Time will tell how this latest royal scandal plays out, but one thing is certain, Avonians throughout the kingdom will be glued to their television sets every Thursday night to see what she says next.

"Bollocks," I mutter, leaning my head back against the leather headrest. I lift my gaze from my mobile phone and out to the streets of Vienna, as we travel toward the United Nations Conference Centre. Oh, to be back in the Caribbean with Will, floating along on the sea together, talking and laughing and making love. It seems impossible that that was only a few weeks ago, when I'm here alone, rain drizzling down while my entire world feels like it's falling apart. But there I go complaining again, which apparently is *no bueno*. At least I can escape the media ugliness for a few days and focus on something important.

I cannot believe the palace went with the exhaustion and dehydration thing. Honestly, that's like the publicist's last desperate refuge. It makes me seem like I'm hiding a serious drug addiction instead of just being a whiny brat.

My phone rings and I see that it is my assistant, Mrs. Chadwick, calling. I sigh and answer it.

"Your Highness, I've got Phillip Crawford from your father's office on the line for you. I'm assuming since you're still en route, you have a few moments of privacy to take his call."

"Certainly," I say, unable to think of a good excuse to say no.

"Very good."

There's a click on the line, then I hear Phillip Crawford's voice. "Princess Arabella, I trust you read our statement regarding your unfortunate comments last night."

Oh, sod off, Crawford. "Yes, thank you. I was just going over it."

"Excellent. Should you be approached by the press whilst in Vienna, please refrain from making any comments on the matter, other than to restate your awareness of your fortunate position, then redirect to your purpose at the conference."

"Yes, obviously," I say. "But it shouldn't be an issue. I'm sure no one in Austria will give two hoots about some comment I made."

"I'm afraid that's not the case. We have it on good authority that a rather large group of journalists are awaiting your arrival in front of the UN building, so stick to the script."

My heart sinks. Of course this would happen. "Is there anything else?"

"Yes, actually. We've got some concerns about the outcome of the conference. We've seen drafts of possible branding and it seems a bit...aggressive. We'd like to suggest some changes for you to bring forward as the Avonian ambassador."

"No, thank you, Phillip. I'm confident that the good people at the United Nations have it covered. They likely don't need a senior royal adviser to assist them." I won't say especially not a man, but we're all thinking it, no?

Phillip clears his throat. "Yes, well, as long as you are part of the royal family, we do need to be cautious in terms of the types of state-ments that we make so as not to cause offence. We specifically object to the phrases 'join the fight' and the repeated use of the word 'demand' in reference to the desires of the organization. We'd like to see the wording softened so as not to evoke images of revolution and/or violence."

Oh for...I am *so* not having this conversation with him. "Sorry Phillip, you're cutting out. I think I might be losing you, but I'll definitely take your comments under advisement."

With that, I hang up and toss my phone into my handbag. As if anyone at that conference will care what the likes of Phillip Crawford has to say. Come to think of it, they probably won't care what *I* have to say either. It's not like I've faced any real oppression in my life. Oh no, I can't wear spiky heels. Who cares?

I'm about to attend a conference filled with incredibly inspiring women who have overcome the most horrific of circumstances, fought for their very survival, and faced racism and inequality every day of their lives. And here I am, Princess Precious, who had the nerve to whine about not having enough freedom. If I even have one friend among these women, I'll be shocked.

Closing my eyes for a second, I wish with everything in me that Will were here with me, holding my hand. Not because I *need* a man. Obviously I don't. I'm perfectly capable of weathering this storm on my own—I hope—but it would certainly be *nice* to have somebody in my corner. Although, after what I've accused him of, I'm not sure he'll ever be in my corner again, and I really wouldn't blame him. Just the thought of him makes my throat feel thick with guilt.

I take my phone out of my bag and read his text for the thirtieth time since I woke and saw it. *Leaving Thailand now. Flying straight to Vienna so we can talk. Kenneth is heading to London, so I'll be going commercial which means it'll take 26 hours including stopovers to get there.*

God, I wish he'd made the tone more clear. Is it a "I'm rushing to you because I'm madly in love with you and I can't stand another minute with this problem between us" text, or is it a "I'm flying directly to Vienna to end it in person" text?

That's the kind of man he is. He'd want to do it in person, wouldn't he? He has a deep sense of honour, in spite of what Arthur thinks. He also would want to get it over with immediately so he could get on with life. Will's the kind of man who'd just say it, like one would rip off a Band-Aid. No big flowery preamble. Just, "We're over."

I tried calling him, even though I knew it was no use. He'll be virtually unreachable until he gets here. If only I could somehow teleport myself onto his plane (looking gorgeous, obviously) so we could talk and kiss and make up properly. Well, not properly on a commercial flight, because those bathrooms aren't exactly sanitary or made for romance and the last thing I need is another scandal. The point is, I'm desperate to see him.

We pull up in front of the building and I realize I was meant to be familiarizing myself with the itinerary for the next few days. God, I really am pathetic. Unable to focus on truly vital topics because I've had a row with my boyfriend. Maybe the advisors were right, and I'm not really cut out for doing anything of high-level importance in the world.

I sigh, hating myself for not being better than this.

The car stops and I see a group of reporters standing around on the sidewalk, a few of them peering through the tinted windows, presumably looking for me. My driver, Norm, lowers the privacy glass. "Do you want us to take you around to the back, Your Highness?"

That is *so tempting.* "No, it's best if I just get this over with." Even though it will suck so hard. "Thank you though."

Bellford, who is in the passenger seat, turns to me. "In that case, Miss, give me a moment to check the crowd over."

I nod at him and he gets out. I sit and wait, my heart rattling my ribcage and my palms going clammy. He taps on the window, then opens the door for me.

I grab my briefcase and mutter, "Come on, dummy. Put on your big girl knickers and get on with it."

18

With Deepest Apologies to Bear Grylls

Will

"WHAT DO you mean you're going to Vienna?" Dwight says.

"Exactly that," I say, walking the long hall of the international flight terminal at Krabi Airport. "Arabella's there for a conference."

"That is absolutely the last place you should be going, number one being wherever Kenneth wants you to go next—"

"London," I offer.

"What does he want you to climb there? The Tower of London?"

"No," I say, dreading the honest response I'm about to give him. "He wanted me to meet with his design team to start work on my own outdoor gear line, but I turned it down."

There's a long pause, then Dwight says, "There's something wrong with the connection because I thought I heard you say you turned down a shot at your own outdoor gear line and that would be stone cold crazy."

"You heard me right," I say, slowing down when I catch up to a family of tourists, who are meandering along, peering into the shops instead of watching where they're walking.

"Was it a crap deal? Because I know you must've had a good

reason to turn down the very thing you've been working so hard for these past several years."

"We never got into talking dollars and cents," I say, wincing yet again at what I've done. "The entire deal was contingent on me being available to go to London for the next few weeks, and I'm not able to do that, so I had to say no."

"What do you mean, *you're not able* to do that?" Dwight asks, making a crunching sound which tells me it's Tums time for him. "Of course you can. I'll happily get you out of whatever small potatoes publicity stuff we've got going on here. Or you could fly back from England for a day or two here and there. We can make this work, William. This is it. This is your moment to take hold of the brass ring and … and …. do whatever people do with brass rings. For God's sake, go to the ticket counter immediately and change your flight. I'll call Kenneth and tell him you made a terrible mistake and that you *are*, in fact, interested in this once-in-a-lifetime opportunity."

"But the thing is, I'm not," I say, then I quickly correct myself. "Well, that's not strictly true. I *am* interested, but the timing is all wrong. I pretty much abandoned Arabella when she needed me most. I can't just leave things for another month and hope she'll be waiting around when I finally get back to her."

"Did you get sunstroke out there or something? Maybe hit your head on a rock? Because I don't think you understand what you're doing right now."

Sighing, I say, "No to both, and yes, I *do* know what I'm doing. It's called the right thing, and no matter how much it hurts, it's what it's going to take to make things work with the woman I love."

More fast crunching, then, "Did she *say* you had to turn this down or something?"

"No, of course not. She would never do that."

"So, she said you *should* take the deal?"

"She would have if I had told her about it."

There's a long, drawn-out sigh, then Dwight says, "Okay, William. You're going to need to walk me through your decision-making process because I am *really* having trouble understanding what in the hell is going on with you."

I stop near a large window, drop my bag, and stare out at an airliner that is pulling into one of the gates. "Dwight, six months ago, this deal would've been the greatest thing that could have happened to me. But now, things are different. I can't just be traipsing all over the planet whenever I feel like it and doing whatever I want. I have to consider what Arabella needs."

"Traipsing? Is that her word for it?"

"No, it's mine," I say. "I had to do the right thing for *us*. Relationships take sacrifice, but that's okay because it's worth it. Besides, another opportunity will come along, I'm sure."

"Really?" he asks. "Another major outdoor equipment company is going to come knocking on your door to offer you your own line of gear?"

"Not likely, but something else will pop up."

"William, your own line of gear is…is the *golden ticket*! It's the gift that keeps on giving because you set it up and for years and years and years, they keep sending you cheques for doing absolutely nothing! Nothing, Will. Cheques with lots of zeroes." He lowers his voice to a pained whisper and adds, "Nothing."

"Dwight, please don't make this harder than it already is. I'm upset enough without you rubbing salt in the wound." I pick up my bag and start back towards my gate. "Now, I'm sorry I let you down. I know this would've been a great deal for both of us, and if I could have made it work, believe me, I would have. But I can't, so I'm heading to Vienna for a few days to straighten things out with Arabella. When I get back to town, I promise, I'll be the very best quasi-celebrity guest of all time."

I stroll past The Travel Shop, only to see a huge sign stating their 30% off sale for Bearz backpacks and outdoor accessories. Speaking of salt in the wound…

"I let you out of my sight for a week and you lose all focus," Dwight says.

"So you're saying you wish I were back living in your guest room?" I tease. "I knew you secretly enjoyed having me there."

"If it's the difference between you throwing away your career and being a disgustingly rich celeb, yes," Dwight says, crunching away. "I'd much rather you were *tethered to my ankle* than have you making horrible decisions. And I know you think I only mean this as your agent, but the truth is, I'm thinking of you right now, *and* your beloved princess."

"Are we becoming friends?" I tease.

"Obviously not," he says. "I want *all* my clients to be happy. They tend to make more money that way."

"Liar. You like me."

"You'll never get me to admit to it, so you needn't bother. Now, are you absolutely sure there is no way I can talk you out of this?"

"I'm positive. Sometimes, a man's got to do the right thing, Dwight, even if it hurts," I say, dodging an out-of-control toddler riding one of those suitcases that's shaped like a dinosaur.

"Yes, but in this case, certainly the right thing is to make as much cash as possible so you can buy her a twelve-carat ring and get her away from her suffocating family."

"A ring is useless without a finger to put it on." I reach my gate, then glance at the clock, realizing I've got another two hours before my flight boards. The seats are jam-packed here, so I turn back the other way.

"Clearly, I can't talk you out of this, so make up fast and hightail it back here as fast as humanly possible. I'll book you some promotional gigs."

"I thought they were small potatoes."

"Not anymore."

Ouch.

I hang up and walk into The Travel Shop. Apparently, I'm in the mood to torture myself with something I'm never going to have. The backpacks are on display near the front, and I stop in front of them and stare. A man comes to stand beside me, taking one off the hook and examining it.

"Don't bother," I tell him. "I lugged that exact one around the jungle for ten days, and I can tell you that after a few minutes, you'll feel it. A good pack should be nearly indestructible and yet undetectable on your back."

He gives me a strange look, then says, "I don't know how they would ever make one much lighter than this." He flicks the tag over, then adds, "At this price, you'd be a fool not to buy one."

He takes the pack and walks over to the till while I turn my attention back to the display.

What a dumb logo. Why would he spell Bears with a 'z?' I mean, seriously, do they think that's super trendy or something?

"Stupid heavy backpack," I mutter before picking it up. Huh. That's actually surprisingly light.

In fact, this is extremely light. How did the one I had in the jungle seem so much heavier when it was empty? I take off my own backpack and slide this one on. And then it hits me all at once. Tingles run up my spine as everything becomes clear to me.

"Those bastards," I say, far too loudly.

Glancing around, I see the man I was just talking to and the woman behind the till giving me strange looks.

"Sorry," I say.

Five minutes later, I'm standing in front of the ticket counter for Avonian Air. "I need to exchange this ticket for your next flight to Valcourt."

———

I'm crammed into the middle seat on my way from Thailand to Valcourt via Qatar and Belgium (with a nine-hour layover in Qatar). That was the only available last-minute flight I could get. The entire trip will take a little over thirty-six hours, which will have me in Valcourt by Monday morning. I can only hope it won't be too late because if it is, Arabella's life is about to be ruined. Her family's too.

The longer I sit and think about what really happened out in that jungle, the more horrified I become. For those in the back row, Dylan must have had audio recording equipment sewn into the backpacks (which accounts for their weight, obviously). The audio probably ran the entire time unless we're really freaking lucky and somehow it lost power at some point. But I doubt it, because even small recorders running on regular batteries could keep going for days.

So, not only do they probably have a whole lot of audio of us having loud, jungle sex, they also have us confessing our deepest, darkest secrets, the worst of which being Arabella's mum's suicide.

Yeah, let that sink in for a minute.

An unbelievably painful family secret—one they've managed to contain for nearly three decades—is about to be spilled on reality television. The more I think about it, the more my entire body courses with rage—not just at the producers and network, but at myself as well. How could I not have seen that coming? I mean, seriously?

How could I allow myself to be a part of this utter trash? I'm not a reality TV guy. I'm a nature documentarian. I'm a professional adventurer. Or at least I *was*. Now, I've been reduced to a Kardashian in hiking boots. And they're going to reduce Arabella and her family to nothing more than a cheap scandal, not to mention forever tarnishing her mother's memory.

And I know what you're thinking – that I should tell Arabella what's going on, but I can't. Not when she's doing work that she's so passionate about for the first time in her entire life. The Equal Everywhere Conference is *so much more important* than what I'm doing (or ever have done, really), so the last thing she needs is another crisis to handle right now. Especially not since I left her to deal with the first one (which happens to be related to this one but is about to get *so much worse* if I can't stop it).

No, the right thing to do is to step up, put a stop to whatever Dylan is about to do, and let Arabella focus on the work she's doing. That's what a good partner does. So that's what I'm about to do.

Well, that's what I'll do in about thirty-six hours. For now, I'll just sit here being used as a pillow by the man to my left who's fallen asleep and now has his head on my shoulder.

19

Princesses, the Paragons of Oppression

Arabella

WELL, this certainly sucks mouldy doughnuts. Day two and I have yet to add anything of value to the conversation. But even worse, my presence here is actually a *detriment* to the cause because the press is camped out in front of the building and the only thing they want to do is keep the conversation about me being a whiny, entitled brat going. They have no interest in interviewing the incredible women here about what the UN is doing to advance women's rights around the world. Sad really.

I'm surrounded by the world's brightest and best—women who have fought on the front lines of it their entire lives, whereas I've spent years feeling put upon because I don't have total autonomy over my wardrobe. I'm afraid that Phillip Crawford and the rest of the advisors were right about me—I don't belong here, which is utterly disappointing.

So far, I've remained a silent observer in a Chanel suit, even though the other women have been very welcoming and do seem interested in hearing from me. Well, most of them anyway. There is one nasty in the group, Dr. Sandra Highbrow (yes, that's her real last name). She's a professor of women's rights at Cambridge and class A be-otch who came right out yesterday at the cocktail hour and asked me what exactly I bring to the table, other than bad press. Those were her exact words. I couldn't even think of a good response, so I just gave a weak laugh, hoping to pass the entire thing off as though I thought she was joking. But she wasn't, which she made very clear by following up her question with, "No, seriously, *what* are you doing here?"

I froze up, but luckily one of the other ladies piped up with, "At the moment, she's trying to enjoy her Cosmopolitan, Sandra. Leave her alone."

To be honest, I should probably go home. The last thing I wanted to do was hurt the cause, which is exactly what I'm doing. I've *never* felt like such a giant wazzer in my entire life. And there's really nothing I can do to fix it, is there? I said what I said, then it got recorded and shared with the world, which means I will forever be known as Princess Precious. End of discussion. For decades to come, when anyone googles me, that stupid clip will come up first. I have never, *ever* been so angry at myself for anything, and instead of setting that aside and managing to find ways to contribute, I keep hearing a voice in my head telling me I'm a fraud, I don't belong, and I can only make everything much worse by being here.

At the moment, we're in breakout rooms. There are ten of us sitting around a boardroom table brainstorming ideas for the next phase of the equality revolution. Well, nine women brainstorming, plus me. Dr. Malika Jelani is leading our session this morning. The topic is assisting women in rural areas in making strides in home-based businesses, something I know nothing about. My phone vibrates in my pocket and I discreetly take it out of my jacket, only to see it's Will calling.

Of course he would call at the exact moment when there is no possible way I can answer. Biting my bottom lip, I glance at Malika, hoping I can make eye contact and excuse myself. But the eye contact makes her think I have something to say.

She gives me a hopeful smile. "Yes, Princess Arabella, you look like you have some ideas to add to our brainstorming session."

"Oh, yes," Dr. Highbrow says. "*Do* share with us how you managed to squirrel away a few dollars by knitting hats out of the sheeple who love you."

Malika, who's standing at the head of the table, folds her arms and tilts her head at Dr. Highbrow. "No, we mustn't do that. Princess Arabella has been every bit as oppressed as any other woman here."

No! Please don't. My cheeks burn. "Oh, I wouldn't say that."

Dammit, I missed his call.

"*Of course* you have," Malika says, then looking around the room, she adds, "Arabella lives in one of the oldest patriarchal subsets of society in human history—royalty. Everything decided by birth order rather than aptitude and life goals, no autonomy whatsoever, not even with regard to her own body. She's even obligated to bear children."

"It's honestly not *that* bad," I say, with a light chuckle. "I know I made some unflattering comments about my life recently, but I really am fully aware of my unusual level of privilege. When I made those comments, I was —"

"Suffering from dehydration and exhaustion?" Dr. No Brows says, wrinkling up her nose. (I'm calling her that because she clearly plucked her eyebrows into oblivion in the nineties, and also because I'm extremely immature when I'm upset. Add that to the list of things I hate about myself).

My phone starts buzzing again and it's all I can do not to leap from my chair and run out of the room.

"She absolutely was suffering that day," Malika says, sitting down in her chair. "Here is a woman who has barely even been allowed to do anything physically or mentally challenging her entire life. So when she managed to break free of those shackles, the first thing she did was test herself beyond the reasonable limits of any human. She has the heart of a true warrior."

No Brows snorts.

"Oh, no," I say, utterly humiliated. "I'm honestly a very average person. And my greatest wish is to find a way to help the truly oppressed."

"Don't you dare! You've been oppressed as much as anyone,"

Malika says. "My friends, we, as a group, need to embrace poor Arabella and help lift her from the depths of her dungeon."

"It's fine, really," I mutter. "I'd be much happier to focus on the needs of the rural women in economically depressed areas."

"And we will," Malika says. "But we must not forget our sisters in need in palaces around the world."

My phone buzzes again, and I glance down at Will's picture, my heart squeezing in my chest. Three calls in a row? Something must be wrong. "I am so sorry, I must take this call. There is an…urgent situation that requires my immediate attention."

Malika looks taken aback for a second, then quickly recovers. "Yes, go ahead, my dear. You can tell us what you were going to say when you return."

"Thank you," I say, standing and rushing out of the room.

Once I'm in the hallway, I swipe to answer. "Hello?"

"Thank God I caught you," Will says.

For some reason, my eyes fill up with tears at the sound of his voice, and I hurry down the hall to a sleek wooden bench. "Are you all right?" I ask.

"Good, yeah. Well, I'm okay. How are you doing?" Will says, his voice filled with the same desperation I'm feeling.

"I feel absolutely awful about what happened, and I really need to see you so badly. When will you be here?"

He pauses for a second. "First, let me say how much I miss you, because honestly, it's enough to fill this entire airport with mushy, gooey emotions. Second, I want you to know that now that I've had some time to cool off, I'm not upset about what happened. I totally understand why you were so confused and upset. It's okay, really."

"No, it isn't," I say, my voice cracking. "I can't believe I levelled those accusations at you. I can barely sleep, I'm so angry at myself. I wish I could take it all back and handle the whole thing over again like a normal, reasonable person."

"Honestly, Belle, I think we may have underestimated Dylan's ability to mess with us," Will says. "And the pressure you're under is insane with the show and the constant public criticism. Add a disapproving older brother, and it quickly adds up to too much for anyone to handle – even a reasonable person, which you are."

I blink quickly, forcing the tears back into my head. "No, I don't think I am, but thank you for saying it anyway," I answer. "I so badly needed to hear that. To be honest, things are not going well with the conference. The press has followed me here and they're ignoring the cause and focussing on my stupidity. Plus, I'm a total disaster. I keep freezing up and have yet to provide any sort of value in any way."

"I'm sure you're being too hard on yourself," he says, and the soothing sound of his voice makes me even more desperate to see him so he can wrap his arms around me.

"Unfortunately, I'm afraid my assessment of my performance thus far is quite accurate," I say. "If you weren't on your way here, I honestly think I'd be ready to pack it in. When do you land? If it's in the evening, I can come to the airport to get you."

"Yeah, here's the thing," he says in a tone that tells me I'm not going to like whatever 'the thing' is. "I have to go straight to Valcourt."

"What? Why?" I close my eyes tightly as disappointment coats my insides like thick paint.

"I can't get into it right now but believe me when I tell you that if I had *any* choice at all, I'd still be on my way to see you right now."

Keep it together. Keep it together. This is not a crisis. War is a crisis. Being forced to flee your homeland to escape certain death is a crisis. This an opportunity to show I can be both reasonable and supportive when life takes a turn. "What happened?"

"Nothing I can't fix but I have to do it immediately."

"So, something bad *did* happen?" My heart squeezes at the thought of anything else going wrong.

Down the hall, the door to our conference room opens up and Dr. No Brows comes walking in my general direction. *Oh perfect.*

I turn my attention back to Will who is saying, "...so sorry, sweetheart. I miss you so much, and if there was any possible way I could be on my way to Vienna right now, I promise I would be. But don't worry about me, okay. You've got enough on your plate. Just focus on the conference and know you're there for the right reasons and that they're lucky to have you. You're smart and kind and you've got so much to offer them. Just trust yourself."

"Thank you," I say, even though inside, my brain is screaming, '*wrong!*'

"My flight is about to leave, but I want you to know how much I love you and how sorry I am about everything."

"Yes," I say, glancing up to see that No Brows is within earshot, so I can't very well tell him I love him back. "Thank you for bringing me up to speed on all of this. Do let me know how things progress," I say in a very formal tone. With that, I hang up.

Well, that was just great, wasn't it? I pulled the Queen Elizabeth handshake when a little Prince Charles ran to her for a hug.

I sigh, then quickly text him. *I'm sorry about the overly formal goodbye. I pretended I had to take an urgent call to get me out of the meeting. One of the other attendees was walking past right when we were wrapping up. What I meant to say is, "I love you so much it hurts, and I cannot wait to be with you again."*

Text from Will: *Back at you, Belle. Go get 'em.*

20

A Deal with the Dylan

Will

"WILL! THE MAN OF THE HOUR," Dylan sings, standing up at her desk. "Come sit. I was thrilled when I got your email. Have you seen the ratings? They are off. The. Charts! And, I have some *big* things coming down the pipe for you, young man! Huge!"

She gestures to a round table in the corner of her office and walks toward it, stopping at the mini-fridge for a can of Red Bull. "Drink?"

"No," I say, folding my arms and remaining rooted in place while she has a seat.

"So, I've been working on something absolutely epic for you. No. *Bigger* than epic, it's—"

"—Did you have recording equipment sewn into our backpacks?" I ask, glaring at her.

"Mm-hmm." She nods, cracking the can open. "Stroke of genius, don't you think?"

Wow, so she's not even going to deny it. "I'd use a different word actually. Unscrupulous or conniving maybe." I tilt my head, then add, "Or evil. Yes, evil is the most accurate, definitely."

Dylan looks taken aback, then she waves off my words as though

I'm nuts. "Evil? Is it evil to make you a star? Is it evil to help put two young people who are perfectly suited for each other together in the wild so they can fall in love?"

"It's evil to record us without our knowledge and you bloody well know it," I say. "What's the secret you're revealing, Dylan?"

"What secret?"

"Cut the crap. You know what I'm talking about," I spit out. I'm definitely treading far over the line of acceptable workplace decorum, but I really couldn't care less. "The one you've been advertising every five minutes."

"I think you can guess," she answers.

I let out a frustrated sigh, my gut tightening. "Her mum?"

Dylan nods. "I can see why you're upset. I get it. You love Arabella and it'll be a bit tricky for her for a few days, but in the end, I promise, it'll be a *positive* thing. It never feels good to keep secrets. It'll actually be quite freeing for them. Plus, it'll open up the conversation on mental illness and suicide. So, when you think about it, we're actually doing a great service for the entire kingdom."

"Don't you dare try to spin this," I scoff. "What you're doing is wrong and you know it. These are *real* people's lives you're about to ruin."

She stands and walks around the table toward me, then perches herself on the edge of it. "You wanted me to make you a star."

Shaking my head, I start to say no, but she talks over me.

"Yes, you did, William. You want to be famous. You want to be incredibly rich so you can spend the rest of your life hopping from one adrenaline rush to the next one," Dylan says. "And I promised I'd get that for you, which is what I'm doing."

"You're unbelievable. I *never* asked for any of this. I just wanted to do my show, teach people about the wilderness, and maybe get some of them out there into nature once in a while instead of sitting around glued to screens their entire lives," I say.

"Well, this is something Ms. Alanis Morissette would call ironic," she says, having a swig of her drink. "You don't want people to get outside into nature. You want them sitting at home watching you. In fact, you *need* them to because if they don't, you can't make a living doing whatever you want whenever you want. Before me, you were a man teetering on the edge of unemployment, remember? The network was about to drop you, but I finally got people to watch. And now, you're upset about how I did it. Maybe you should just say thank you and be glad you're about to have all your dreams handed to you on a silver platter."

I set my jaw and glare at her, my mind spinning as I search for a way to make her listen. As badly as I want to lose it and start yelling, the wiser part of my mind is telling me I have to play nice here. I have everything to lose, but more importantly, so does Arabella. "I don't want it this way, Dylan. I'd rather be broke for the rest of my life than to hurt Arabella like this." I let my shoulders drop. "Please, Dylan, please don't do this to them. There are other ways to get ratings."

She scrunches up her nose. "I wish I could help you, but the execs love it. Victor and Kira almost died, they were so excited. They'll never give it up."

"Let me talk to them," I say. "I can convince them that this is the wrong thing to do."

"Doubt it," she says with the phoniest apologetic face I've ever seen.

"They'll sue you."

"They'll lose," Dylan says. "The contract you and Arabella signed is absolutely clad in titanium, never to be undone."

"Come on, Dylan, you're a better person than this," I say, even though she's not and she probably knows it. "Don't you feel the least bit bad about what you're about to do? They're going to suffer for the rest of their lives because this thing will get played over and over forever. Even little James and Flora are never going to get out from under this. It's the kind of story that never dies."

"There's a price for fame, Will. Paris Hilton—sex tape, but now a successful businesswoman," she says. "Same with Kim. In fact, her entire family hitched their star to her booty, and look at how amazingly it's all turning out for them. Kylie's a freaking billionaire, Will. A *billionaire*. Think of what you could do with a billion dollars! You could save all the elephants and bees or whatever you're worried about saving. You could buy a small country and turn it into an enormous obstacle course. Trust me, compared to what some people go through for fame, you're getting off easy. John Wayne Bobbitt had to have his penis thrown in a ditch to get famous. This is *peanuts* compared to that."

"Jesus, Dylan! I don't want to be a billionaire." I throw my hands up in the air. "You're about to *permanently ruin* the life of the woman I love. Permanently. Forever. Never to be undone. I cannot stand by and let this happen."

She makes a clicking sound, then says, "But the thing is, it already happened."

Every hair on my body stands on end and anger rushes through my veins. "I'll stop doing any more promotions."

"We'll sue you."

"I'll...I'll tell everyone what you're doing, and no one will ever want to work with you again."

"That'll only make me bigger. Wealthy desperate people will *always* be in need of someone who's willing to get her hands dirty."

Bugger, she's right. I sigh, then lower my voice. "I'll do anything."

Oh, that seems to have worked because she's tapping her chin with her finger while she stares at me. "Anything?"

"Anything. Name it."

A slow smile spreads across her face, causing my stomach to turn to stone. I've just made a deal with the devil, haven't I?

21

Apricot Jam, Dragon-Slaying Virgins, and Painful Pep Talks

Arabella

"Somebody better be dead," Gran says into the phone. "Because there's no other acceptable reason to call me at this ungodly hour."

"It's nearly 8 a.m.," I say, staring out the window of my hotel room into Am Hof Square.

"Exactly."

"I'm sorry, I just really needed to talk to you. It seems like the entire world is falling apart and I feel very much alone."

"That's because you got used to all that regular shagging," Gran says, "And now that you haven't had it for a while, you're upset. Buy a vibrator and a dirty book. You'll be fine."

"Gran!" I say, wondering why I bothered to call her in the first place. "I wish just once you could sound like a regular grandmother—the kind who bakes bread and comforts her grandchildren when they're having a rough go."

"Oh, sweetheart, if you wanted that, you really should've been born into a different family. Hang on for a minute. Now that I'm up, I'm famished." I hear her ring her bell, then start her breakfast order

—steel cut oats with berries and Earl Grey tea. Since her heart attack, she starts all but one morning a month this way.

I look out at the Mariensäule, a statue of the Virgin Mary set on a tall pillar in the centre of the square. Under her feet is a dragon with an arrow through his back. I sigh, wondering how she managed to vanquish her dragon.

Oh, Arabella, dramatic much?

Turning from the window, I glance at my untouched meal of palatschinken, which are, in my humble opinion, the world's most amazing crepe-like pancakes. They're filled with apricot jam that's been infused with Viennese brandy. I also ordered a side of apfel-radln, which are fried apple rings, going all-in on carbs and icing sugar in an attempt to lift my spirits.

Gran clears her throat and comes back on the line with me. "All right, since you've already started my day on the wrong foot, you might as well tell me what's up your tush."

"Oh, thanks," I say sarcastically. "Honestly, I don't even know where to start. There are just *so* many things going wrong. Will and I haven't seen each other in close to two weeks and we've had a huge row—"

"—Tessa told me how our Arthur lent a hand in that. Tosser."

"Right? He got me all worked up and I said the most awful things when I spoke with Will, and even though he says he forgives me and our conversations since have been quite lovely, I really won't know if we're truly okay until I see him face-to-face. He was supposed to come here, but he went to Valcourt instead and I have no idea why. He said it was unavoidable, but I honestly don't know what could be so bloody important. And I hate myself for even worrying about it because there are so many more important things in this world to focus on, like poverty and disease and violence, not 'is my boyfriend mad at me?'" I say, taking a deep breath and continuing my rant. "Plus, I'm surrounded by all these amazing women which only serves to highlight the fact that I've never really done anything of conse-quence my entire life. Literally nothing that any other person couldn't have just slid into my place and done. And I'm supposed to have turned into this brave champion of women's rights, but the truth is, no matter what I did in my fleeting moment of courage in the jungle, I'm still the same old unremarkable me. So, what should I do?"

There's a long pause, then Gran says, "Oh, are you done? I stopped listening somewhere around the word boyfriend."

"*Seriously*, Gran?"

"No, not really, but good God, can you ever go on with the whining. That might be the one area in which you do have extraordinary talents."

"Forget it," I say, with a sigh. "I'm sorry I woke you."

"Oh, fine," she says, reluctantly. "I'll try to help. First off, you're not unremarkable. It was a very unkind thing of me to say and I only half meant it."

"No, don't backtrack now," I say. "You were absolutely correct about me. "

"Come now, you're being too hard on yourself, which is my job. If you keep this up, you'll put me out of business."

A tiny smile escapes my lips.

"Now, one issue at a time. Let's start with the least important thing and work our way from there."

"Which is?"

"Your love life," Gran says. "Before you allow yourself to be all upset about your young man not rushing to you for make-up sex, you need to decide if he's worth the trouble, because as far as I can tell, he's creating a considerable amount of it."

"Of course he's worth it!" Now, I'm mad.

"Why?"

"What do you mean, why? Because we're in love."

"But, *why*? I'm not trying to be difficult. Being a royal and being happy are generally not compatible. You need to be one hundred percent certain that he is a man with whom you can go the distance— and let me tell you, the distance is really bloody far, especially if you both live to be as old as me."

Sitting down on the window seat, I trace the statue on the glass with my fingertip. "He's it for me, Gran, even though being with him is going to be ridiculously difficult. He just gets me, you know? And when he looks at me, it's like the rest of the world disappears. And I never feel as alive or as content as I do when we're together."

"Not a bad start, but a lot of that wears off."

"Great, thanks," I say, rolling my eyes even though she can't see me. I think for a few seconds, then say, "He's the first person to believe I'm strong."

"Poppycock. I've always known that."

"Okay then, he's the first *man* who's ever believed in me. Like, really *believed* I'm capable of tackling anything, no matter how hard," I answer. "It's intoxicating to have someone with that kind of faith in you—someone who offers you freedom and excitement. And it's not only the adventure stuff—we also have so much fun together. We laugh and joke around and I can be myself, Gran. Not anyone else's version of me but the person I really am. So, yes, he's worth the trouble."

"That's a shame, really," she says. "It would've been so much easier if you'd fallen for, say, an accountant, or a doctor. But since you've gone and fallen for exactly the wrong sort of man, the two of you need to sit down and talk. Set up some rules for your relationship, including, but not limited to, ignoring other people's opinions about your relationship, except mine, obviously—"

"Obviously."

"And having a maximum number of days apart that you won't go over for anything," she says. "And *never* underestimate the power of the media to tear two people apart—it's their favourite pastime and the very best way to sell ad space. Start with that and go from there. You'll be fine."

"Thank you," I say, relief sweeping over me, before quickly being washed away by worry again.

"Now, let's move onto your conference, at which you're clearly failing spectacularly."

"Yes, let's," I say, glad that no one can see I'm pulling a pouty face. "It's the last day, and I really must come up with something, *anything* at all really, to prove I belong. I thought that when I was finally presented with something truly important to do with my life, I'd be so good at it. But I'm awful. I freeze up when it's my turn to contribute. Oh, God, maybe it *was* a bit of a stretch for me to think I could take on something like this."

"Rubbish," Gran says. "You're every bit as intelligent and brave as you let yourself be. The problem with you is that you tend to stop short of the point where your potential is just picking up."

"Exactly. So, how do I stop that?"

"You just have to say, fuck it."

My shoulders drop. "Oh, is that the secret to life?"

"A happy one, yes," Gran says. "Now, you dig into those crepes and apfelradlns while I talk."

"I'm having a bowl of porridge and some berries," I lie, sitting down at the table.

"Sure you are," she says, "And I haven't been with another man since your grandfather died. Now, shut up so I can tell you what your biggest problem is. Your entire existence revolves around the fear that you might offend somebody or that— *gasp*—somebody won't like you, which leaves very little room in your life for doing anything of consequence. And that's precisely what's stopping *you* from having anything of value to say. You're terrified of being criticized by those women who *you* think have more of a right to an opinion than you do."

I hear a slurping sound, which means she's testing her tea to see if it's her preferred temperature. "The truth is, you *do* know the experience of being a woman. You face it every single day, in the way that your father and Arthur and the senior advisors treat you like a child, trying to protect you from anything bad that could ever possibly come to fruition, in spite of many years of me telling them to stop. You're so busy listening to them that you've never made room to hear your own voice."

I pick up my fork and knife, and slice into one of the pancakes, letting some of the jam ooze out the sides while she talks.

"Stop worrying so bloody much about what anyone else thinks of you or you'll wind up doing the same banal thing that countless generations of women have done—stay in your safe zone, trying to never offend anyone. Now, you can carry on doing that, or you can go out and live a great, big, juicy life filled with adventure and fun and celebration and laughter. But none of that can happen unless you let go of the need for approval. Are you with me so far?"

"Barely keeping up, but I'm there."

"Good enough. Start with today. If you want to end this conference on a high note, stop worrying about what those other women in the room think of you. You can't change who you are or what type of upbringing you've had any more than someone who was born in a slum in Calcutta could. There is a fiery woman inside you dying to get out. You need to let her."

"Okay, okay," I say, nodding enthusiastically, even though she can't see it. "I am going to do exactly what you said Gran, thank you."

"No, for God's sake, Arabella!" Gran barks. "Did you not hear a word of the tremendous speech I just made?"

"Of course I did. I was listening very carefully and I intend to take your advice."

She lets out a frustrated growl. "If you actually understood what I meant, you would've told me to fuck off and mind my own business because you could sort this out for yourself."

I burst out laughing. "I could never say something like that to you."

"I'm serious. Tell me to fuck off or to bloody well shut up and let you be."

"No, I couldn't—"

"Sure you can, and quite frankly, you *should*. I can be quite awful to you at times."

"All right, fine. Stop being so nasty, Gran," I say, feeling terrified and exhilarated at the same time.

"Watch yourself, child," she answers sternly. "I won't put up with any cheek from the likes of you."

"But you—"

"I know what I said, but I changed my mind. Be a hardass with everyone else in the world. Just not with me. Now, you eat your pancakes and go be incredible. Or don't. If you'd rather not, don't be incredible today. Sit there like a very pretty dummy and wait for the entire conference to be over, then come rushing back to your boyfriend, like the very good girl you are."

22

When You're Going to Jump the Gun, Make Sure You Bring Friends...

Will

"*THIS* YOU WANT TO SIGN?" Dwight takes off his glasses and rubs the bridge of his nose. It's late in the evening and we're sitting at his kitchen table. He's just finished reading over the twenty-two-page contract drawn up by the lawyers at ABN. "This absolute rubbish contract? When you turned down the deal of a lifetime literally three days ago?"

I give him a firm nod, even though my gut has been churning since yesterday morning in Dylan's office. "Definitely."

"You're the worst client I've ever had," he says, but I can see in his eyes he doesn't mean it. "Bar none. No one is as excruciating as you." He drums his fingers on the table and sighs. "These people don't play nice, Will. Look what they were going to do to Arabella. And now you're tying yourself to them—*exclusively*, I might add, which almost certainly means lost opportunities—for *three years*. That's a lifetime in this business."

"I don't have a choice," I say, my muscles tensing up at the thought of what I'm doing.

"Exactly my point. Any time you're strong-armed into a deal, you're not going to be the one to come out on top," he says. "And in this case, they're absolutely taking advantage of the situation to lock you in for a pittance compared to what they should be paying."

I brush aside his words, knowing that facing the truth of what I'm doing will only make things much worse. "I can't let myself worry about any of that. Not with what's at stake."

He picks up the contract and thumbs through it again, shaking his head. "It's very admirable of you to want to shoulder the burden on this one, but I can't help but think if you just talk to Arabella—"

Holding up one hand, I say, "I'm not changing my mind. This is my chance to step up and do what needs to be done. And after the way I took off on her when Kenneth came along, I don't care if they asked me to sign a thirty-year contract, I'd do it if it would save her and her family from permanent public humiliation."

"What if we go to one of the staffers at the palace? Or Prince Arthur? They might have some way to make this go away." Dwight stands and swipes his mug off the table, then walks over to the counter to refill it with more tea. "I'm not sure if you're aware of this, but those royals actually have a fair bit of clout."

I manage a wry grin before shaking my head. "They dislike me enough as it is, Dwight, but at least I have a chance to win them over eventually. If I make them responsible for this mess for my own profit, they'll have every reason to hate me forever."

Returning to the table, Dwight sits back down across from me. "This is going to suck *hard*. You're selling your soul to the world's most evil, not to mention irritating, television producer. You're aware of that?"

"I am."

"The promotional schedule alone will be god-awful. Have you even looked at what they've got you doing over the next three weeks?"

Shrugging, I say, "Small price to pay."

"Speaking of pay, what they're offering is a disgrace."

"You've already mentioned that," I say, pulling the contract toward me. "But in all fairness, this *World's Best Survivor Challenge* they're proposing comes with a hell of a nice prize."

It's rather exciting actually – it's a competition of all the top adventurers in the world and the purse is a cool million. The best part is that they want Arabella and me to compete as a team.

"*If* you win, which is a gigantic if," Dwight says, concern written all over his face. "As your agent, I feel obligated to tell you that there is no way out of this non-compete clause."

"And as my friend?"

He stares at me for a moment, then says, "As your friend, I say you're doing the right thing for the right reasons, and if she doesn't propose *to you* after all this, she doesn't know what an amazing person she's got."

I smile at him and click the pen, then start to sign before I can change my mind. My heart pounds in my chest as I go through each page one by one, initialling as needed. When I finish, I say, "I knew you loved me."

"Let's not get carried away."

—————

The next morning, I was up at four a.m. to get to the ABN studios for a spot on their Breakfast Television show, where I showed a sleepy audience how to make a one-person emergency tent out of a garbage bag. Next, I hurried across town to judge a baking contest (the real winner was me because I hadn't had time to eat before I got there). After that, I crammed for my spot as a guest commentator at the Valcourt United vs. London Bulldogs football match (which was a little harrowing since I'm not exactly an expert). Finally, I was off to the stadium for four hours to sit behind the sports desk and talk sports, then back to Dwight's to drop into bed just after ten p.m. because this morning, I had to get right back on the promotional circuit.

But it's a small price to pay because agreeing to all of that meant I got to watch the rest of the episodes in the editing booth and nix anything that would be humiliating for Arabella and/or her family. Each cut was a fight, but I came out victorious in all but two pretty minor things. I'm a little tired, what with the editing and PR work, but honestly, I feel positively victorious.

In a funny way, this whole crappy secret audio recording thing has helped me feel like I finally deserve her. Can I buy her a mansion and a fleet of luxury cars? Not yet. *But* I stepped up and protected her when she needed it most. The best part is, she didn't have to experience the horrifying drama of it all because I was able to handle it without her knowing. Protecting her from the pain and sadness of it all and the absolute terror of having given away her mother's secret is what a good boyfriend does. And I am that boyfriend—the kind who handles things, who eases the burdens of the one he loves. He does not make things worse.

I know now, without a shadow of a doubt, that I've got what it takes to be the husband she needs, which is why I'm at La Pearls Fine Jewelers at this very moment, about to pick out the perfect ring so I can propose to the perfect woman.

She'll be flying in late this afternoon, and I've decided to do it tonight. It just makes sense, really, when you think about it, because we're meant to be together and when you know it, you also know there is no point in waiting, not even one extra day. Because you want your life together to start as soon as possible.

It's taken a lot to pull it all together—I had to enlist Dwight's help in order to come up with the perfect plan. And he really came through in a very big way. Turns out, one of his fellow agent friends has a certain famous actor as a client who happens to have a secluded beach house an hour from Valcourt. I'm sorry I can't tell you who he is because I've been sworn to secrecy. But I could give you a hint. He was in a certain movie called *Inglourious Bastards*. No, not Brad Pitt. This guy also won an Academy Award for his role in *Django Unchained*.

Anyway, his place is just sitting there empty and Dwight called his agent who called Christo—whoops! I almost said it. Anyway, turns out he's a big fan of my show, so he said we absolutely could stay there as long as we want since he's off filming a movie I can't tell you about. Can you believe it though? *He's* a fan of *mine*?

I've rented a Mercedes with dark tinted windows so I can sneak Arabella out of the palace without the press spotting us. I'll whisk her up the coast, wine and dine her, and bam! Will you marry me? Yes, yes, I will.

And just like that, everything is going to be incredible.

But first, the ring.

I knew it would be impossible for me to pick it myself, so I've enlisted a crew—Dwight is here with me at the store, and I'm about to patch my family in via Zoom so they can help with my selection. Ah! There they are now.

"Hi guys!" I say as the faces of my brother, Harrison, his wife, Libby, my sister Emma, her husband, Pierce, and our de facto mum, Rosy Brown, all come into focus on my mobile screen.

The somewhat snooty salesman has gone to the back to bring out a tray of what he called 'next level' rings. When he returns, he glances at my phone and rolls his eyes. "Perfect. You're shopping by committee because that's always so efficient."

Honestly, I'm in too good a mood to care how grumpy this guy is.

"Will, are you sure you're ready for this?" Harrison asks, scrubbing the back of his neck with one hand. "I mean, it was literally three weeks ago that you had to crash on your agent's couch because you didn't have the cash to get your own place."

Surly Salesguy raises one eyebrow at me.

I chuckle nervously. "No, I was staying with Dwight because I was waiting for my big bonus check to come in, and it did."

"But, blowing it on a ring, Cuddle Bear?" Rosy asks. "That girl's got enough diamonds. You should put a downpayment on a house."

"I can do that too, Rosy," I say with a grin. "Dwight's here…" I point the screen at him. "Say hello, Dwight."

"Hello, family," he says. "Don't worry about Will. I'm keeping him out of trouble."

"And he signed me for another set of commercials—this time for Merill's—plus, we just landed a contract for a new survivor challenge competition that films in Greenland in two months. Arabella and I will compete as a team."

"Greenland in November?" Emma asks, wrinkling up her nose. "What does Arabella think about that?"

"She doesn't know yet, but trust me, she'll be *thrilled* when she finds out. Absolutely thrilled. She's been dying to get back out into the wild since she came home."

Libby gives Harrison a swat on the arm. "I told you he knew what he was doing."

"I can't help it. I have to ask," he says, rubbing his arm.

"No worries *at all*," I say with a huge grin. "I totally get it. In fact, I'm glad you asked because I'm sure you were all wondering, so it's best to get it out in the open. But now that we've set that issue aside, we can all get on with the big decision."

Emma holds up her hand. "Have you narrowed down the styles at all?"

"Nope. I don't have the first clue," I say. "What do you guys think a woman like Arabella would absolutely love? Like, absolutely blow her mind because she loves it so much?"

"Well, considering that none of us really know her," Emma says, "It would be difficult to say."

"Okay, fair enough," I say, nodding. "In that case, let me describe her for you. She's like the warmth of the sun on a chilly winter's morning. She's like the most refined, elegant, sophisticated, well-educated, well-spoken woman I've ever met, but who also has this deliciously adventurous, kickass fierceness to her that is irresistible. She's smart and witty and kind-hearted and sensitive and... caring... and she calls me on my bullshit, and I don't know if any of this helps in picking out a square cut or emerald drop or whatever the hell these things are called, but I just can't help but brag about her." I glance at Dwight. "Do you think she'll say yes? Because the more I think about how incredible she is, the less likely it seems that she'll want to marry me."

"Cuddle Bear! Of course she'll say yes," Rosy says. "You're perfect. Any woman would be lucky to have you—royal or not."

Emma glances at Rosy and rolls her eyes. "I wouldn't go that far. Ask the salesman what their return policy is."

Sales guy chimes in with, "One week, subject to damage."

"William, have you thought of going with an antique? Something really special, maybe with a romantic history to it?" Pierce asks.

I nod. "Thought about it, but she's just so modern and so ready to forge a new path for herself, I feel like something brand-new that's never been worn before would be best. Something that says fresh start. It's you and me in this forever."

"Good Lord, Will, take it down a notch before we all start getting nauseous," Harrison says.

"Righto, sorry," I say. "I'm just beyond excited."

"Yeah, we got that," Emma says.

I aim the phone at the black velvet tray and smile down at the shiny rocks, each one absolutely dazzling under the bright lights. God, those lights are hot. Or am I actually flushed with excitement?

My entire family starts talking at the same time, trying to point out which ring they like. The salesman sighs and speaks loudly in the general direction of my phone. "One at a time, if you please."

There's a pause, then they all start up again, and I find myself chuckling.

I'm giddy.

I mean, like actually giddy for maybe the first time in my entire life.

Best. Day. Ever.

23

Plagiarizing Your Potty-Mouthed Grandmother is Always a Good Idea...

Arabella

"Welcome, everyone, to our Equal Everywhere Wrap-up Session," Malika says into the microphone.

We're in a large, bowl-shaped auditorium and she, along with five other conference leaders, are on the stage, with the other ninety of us in the audience.

She pauses and looks around the room, smiling. "What a wonderful five days it's been—sisterhood at its finest. We've made new friends, we've laughed, we've cried, we've healed, we've shared our experiences. But more than that, we've started down the path of changing the world for our daughters and granddaughters so they may never know a world where they are considered less than. Today, as we wrap-up, I'm going to call on those of you who haven't yet said your piece, because it takes every voice to make a difference."

Oh, crap. That's me, isn't it? Yup, she just gave me a wink. Bollocks.

"But, first, we'll start with each of our breakout group leaders who will give us an overview of the most poignant ideas that surfaced as we peeled back the layers of the inequality onion."

Phew! Thank God. I've got a few extra minutes to think. I'm sure something will come to me while I listen to everyone else's ideas. Something I can tweak or change that could be of use.

The first group leader gets up and takes the podium. *Okay, concentrate, Arabella.*

"I want to start by saying what an honour it's been to…"

Blah blah blah. Get on with it.

My mobile buzzes and I sneak it out of my pocket. Aww, a text from Will. *Can't wait to see you tonight. I have all sorts of plans for us. Are you still landing at six?*

Me: *Yup. This finishes at two. I miss you so much, I'll literally sprint out of here.*

I grin to myself, then glance up, only to make eye contact with Dr. Highbrow, who gives me the raised no brow. At least I think that's what she's doing. It's so hard to tell from back here.

Straightening up, I set my expression to 'very much paying attention' and turn my eyes to the stage.

"…in conjunction with, not in opposition to, our male counterparts around the globe. The concept is to help men see what's in it for them when we do well…"

I wonder what Will's got planned. Whatever it is, I'll love it. Gosh, how is it only eleven o'clock? Six p.m. is so far away. Focus, Arabella!

I should really take notes. I dig around in my briefcase and take out a pad of paper and a pen, disturbing the woman next to me. She purses her lips at me, and I whisper, "Sorry," to her.

Okay, think. Think. What's the best way to permanently solve inequality?

———

All right, so I managed to make it through the first half of the session without being called on. (Thank goodness, because inequality is a tough nut to crack.) I sat alone at the luncheon to give myself time to ponder. By dessert, all I'd come up with is, "Believe we can." It's shit, I know.

Now we're back in the auditorium, trying to hash out a slogan we can use going forward. We're running thirty minutes behind schedule, which means I'm going to have to duck out before it finishes so I can make my flight.

Oh, great, Dr. Sandra Snooty Pants is taking the stage. Of course she is, since she knows so much more than anyone else. *I'd* rather be up there than have to listen to her. Okay, so that's a lie, but you get me on account of the fact that I've established how much I hate her.

"My fellow women…"

Her *fellow* women? Ironically sexist, no?

She goes on for nearly the entire twenty minutes I have left, which, quite honestly, is a huge relief. I can sneak out without having humiliated myself. I haven't actually done anything of service either, but when those are your only two options, I'll take the first one.

I gather my things, then stand, apologizing to each woman in my row while I sneak past them. I get to the aisle and am turning away from the stage and toward the exit, when Dr. No Brows says, "Oh, Princess Arabella. Sneaking out early?"

My entire body heats up with embarrassment and I turn to her. "I'm afraid I'm going to miss my flight."

"That's okay," she says, with a nasty grin. "I'm guessing you didn't have much to add to the conversation anyway."

I stiffen up and stare at her. "Actually, I do."

No, I bloody well don't. Why the fuck did I say that?

"Really?" she asks. "Why don't you come up and share with us?"

"Fine. I have a couple of minutes," I say, walking slowly down the steps to the stage. My legs feel like two cooked spaghetti noodles, and for once, I'm glad I'm in boring one-inch heels. When I reach the front, she hands the mic down to me and I turn to the crowd and clear my throat.

"Good luck," she whispers, but we all know she doesn't mean it.

I stare around at the women in the room, feeling as out of place and on the spot as I ever have. Lunch feels heavy in my stomach and I'm cold and sweaty at the same time. "I um…my experience is not… I haven't been…over these last few days I've been wondering if a good slogan might be…" *Shit! Say something!* "Fuck it," I say into the mic.

A few gasps are heard from around the room, along with some giggles.

In for a penny, in for a pound...

Raising my voice, I say, "That's obviously not an official UN slogan, but it could work as our own secret slogan to propel us forward in our mission. The truth is, as women, we care *too much*—about what men think and about what each other think..." I glance at Dr. Highbrow, who looks scandalized. "We worry about making sure we fit whatever mould our families and society deem acceptable. We concern ourselves with the happiness of everyone else in our lives without giving thought to what would make *us* feel fulfilled."

I pause and look around, seeing some nods in my direction. Taking a deep breath, I decide to really go for it. "And...and, frankly, it's all so stupid. I mean, think about it, if more women throughout history had found the guts to say 'fuck it, I'm going to do what *I* want,' men would be far more responsible, and children, far less helpless."

Yes, I'm stealing from Gran, but I promise to include my own thoughts here as well. "If every woman in history hadn't taken a back-seat to every man, don't you think the world would be a slightly better place? With more equality, more justice, fewer wars, and fewer weapons? I say the answer is yes, which is why I also think *Fuck It* is the attitude required by the times. Obviously, we could massage the wording in public, but the sentiment must remain. Because when our entire existence revolves around the fear that we might offend someone or that we won't be liked by everyone we meet, or that we're not thin enough or pretty enough, it leaves very little room in our lives for doing anything of consequence. Trust me, I know this one by heart because all I've done in my life is obsess over what other people think of me. Well, that, and follow rules laid out for me hundreds of years ago by the men in charge. I've been a very good princess, always doing what I was told instead of what I wished to do.

"In fact, this entire conference, I've let the fear of being criticized by all of you—women who are far more accomplished than me—stop me from participating because I was afraid of making a fool of myself. No more, I say. Fuck it!" I shout, this time being met by scattered cheering.

"Yes, fuck it! I refuse to do what countless generations of women have done—stay in my designated safe zone, trying to never offend anyone. I need to hear my own voice and speak my own truth and stop listening to my father or my brother or any of the dozens of senior royal staff or the media with their opinions on every aspect of my life, or worrying about what Dr. No Brows – err, Highbrow – here has to say about me. Fuck it. I don't really care what you think." I look at her. "You've been most unwelcoming of me this entire time and I don't appreciate it. Your judgment of me is both harmful and hypocritical, so fuck off because I'm going to go out there and live a great, big, juicy life filled with adventure and fun and celebration and laughter. I'm going to do important things and help other women who decide to rise up to their true destinies as laid out by no one else but themselves."

I draw a deep breath, and smile as applause breaks out around the auditorium. I soak it in for a moment before realizing I'm going to miss my flight. "Thank you. Thank you. Now, I must run because I have a plane to catch and there's no way I'm missing it because I haven't seen my super hot boyfriend in weeks and I need to go get some."

A few people cheer and others seem slightly offended, so I hold up one finger in the air as though punctuating a great speech and raise my voice again. "But I'm not rushing home because *he's* expecting sex and I want to please him. I'm rushing home because sex is exactly what *I* want to do today!"

With that, I drop the mic and stride up the steps of the auditorium to the back doors where Bellford is waiting. Women in the aisle seats high-five me as I go, and I shout, "Yes, ladies! Fuck it!"

I stop so one of them can get a photo with me. "I refuse to let anyone plan even an hour of my life again! From now on, it's my way or the highway!"

I run up the last few steps, push the door open, and rush out with Bellford next to me. Once we're alone, I say, "Oh my God, I can't believe I did that! What did you think? Too much cursing?"

He tilts his head and opens his mouth, but I cut him off. "You know what? Don't answer that. Turns out I don't actually care. No offence."

"None, taken, Your Highness."

"Oh good, because I'd hate to offend you. You really are so dear to me."

"Of course, Miss," he says as we hurry down the long hall. "But, may I say what a pleasure it was to see you break out of your shell like that?"

"You approve, then? No, doesn't matter. Anyway, that felt amazing! Honestly, I knew I had some grit to me when I was in Zamunda. I mean, I really was quite fierce by the end, but it's easy to be fierce in a life that's not your own and entirely another thing to be fierce in a setting like this. This is high stakes, Bellford," I ramble on as we near the front doors. "This is me bidding farewell to the timid, people-pleasing princess I used to be once and for all. I just dare anyone to try to tell me what to do from now on. They're really going to have it coming."

24

The Best Laid Plans (For Getting Laid...)

Will

OKAY, so things haven't exactly gone the way I hoped, but that doesn't mean tonight's not going to be incredible. As it turns out, one cannot simply pick up a princess and take her on an overnight date in his rented Mercedes. At least not without said car being given a one-hundred-point inspection by a royal mechanic, which, due to the hour, would've meant Arabella and me waiting until the head mechanic could finish his dinner, then drive back to the palace. Rather than delay things, I opted for the alternative, which was to borrow one of her family's many vehicles. Apparently, the only one they were willing to part with for the night is a very boring sedan, even though there are three Porsches, one classic Mercedes Gullwing, and a Lamborghini sitting in the massive garage. Not that I'm complaining about driving a Rolls Royce, mind you. But they're not exactly sexy, are they? Also, borrowing a car from your girlfriend's father so you can take her out is beyond demeaning for a man in his thirties. I could almost imagine my voice cracking as I say, "Don't worry, Sir, I'll have your daughter home before curfew."

The other thing that happens when you take a princess out is that you must bring along chaperones. In our case, this includes her head bodyguard, Bellford, and her regular armed driver, Norm, who are following in a Mercedes. Behind them, another car bearing the two nightshift guards, who will be periodically checking the property and outside of the house throughout the night, but will otherwise remain in their vehicle overnight, which is just plain weird, not to mention unnecessary, if you ask me. I'm pretty sure I can keep her safe in a house, for God's sake. We'll be inside having the most romantic night of our lives while two men wait outside. The entire thing has me slightly nervous and I keep checking the speedometer to make sure I'm not going even one click over the speed limit.

All of this seems very natural to Arabella, who has her head leaned against the seat with a contented expression on her face as she rests her delicate fingers on my thigh. But for me, it's awkward AF.

I'm going to have to figure out a way to forget they're out there so I can give Arabella one-hundred percent of my attention, if you get my meaning. But honestly, just knowing they're going to be out there the entire time (and that they'll know what we're doing) gives me a squishy feeling, like one gets when you watch a video compilation of guys getting bagged.

Okay, none of that, Will. Buck up. After tonight, we'll be on our way to freedom from her family, and our perfect new life can begin.

Smiling over at her, I pick up her hand and give her a kiss on the knuckles. "It's so nice to be able to do that."

"Agreed. These last couple of weeks have been absolute torture," she says. "Especially with that awful fight and not being able to make up with you properly. Let's hurry up and get wherever we're going so I can show you exactly how sorry I am."

It's been so long that my entire body reacts to the thought of her showing me anything. "You have no idea how badly I want to speed right now."

"Then do."

"No way. Not with the men in black following us," I say, glancing in my mirror again. "They'll definitely rat me out to your father if I'm endangering your life."

"They will not," Arabella says. "Bellford's a good egg."

"Oh yeah?" I say, glancing at her. "Then why did he tell me if I do anything to risk your life, he'll make sure your father finds out?"

She purses her lips together and makes a groaning sound. "Did he really? Well, I'll have a little talk with him when we get back home."

"Look at you being all tough."

"I rediscovered my inner Furiosa when I was in Vienna and came back bound and determined not to let *anyone* tell me what to do ever again."

"I'm impressed, Your Highness." I say, squeezing her hand a little. I'm also thrilled, because if she's in her 'I'm a force to be reckoned with' state of mind, she's far more likely to agree to a) marrying me, and b) *The World's Best Survivor Challenge*. I haven't mentioned it yet because it seems like the kind of thing that requires exactly the right moment. Not that I don't think she'll want to come, because I'm sure she will. Although she may be a little irked to find out Dylan will be the showrunner on that one. Also, I'm not exactly sure if she'll be excited to spend a month in Greenland in November. But, we'll cross that bridge when we come to it.

Oh, I picked out the perfect ring, by the way. The moment I saw it, I just knew it was the one for her—it's got a round brilliant-cut diamond with several smaller diamonds set in an engraved platinum band that is meant to invoke the beauty and flow of the Avonian Wild Fern. Currently, it is safely zipped into my shaving kit, waiting for the perfect opportunity to surprise her. I spot the sign for Half Moon Bay, and slow down to make a left turn, signalling far earlier than I normally would.

"I cannot *wait* to get you to the beach house and get you naked," Arabella says.

"Get *me* naked? I'm going to be the one getting *you* naked."

"I don't think so, sir. I've had five lonely nights in my hotel room in Austria to come up with all kinds of things I want to do to you."

"Really?" I asked, smiling down at her. "In that case, we might have to see if we can stay an extra couple of days."

We reach the small village and wind our way through the tree-lined main street, and past all the quaint seaside homes. I try to relax and forget about the cars tailing us, but that seems about as likely as... well, something that's not very likely.

"This is lovely," Arabella says. "I've actually never been out this way if you can believe it. My friends used to come to Half Moon Bay to party when I was in uni, but I was never allowed to go."

"Well, we'll have to be especially wild then to make up for it."

She grins at me, then turns to look out the window as we leave the village and continue on down toward the cove. The farther we are from town, the larger and more spread out the cabins and homes become. By the time we make our left turn onto Seaview Lane, I find myself feeling almost giddy with excitement. This is going to be one of the greatest nights of both of our lives.

"Do you think he might keep his Academy Award here?" she asks as we pull into the driveway of a large two-storey beach house with a wall of tall windows and a steep roof that peaks at the centre of the structure.

"I'd imagine he keeps it in his flat in London or some such," I say. "But if it is here, we should take turns giving acceptance speeches."

"Oh, yes! That sounds delightful. And we'll finish them with 'Kids, get to bed. It's way past your bedtime,'" she says, pretending she's holding an Oscar.

I laugh as I park the car, then take the keys out of the ignition just as Norm and Bellford pull up beside us. Oh, good. They found the place.

Pocketing the keys, I say, "Let's go."

Arabella shakes her head. "They'll need a few minutes to check the house and secure the grounds," she says, apologetically. "But as soon as that happens, we can pretend we're completely alone."

I smile and nod to hide my slight irritation. "I'll give them the keys."

———

"I can't believe we didn't even make it up the stairs," I say, panting slightly. "You weren't lying about getting my clothes off fast."

She trails a finger down my bare chest and gives me a satisfied grin, looking thoroughly relaxed, even though we're on the tile floor in the foyer of the house. "I can't tell you how badly I needed that," she says as we both stand and start picking up our clothes.

She tugs her wool dress over her head and pulls it down. "That sounded terrible, as though I meant it in the 'I'm using you for sex' sort of way, but in reality, I meant it in the 'I really needed to feel close to you,' sort of way."

I pull my jeans up, then lean down and give her a lingering kiss. "Don't worry. I always know what you're thinking."

"Really?" she asks, giving me a quick peck on the lips. "What am I thinking at this very moment?"

"That you would kill for some river fish and yam tubers," I say with a grin.

She laughs. "How did you know?"

I slip my arms around her waist and pull her to me. Ah, having her pressed up against me again is the sweetest of relief. It's enough to make me completely forget that I gave up a lucrative outdoor gear line. Kenneth who, right?

I am finally happy again. I lower my head down and we snog some more.

When she pulls back, she gives me a skeptical look. "That's not what you're making for dinner, though, is it?"

"No," I chuckle. "I think we've both had enough of yam tubers for quite some time. What I'll be preparing is a surprise, and it'll be a nice one, I promise. Hopefully enough to make up for taking off to London, then Italy, then Thailand."

"Don't forget, back to Avonia instead of Austria," she says with a wink.

I feel my jaw tighten a bit with irritation, but then remind myself it's not her fault that she's holding a bit of a grudge about that one. After all, she has no idea what I saved her and her family from.

———

An hour later, we're sitting at a table outside on the large deck attached to the house, under the heat of a patio lamp. Gentle waves lap against the shore, and the stars are out in full force as we finish our dinner of grilled lobster, roasted vegetables, and garlic smashed potatoes (all recipes I got from Emma). I'm a little on edge, expecting one of her bodyguards to come walking around the corner at any moment, but so far, they've kept their distance.

Arabella and I have finally managed to properly catch up. We sipped wine while I cooked, and I gave her the highlights and lowlights of my globe-trotting with Kenneth. Arabella told me all about the conference and we had a few laughs about the horrible Dr. No Brows. Dinner has been a fun combination of flirting, saying annoyingly mushy things to each other, and her telling me what an amazing chef I am. So far, Operation Propose to the Princess is a go.

Arabella sighs happily. "What a perfect evening, out here under the stars, alone. This is exactly what we needed."

"I want to give you a lifetime of perfect evenings, just like this one," I say, my heart beating faster. *Dammit, I should've put the ring in my pocket because this is the exact right moment. Maybe I should run in the house, then come back and just ask her?* The thought makes my heart skip a couple of beats. That's it. I'm doing it. "I'm going to go get dessert. I'll be right back."

"Oh, let me help," she says, starting to get up.

"No, you relax right here and enjoy the stars. I want to surprise you."

"All right. But bring more wine."

"How about champagne? I think we need to celebrate your success."

25

How to Ruin the Perfect Date...

Arabella

I LEAN BACK in the wicker chair, feeling the warmth of the propane lamp on my cheeks. I turn to look through the window, and see him rushing around the kitchen, with a giant grin on his face. *A lifetime of evenings like this.* There is nothing I want more. Our big fight when he was in Thailand seems like ages ago, even though technically, it's only been a week.

Huh, I guess we should probably talk about what happened. I was so relieved to see him and still so high from what happened in Vienna that I completely skipped the bit where we figure out how to avoid this type of fight in the future. And now that I think about it, a lot has gone wrong in a very short period of time, and he still hasn't explained why he came back to Avonia instead of meeting me in Vienna.

My mind wanders to the auditorium this afternoon, and my words about hearing your own voice make me realize we've had a rather fraudulent date so far, including the sex. We've put the cart before the horse, and as much as I hate to, I need to right things if I want to be the woman I told all those other women I am. My gut tightens a little at the thought of speaking up. The last thing I want to do is ruin this wonderful evening Will's put together.

But surely I can find a way to calmly speak my mind, and keep things light and airy, so we come out the other side stronger. Yes, of course I can.

The door opens and Will comes outside carrying a tray with a bottle of champagne, two flutes, and two plates of cheesecake. He grins at me as he crosses the deck. "Your favourite—New York-style topped with blueberries."

"You remembered," I say, watching as he sets the tray on the table and sits kitty-corner to me again. "You've really pulled out all the stops to make tonight incredible, and I want you to know it means the world to me."

"Of course I would," he says, reaching for my cheek. He rests his fingers gently on my skin while he talks. "The last few weeks have been awful for you and I wanted to make up for not being here. You're the most important person in my life, Belle, and I am always going to put you first."

"I feel exactly the same way, Will," I say, taking both of his hands in mine. "Let's never fight again."

"Agreed."

"That was absolutely the worst feeling I've ever had," I say, lifting his hand and kissing his palm. "Being so far away and needing so desperately to fix things. Which is why I think it might be wise to set up some ground rules for our relationship. You know, so we can avoid anything like that again."

He pauses for a moment and glances at the champagne bottle, then back at me. "Okay, ground rules. What do you have in mind?"

"Nothing crazy," I say with a reassuring smile. "But I was thinking we should do something Faith Hill and Tim McGraw do. Oh, are you familiar with them?"

"Vaguely."

"They're both famous country singers from the US, and they've managed to stay married for decades in spite of their fame. They say their secret is that they never spend more than three nights apart. Now, I'm not saying that we would have to follow the *exact* same rule as them—I know sometimes your work will take you away for several days at a time and mine will too. It's just an example, more than anything."

"So, not three nights then?" he asks. "What are you thinking, maybe eight?"

"Sorry, no, I didn't mean for us to pick a set number of nights. I know that likely wouldn't be possible. But maybe we should come to some sort of agreement about *how we decide* which opportunities we take and which ones we turn down. I'd like to make those decisions together, especially if it involves one of us having to fly off somewhere."

"Okay, deal," he says, leaning in and giving me a kiss.

Mmm. Lovely. This is going well, isn't it? I'm so glad I brought it up. "Perfect. So, we won't say yes to any more trips without discussing it first."

"Exactly, from now on, we check with each other." He smiles while he places the cheesecake in front of each of us.

"Yum," I say, picking up my fork.

Will digs into his dessert, and as his first bite is on his way to his lips, he says, "Glad that's settled."

"Me too." I let out a sigh of relief. "We just have to get better at communicating with each other, is all."

He swallows, then nods. "Absolutely, it's probably more of a habit than anything, right? Neither of us are used to being accountable to someone else."

"Well, you less so than me, really. I'm accountable to an entire kingdom," I say with a light chuckle.

"Right. I guess it's something *I* need to work on then," Will says, his smile fading. "Although now that I think about it, I did try to get a hold of you several times before I agreed to go to London, but you didn't pick up so I had to make a decision."

"True, true," I answer, feeling a chilly breeze at my back. "But that's obviously not a normal situation—having someone call you at the last minute like that. So it won't be a problem in the future."

"Exactly," he says, then he narrows his eyes a bit. "But just to be clear, you do agree it was the right call for me to go, right? The commercial was a big step forward for us as far as being able to be financially independent."

I lift my first bite to my lips, then set it down again. "Sorry, darling, I'm a bit confused. How exactly?"

"Well, it was an incredible opportunity for me, and I'm now in a position where I need to earn a lot more money than I have in the past," he says, clearly trying to sound casual, even though I know I've touched a nerve. "These types of chances don't come along very often, believe me. In fact, I've been waiting for years for something like that, so when it happened, I had to take it."

He slices into his cake with the side of his fork, then scoops up some blueberry sauce.

"But sweetheart, we have money."

Will pauses, midbite. "To be fair, *we* don't have money. Your family has money and theirs comes with all sorts of rules and obligations and strings attached. Mine will mean freedom and independence and us living exactly the way we want to for the rest of our lives."

Oh dear. He definitely thinks I'm going full Megxit. I set my fork down, the buttery lobster suddenly sitting heavy in my stomach.

He gives me a hopeful smile. "I want to start a life with you, Belle. I want to give you everything you ever dreamed of—adventure and freedom and the ability to make your own decisions and spend your days doing whatever you want. It's why I went to London in the first place. And Italy, and then to Thailand. And to be honest, if I had gone back to London with Kenneth, I'd be well on my way to having my own outdoor gear line, which would have set us up for life. But I knew you needed me, so I rushed back."

"He offered you your own line of outdoor gear?" I ask, my heart pounding in my chest.

Shrugging, Will says, "Yeah, but I would have had to spend at least a month in England hashing out the details and there was no way I was going to do that to you, not with how bad things have been going since the show started."

"Oh, Will, I don't know what to say." I reach for his warm hand and squeeze it. "That must have been such a disappointment for you."

"It's okay. I always land on my feet," he says, lifting my hand and brushing his lips across my knuckles. "Besides, ABN has offered me a three-year contract which will mean steady money. It's not 'buy our own castle' cash, but we could probably afford something nice."

"Was the deal from Abernathy a 'buy our own castle' deal?" I ask, even though part of me doesn't want to know.

"Pretty much, but there wouldn't have been any point in having all that cash if I didn't have you to help me spend it?" He leans in and gives me a kiss, and I know, without a doubt, that this man loves me.

And I love him so much. "I can't believe you gave that up for me."

"You're worth it. I'd give up my life for you." He pulls me onto his lap, and we snog each other senseless for a few minutes, but as we're kissing, there's a tiny voice in my brain screaming that I'm kissing him under false pretenses. I'm letting him think he's going to be the one bringing home the bacon when in fact, I can more than afford to buy the entire pig farm.

The voice grows louder now, telling my lady bits to cool down because he may have turned down the deal to rush to my side, but that's not where he ended up, is it? Lady bits are begging brain to shut up, but brain refuses, and, in fact, starts shouting.

I pull back and stare at his impossibly handsome face. Fuck me but being a strong independent woman sucks dirty tennis balls sometimes. "I'm sorry, but I do need to ask you something. And I'm not trying to start a row and I don't want you to think I don't appreciate you giving up the Abernathy deal for me, because I do. I utterly, completely do. Incredibly romantic grand gesture really."

"But?" he asks, his hands sliding off my body and onto the arms of the chair.

Deciding it's far too awkward to have this talk whilst sitting on his lap, I get up and sit down in my own seat again. "It's just that you *didn't* come see me when you left Thailand. You came back to Valcourt to do promotional work for the show. And I'm having a bit of trouble understanding how *that* was for me." As soon as I say it, my hurt starts to bubble to the surface.

"Look," he says with a deep sigh. "I had a very good reason for coming back here, but I really don't want to get into the details, okay? Can't it just be enough that I went zipping all over the world to give us a better life, but then when you made it clear you needed me, I was willing to turn down the biggest opportunity of my life? And I *fully intended* to meet you in Austria, but something really bad happened and I needed to come back and deal with it immediately."

I stare at him for a moment, trying to process what he's saying. I nod my head a little, then shake it. "Yes, the thing is, I really *do* need you to tell me what was so bloody important, because judging a baking contest and going to a football match doesn't fit my definition of urgent."

"That's not why I came back. Something *else* happened." Will rakes one hand through his dark hair, frustration written all over his face. "To be honest, I think it's better for you *not* to know about it because it'll only upset you," he says, quickly adding, "Now, I know that's not going to make you happy to hear because you're an independent woman, but please trust me on this one, okay? Some shit went down, and I dealt with it so you wouldn't have to."

I fold my arms and harden my gaze, shivering a bit from the cold and the emotion of it all. "What shit, Will?"

He pauses and looks out in the direction of the water for a moment before answering. "It's not going to make you feel better."

"Tell me anyway," I say in a calm tone that surprises me.

Will looks into my eyes. "They have audio of our entire time in the jungle."

Every cell in my body freezes while my mind races to comprehend the severity of what he's just said. "Everything?" I ask in a whisper.

"Yes, but they're not using it. They wanted to include some kissing and rustling sounds, but I forced them to cut it."

I search his face, seeing there's more he doesn't want to tell me. "I don't understand. How did you find this out?"

"After you...*called* to tell me about the audio of us on our first night, I kept racking my brain, trying to figure out how I could've accidentally recorded that. I was so sure I had taken the batteries out of the GoPros. Then, when I was at the airport in Thailand— about to get on a plane to Vienna—I wandered into a store and saw one of those Bearz backpacks. When I picked one up, it hit me. The backpacks aren't heavy at all. They're actually surprisingly light. I realized that Dylan had the crew sew recording equipment into them."

My limbs go numb as reality sinks in. "That skanky ho," I say, suddenly furious. "Does she have no soul at all?"

"Apparently not," he says. "And don't worry, I made sure she knows it. I told her what she did was conniving and evil."

My mind is spinning so fast, I wish I had skipped that last glass of wine. Memories of our time in the jungle come back in large chunks, each one feeling like a brick falling on my head. "But...everything we *said* to each other out there." I gasp loudly and clutch my hand to my upper chest. "They all listened to us having sex! The whole production team?!" I feel dizzy with rage and humiliation. "Over and over again. Do you even realize how much sex we had out there? And they..." I stop myself, feeling my eyes fill with tears of embarrassment. "So much sex."

A light coughing sound comes from the other side of the yard. Will and I both turn to see Bellford walking along with a flashlight. Oh terrific. Now he's heard about the sex.

Will purses his lips and gives him a look of utter resentment. "Perfect timing. So nice to be surrounded by staff at a time like this."

I stare at him for a moment, my rage turning toward him. As if I really need to hear him complain about my security team right now. "He's just doing his job," I snap.

"A completely unnecessary one if you ask me."

"Oh really? You don't think it's necessary for me to have protection?"

"Not when you're with me."

I roll my eyes. "Do you have any idea how many death threats are made against my family each year? Or how many lunatics out there would kidnap me to get at my father?"

"Well, no one is going to get near you with me around."

Okay, my mind is literally about to explode. "Are you serious right now?" I scoff. "My need for a security team is no reflection on your manhood, Will, so just get over yourself already."

"Could you please calm down?" Will says, glancing at Bellford, who is now walking along the shoreline. "He can probably hear you."

"Calm down?" I whisper yell. "Calm down? Sure, of course, sweetheart," I say, giving him a phoney smile and blinking quickly. "I just found out that several people at a major television network have spent *hours* listening to us do it, and that you kept it all a secret from me when I had every right to know. And now you've decided I don't require a security team even though you don't know the first thing about being a royal, but yes, of course I'll calm down because I certainly wouldn't want to be some hysterical female who's prone to overreacting."

"Sorry if I don't like constantly being surrounded by your staff, but in case you didn't know, regular people don't live like this. They have something really nice called *privacy*."

Wow. Just wow. "Sarcasm is hardly going to help things."

'Think back about twenty seconds. I'm pretty sure you're the one who got sarcastic first."

Shit. He's right. "Well, you don't have to stoop to my level!"

"Look," he says, glancing at Bellford. "This may be normal for you but I sure as hell don't want to have *them* around all the time."

"Well, unfortunately, *they're* part of the package, so deal with it," I snap. "And you know what? If they had been in the jungle with us, they certainly would have found the bloody recording devices and we wouldn't be in this mess!"

"Oh, *really?*"

"*Really.*" I stand up and start clearing the dishes. "But I just had to run off, thinking I knew better, didn't I? Thinking I didn't need them when very clearly I did."

Will gets up and starts to help me load the dishes onto the tray, including my sad little uneaten piece of cheesecake. "They wouldn't have been able to stop this."

I freeze in place. "Of course they would have. What do you think they do? Just stand around with guns strapped to their hips waiting for danger?"

"Well, don't they?"

Letting out an irritated sigh, I say, "That's only in movies. In real life, your security team spends most of their time making sure every situation you're about to enter is secured, which includes sweeping rooms and…other things for recording equipment."

"No need to be condescending."

"Sorry!" I yell. "I'm just…furious that I put myself in that situation and now…Argh!" I can't even say it. My entire head and neck heat up with humiliation. "And I'm mortified, Will. Totally and utterly mortified."

Will blows out a long puff of air. "*This* is why I didn't want to tell you what was going on. I knew you'd get upset."

"Of course I'm upset! What I can't figure out is why *you're* not. We were totally violated by that…that…bitch." "She needs to pay for this. We can't just let her get away with it."

"I *am* angry," Will says. "I'm furious actually. But I also know when I'm beat. Dylan won. I had no choice but to play nice so I could make it all go away."

"You *did* have a choice, Will. You could've told me," I say, raising my voice again. I pick up the tray and clomp to the door, my fury picking up with each step. "Because if I had known, there would've been no playing nice and she would've gotten what's coming to her for once!"

"Believe me, I wasn't exactly easy on her," Will says, opening the door for me and moving aside to let me in. "She'll think twice before she tries something like that with us again."

I stop in my tracks, holding the heavy tray. "Wait. Did you already sign the deal?"

"Yes, I already told you that."

"No, you said they *offered* you a three-year deal. You didn't say you accepted."

"Well, that's what I meant," he says, shrugging. "Sorry if you misunderstood."

Setting the tray down on the counter much harder than necessary, I turn to him. "Tell me everything. What they had on us, what you agreed to, *everything*."

"I agreed to do an exclusive contract with ABN for three years, including whatever promotional stuff they need, and…I also had to sign us up for another series."

My jaw drops and my eyes fly open, but before I can say anything, Will holds up one hand. "Hang on. Don't get mad before you know what it is."

"How about if I decide when I get mad?" I say, shooting daggers at him with my pupils.

Will closes his eyes for a second, then starts to explain, sounding far too calm. "It's actually going to be pretty amazing. It's called *The World's Best Survivor Challenge.* You and I will compete as a team against the best of the best. The prize is a million dollars and, even better, it'll get you away from your family for a month and give us a chance to be back out in the wilderness together."

I cross my arms and let my nostrils flare. "And you said yes on my behalf without talking to me about it?"

"I had to if I was going to save you and your family from a shit ton of embarrassment."

The words 'save you' stick in my brain, bouncing around until I'm furious. "Do you actually believe I need to be saved?"

"In this particular situation, you did," he says. "And don't turn this into some patriarchal, 'he's trying to run my life' thing, because it wasn't like that. I, of all people, get how tough you really are, but because I had left you to deal with the fallout from the show, and because you were tied up at the conference, I decided to do what any good partner would do—which was to handle it on your behalf. If I had waited until you came back, it would've been too late."

"That's a decision we should have made together! You knew how to reach me. You should have told me what was going on so *I* could decide if I should leave the conference or not."

"Oh, for God's sake," he says, his voice rising. "I've been flying all over the world trying to make a better life for you, and trying to protect you from the enormous hurricane of shit that was about to come your way—and trust me, it would've been a game changer for your family—but instead of being grateful, you're actually pissed at me."

"I could have stopped them!"

Will raises his voice. "How exactly? Because turning on the water works wouldn't work on someone like Dylan."

"Water works? Wow. Nice, Will," I say, my voice shaking with anger. "I would have used my position and power to threaten the network. And it would have worked too. And I wouldn't have had to sell both our souls back to the devil."

"What are you talking about?" he asks, walking away from me and pacing. "I made an incredible deal for us. I spent over seven hours sitting in an editing booth, fighting with her over every tiny bit of audio. And in the end, I won. They're not going to air the part where you told me your mum committed suicide!"

I gasp and my entire body goes numb.

"Yeah, that's what the big secret was. Your mum's death. Do you have any idea how hard I had to fight for them to give that one up?"

"Oh my God," I whisper, feeling like I've been punched in the gut.

"It's the *first thing* I thought of when I realized what they had done," he says, his voice quiet now. "I was standing in that airport holding that stupid backpack, and I remembered the moment you told me the truth about your mum. And immediately, I could see a future of hurt and anger for you and your pain becoming something public for people to judge and poke fun at. So I literally ran to the ticket counter, spent thirty-six hours on planes, and went directly to the studio the second I landed, and I *made* them take it out. Me. And I managed to get them to sign an agreement so they'll never share it. And here you are, totally pissed at me for doing the right thing. I didn't sell either of our souls. I turned a crisis into an opportunity."

I cover my face with both hands and close my eyes, exhaustion overtaking me. "This is too much," I whisper.

"I know it is," he says, his tone becoming more gentle. "I've been living it for days so you wouldn't have to. But it's okay now. I fixed it and no one will ever have to know."

"I'm the one who betrayed my family. I should've been the one to fix it."

"In the end, does it really matter?"

"Yes, it does." I pick up his plate and dump the rest of his cheesecake into the garbage, then toss out mine, even though it looks so delicious. Soon, the two of us start doing the dishes, silently stewing while we work.

By the time the dishes are put away, we're both moving slower and more carefully, and the mood has shifted. I'm less angry but that feeling has been replaced by utter defeat. I turn from the sink and lean against the counter.

Will leans against the island opposite me with his head down. Rubbing his jaw, he says, "I needed to be the hero this time, not just for your sake, but for myself, too. Do you know what I loser I felt like after the pre-show? Having the world know you bought me a yacht and all I've given you is a stupid shell?"

"Do you think any of that matters to me?" I ask.

"But it matters to me. It matters to your dad who could barely be bothered to talk to me, or your brother, who went out of his way to make sure I know I'm not good enough for you." He lowers his tone and looks at me with an earnest expression. "I want to give you the life you deserve. I want to give you your freedom so it can just be the two of us again."

The words come out before I can stop them "I don't want my freedom."

His head snaps back. "What?"

"I know I said I wanted to get out, but I don't. Not anymore," I say. "The truth is, my life is much better now than it was when I met you. I'm finally calling my own shots and doing important work for once, and I can't give that up."

His face hardens. "Wow, and you're sitting here accusing me of keeping secrets when you've been holding onto a pretty big one."

"I haven't had a chance to tell you I changed my mind because you haven't been here," I say in the most accusatory tone I can muster.

"Excuse me for flying all over the world trying to make a life for us."

"Oh *please*," I scoff. "You've been flying all over the world doing exactly what you want to."

"What? Is it a crime to love my job?" he asks.

"No, but please don't pretend *everything* you've been doing is for me when a lot of it is actually for you."

"It's for *us*. So we can have the kind of life we want," he says. "Or at least the life I thought we wanted, but apparently you've changed your mind now."

Urgh. Why did I ever say I would go Megxit? Stupid, Arabella. Stupid. "It's not like I've planned out every detail of our lives or something. I just don't want to give up the work I'm doing. I have a lot of responsibilities. It's not so simple to walk away from it all."

Will sighs. "I'm not saying you have to, but the work you're doing —no matter how important it is, doesn't come with a salary. Mine does."

Of all the pigheaded, shit things to say. "Why does this have to be so bloody complicated? We don't ever need to worry about money. Shouldn't that be a good thing?"

"You can't seriously think I'm going to live off you for the rest of my life!" he says, raising his voice. "I can't do that. Not if I'm going to have an ounce of pride left."

"I'm asking you to give up the illusion that money will somehow make you worthy of me, when the truth is, you already are."

He shakes his head. "Money is only an illusion to people who've never had to worry about it. For the rest of us, it's really fucking real."

His words cause my stomach to turn to stone. "So, we have to be like everybody else? Worrying about other people's opinions about our relationship and wasting our time building our own fortune when we already have one just sitting waiting?" I take two steps toward him and put my hand on his arm. "Can't we be different?"

"No," he says. "We can't. I'd never be able to look at myself in the mirror if I was sponging off your family."

I slide my hand down to my side, and in that moment, I know the truth that I've been avoiding for weeks. And it's all suddenly and horribly obvious. This isn't going to work. "So I guess you've got your mind made up then. There's no room for negotiations on this one."

"I'm sorry, but I refuse to be a leech. If you can't understand that, I don't know where we go from here."

"I do."

"Yeah? Where?" he asks in a nasty tone.

"We have to end it."

"Are you serious?"

Tears of frustration fill my eyes. "I am. You're treating me exactly like my family does—like a child."

"Just because I want to earn my own money?" He lets out an angry laugh. "This is insane, you know that, right?"

"It's not just that," I say, feeling suddenly very sober. "First you tried to hide the truth about the recordings, then you signed me up to film another series without asking me, and now you're refusing to even consider building this life together on terms that are acceptable to both of us." My voice cracks but I continue on, forcing myself to pull it together. "You pretend you believe I'm so strong, but deep down, you see me as weak. As someone who needs to be shielded from bad things, someone who can't handle knowing what's really going on in my own life."

My heart pounds in my chest as I realize what I have to do. "This isn't going to work," I say finally, and I can literally feel my heart breaking when the words come out.

"Come on," he says. "This is just a fight, but it's nothing we can't solve."

I shake my head. "No, we can't. I love you, Will. I love you more than I've ever loved anyone, but we don't want the same things. I want someone who shares everything with me and respects me utterly and completely. You want someone who wants to let you make all her decisions and who wants to be sheltered from reality. I'm sure she's out there somewhere, but she certainly isn't me."

"Don't say that," he says, walking toward me and putting his hands on my upper arms. "We've been through worse things. We'll get through this."

"I'm afraid we won't. The truth is, when we were in the jungle, the only reason we got through that as a team was because you had a broken leg. Otherwise, you would've taken the lead the entire time, and you would've loved having me following you."

"What are you talking about?" he says, wrinkling up his nose. "That's not how it happened. You rescued me out there—you did what you had to do to save my life. And I just did what I had to do to save your family. That's what people do when they love each other."

"They also work as a team. They don't keep secrets. They trust each other to be capable enough to handle things so they can take on life together."

"We can do that," he says, rubbing my arms.

Tears slide down my cheeks but I leave them there. "I don't think we can. You're never going to see me as an equal partner, which means I'm not the right one for you."

"No, that is not true, I promise you," he says, crouching slightly so we're eye-to-eye. "Remember the conversation we had on the plane coming back from the Caribbean? We knew this was going to be hard. We knew we'd be tested to our limits with the media and your family and whatever tricks Dylan had up her sleeve. And we promised each other not to give in or let them ruin what we had."

"This has nothing to do with the show."

"Are you kidding?" he asks, straightening up. "It has *everything* to do with the show. Don't let them win. Come on, I'm never happier than when I'm with you and I know you feel the same way. We have some things to sort out, for sure. But we'll manage. We just have to survive the next few weeks, then we can get back to where we were."

He pulls me in for a hug, and I inhale the scent of his skin, my heart squeezing at the thought that I'll never be in these arms again. "What we have only works when we're alone in the jungle or on a yacht in the middle of the sea, which isn't how life is. Real life is filled with obligations and responsibilities and compromise...and...we're just too different, Will."

He pulls away, letting his hands drop and stares at me, his face filled with pain. "So that's it then?"

I nod. "I'm sorry. The thing is, I'm only just beginning to find my strength, Will, and if I'm with someone who puts me back in my safe little box, I'll never find out who I can really be. If I stay with you, I'll let the person I truly am die. And I can't do that, Will. I'll end up hating myself and you."

"I can't believe you're willing to throw away what we have because I did one thing you didn't like," he says, his voice filled with bitterness. "Jesus! It's not like I cheated on you or something. Everything I've done has been for you, Belle. *For you.* I gave up millions of dollars for you. I signed a shitty *three-year* deal that'll have me beholden *to Dylan* for you. And yet, you actually want to give up on us. Do you even hear yourself right now?"

I close my eyes, shutting out his words. "I'm sorry, Will, but the fact that you can't understand what you did wrong proves we don't belong together. You're never going to see me for who I am, which means you'll never love me the way I need to be loved."

"Fine, go then, because clearly nothing is ever going to be enough for you."

"I'm so sorry, Will. I hope you can understand."

"No, I really can't," he says, digging into his pocket and pulling out a small black velvet box. He slams it on the counter. "This is *not* how I thought tonight was going to go."

Shit. He was going to propose. Shock and pain vibrate through me. I stare at the box knowing that the life I thought I wanted is sitting right here within my grasp. But that life was a fantasy and the reality is not one I can live with. I force myself to turn away from him and walk to the front door before I can change my mind. I pick up my overnight bag and am about to walk outside when I hear his voice. "You're letting them win. You know that, right? Dylan, the media, my stupid wild girl fans, *your brother*. You're letting them all win."

I freeze with my hand on the doorknob, but I don't turn around because I don't think I can handle seeing his face right now. "No, I'm not. If I stayed with you, it would be on your terms. I'm letting myself win for once."

With that, I turn the knob and walk out into the cool night air, the screen door slamming behind me.

I sob once, then hold my head high and walk over to Norm and Bellford, who are standing next to the car smoking. They quickly put out their cigarettes, and Norm rushes to open the back door, while Bellford takes my bag and puts it in the boot. Neither of them says a word, for which I'm grateful. I get in and settle myself in the backseat, waiting until the doors are closed and the lights go off before I let the tears pour out.

26

I'm Totally Fine, Thanks for Asking...

Will

"ARE you sure this is a good idea?" Dwight asks, staring down at me with his arms folded.

I'm sitting on his couch and I just turned on the telly to watch episode three of *Princess in the Wild*, which is going to start in about three and a half minutes, give or take. "Of course, it's not a good idea," I say. "But when has that ever stopped me from doing anything?"

"Why don't I watch it for you to make sure that Dylan kept her word. You could... I don't know, maybe go for a nice, long run, perhaps to a certain palace where you could attempt to make up with the love of your life?"

"Nope. I'm really the only one who knows what we agreed to. Besides, it's not gonna bother me *at all* to watch this—I wasn't really all that attached to her."

"Yes, sure, sure," he says, sounding anything but convinced. "It's just that I can't help but remember all those things you said about her being like the warmth of the sun on a cool winter's day and all that. Remember? When you were spending a massive wad of cash on an engagement ring for her? Like about thirty hours ago? And now... you're saying you were never that attached. You can see why I'd be confused."

"When I make up my mind, it's done," I say, getting up and walking over to the kitchen. "You know what I need? A boozy smoothie. One of the guests at the resort ordered it from me years ago, when I was working at the beach bar. It's brilliant really. Ice cream and straight bourbon. Can I make you one?"

"Thank you, no."

"Are you sure?" I ask, smiling at him. "You won't know what you're missing out on if you never try."

Holding up one hand, Dwight says, "I'm still rather full from dinner."

"More for me." I open the vanilla ice cream carton and free pour bourbon directly in until it's nearly full. I grab a spoon from the drawer, then make my way back to the couch, seeing Dwight visibly stiffen.

"Remember rule number eight?" he asks. "No eating in the... oh, I see you're just going to do it anyway."

"Don't worry. I have very steady hands," I say, stirring the concoction. "Well, at least until I finish this. I'll be shitfaced by then."

When the theme song starts up, it feels like my heart is being literally ripped out of my chest by that bad guy in that Indiana Jones movie. You know the one, where that guy rips that other guy's heart out of his chest while he was still alive. Yeah, seeing her face feels about that good.

And...there she is in a gown getting out of a limo. The woman I was about to propose to a mere twenty-four hours ago, looking too beautiful to be real. I continue watching while I stir my snack. Finally, the theme song ends and a commercial starts up, temporarily relieving me from my misery. "See the trick is, you stir in the booze until you can drink it. It's a very efficient way to get drunk compared to spoonfuls." Looking around, I see that Dwight's not here. I shrug, then take a swig of the carton.

He returns with his arms full of blankets. "Get up."

"It's fine, I'm not going to spill."

"Up."

I do as he says and watch in wonder while he puts a sheet down on the couch, then an old blanket over top. He smooths them out until he looks satisfied. Finally, he nods. "Okay, you can sit down. But this is a *one-time* thing," he says in a warning tone.

My phone lights up and starts buzzing on the coffee table for the eightieth time today. It's a FaceTime call from Harrison, who I'm sure has gathered the rest of the family to find out how my big proposal went. I ignore it and have another few more gulps of my boozy smoothie. With any luck, I'll be completely drunk by the time the second set of commercials roll.

"I don't think they're going to stop calling. Do you want me to answer and let them know what happened?" he asks.

"Sure, I don't really care." That's not true. I absolutely care. I've been avoiding the call because somehow, telling my family makes the whole thing feel like it's actually happening. And if it's actually happening, I'm going to have to feel things I don't want to, like pain and anger and, well, a whole bunch of other sappy things that men like me don't experience.

Dwight swipes the screen. "Hello, family," he says, aiming for an upbeat tone.

"You?" I hear Rosy's voice. "Where's my Cuddle Bear?"

"Right here," he says.

Out of the corner of my eye, I can tell he's aiming the phone at me, but I won't look. Instead, I keep my eyes glued to the telly.

I hear Harrison's voice next. "Uh-oh. Is that a boozy smoothie? Straight from the carton?"

"I'm afraid so," Dwight says, sounding grave.

Emma says, "I take it things didn't go as planned last night."

"Quite the opposite, I'm afraid," Dwight says.

I decide it's time to interject. "It's not a big deal, I'm already over it, and I'm pretty sure I can return the ring because it's been less than a week."

Dwight lowers his voice. "Yes, he didn't want to do that today. He wasn't quite ready."

"I was just too busy," I say, sounding defensive even in my own ears.

"Cuddle Bear, what happened?" Rosy asks. "I can't believe that girl would have the nerve to say no to you."

"Oh, I didn't ask. It was over before I could get to that part," I say, wiping the sticky, cold liquid off my chin. "It's fine, really. It's better to find out now than five kids from now. Although come to think of it, we only would've had two. It's nobody's fault. We're just too different. You needn't say anything bad about her."

Dwight chimes in with, "Yes, I made that mistake earlier today. Not a good idea."

"Is there any chance she'll change her mind?" Harrison asks.

"Why does everyone assume she dumped me?" I ask, feeling very irritated.

"Well, it just seems rather obvious," Emma says. "After all, it was only yesterday that you were comparing her to the sun and the moon and all of that, so it would be rather odd if you had suddenly changed your mind."

"Also, the boozy smoothie is a bit of a tip-off," Harrison adds.

"I did not compare her to the sun or the moon. Well, maybe the sun," I say. *Stupid falling in love.* "But you needn't worry because I'm never going to make that mistake again."

"So, are you still going to compete in Greenland together or is that off too?" Emma asks.

"I don't know," I say, suddenly realizing we may have a bigger problem than I thought because if she doesn't compete with me, the agreement I made with the network is kind of null and void, isn't it? "It's all pretty new, so imagine it'll take a few days to sort everything out."

"No matter," Rosy says. "If you need a partner, I'm sure Emma here would be up for it."

"Oh," Emma says, "That would be fun! Harrison, could you give me a couple of weeks off to go help out our little brother?"

"Sure," Harrison says. "Anything, you need, Champ," he adds, like the good father figure he is.

"I don't think the network is going to let me choose," I say. "But

I'll float the idea and see if they like it. Anyway, the show is on so I should go."

"He means he needs us to shut up so he can continue torturing himself," Dwight says as quietly as he can.

"I heard that. If you'd like to continue talking about me behind my back, please feel free to take the call with my family in the other room."

I assume he'll ring off, but instead, he stands and starts walking down the hall. "So, Emma? Do you have an interest in a television career?"

27

The Stages of Surviving a Breakup...

Arabella

THE SHOW ENDS and I turn off my telly, then glance down at my white duvet, only to see it's covered in crisp crumbs and used tissues. I should not have watched that. That was the worst idea I've ever had, possibly even more so than the time I decided to sneak away with a handsome adventurer/nature documentarian. Well, obviously not *more* than that, because if I'd never done that, I wouldn't have this gaping wound where my heart used to be.

The last twenty-four hours, I've been like one of those perpetual motion machines that just keeps going back and forth, slightly faster each time. *I should call him and tell him I made a huge mistake. No, that would be the huge mistake. I did the right thing.*

What's done is done and I did it for the right reasons, so no matter what, I am not going to rush across town and beg him to take me back. And I'll tell you what else I'm not going to do: a) mope around for weeks like a love-sick duck whose mate got hit by a car (Have you seen that video? Tragic); b) go on and on to anyone who'll listen about how I thought I had the perfect love and now I've lost it; c) run to Will and beg him to take me back. Oh, I said that one already, didn't I?

Anyway, I'm not going to cry about it. Much worse things have happened in the history of love and much worse will happen in the future.

So, here's a quick list of what I *am* going to do: a) sleep well (no staring at the ceiling or moaning into the silent darkness of the night); b) exercise every day (except today because I needed time to recover, but starting first thing tomorrow, I'll be hitting the gym); c) eat well (again starting tomorrow, since this evening has been the world's most pathetic festival of carbs and salt); and d) get on with it, just like any strong woman would.

Yes, in a couple of days, I'll be on top of the world. In a couple of months, I'll barely remember Will's eye colour (brown like perfectly-brewed coffee), or the smell of him (sandalwood, leather, and fresh cocoa), or his smile, or the way he gets that dimple only on his right side when he finds something amusing. Anyway, obviously I know these things now, but very soon, poof! They'll disappear.

So, yes, I'm doing very well, thank you.

My phone buzzes and Will's face appears on the screen. Pain! I took that shot just off the coast of Rarotonga. His hair is all wet and sexy because he just climbed back on the yacht after going for a swim.

Oh God! What do I do? Do I answer? What if he wants to yell at me for breaking his heart? No, I'm not going to pick up. Not after all those crisps. I'll wind up begging him to get back together. I'll ignore it.

Stop ringing, phone! That's enough. Go away.

Oh, now it actually did stop ringing and his face disappeared. Good. But also bad, because he's gone again, never to return.

Hmm, except now, via text.

Arabella, pick up the phone. I'm not calling to fight with you or to beg you to get back together. I need to talk business.

The phone starts to buzz again, and I'm faced with two options: answer or decline.

I hit answer, my heart bubbling up to my throat. Trying to sound casual, I say, "Hello."

"I just…wanted to let you know they didn't include anything I told them not to," he says, slurring his words slightly. "In case you didn't watch. I was watching to make sure, but they didn't do it."

"Are you drunk?"

"Very—boozy smoothies."

"Sounds disgusting."

"It can be, but if you have enough of them, you won't care anymore," he says. "You want the recipe?"

"Uh, no thank you."

There's a long pause, then he says, "Listen, there's something else but I can't remember what it is…"

You love me? You realize how wrong you were and want to start over?

"Oh, now I remember. It's about the World's Surviving Best Greenland Challenge. I'm willing to pair up for that—strictly professional, that is. I'm pretty much over you already so we'd be fine by November fifteenth when fliming starts. Milfing. F-ilm-ing," he says slowly, annunciating each syllable.

"I don't think that's such a good idea, Will," I say, my heart breaking to hear him like this. "And even if it were, we're hosting the annual Order of Avonia gala that night."

"Righto," he says, putting on a posh accent. "You have an important gala, so you'll be all dressed up in a beautiful gown. You don't want to go to Greenland, not with the likes of me anyway."

"It's just best not to let ourselves get confused."

"Totally. Listen, remember that deal I made with the network so they won't share that awful secret about your mum?"

"Yes, obviously."

"Good, I thought you might. Anyway, do you want to tell them you're not coming to Greenlandia or should I? Prolly best if you do it since you have powerful lawyers and all that in case they say we're reneging on the deal."

"Sure, I'll handle it first thing tomorrow."

"Terrific. So, that's it then, I guess we don't have any reason to talk again."

"Well, we'll see each other at the finale after-show," I say, closing my eyes as I realize how shitty that's going to be.

"Unless you can get yourself out of it," he answers.

"I don't think I can."

"Are you sure? You're very powerful with your power and your money and your kingdom."

Anger flares up, and I'm about to say something when he continues. "No matter, we'll both be fine by then. Did I tell you I'm pretty much over you already?"

Christ. He's a total mess. "You did."

"Excellent, I wrote that one down on a little piece of paper so I wouldn't forget. I can check that off now."

"I'm glad."

There's another long pause in which I hear his breathing fall into a steady rhythm, almost like it does just before he falls asleep. I sit motionless and listen to it, wishing I could undo what's been done. Suddenly, he speaks up. "So, if there's nothing else then, I should go. I have to be up early. I wrote that down too in case I started getting all sappy or something."

"Smart thinking," I say. "I don't think there's anything else."

"Okay then," he says, "Thanks for calling."

I'm about to tell him he called me, but then I realize there's really no point. "You're welcome. Good night."

"Night, my sweet Belle."

Okay, that was awful. Breathe, Arabella, breathe.

That was the worst of it. From here on out, onward and upward. No whining or complaining. Just chin up, get on with it. Be stoic. Suffer in silence. Leave my feelings at the door when I go out each morning.

————

"Kira Taylor here."

"Kira, it's Arabella," I say, glad I was able to take the VP of Unscripted Television at ABN by surprise. If she'd known I was calling, she'd be ghosting me big time. "We need to talk."

"Listen, I didn't know about that whole audio thing until *after* the show was edited, and by then, it was really too late to do anything about it, given the tight timeline," she says quickly. "And in the end, it all worked out for the best since we've come to an arrangement that allowed us to remove the um…more sensitive things."

"You still tried to screw me over in a most hideous way," I say, looking at the mirror on the wall of my office and giving myself a stern glare.

"Yes, well, that's show biz, right? It's an all-out battle for ratings. When someone hands us a bombshell like that, it's basically irresponsible not to use it, since our mandate is to protect the interests of the shareholders and all that…" Her voice trails off, and I know I've got her right where I want her—feeling guilty.

I remain silent and let her squirm on the line a bit. She finally speaks up again. "And none of that matters to you, does it?"

"Not even a bit."

"So, are you calling so I can apologize because I really am very sorry about what almost happened, and I assure you, no one will ever breathe a word. The only people who know are Victor Petty—you remember Victor, yes? My co-vice in Unscripted?"

"Yes."

"And Dylan Sinclair, of course, who, although a total genius, I have to say, scares me a little."

"What about the editing staff and promotions?"

"Them too, but they won't say a word or they'll be fired immediately," she says. "Didn't Will go over all this with you? You sound out of the loop."

"Yes, he did, but I wanted it straight from the horse's mouth." That was a subtle shot because Kira once told me she hates her front teeth on account of them being rather large. See? I can be nasty when necessary. "You need to know I'll sue if any of that gets out. And I'll win. And even if we lose, we have a *deep* reserve fund for legal proceedings so by the time we're done with ABN, the entire network won't exist."

"That's not going to happen."

"You know what else isn't going to happen?" I ask, my heart pounding wildly. "Me participating in that survivor challenge show."

"Right. Because you never want to work with us again?"

"Can you blame me?"

"No, I can't."

"I trust it won't be a problem if I drop out." God, I'm a badass. I mime smoking a cigarette in the mirror, then say, "No repercussions for myself or my family?"

"You have my word."

"Excellent."

"But, does this mean Will isn't going to be part of the show either?" she asks. "Because his participation really is integral to the deal we made."

"Will's still in."

"And you're okay with that?" she asks.

"Totally. I'd never get in the way of his career," I say, not wanting to admit we've broken up.

"That's very mature and reasonable of you."

Aww, that was sort of sweet, wasn't it? No! Stay strong. "That's me. Both mature and reasonable, but also deadly serious about protecting my family."

"Duly noted."

―――――

From: Princess Arabella

To: Arthur, Tessa, Father, Gran, Mrs. Chapman, Phillip Crawford

To Whom It May Concern,

   Just a quick note to let you know that Mr. Banks and I have decided to part ways. I'm doing fine with this decision and would appreciate it if no one would bring it up. It's for the best and I would prefer to swiftly move on.

   Best,

   Arabella

There, that ought to do it. I'll just send that email and I'll never have to talk about it again. Perfect.

Send.

My phone rings. Tessa's calling. I push the speaker-phone button and say, "I'm fine, I promise."

"Cut the crap," she says. "It's not possible to go from madly in love to utterly detached overnight."

"Maybe for some people, but when I make up my mind, it's set. Now is there anything else you wish to discuss? Because I'm really quite busy today. The conference set me back on my correspondence."

"Fine. If that's how you want to be, I'll leave you to it," Tessa says. "Just know that I'll be here when you're ready to fall apart."

"Won't happen."

"Good God, you are so much more like your brother than I ever thought."

"Am not."

"Are too, but I love you both anyway."

With that, she hangs up. I stare at my computer screen, knowing I'll likely have a parade of concerned family members and the P.R. gurus trying to see me all day, which is exactly why I sent the notice when I did—because I'll be in meetings from now until after five this evening. My hope is, by then, they'll have forgotten about this and moved on with their lives so I can avoid *that* conversation.

Ha! And here is my first appointment now. Oh, no it's not. It's Mrs. Chapman. I hope she doesn't want to talk about my silly break up. She strides across the room, holding a file folder.

"Oh, I hope you're not going to bring up the email I just sent because I really don't want to discuss it."

"I hadn't planned on it," she says.

"Good, because I've written all I plan to say on the matter," I say, taking the folder from her.

And then, for some strange reason, I find myself telling her the entire story from start to finish (save the bit about my mum). I go on and on, even though I know I should stop, but she's such a wise person that I'm hoping she'll have some nugget of wisdom that will save me from my grief. Also, she can't tell anyone on account of the NDA the staff had to sign.

Finally, I end by saying, "So, it was very clear that, although he's undoubtedly a good man, he's not the right man for me. I truly need someone who sees me as more of an equal partner than what Will's willing to do. Oh, that's funny, I just said Will's willing. Anyway…"

Mrs. Chapman blinks at me a few times, then says, "The Minister of Education is here to discuss your participation in National Learning Day."

Oh fuck. "Brilliant, please send him in."

Okay, that's it. Not another word about him.

———

"…It's been a week since we broke up. Well, if you want to get technical, it's actually been eight days, six hours, and twelve minutes, but who's counting? Ha ha. Certainly not me. And don't worry, I'm not devastated at all. In fact, I feel very strong. Very strong indeed, knowing that I made the very best choice possible for the new me. We women have to learn to hear our own voices. Yes, that's the secret to greatness. But just out of curiosity, do *you* think I made the right decision?"

Yvonne, my maid, stares at me, her arms full of clean towels.

Apparently, I'm not done just yet…

She gives me a thoughtful look. "I…well, honestly, Your Highness, if you don't mind me saying, it seems to me that, other than his unfortunate decision not to tell you what was going on, he did act as a very good partner in that he knew you were busy with something of vital importance, so he quickly changed his plans and took care of something on your behalf. Depending on how you look at it, he actually *was* viewing you as an equal because he was valuing what you were doing in Vienna. My boyfriend never would have stepped up like that, to be honest. He would've insisted that I come back and deal with it myself. But then, my job isn't as important as what you're doing for the United Nations, now is it?"

"No, it's absolutely vital, Yvonne. I probably don't tell you often enough, but I appreciate you greatly."

"Thanks, Miss. I should get going though. My shift ended half an hour ago."

"Right. Sorry to have kept you."

"That's all right," she says, walking to the closet to deposit the towels. "Good luck with your decision."

"Thanks."

Well, bugger. Now *I'm* confused.

28

All by Myself...Don't Wanna Be...

Arabella

How long does it take to feel human again after a breakup? I'm asking for a friend. Because, although I'm completely fine, she's a hot mess. She spends her nights lying awake, staring at the ceiling whilst second-guessing her decision to break up with him. Poor pathetic thing—I'm so glad I'm not her.

I mean, these haven't exactly been the happiest of days, and I do find it the teensiest bit difficult to concentrate on work, even though I've packed my schedule so tight, there's not even a second to think about you-know-who. It's a good thing really, because it's allowed me to keep it together during the day, head held high, as I race from thing to thing with a bright smile.

But, honestly, as evening draws near, I find myself filled with an ever-increasing sense of dread, knowing I'll be going back to my empty apartment where I'll face another evening very much alone listening to Celine Dion. You may be saying to yourself, "why doesn't she spend time with her Gran or her father or Arthur, Tessa, and the kids?"

Simple really. I need to avoid my family since there is *no way* I'm going to fall apart in front of any of them, in spite of what Tessa said last week. I've set out to prove that a girl doesn't have to dissolve into a blubbering mess every time she parts ways with a man. And with the exception of blabbing to Mrs. Chapman and Yvonne and, well, a few other staffers about the whole thing, I'm winning.

If you call winning avoiding the people who love you most, which in this case, I do. Mostly.

So, as you can tell, I'm doing really well, all told.

Except for the empty nights alone. And the fact that now I not only have lingering feelings of missing Will, I also miss my family. And there are moments—fleeting as they may be—that I wish I could go back and change everything. Like right now. I've just finished eating a very dull meal of broiled chicken, Waldorf salad, and grilled asparagus while I scrolled through my Pinterest feed on my mobile.

Now, I'm left tapping my fingers on my table while I stare around. Maybe it's bedtime. Let's see…nope. It's only twenty to eight. A bit early for that. Last night I went to bed at seven and it was awful because that meant listening to the clock tick for over four hours before sleep finally came.

You know what? Tonight I'm going to trust myself and go see Tessa and Arthur. It's Thursday evening and I need something to distract me from turning on the telly. Because if I don't, I'm definitely going to polish off a bottle of wine while I watch *Princess in the Wild*, which would lead to uncontrollable sobbing and puffy eyes tomorrow. No thank you.

I walk to my bedroom and change out of my suit and into my cosiest pair of sweats, glancing out of the window to see the moon low in the sky. I feel a pang in my chest, thinking of all the nights we lay out on the deck of the yacht, laughing and talking and just generally being deliriously happy. *Oh, shut up, brain!*

Five minutes later, I find myself knocking on Arthur and Tessa's door. It swings open a moment later, and my brother stands before me in jeans and a T-shirt, clearly settled in for the evening. "Arabella! I was wondering how long you were going to continue pretending you're fine."

He steps aside to let me in, and there's something about the smirk on his face that causes me to stiffen up.

"I am fine," I say. "I've just been very busy."

"Very busy telling everyone and their uncles' dogs about your breakup?"

My face turns red and I walk directly to the bar to pour myself a gin and tonic. "I've done no such thing," I lie. "Why? What have you heard?"

"I hear everything," he says, following me into the living room, picking up scattered toys and loading up his arms. "Apparently, you've been polling the staff for their opinion on whether you should've dumped his arse or not."

"Not polling," I say. "More like, seeking out new perspectives."

"Sure you were," Arthur snorts as he drops the toys into a large wooden box, then he starts collecting some board books and stuffed animals. I watch him in this very simple domestic act, then glance around, realizing that this is what a happy home looks like—two people who love each other in spite of their differences and work together to give each other and their children the best life possible. My nose tickles with emotion, and I draw a deep breath to stuff those pesky feelings back down where they belong.

"But seriously, Arabella," Arthur says, "How are you? For real?"

"Great. Honestly. I was a *little* upset at first, but overall, I'm very happy with my decision." I take a quick swig of gin to help swallow my lie. "Yes, quite pleased indeed. We were utterly wrong for each other. As much as I hate to admit you were right about something, you may have been right about us."

"Excellent," he says, picking up a large blue stuffed bear and holding it on his hip like he does one of his kids. He crosses the room with it and sets it on a toddler-sized rocking chair, then pats it on the head. "In that case, you probably won't mind if we watch your show."

"Is that tonight?" I ask. "I completely forgot about it."

"Wow, impressive," he says, walking over to the coffee table to pick up the remote. He stares at me while he turns on the television, clearly thinking we're in a game of emotional chicken and I'm about to lose. Well, not today, Arthur. Not today.

"Throw it on if you want to," I say with a shrug.

"I think I will," he says, pressing buttons on the remote until he gets to ABN.

"Where's Tessa? I was hoping she'd be here."

"She's down at the gym with Xavier doing a last-minute workout before our trip."

"Oh, I forgot that is this weekend."

"She certainly hasn't. The poor woman—getting absolutely lambasted by the media at every turn."

"Bastards," we both say at the same time.

Arthur grabs a beer from the bar fridge and sits down on the couch. I pick the same spot on the loveseat that I chose when we watched episode one here in this very room. The theme song starts up, and when we get to the bit where they show lots of clips of Will without his shirt on, I lean over and pick up a copy of Parenting magazine off the coffee table and start flipping through it casually. "What's happening with you these days?"

"Same old, same old. Running a kingdom, blah blah blah," Arthur says. Muting the commercial, he adds, "I got a strange call today from a man named Dwight Anderson."

I freeze in place, staring at an ad for diaper rash cream, then force my voice to sound bored. "Will's agent? Whatever did he want?"

"Oh, are you sure you even want to hear this? I mean, since you don't care and all…"

"Well, I have no personal interest in it, but if one of Will's people is bothering you, I'll put a stop to it."

"That's all right, I didn't mind, really. Interesting fellow with quite a sad tale of a devastated young man camped on his couch, drinking a disgusting-sounding concoction called 'boozy smoothies' every night until he passes out."

I swallow hard, then say, "Well, I'm sure it's only temporary. He'll move on soon."

"He told me what Will did to save our family."

"Don't sound too impressed," I say, glancing up at the television, only to see Will's perfect face and get shot in the heart like that dragon under the Virgin Mary's feet. *I'm the dragon, aren't I?* "He didn't do anything that won't help his own career immensely."

"Arabella, he did the right thing. He stepped up when you needed him to. And as much as I hate to admit it, he may have saved our family from irreparable harm—harm that *you* would've been responsible for, by the way."

"I didn't come here to be lectured."

"I know that. You came to pretend everything's fine and try to fool me into thinking you've never been happier."

I open my mouth to object, but Arthur holds up his hand. "Don't even bother. Unfortunately for you, you're far too much like me for your own good. It appears as though you suffer from the family affliction of an abundance of pride mixed with an inability to admit when you're wrong."

"I certainly do not. That is such a man thing to say—assuming you know my mind better than I do."

"It most certainly is not," Arthur says. "I'm merely returning the favour that you did for me when Tessa and I broke up and I was too pigheaded to apologize."

Dexter wanders over to me and sticks his snout in my lap, knocking the magazine out of my hands. I reward him for his pushy behavior with some scratches under his whiskery chin.

"It's not the same," I say. "When you two broke up, it was because Tessa didn't believe she could ever fit into our world and you weren't exactly making her feel welcome. *I* called it off with Will because the thing that made us so right for each other turned out to be a lie. I mistakenly thought he believed me to be strong and capable, but the truth is, he never did. Or, if he did at one point, he stopped believing it. Either way, the result's the same."

On the screen, the clip of some bonobos hiding from the rain in a tree plays, bringing me right back to that moment when he handed the camera over to me for the first time and told me to narrate. I remember how I froze up at first, and he told me to pretend I was talking to my gran, describing what I was seeing, and how that simple instruction freed me of my fear of messing it up.

"It's hard being a man in the new world," Arthur says, having a sip of beer.

"Oh boo-hoo," I say. "I feel so sorry for you."

"I'm serious. We have an innate need to protect the ones we love, and that's hard to shut off. And if you can't manage to turn it off, you wind up sending a message you don't intend. I suspect that that was the case with Will."

"Oh, so you're suddenly a big fan of his?"

"I wouldn't go that far, but I would say I'm immensely grateful for what he did for this family, and I understand why he did it."

"Maybe you should date him then."

"Ha ha," he says. "But truthfully, Arabella, his heart was in the right place, and what he did has definitely won me over—which is not an easy feat."

"And he lost me in the process," I say. "Also difficult to do."

I stare up at the screen, watching as we mug for the camera in our lean-to, my heart squeezing at those happy, carefree faces. How was that me? "At this point, it doesn't matter if he was worth it or not. I've pushed him away, and it's too late to go back."

"Yup, I suppose that's true," he says with a sigh. "Nothing you can do now. It's not like you could call, text, or email to ask him to meet you somewhere to talk."

"Not doing it," I say.

"Probably best not to—you'd have to apologize and be honest. Messy business, that."

"Exactly."

"Then, you'd have all that happiness to deal with, possibly for the rest of your life."

"Sounds horrid."

"Oh, it is," Arthur says. "Believe me. It can be a little much sometimes. I mean, there are literally moments when my heart is so full of love, it feels like it might burst. You don't want that."

"Definitely not."

"Excellent, then carry on."

"I fully intend to."

"Good show."

"Shut up."

29

The Lonest of the Lone Wolves...

Will

WELL, I guess that's it then. I told myself if she didn't call by the time we showed up to film the finale after-show, that I'd give up on her. And since Dwight and I just pulled up in front of the studio, it really is over. He parks the car, then takes the key out of the ignition, but instead of getting out, he leans back and looks at me. "You okay?"

"I will be once I get this over with." I stare out the window at the brick wall in front of us. There's a sign posted on it that says visitor. Although, it's referring to who can park their car here, it seems very appropriate for the moment, considering I was no more than a visitor in her life. Oh, wow, that was both pathetic and dramatic.

Dwight sighs. "I wish I could tell you that you didn't have to do this, but you do."

"I'll be fine, so long as I can get through taping without embarrassing myself by…." I stop myself before I say begging her to come back. Luckily, Dwight doesn't finish my sentence for me. At least, not out loud.

I tap my fist on my knee a few times, trying to distract myself from the tsunami of emotions I know is about to bear down on me. "Could you do me a favour, Dwight?"

"Anything for my favourite client."

"Oh darn, I thought you were going to say your favourite room-mate," I say with a slight grin.

"Not a chance," he says. "Now, what do you need?"

"Can you stay with me in the dressing room before the show? Last time they had us in a shared green-room, and since we haven't made it public yet that we're not together anymore, I'm pretty sure that's going to happen again."

"Sure thing," he says with a nod. "Let's go get 'em."

We open our doors, and before we get out, I say, "Hey, I'm sorry you had to deal with me while I was temporarily pathetic."

"That's all right," Dwight says. "It actually made me feel slightly better about my own foibles."

"Glad I could help," I say with a little chuckle. "You've been a good friend to me."

"It's been an honour," he says. "Not one that I want to repeat… but still."

We get out of the car and start toward the studio doors. I find myself moving slowly for reasons I don't care to analyze. It's got *nothing* to do with the fact that she hasn't called yet. Really, it's probably because I have to steel myself for the evening ahead. "How long do you think this whole thing will take?"

"About three hours. Maybe three and a half, I suppose, if you end up chatting backstage after, which I would definitely suggest since all the bigwigs are going to be here."

"Right, brilliant." Maybe she'll leave. She's good at that.

Three hours, then Arabella and I will be out of each other's lives forever. And after that, I can get back to lone-wolfing it. "The truth is, I'm better off without her."

"Absolutely," Dwight says, sounding utterly unconvincing.

I stuff my hands into the pockets of my jeans to shield them from the chilly fall air. It nips at my nose and makes me long for the warmth of home. "I think I'll head back to Paradise Bay when this is over. I can really focus on working out and preparing for the survivor challenge there."

"I'll see if I can make that happen for you, but I'm pretty sure Dylan has you booked up until almost the last day before you go to Greenland."

We reach the door, and I stop to tie my dress shoe, even though the laces aren't technically undone.

Come on, Belle. Just pick up the phone and call me.

Nope. Still nothing. "Yeah, I'm definitely better off without her, don't you think?"

"You already said that," Dwight says gently. He turns to me. "Go in there tonight with an open mind. You never know what could happen."

"As much as I'd like to have an open mind, I don't think my heart can take it." It was over when she left me at the beach house. "It's for the best. Really, it is. We're just too different."

He reaches for the door handle and gives it a tug, saying, "Then why haven't you taken the ring back yet?"

With that, he walks inside before I can say anything, leaving that thought hanging in the wind.

———

"We've got about twenty minutes until show time," the assistant director says as she leads us down the hall. Bellford stands just off to the side of the room we shared last time, and thankfully, he gives me a quick nod, then stares past me, his face expressionless. My heart lurches at the sight of him because it means she's really here.

"Your dressing room is fully stocked with beverages and hors d'oeuvres, but if you need anything else, just let me know. My name is Rainy. Pick up the phone, hit three, and you'll get me."

"Thank you, Rainy," I say, giving her a broad smile.

"Princess Arabella is already in there," she says. "But I suppose you already knew that."

"Right, of course I did."

My palms start to feel clammy as Rainy opens the door, and I glance over my shoulder to make sure Dwight is with me, only to see him going back the way we came in. He turns and gives me a thumbs-up. *That wanker.*

I walk in, expecting to see Arabella sitting at the makeup table or perhaps on the couch, but she's nowhere. The door closes behind me, and I realize I'm alone so I let out a long exhale, leaning with both hands on the back of an armchair. "Just get through this and whatever you do, *do not* try to get her to come back."

I hear a flushing sound and realize that she must be in the loo. Oh great, she probably heard me. If she did, it'll be considerably more difficult for me to pretend I'm not as pitiful as I am. A fuzzy memory of me calling her my sweet Belle on the phone creeps forward in my brain, causing my face and neck to feel flushed.

The door to the loo opens and Arabella starts to walk out, then stops in her tracks when she sees me. "Hello," she says softly.

"Hey," I say, sounding stiffer than I'd like. I'm supposed to be the happy-go-lucky, everything rolls off my back guy. "How've you been?"

"Really well, thank you," she says, tilting her head and using that tone she does when she's greeting someone new. Polite. Detached. Beautiful. "You?"

"Busy. Lots of promotional stuff going on every day... and I've been working out pretty hard for the survivor challenge show next month, so..." *So what? Finish your sentence, you tit!*

"I'm glad we're able to have a moment alone," she says.

My heart speeds up, but then she continues with, "I suppose we should decide how we're going to play this."

And my heart is crushed again. "Oh right, because we haven't made it public yet that we're both back on the market."

She stiffens slightly at the 'back on the market.' "Precisely."

"I think we should just be honest," I say, fidgeting with the button on my suit jacket. "Pretending never works out. You end up getting caught anyway because the truth has a way of getting out."

"Agreed," she says. "Although some secrets can be kept longer than others."

A tiny flicker of hope appears in my chest, and I search her face for meaning. It takes me a second to realize she's talking about her family's secret, not ours. "You're referring to the audio recordings."

"Yes," she says, her face filling with emotion. "I realized I never did properly thank you for what you did for my family, and that was wrong of me."

"Don't worry about it." *Don't worry about it? That's all you have to say? How about "Too little too late, Your Highness," or some other snippy thing that lets her know she hurt me.*

"I do worry about it. It was a big sacrifice you made, and I…think about it a lot."

And you're still in love with me and you want to get back together. Say that. "It's a great career move for me, honestly."

"Anyway, you're right. We should be honest if they ask us about our relationship status. We can give them the whole 'we've parted ways amicably and we wish each other well, but our lives are taking us in different directions at the moment.'"

"Sounds like utter bullshit, but I imagine it's the classy way to go, isn't it?" I ask with a slight grin.

She laughs, and for a second my whole world lights up, then her face grows serious again. "I realized I still have that sweater of yours that I borrowed."

I nod. "You mean when we went to that Yoda Guy exhibit in St. Maarten?"

She smiles and nods. "Remember that woman with the *I May Be Wrong but I Doubt It* shirt?"

"God, she hated me."

At the same time, we both say, "You're not meant to touch the swords!"

We laugh at the memory, and everything feels perfect for a second, followed by the most excruciating pain.

When the moment passes, Arabella clears her throat. "Anyway, I'll have someone return it to Dwight's…I mean, if you're still staying there?"

"At the moment, yes." I stare a little too long and feel my resolve slipping. Fucking Dwight ditching me like that. "Keep the sweater," I say, managing a grin. "If you don't, I'll feel like I have to return the yacht."

Arabella busts out laughing and shakes her head. "You owe me nothing."

There's a knock at the door and Dylan comes barging in, wearing a headset and carrying her iPad and a Monster Energy drink in one hand. "Here are my stars!"

She makes a beeline for Arabella and tries to go in for a one-armed hug, but gets cut off by a palm out.

"Don't even," Arabella says in a warning tone. "Not after what you tried to do to my family."

"I get it, believe me," Dylan says. "You're a fighter, and I threatened to hurt your family. *Of course* you would react like that. It makes nothing but sense for you to be upset with me."

"Precisely. Now, say what you came in here to say and get out because you and I are done."

"I wasn't going to stick around anyway," Dylan says. "There is just *so much* to do when you're running a production this big. You have no idea. Anyway, super excited about tonight, although now that I'm in here, I have to say, your energy is not what we're looking for." Dylan wrinkles up her nose. "I need happy faces. I need excitement. I need the two of you being proud of yourselves and proud of each other, and I need Will to be absolutely incredibly excited about the world's best challenge coming up." She sings that last part. "You really have to sell it, Will, because the network is spending a fortune on it."

Arabella and I exchange a look of irritation which Dylan seems to catch because she falters slightly, then says, "Anyhoo, I gotta get back out there. I just wanted to make sure my two stars were all lined up."

She pokes me on the chest with one finger and says, "Especially you. Because you are the biggest star in the night sky. And by that, I mean primetime."

With that, she rushes out the door, leaving a waft of strong fruity perfume lingering in the air.

"I thought you were going to punch her there for a minute," I say

"You know that's not my style," she says with a grin. "I'm more of a 'shove her in the face' type of girl."

Do not do it, idiot. Do not even think about saying it. She's the one that broke

up with you and not the other way around. She's the unreasonable ender of things, and your only job tonight is to protect what's left of your heart. "How are things at the UN?"

Arabella smiles. "Wonderful. Very challenging, lots of work, I love it."

And I still love you. "Did they go with your motto in the end?"

"Not as such," she says with a chuckle. Her cheeks redden a bit and oh wow do I ever want to kiss her. "They went with unstoppable, united, uplifting."

"Yours is better."

There's another knock on the door, and Rainy pops her head in. "Are you ready?"

Well, that's the question of the day, isn't it?

———

Okay, I made it through the introduction, and I've gotten the lay of the land here. And it's not good—Arabella and I will be sitting on stage on that stupid red loveseat from the game show while the finale plays. Oh, *and* there will be cameras on us the entire time, filming our reactions, so that's great, isn't it?

I kind of wish I had taken acting classes when Dwight suggested it because I don't know how I'm going to get through this, especially considering that there is a serious lack of boozy smoothies here.

Urgh. I'm sitting so close to her I can smell her perfume and feel the warmth of her arm next to mine, but I can't reach out and cover her soft hand with mine. I can't lean in and give her a gentle kiss on her temple or lean back and put my arm around her shoulders. Instead, I have to sit here with this stupid smile frozen on my face for the next hour and a half while I watch myself fall in love with the woman next to me who suddenly stopped loving me.

The theme song starts up, and the audience breaks into wild applause. I should be enjoying this moment. My career is finally taking off. But every second of this evening will be fake nails on a chalkboard.

———

Footage of her passed out in front of the tent, looking half dead, starts up. I hear myself pleading, *"Do not die, Arabella! You can't die."* And everything comes back to me—the knowledge that I am absolutely in love with her and the terror of losing her were all there in that moment.

"Wake up, okay?" I beg, my voice breaking. "Come on, Arabella! Wake up!" I shout.

Her eyes flutter and she whispers, "Don't be mad."

"Never. I could never be angry with you."

She gives me a weak smile, even though her eyes are still closed. "Thank you. I love you, Will. I did it for you."

"Did what, Belle? What did you do?"

Then a shot of the satellite phone smashed with a rock on top of it and my voice again. "No, no, no, no, no. Tell me you didn't."

"We can make it. I just need a bit more time." Her head lolls to the side and she passes out again.

The audience gasps, even though clearly she's fine because she's sitting right in front of them, and I'm forced to relive one of the scariest moments of my life—the fear of losing her. It's sort of ironic because she's not dead but I lost her anyway. I'm not even pretending to smile anymore. Fuck it. This is too hard. The camera man moves in for a closer shot, and I have the urge to swat him away, but I do nothing. I just sit here with one hand on each knee wishing this was already over.

———

Oh crap. We've just watched the big fight on the raft after Arabella ate the berries. I definitely come off sounding like a real arsehole in that one, but honestly, after spending an entire night trying to keep her alive while navigating our way down the river in the dark? I had a right to be angry.

Blech. Now we're at the river's edge in Wasapi, the town where I was going to take her to the hospital and call it quits. I'm telling her there's no way we can make it to the finish line, not with her in her weak condition.

She lifts her chin at me. "You're such a coward."

I bark out a nasty laugh. "I'm a coward?"

"Yes. Sorry to be the one to have to tell you this, but you are. You think you're so BEEPing brave out here doing manly things in the wild, but the truth is, you're just hiding from any real type of life and responsibility. You have set it up so you have the perfect excuse for never getting attached to anybody. You're a crap brother, you're a crap uncle, and you'd be a crap boyfriend."

Her words hit me hard as the reality of how I've spent the last few weeks of my life sets in. Maybe I have been running.

"Fine. You quit. Do what you want, but I'm not giving up." She stands, looking strong now as she steps off the raft.

The studio audience cheers, and I feel like a total schmuck.

Arabella holds her hand out to me and says. "Give me the BEEPing map. I'm going to go take a piss, then get back across this river and through that jungle to the finish line. If you want to go into town and cry in your beer, you be my guest. I don't give a BEEP what you do. But I'm going to prove that I can finish what I started."

"You cannot do this alone."

"Then I'll gladly die trying, because I refuse to be the reason that your friends lose their jobs or your brother loses his boat," she says. "And there's no way I'm going home with my tail tucked between my legs so everyone I know will say, 'Yup, we were right about her. She's so delicate she can't even eat some berries.'" Leaning in, she tries to look menacing. "So, either get your weak arse out of my face or be a man and come with me. I don't care what you choose, but you are giving me that map."

And cut to commercial. The audience breaks into applause with some scattered shouts of, "yeah, girl!" and "you told him!"

I glance over at Arabella and she gives me a sheepish grin, clearly not knowing that that was the moment I knew without a doubt that she was the one for me. I fight the urge to ask her if we can give this another try, but I do let myself lean in and whisper, "Tiny but fierce."

Her eyes soften and she glances at my lips for a second before a makeup artist swoops in to powder her forehead.

———

And now…the bit when I fall in the ravine and break my ankle like a complete moron. It's dark, so there is only audio, for which I'm glad because I know I was wincing a lot down there.

"What do I do, Will? You're the guy who knows how to get out of these situations. Tell me what to do and I'll do it. Do I go back for help? Or is there some way I can get you out of there? Just tell me and I'll do it."

"Just stay put. It's the safest choice," I answer. *"There's no possible way you can navigate your way out of here. Not at night, anyway. Cover yourself with a sleeping bag and try to get some sleep. At first light, you start walking."*

"I'm not leaving you here."

"You're going to have to. It's my only chance of making it out of here alive. Yours, too."

There's a long pause, then I speak again, sounding calm and quiet. "Arabella?"

"Yes?"

"I'm probably going to pass out, so if I do, I want you to promise you'll leave as soon as the sun comes up. Just go. Do everything I taught you so you can get out of here."

"No, I don't want to leave you. There must be a way to lift you out of there."

"There isn't. I can't walk and you can't carry me. You're already defying the odds to have made it this far after being so sick."

The scene cuts, then a new one starts up again. The sound of the birds tells me it's early morning in this part.

Arabella's panicky voice is heard. "Will?!"

"It's time. Get going, okay?" I say.

"Can't I—?"

"No. If there was a way, I'd have thought of it by now. But, there's still a chance that you can make it back and someone will find me in time."

"But—"

"You can do this, Belle. I know you can. Forget all that BEEP I said to you yesterday. I was just angry and hurt and … being a BEEP. I didn't mean any of it."

"I'm so sorry, Will. I didn't mean anything I said, either. Well, that's not entirely true because I do think you have commitment issues…"

The audience laughs, and I feel my entire head heating up with embarrassment.

When they quiet down again, I hear my voice. *"...It's about a five-hour hike from here straight east. Do you remember what I said about how to make sure you're not going in circles?"*

"Yes," she says, sniffling. *"Pick an object in the distance, keep my eyes on it, and when I reach it, pick a new one. And then keep turning back to make sure the last one is behind me."*

"That's right," I say. *"You've got this, Belle. I know you do."*

"I hope so."

"I know so. You can do this. Just think of everything you've done over the last nine days. You've rappelled from a helicopter into the jungle, swung from vines into a lagoon, free-climbed down steep cliffs, you've hiked for over ten hours straight at night. You made it this far. You'll make it out."

"Okay, I'll go, but you have to promise me you're going to survive until I get back with help."

"No problem," I say.

"Will, I'm going to go now. But before I do. I just wanted to say...thank you."

"Buy me a beer when we get to town."

"Okay," she answers, letting out a small chuckle. *"I'll be back for you before you know it."*

"Yes, you will. You can do this, Arabella."

"How are you so sure?" she asks.

"Because you've always been able to. You just needed a reason to try."

A resounding "awwww" is heard around the studio, and I glance down at Arabella's hand, very much wanting to reach for her. When I look up at her, she's staring at my hand too and I know deep down, she's not over me.

———

Bugger. They're playing my stupid sappy 'goodbye to everyone I love' recording. I knew it would happen, but honestly, it's just so awful to have to sit through this.

"...Arabella, if you see this, I didn't mean all those BEEP things that I said.

I lied to you when we were playing truth or dare. I do have a fear and you already know what it is. I'm afraid of letting anyone get close to me. I am a complete coward and I've done exactly what you said I did, which is to set my life up so I could sidestep love completely. When you were sick, I thought for sure I was going to lose you and the pain of it made me even more certain that I don't have what it takes to go the distance with anyone. I can't do it because you never know how long you've got with someone, and I can't be the one left behind. You were right. I'm too weak for that.

"But I want you to know these past days out here with you have been the greatest of my entire life. I have never felt anything close to what I feel for you, and if I had made it out of this alive, I would sweep you up into my arms and never let you go. For what it's worth, I love you, and I want you to go on and be the totally kickass version of yourself I watched come to life out here. Don't let anyone underestimate you. But if they do, you show them who you really are. You're fierce. You're brave. You are a warrior. Thank you for trying to save me. Please don't spend a moment feeling guilty for how things ended up, because there is nothing you could've done."

Arabella's voice is heard. "Well, that's a little insulting. You assumed I'd fail."

A cheer erupts, filling the room and making Arabella laugh. She looks adorably thrilled by their reaction. You know, for a total harpy.

———

I've almost made it now. We've been watching her drag me through the jungle and down the road, all set to inspirational classical music for about three minutes. Oh God, now we're at the part where I tell her the time already ran out. This is so hard to watch because all the feelings come rushing back and I'm overwhelmed with an incredible sense of pride and love for her. I can feel my heart breaking for her, just like it did that day, and I want to wrap her in my arms and tell her it's okay, even though it's in the past and the very last thing she wants is my arms around her.

I want to whisper that I'm proud of her. I want to whisper that I'm still in love with her. I feel a shift in the emotion between us. It's the closeness that we shared out in the Congo and the closeness we had until a few weeks ago, when everything felt possible and perfect. But what if it's all in my mind?

Almost there. It's the dramatic ending, where she pulls me over the last hill and the reporters and medical staff all start rushing toward us. It's pouring rain and she is a force to be reckoned with, while I am pretty much dead weight. She's yelling for an ambulance for me, and I feel a lump in my throat while I watch her. Forgetting everything that's happened in the last few weeks, I reach out and take her hand in mine and squeeze it. "Thank you," I say to her.

She smiles up at me and squeezes my hand back, tears filling her eyes.

But then I remember and pull my hand away, digging my nails into my palms to stop myself from telling her I still love her. Finally, the theme song starts up, and the audience bursts into applause, rising to their feet for a standing ovation. I stand and hold both hands out toward her for the audience to cheer for her. She bows and then does the same for me, as though we're just two actors who have wrapped up a Broadway play.

Okay, the worst is over—I hope. Now we just have to get through the after-show and I'll be fine. One more hour. Then, I get to spend the rest of my days trying to forget her. *Wunderbar.*

30

That's All Folks...

Arabella

"WELCOME to the *Princess in the Wild After-show*! I'm your host, Dylan Sinclair. Over the past five weeks, we've followed Will Banks, professional adventurer, nature enthusiast, and survival expert, as he first led, then was *rescued* by, Avonia's own Princess Arabella, Duchess of Bainbridge. We've seen them make their dangerous and often romantic journey through the jungles of Zamunda," Dylan stands in the aisle at the back of the theatre, the spotlight on her. "They've faced giant rats, bats, and amorous bonobos, but most of all, they faced each other."

She starts walking down the steps toward the stage, fanning out her hand, and I have to say I really hate this woman with a passion. "Two opposites from completely different worlds—completely different *sides* of the world, in fact—who had to learn to meet each other halfway. We've seen Will go from arrogant and condescending to patient teacher, and then finally, to patient in danger. We've seen Princess Arabella go from being a whiny, pampered debutant to becoming a true warrior who literally dragged her partner to safety to save his life." She pauses to let the audience soak in her dramatic opening.

"It's been an emotional journey. It's been funny. It's been heart-warming and it's been terrifying. But mostly, it's been damned exciting, am I right?" she asks.

The crowd enthusiastically applauds.

"I want to thank everyone who's been tuning in every Thursday night because each one of you has helped to set a record. We are happy to announce that this is the highest-rated show ABN has ever had." Dylan pauses for a round of applause. "Better than that, the *last three episodes* have been the highest rated programs in their slot in the following countries: England, Scotland, Ireland, Belgium, the Netherlands, Germany, Italy, France, Portugal, and of course, here in Avonia.

"Over the next hour, we are going to bring you viewer reactions as well as hear from Princess Arabella and Will themselves to find out what were their worst and best moments out there—although I think we can guess that one!"

The audience laughs and Dylan nods at them. "Oh, yeah, these two got busy, didn't they?"

Dear Lord, please make her stop. I really prefer to *not* have people talking about me getting busy, but then again, I suppose if I didn't want people talking about it, I bloody well shouldn't have done it. Truth be told, I could use a few minutes alone to splash some water on my face, cool down a bit, and get my emotions in check. I knew being around Will would be difficult, but I hadn't thought about what it would be like to be in such close proximity or just how excruciatingly intimate this entire evening would feel. Why does he have to be so bloody handsome and smell so intoxicatingly delicious? Why?

The combination has completely scrambled my brain, which is going to be a problem, because I'm about to be asked all sorts of questions that I'd rather not answer. And for some stupid reason, I don't really feel like telling the world that we're not together anymore. Somehow, letting them believe the lie that what they witnessed was true love seems kinder than letting them down.

"We've got a busy hour ahead of us," Dylan says. "So let's get started."

The screens light up again, and they show footage of me coming over the hill all sweaty and soaked from rain and covered in mud with my teeth bared like I was heading into battle. We hear one of the reporters, shouting, "They're here!" and me screaming for an ambulance. They freeze the video there (with my mouth open as wide as possible, obviously) and Dylan turns to me. "What were you thinking at that exact moment, Your Highness?"

I'd much rather tell you what I'm thinking at this exact moment. "Oh, so many things. Until we got to the top of that last hill, I wasn't sure if we would make it, to be honest. I was almost out of strength and was terrified that because of the bad decisions I had made, Will was going to die. It was just such an emotional thing to bring him over that hill and see the ambulances and all the people there waiting to help us. It was probably the greatest relief of my life."

"Lovely," Dylan says. "Now, some people have suggested that you were likely on some type of steroids or performance-enhancing drug to allow you to do what you did. Do you care to comment on that remark?"

Will clears his throat. "I don't think she should have to. That's obviously a cruel fabrication, and quite frankly an affront to women everywhere to suggest that she wouldn't have been able to step up and do what needed to be done in a life-and-death situation. It's insulting really," he says, then glances at me, his face blanching a little when he sees my deadpan expression. "Just like me speaking for her just now. Insulting."

I smile and say, "I've never used any performance-enhancing drugs, unless you count caffeine, which frankly I could've used that day."

The audience laughs again, and I feel a sense of pride for managing to say something witty for a change.

Dylan continues. "And Will, you have taken *a lot* of heat on social media for falling in that ravine in the first place, and for allowing yourself to be rescued by a princess. Have people been especially unkind about it to you in person, and if so, do you think it's because of who she is?"

"You know, in hindsight, I should've fought harder to stay in

Wasapi, which would've brought both of us to safety, instead of allowing ourselves to end up in such a perilous situation. That would've been the smart thing to do, so, I definitely deserve the criticism there. Also, I let my frustration overtake my logic, which is always a huge mistake. Had I not, I would've been a lot more careful and I wouldn't have fallen, thus putting Arabella in the situation she was in. Whether or not I'm taking extra heat because she's a princess, I guess some people find that funny, but I don't. Being a princess isn't who she is. It's the position she was born into, and those things are very different. People often underestimate her—I know I did. But Arabella is so many things—she's intelligent and thoughtful and fun, and when she has to be, she's absolutely as fierce and capable as anyone I've ever known."

The audience claps, and I do my best not to think about what he's just said about me. He almost sounded like he meant it—that he does really believe I'm strong. But we all know that's a pile of horse pucks. Right?

"Okay," Dylan says, walking to the front row. "We've got a question from your number one fan, Will, Hannah of the *Will's Wild Fangirls* website and blog."

Dylan holds the mic in front of Hannah's face while Hannah leans toward it. "This one is for Princess Arabella: Do you regret eating those berries because it seemed like a really stupid thing to do? Like, I never would have done that if I were with you, Will. You told her not to eat the berries without checking with you, but she did anyway, then she lied about it."

Can I go home now? "Thank you for your very blunt question. Or was that a comment?" I say with a chuckle.

The audience laughs as well, and I have to say it feels nice that I've won them over.

Hannah looks positively livid while she waits for me to give her a proper answer.

I offer her an easy smile. "Of course I regret it. It's one of the biggest regrets of my life because I could've died, but even worse than that, I put Will's life in peril, and there is nothing acceptable about that. I also caused us to miss the deadline and cost him and my charity a substantial payout, which still bugs me to this day."

Dylan moves the microphone back to her own mouth. "Would either of you be willing to do something like this again to see if you can redeem yourselves?"

Will says, "Absolutely," while I say, "We'd have to see what the challenge was."

"All right, after this commercial break, we'll be back with the huge announcement you've all been waiting for!" Dylan says. "We're also going to find out what's in store next for these two lovebirds. You won't want to miss that, so stay tuned."

The red light goes on and Dylan makes a beeline for backstage while Will and I remain rooted in our seats. The audience starts to chat amongst themselves.

"Thank God that's over," I mutter

"Agreed," Will says, tugging at his tie.

"What a horrific evening. The worst part is you're really the only person I can cry to about all of this, but I can't really do that, now can I?"

He pauses and stares at me for a second, his eyes filling with hope. "Do you need to cry? Are you upset?"

"I didn't mean *cry*. I meant complain. I'm fine. Honestly."

"Right. Sure. I know you probably don't care about my opinion, but you're doing great up here. The audience loves you."

"Not everyone," I mutter, glancing at Hannah, who is glaring at me while she talks to the person next to her.

Will snort laughs, and it's not a particularly attractive sound, but somehow it does me in because I remember how fun we are together. It's all I can do this whole time to remind myself that what we had only works when we're alone.

Dylan walks back out onto the stage, but this time she brings Veronica Platt with her. The lights come back on brightly, and Veronica glances over at us. "You two are doing great. Really great stuff."

Dylan turns to the camera and says, "Welcome back to the *Princess in The Wild After-show*! We've only got about ten minutes to wrap things up and to make our special announcement and it's such big news, we've brought out ABN's head news anchor, Veronica Platt!"

Veronica smiles and waves at the crowd while they applaud. "As you know, *Princess in the Wild* has been a massive hit, and because of that, ABN is launching a brand-new channel dedicated to both classic and new nature documentaries, adventure movies, and physical challenge reality TV shows!"

More applause, then she continues. "This is a wonderful opportunity for Avonians to participate for the first time in shows like *Survivor*, *The Amazing Race*, and *Avonian Ninja Warrior*."

The crowd explodes with excitement, even though likely no one in this room other than Will is ever going to be featured on that channel.

When they quiet down, Veronica says, "And I have another huge and more personal announcement which no one knows about, not even anyone over at the news desk. I will be leaving ABN News to become one of the executive producers at the Avonian Nature Network. As much as I've enjoyed my time as head anchor, I felt it was the right moment in my life to start a new chapter and challenge myself in interesting and exciting ways. Starting with…" she pauses dramatically, and on the screens the logo for *The World's Best Survivor Challenge* appears in bright yellow letters.

"We at ANN are thrilled to be bringing you a challenge show so harrowing, only a few people on the planet are considered capable of participating – it's called *The World's Best Survivor Challenge*. We start filming next month in a secret location which we'll reveal to you at the very end of this episode. Eight contestants from around the globe— each of them paired with one of the world's foremost experts in survival—will compete for a prize of one million dollars!"

More applause.

"And obviously our very own Will Banks is one of them."

I sit, wishing they'd let me go now since my bit is over. As happy as I am for Will, having just watched us fall in love on-screen, my heart can't take the thought of him competing with someone else. And I know *I'm* the one who ended it, and I stand by that decision, no matter how gut-wrenchingly awful it seems at the moment, but that doesn't mean I want to think about him falling in love with someone else. Not that he'll necessarily fall for his partner. It could be a man or a woman who he won't fancy at all, really. Or it might be the perfect woman for him, and I'll just have to wish I were mature enough to be happy for him if he finds love again soon.

"Now, I know what you're thinking," Veronica says. "You're wondering why I didn't say Princess Arabella's name since she clearly has proven herself to be capable. But I'm going leave that to her to explain."

Oh crap. Me again? "As much as I wish I were able to join in all of the excitement, I have recently taken on an important role as the Avonian ambassador to the United Nations Equal Everywhere Campaign. Therefore, I will be extremely busy with that work, fighting for equality of girls and women all over the globe."

Veronica looks around the audience and says, "I don't know, audience, what do you say? Are we disappointed?"

The audience doesn't seem to know what to do, so some of them clap, some shout "yes," and several boo.

Oh, how lovely.

"That's okay," she says, gesturing for them to calm down. "That's okay because I'm about to bring out the surprise competitor who is going to be joining as Will's partner. Even Will doesn't know who she is so he's going to find out at the same time as you! Let's meet her, shall we? Roll the clip."

No, let's not.

A video starts, featuring a young brunette woman running at a vault. She does some spectacular flippy thing and sticks the landing. The scene cuts to her now wearing an *American Ninja Warrior* tank top that quite frankly is rather tight and a pair of barely-there black booty shorts as she flings herself at an enormous swinging ball, Miley Cyrus-style, then leaps off it onto a moving suspension bridge. The voiceover starts up while we watch her do death-defying feat after death-defying feat. "Gymnast, three-time Parkour World Champion, stunt woman for Bree Larson in the *Captain Marvel* movies, Sports Illustrated swimsuit model, and certified life coach. Please welcome the beautiful, the strong, the brave Amanda Jenkins!"

The gorgeous brunette steps out onto the stage, dressed in a black minidress with spaghetti straps and heels I'd never get away with. She waves at the audience with not even the tiniest bit of a bingo wing flapping under either arm. She's so incredibly fit that her stomach isn't just flat, it's *concave*. Well, isn't this a kick in the box?

Will and I stand to greet her while she walks over with a huge grin on her beautiful face. She and I do air kisses and I tell her it's lovely to meet her, which is clearly is a big, fat lie.

Then she turns to Will and gives him a massive, boobsy hug and says, "Oh my God! It is amazing to meet you. I am such a fan. You have no idea."

"The pleasure is all mine," Will says. "I've been following your most impressive career. I can't believe you've accomplished so much at such a young age."

Has he? Has he really been following her career? Because if so, he sure as shit didn't mention it to me.

"I'm not that young, I'm twenty-six," she says with a giggle. "Anyway, we are going to have *the best time* in Greenland."

Veronica clears her throat. "Okay, you two will have loads of time to get to know each other over the next few weeks, but we are trying to film a live show. I'm going to need you to have a seat."

A stagehand brings out an extra chair, and I start toward the loveseat, but Amanda scoots in front of me and steals my spot. *Seriously?* I manage to maintain my smile as I go sit in the third-wheel chair. Not wheelchair, sorry. It's just a regular chair. I mean, *I'm* the third wheel sitting in this dumb chair. Whatever, this sucks.

Veronica is positively bursting with excitement as she addresses me. "Princess Arabella, are you jealous that Will is going to be competing with another woman—especially one so beautiful and talented—given how the two of you met and fell in love?"

"I'll be extremely jealous," I say with a phoney smile. "But only because I'll be missing all the fun."

"So, you trust him?"

I suppose now would be the perfect time for me to admit that we're not together anymore. But instead, I find myself saying, "There's no one on earth that I trust more."

———

I'm lingering here in the studio even though filming ended over twenty minutes ago and it's horribly awkward because I'm standing here alone, literally in the corner, while the network executives surround Will and Amanda. I feel too out of place to join the group and none of them seem keen to come over and hang out with the wallflower. There's really only one person I want to come talk to me and he's far too preoccupied. Also, I dumped him, so…

I just hang around pretending I'm very busy. I've already scrolled through my IG feed whilst keeping a very serious expression on my face (in the fashion of a model pretending to be a librarian). I've stared hard at a spot on the floor and rubbed at it with the bottom of my shoe as though I'm considering purchasing the network and my decision rests on whether or not that spot is permanent. I've also done the 'just looking through my handbag for my car keys' thing, even though I'm not fooling anyone because princesses who ride in limos don't actually have car keys.

What else did you lose in there, Arabella? Your dignity?

Yes. Yes, I did.

I look back up at the group. They're chatting and laughing like a bunch of smug lawyers celebrating a class action lawsuit victory. Blech. That Victor Petty just slapped Will on the back, and they're chuckling away like old buddies. *Don't fall for it, Will. None of these people care about you. They only care how much money you can make them.*

I should be happy for him, I know that. A good person would be, but somehow I don't have it in me. I should go. The humiliation grows exponentially by the minute. *Just turn and walk out, Arabella. There's nothing left for you here.*

Although if I give him a couple more minutes, maybe he'll walk over and I can talk to him for just another minute or two. I'm not quite ready for us to never have a reason to see each other again.

Oh God, this is it, isn't it? As soon as I walk out of this building, this is *actually* over. For real.

But isn't that what I wanted?

How can I be so confused? I've spent the last two weeks absolutely kind of sort of positive I'd made the right choice, but the second I saw him tonight, all those excellent reasons for breaking up vanished. It doesn't help that I had to spend ninety minutes sitting so close to him that I could smell his manly scent. Sigh. I suppose watching us go through what we did out there in the jungle didn't exactly make it easier—seeing myself at my toughest and happiest. Hearing us laugh and kiss and talk about everything and nothing. He believed in me out there. He did. It was written all over his face. If only he hadn't stopped. But maybe he didn't and I've gone and fucked up the best thing that ever happened to me?

Bellford approaches me. "Your Highness, if you'd like to leave, Norm says the crowd has dispersed outside and he's pulled up along the side door."

"Righto," I say, giving him a quick nod. "I think I'll stay for a few minutes in case they need anything else from me, like photo ops or some such."

Who am I kidding? Nobody is going to need me for photo ops.

"Very good, Miss," he says, then takes a few steps away and talks into his sleeve to give Norm the heads-up.

I should leave. I'm making a total arse of myself here. But if I stay, maybe we can talk and maybe that'll lead to us going for a drink and maybe that drink will lead to us kissing and that kiss will lead to us starting over. And maybe this time we'll get it right. I'll make things easier for him instead of harder, and we'll live happily ever after and we'll prove that a person really can have it all.

Oh, now wait just a bloody minute. Amazing Amanda is touching Will's arm and they only met like ten seconds ago. Oh, really, Amanda? If we were still a couple, I would *not* be happy about him spending however many days in the wilderness with the likes of her. She's clearly making a play for him, which, if you think about it, is a pretty shit move considering the fact that the world thinks we're still a couple.

Dylan comes over and stands next to me, holding out a can of Red Bull for me. "I thought you might be thirsty."

"No, thank you," I say, stiffening up.

"I wanted to apologize for what I tried to do to your family," she says in a rare moment of humanity. "When I get on a project, I'm like a dog with a bone. I don't know when to let up."

"Indeed."

"ABN hired me to make Will a star, and that's what I'm doing," she says, cracking open the can and taking a swig. "He's got what it takes to go all the way. Handsome, likeable, smart, and daring. He's the whole package. But you already know that."

"Yes, of course." I watch as Amanda says something that makes Will laugh. Oh, yes, I'm sure she's terribly clever on top of being a super-human, sporty bendy woman who flies through the air with the greatest of ease.

"They'll make a good team," she says. "They definitely don't have the delicious sexual tension that the two of you had, but with any luck, they'll win."

"I hope they do," I say. "He deserves a win."

"He does. He's a good man. Plus, people love the whole orphan-makes-good angle. Really plays well on the telly," Dylan says. "If you don't mind me saying, Your Highness, you two are incredible together. Right up there with Fred and Ginger or Tom and Rita." She smiles at me. "If you ever want to do another show together of any kind, just let me know. I have So. Many. Ideas for the two of you."

My answer must be written on my face because she says, "Probably not. Not with me, anyway."

"Quite right," I answer, then I can't help but feel a teensy bit bad. After all, she did apologize, and she also agreed to keep my family's secret.

"Anyway, thank you for being so supportive of what Will is trying to do with ANN," Dylan says. "There's a lot riding on his shoulders and it's easier for everyone that he has someone as understanding as you."

But he doesn't.

"I should get back to the gang," she says. "There are deals to be made."

"Yes, of course."

She starts to walk away, but I stop her. "Dylan."

When she turns, I smile. "Thank you for not airing the truth about my mum. I know it would have been an incredible coup for the network."

"It would have, and I'm not going to lie, it hurt like hell to give that one up. But the truth is, when Will begged me not to do it, I just couldn't go through with it. Call me a romantic, but to see a man like him willing to do anything for the woman he loves, well, it just got to me." She has a long gulp, then says, "And we're going to keep him so busy, he'll more than make up for us losing the big scoop. He'll be earning us money for years to come. Years. I'm going to make him the biggest thing since Air Jordans."

With that, she walks back over to the group, her words bouncing around in my head while I stare at him. He begged her. He was willing to do anything. And now, he's got the fate of an entire network resting on his broad shoulders. And I need to let him go do what he needs to do because if he has me to worry about, he won't, will he? He's finally on his way, and I can't let him give up his dream for me. Not again. Even if I did make the mistake of a lifetime and even if I'll never find happiness again. I must let him go.

I watch him for another few seconds, and finally, he glances at me. I smile at him and mouth, "Go for it," then turn and gesture to Bellford that it's time to leave. I force myself to walk out without turning back for one last look.

I mean, technically I can see him whenever I want since there are literally hundreds of videos and photos of him all over the bloody internet.

I shouldn't look, but I will.

31

Diamonds, Goose Down, and Busy Body Brothers

Will

One Month Later

"DID YOU START PACKING YET?" Harrison asks. I'm in my bedroom at Dwight's and I have him on speaker phone.

"Just started," I say, pulling my suitcase out of the closet.

"How have you been?" he asks. He's still got that irritating 'I'm worried about you since you lost the love of your life' tone happening and no matter what I say, he won't believe that I'm fine, which I am.

"Great. I'm really excited about the show—I've been working out hard and studying up on the terrain, as well as the flora and fauna of Greenland. I've got a great partner, so all in all, it seems like we're in a good position to take this thing."

"Good for you, Will. It's almost like everything's going your way these days."

"Yup," I say, dumping out the bags from my shopping spree earlier this afternoon onto my bed. I start ripping the tags off with my teeth, even though I know you're not meant to do that. "I've stocked up on thermal underwear and got myself a Canadian goose down coat. The only thing I wish is that we weren't filming in such a cold climate."

"Is that the *only* thing you wish?" he asks.

I roll my eyes. "Let me guess, inquiring minds want to know."

"Yeah, Emma and Rosy are both pissed that you aren't returning their calls."

"If they want me to return their calls, they're going to have to stop asking me about Arabella."

"I'll let them know. In the meantime, they've given me a list of questions for you since they knew you'd answer my call."

"Seriously?" I say, starting to roll my new wool socks into tight little balls and tossing them into my suitcase.

"Hey, dude, you really can't blame me. Unlike you, I can't ignore them due to proximity," Harrison says. "Now, I'm supposed to find out if you've heard from her at all."

"Nope. Not since she snuck out after the finale."

"Okay, so I imagine they'll have a follow-up question for that, which is whether you've tried to reach out to her."

"Tell them I haven't," I say, opening the top drawer of the dresser. "Let me guess—the next question is going to be why and the answer to that would be because it's over and that's that. The truth is, mate, she was right about us. We are too different, and we really don't want the same things in life."

"Too…different…same things in life," he says slowly.

"Are you taking notes?"

"Wouldn't you?"

"No, I'd tell them I couldn't reach you. Now, how's my little Clara Bear doing? Can I talk to her so she doesn't forget her uncle?"

"She's not here. It's Emma's day off, so she and Pierce took her to the zoo. I think he's trying to talk her into having a child so he's hoping heartwarming experiences with my daughter will do the trick."

"You should tell him that's not how babies are made."

Harrison laughs. "I'll be sure to do that. Now the next question is from Rosy: Did you finally take the ring back because if you didn't, by God, why haven't you done that yet? You paid a small fortune for that thing and she'd feel a lot better if you were to have spent that money on a down payment on a house on her street. I guess one just came on the market that she wants to show you."

Now it's my turn to laugh. "Really? What's the house like?"

"You're avoiding the question, Will, which leads me to believe you have *not*, in fact taken back that five-carat rock."

"I forgot. I've just been so busy preparing for the show."

"Freud would have something to say about that," Harrison says. "Actually, you wouldn't even need somebody with a psychiatry degree to have something to say about that. Your average house cat could probably figure out that you're still holding out hope."

"Well, your average house cat would be wrong because I've only had a month to prepare for the biggest challenge of my entire life and the possibility of winning a million freaking dollars, Harrison."

"You could buy a lot of rings with that."

"Not doing that again. Once is enough for this guy." Clearing my throat, I say, "Okay, I really have to run because my flight leaves in two hours, and I promised Dwight I'd wash and dry my sheets and towels and put the bed back together before I left."

"Okay, last question, then I'll let you go," he says. "Also, from Rosy: Who's this Amanda woman and is she interested in getting married and having babies with you?"

"Amanda is my partner on the show and nothing more. She has a great life back in the US that she'll be returning to as soon as this whole thing is over. She and I are currently, and will remain, strictly professional."

"Okay, she's going to want to press the issue a little," Harrison says. "And if I don't point out that you said the exact same thing about Arabella, I'll never hear the end of it."

"I was lying about Arabella. But with Amanda, it's true. She's a really nice person, but she's just not the one for me."

"Okay, follow-up to the follow-up," Harrison says with a sigh. "Is that because *Arabella* is the right one for you?"

Sighing, I say, "No, it's because there is absolutely no spark there whatsoever. She really feels more like a younger version of Emma to me. And also, if you refer to my earlier answer about never wanting to go down that road again, it will hopefully help resolve all curiosity on everybody's behalf." I take the ring box out of my drawer and open it, staring at it for a moment. Yup, still hurts. "Okay, I really gotta run. I'm going to try to come home as soon as we're done filming, but unfortunately, with the contract I'm under, it's not really up to me. If they need me to come back to Avonia first, then that's what I'll have to do. But make sure you give everybody there a hug from me and tell them all I miss them because I do."

"Okay, I'll pass the message on," Harrison says. "Stay safe out there, okay, little bro?"

"Will do."

"You better, because you won't have a princess with you to rescue your sorry arse."

"Just had to get that last shot in, eh?"

"Sorry, couldn't help it. But seriously, take care."

I finish packing, then pick up the last thing left on the bed—the ring box. Dammit. What do I do with that? It's not like I can bring it with me. I take it to the kitchen and write a note for Dwight, who is up in Didsbury visiting his mum right now.

Dear Dwight,

Thanks for letting me stay. It's been a blast. Sorry about eating all your ice cream and drinking all your bourbon. I need you to hang onto the ring for me since I ran out of time to take it back. You'll find it behind the ice cream carton in the freezer.

Catch you soon,
Your favourite roommate,
Will

32

Wherever You Are in Life, Pretend It's Exactly Where You Want to Be...

Arabella

ABN Evening News with Giles Bigly

"GOOD EVENING, I'm Giles Bigly, and welcome to ABN's Evening News. Our top story this Saturday, November fifteenth, comes to us from Valcourt Palace, where preparations for the Order of Avonia Gala are under way. The annual event takes place tonight at eight p.m., where seven new inductees will be granted the Order of Avonia. We'll go live there in just a bit, but first, over to former news anchor Veronica Platt, who has agreed to be our woman on the street tonight while we're looking for a replacement for yours truly. Veronica is joining us live from the Valcourt Airport where, in roughly one hour, she and the cast and crew of *The World's Best Survivor Challenge* will be boarding a flight to Greenland. Veronica, tell us what's going on."

Veronica stands in front of the sliding doors at the airport next to her suitcase, holding a microphone. "Oh, now I get it. That really *is* irritating when the anchor tells the entire story."

"Isn't it?" Giles asks with a bright smile.

"Quite. Anyway, it's going to be a crazy fun night for the cast and crew of *The World's Best Survivor Challenge*. We've chartered a flight to take everybody over, and we'll be filming as our competitors get to know each other. There should be lots of trash talk and jockeying to see who's the top dog. But I doubt anyone will be getting much sleep."

The camera pans to a group of people all talking excitedly at the gate. "As you can see, all the greats are here—Survivorman himself, Les Stroud, Bear Grylls, Laura Zerra and E.J. "Skullcrusher" Snyder from Discovery Channel's *Naked and Afraid*. We also have Mykel Hawke, Amanda Jenkins, and of course, ABN's own Will Banks, who is favoured to take the million-dollar prize along with Amanda."

"I don't know," Giles says, shaking his head. "I have to say, my money's on Les Stroud for this one. He grew up in Canada, and Will just doesn't have the experience to best him in a cold climate."

"Well, only time will tell, Giles," Veronica says. "But I, for one, am rooting for our homegrown hero."

"I'm sure you are," Giles answers. "Thanks for that fascinating bit of journalism, Veronica, and enjoy your stay in Greenland. I hope you packed your parka. I heard it's minus fifteen degrees Celsius there at the moment."

Veronica's smile morphs into a look of dread, complete with flared nostrils and dead eyes. "It'll be grand, I'm sure."

"Why wouldn't it be? Well, you have fun. I'll just be right here in this warm studio behind this solid desk. We'll be back after a word from our sponsors."

The feed cuts and a commercial for inflatable wizarding hats for cats starts up.

———

"Ugh, why did you let me watch that?" I ask Nikki, who is putting the finishing touches on my hair. We've opted for a rose-shaped braided bun with a few loose pieces to frame my face.

"You're the one that put it on," she says, her words muffled slightly by the bobby pin between her teeth. "But I'm not sorry we saw it. That's one Bear I'd hibernate with."

"Take it from me—the last thing you want is some outdoorsy survival guy. Sure, they seem all dangerous and exciting, but they're not exactly marriage material."

"Who said anything about marriage? I'd settle for a few months of caveman sex," she says, taking the straight section of hair near my cheek and rolling it up with the curling iron.

"Not worth it," I answer. "You'd end up getting too attached, and, if you're not careful, you'll end up with five kids to look after while he's off swinging from vines in the Amazon."

Nikki carefully pulls the iron out of my hair and checks to make sure it's got just enough bounce. "Who are you trying to convince? Me or you?"

"You, obviously," I say. "I already know this by heart."

"Done," she says, stepping back and smiling at me in the mirror.

I look at my reflection and see a very sophisticated, wildly unhappy princess. "It's beautiful. Thank you."

"Any time," Nikki says, starting to pack up her things. "Do you need any help with your dress, because if not, I thought I'd swing by Tessa and Arthur's and see if Xavier's still there."

Chuckling, I tell her I'm fine and to have fun.

But as soon as she leaves, that awful feeling overtakes me again— it's a blend of utter emptiness mixed with absolute restlessness that I'm filled with each evening. So typical—I'm fine during the day when my mind is busy with the Equal Everywhere Campaign. Anyway, I am happy with my life. Really, I am. Mostly when I'm around other people doing things that make me proud. But when I allow myself any time to think at all, I have to face the gaping hole where my heart should be.

I've tried everything, but nothing works. Actually, I've only tried two things. I did a PGX workout once (which was terribly painful). The rest of the time, I've gone with calling down to the kitchen for various night snacks—burgers, fries and milkshakes, pizza, chocolate torte, and the odd pecan tarts. Hmm...I could go for one of each right now, because I am absolutely miserable to be dressing up in an elegant gown to attend what could be a very romantic autumn ball with Gran as my date. I thought my days of dating my grandmother were over.

That came out wrong. Attending formal—oh, you know what I meant.

Anyway, thanks to stupid Giles Bigly, I'm now keenly aware that Will is about to board a plane on which at least half of the passengers will want to shag him. Not that it's any of my business. He's off to have another adventure and I'm off to do exactly what I've always done, even if the royal reins have been loosened and I'm starting to be known as someone with enough grit that, instead of people comparing me to my mother, they're comparing me to my feisty gran.

But the crap thing about getting exactly what you want is that if you let go of the person you want to share it with, it doesn't seem to matter that much. And I know logically I did the right thing for both of us by ending it with Will. He's now able to be free and follow his dreams, and I'm able to know without a doubt that I have the strength to stand up for myself and hear my own voice. Only that voice keeps telling me I missed out on my one chance for a life with the man I love, and that if only I hadn't acted so rashly and if I'd trusted my strength, I could have made it work. But it's too late because he's probably boarding the flight now and I'm about to squeeze into this gown (and I mean squeeze because the late-night junk food fests aren't nearly as good for the waistline as late-night shag fests), plaster a fake smile on my face, and pretend I'm happy.

Oh, whatever, you big baby. Get on with it.

I trudge over to my dressing room and go in search of my boring beige heels. No one will see them and the truth is, they're probably a lot more comfortable than some gorgeous four-inch Valentino Garavani pumps.

Ah, there they are, Old Beigeys, waiting for me on the shelf, like the faithful shoes they are. Nothing wild or scary about them. Just nice fitting and dependable, like the sort of man I should find. Maybe I should see if the Earl of Wemberly is coming. He may have gotten his breath fixed by now after he found out what I said about him on the telly.

Maybe not.

33

Would You Rather...

Will

"OKAY, PEOPLE!" Dylan calls. "It's time to board the party plane! Whoops, I mean the plane full of the world's best survivors."

The group starts to pick up their bags and file toward the ramp, excitedly chatting to each other. I should be more thrilled than I am. I just finished having a 'would you rather' conversation with E.J. Snyder and Les Stroud about which would be less appealing: being stranded in Antarctica with Paris Hilton or being dropped into a well filled with Arizona bark scorpions. Les went with the scorpions. He's not wrong.

I *am* happy, but not in the way I thought I'd be. There's this underlying sense of blah that I cannot shake, no matter how hard I work out or how fast I run.

I end up in line next to Veronica and Dylan. "Hi, Veronica, Dylan," I say with a polite smile.

"Hi," Veronica says.

Dylan leans in. "I was just saying to Veronica that if ever I'm going to be on a plane that crashes, *this* would be *the one* because it's *filled* with incredible people who can bring us all to safety."

"Sure, unless the plane explodes in the air," I say casually. "Then there's really not much anyone could do."

"Well, that was a little macabre," Dylan says, laughing and hitting me on the chest. "Are you the dark horse in the race?"

"I have no idea what that means," I say. Turning to Veronica, I smile. "Are you excited to be starting out on your new venture?"

"Oh my God, yes," she says. "If I were still on the news desk, I'd be covering that boring gala at the palace tonight. I bet you're not too sad to be missing that, are you?"

That's a loaded question. How do I answer that one? "Yeah, I'm not exactly a suit and tie kind of guy."

"Was Arabella upset that you aren't going with her?"

"Oh, you know her, she's such a trouper. Not one to complain." I suppose at some point, I should stop pretending we're still a couple, but to be honest, if people assume she and I are still together, it'll make this trip a whole lot easier. The last thing I need is any sort of romantic anything to mess things up. Clearly, I don't make good decisions when I'm in love.

"I heard through the grapevine that Arabella's going with her gran," Veronica says. "Those two are so sweet together, don't you think?"

"Very."

We step through the door of the plane and are greeted by the flight crew, who are all lined up, looking slightly wary of the excited energy boarding the aircraft.

"Okay, people!" Dylan yells. "You will see that we've placed pieces of paper with your names on the seats. You are not allowed to sit near your partner on the flight because we don't want you strategizing before we get there. Find your name and take your seat so we can get going!"

I scan for my name, hoping I'll be sitting with Mykel Hawke. He seems pretty cool. Actually, anyone but Dylan or Bear would be good. He and I haven't spoken yet, but he certainly gave me a look in the airport that showed he most definitely heard what I had said about his backpacks during the show. Awkward.

I feel a tap on my shoulder and turn to see Veronica is still with me. "Look, we're sitting together!" She points to our seats about halfway along the plane.

"Brilliant," I say. "Window or aisle for you?"

"I'm totally an aisle girl," she says. "I just love talking to people."

"Perfect because I'm a window guy."

We make our way to our row where I stow both our bags and take my seat.

Veronica sits next to me and leans in, lowering her voice. "I hope you don't mind me asking, but are things okay with you and Arabella? I have a source at the palace who said they haven't seen you there in weeks and that the princess has been absolutely miserable."

My body goes numb, but I fight to look totally happy. "Well, we've both been so busy, but things are absolutely fine. Just as they should be."

Narrowing her eyes, Veronica says, "You sure there isn't something going on? My source said she's been extremely quiet, totally distracted, and ordering giant amounts of desserts for herself every evening. It has all the hallmarks of a breakup."

Before I'm forced to answer, Veronica gets distracted by one of the producers, who needs her to go to the back of the plane and talk about some planning thing. I stare out the window, trying to absorb what I just heard. She's miserable. That shouldn't ignite a fiery hope in my belly, but it does. She's not over me, which works out well because I'm not even close to being over her.

I think about the promise I made to her that she would never be without a date again, and I can picture her now, getting ready, feeling like a complete loser, even though she'll be the most beautiful woman there. And there will be about a hundred eligible men all vying for her attention, now that they've seen how boring she's not. The thought makes my blood run cold.

Dylan comes down the aisle, shouting instructions with an open-mouthed grin.

She stops next to me and says, "Isn't this amazing?! Can you believe *I* put this together when only six months ago, I had never directed anything in my entire life? In fact, I had never even *worked* at a television network? I have to say, I'm quite pleased with myself."

How unusual for you. "Well done," I say, forcing a smile on my face.

She grins at me and points. "My money's on you, Will Banks, my protégé."

Then, she turns and starts yelling again, causing everyone within a three-metre radius to wince visibly. "Now, *do not* worry about getting up early tomorrow because the plan is to party it up tonight, get to know each other, and have the best time of our lives. The next two days are just to relax and recover for the competitors while the crew starts setting up. You can do some sightseeing or working out or whatever. Just make sure you forget about the cameras and have an epic time!"

Suddenly, the thought of staying on this plane for the next ten hours feels like it's going to suffocate me. I can't do this. I cannot leave things the way they are with Arabella, not when there's even the tiniest possibility she may still love me. Not when I'm so desperately in love with her. The truth is, I don't want any of this without her. Not fame, not the money, not the next sixty years on this planet. Nothing.

I need to get the hell off this plane. Now. But that would be career suicide, no?

My heart pounds in my chest, and I pull my mobile out of my pocket and dial Dwight's number.

Dwight picks up on the third ring. "Yes, I'll book you the next flight to Nuuk. It leaves in twenty-two hours, so you'll have to make up with her fast."

I laugh, feeling genuinely excited for the first time in over a month. "I was hoping you'd talk me out of getting off the plane."

Sighing, Dwight says, "That's what a good agent would do, but I'm afraid you're turning me into an exceptionally awful one."

"But a really amazing friend."

"Should I take the ring out of the freezer?"

I consider it, my heart beating like it does when I'm about to base jump off a cliff. "No, I think that would be a little presumptuous."

"Good point."

"This is the right call, isn't it?" I ask him.

"Only if you want to be happy," Dwight says.

"I do, but even more than that, I want her to be," I say, standing and opening the overhead bin. "Do you think I can make her happy?"

"Probably," he says, sounding slightly disgusted. "Women seem to like muscle-bound, daring men who are also really thoughtful and caring."

"Aww, thanks, Dwight."

"If you ever tell anyone I said that, I'll go public with that poem you wrote her."

My cheeks go instantly hot at the memory. "Duly noted."

"Okay, now get going. Your princess is on her way to a ball without her Prince Charming."

"I'm on it." I stand and get my bag, then quickly start toward the exit.

Dylan calls to me, "Will, what are you doing? Everyone needs to sit in their assigned seats."

I turn back. "I'm not changing seats. I'm getting off the plane. There's something I have to do that can't wait."

"No," she says in a stern tone. "You have to stay on the flight. Filming starts now."

"Sorry, Dylan. I'll be there in time for the actual competition, I promise."

"But I need to have footage of you on the plane with everybody else," she says, squeezing her way around some of the other people so she's now standing in front of me.

I put my hands on her shoulders and smile down at her. "You of all people can spin this into something amazing. I will see you in a couple of days." With that, I pivot and press on down the aisle as fast as I can.

34

Octogenarians Showing Too Much Cleavage...

Arabella

"WHICH ONE DO you think is sexier?" Gran asks, standing in her slip, holding up two dresses—one of them a sparkly black and the other a royal blue with a plunging neckline (which I'm not convinced is meant for an octogenarian, but I'm not going to tell her that). "The black is very sparkly. I quite love it."

"You just don't want to see me with the plunging neckline," Gran says. "But I'll have you know, my cleavage is quite youthful. At least, that's what the men say."

"Brilliant." I sit down on the tufted bench in her dressing room while she disappears behind the screen. "You're going with the blue one, aren't you?"

"But don't take it as an insult, dear," she says. "It's not your fault that you've gone back to being completely dull. Old habits are hard to break and all that."

"I have *not* gone back to being boring," I say, then glance down only to realize that my beige shoe is poking out from under my dress. I quickly tuck my feet under the bench to hide them. "I've just gotten very busy doing extremely important things."

"If it makes you feel better, just continue to tell yourself that." Gran appears from behind the screen, wearing the blue dress of course. Good God, that's a lot of old lady cleavage. She turns and points to her back. "Zip me up."

I stand and do as she asked, a sense of utter doom coming over me as I realize this is going to be it for me for the rest of my life—or even worse, only for the rest of hers.

She turns and stares at me for a second, then shakes her head in disgust. "Christ, you're miserable."

"I am not. I just have a lot on my mind, but I'm really quite happy."

"Whatever for?" she asks. "If I had your life, I would be utterly despondent."

"Thanks for that," I say.

"Ridiculous," she says, walking over to her wall of cubbies and selecting a gold clutch. "Here you are *in your prime* acting like an old lady—one without any imagination or adventure in her bones whatsoever."

"That's not true. You're the one that told me to hear my own voice, and my voice told me that I was better off on my own than with someone who was going to treat me like a child."

"That wasn't your voice. That was your fear talking," she says, "What I was hoping you'd get from my speech that day was that you need to listen to your heart, your gut, *and* your brain."

"Well, you could've bloody well said that," I snap. "I've gone and dumped my one shot at any type of excitement in this life because I thought I was meant to be doing the sensible thing."

"I never once said to be sensible," she says quickly. "In fact, I've been trying to tell you the exact opposite for years now, only you're too frightened to try."

"That's not true. Look at my speech at the UN. That was quite the departure from proper decorum, and it worked too," I say. "Because the new slogan is 'Unstoppable. United. Uplifting.'"

"I quite like that," Gran says with a nod of approval. She walks over to her dressing table, where a large velvet box waits for her. Opening it, she picks up a pearl and diamond necklace and holds it up to me. "Be a dear and help me get this on. My date will be here soon."

"Your date?" I ask.

"Yes. My heart surgeon retired, so he was free to ask me out finally."

"Dr. Clarke?"

"Yes, he's such a doll."

And he's likely twenty years younger than her. I sigh, feeling a surge of irritation welling up in my gut. "Well, you might have mentioned that. Now, I have to go by myself, which is *far* more embarrassing than going with you."

She wrinkles up her nose at me. "Is it?"

"Of course, it is," I snap. "People think it's sweet that we go together."

"That's only what they say to your face," she says, making a clicking sound with her teeth. "The truth is, you were always going to stand me up tonight because, in a few minutes, you're going to realize you've made the biggest mistake of your life and you're going to rush to the airport to try to catch your man before he takes off with all those fit women to Greenland."

"That's ridiculous," I scoff. "You really think that I'm so silly and jealous that I'm going to rush off and beg him to come back just because he might end up with someone else?"

"No," she says. "The silly and ridiculous part has been how you've been behaving over the last month. But you're about to pull your head out of your arse because generally that's what people do when the doomsday clock on your relationship is about to strike midnight."

"I'm not... there's just simply no way... It's too late."

Then why is my heart beating so fast right now?

"It will be if you don't hurry."

"He'll never take me back," I say. "Not after how I treated him."

"Of course he will," she says, plucking a tube of lipstick off her table and popping the lid off. "You're going to find him and tell him the truth, which is that you got very scared."

"I wasn't scared. I was furious."

"Liar," she says, smearing the red lipstick on her bottom lip. "You were terrified that if you stayed with him, you'd let him replace your brother as the person who calls the shots in your life. But the irony of it is that, by dumping him, you proved you'll be just fine with a strong man by your side. Although, because you're too stupid to have figured it out, it could very well be too late by now."

I sit back down on the bench, feeling my entire body grow slightly weak at the revelation. "Oh my God, you're right."

"Of course I am," she says.

"If you knew this, why would you keep it a secret? Don't you think this would have been information that would've been useful to me, say, a month ago?"

"I'm rather busy, I can't go around fixing everyone's love lives all the time," she says, standing and walking over to the mirror to double-check her lipstick. She smacks her lips together, then pops a finger in her mouth to wipe away the excess. "Besides, for once I thought I should leave you to it, so that you could figure something out on your own for once."

"Such a disappointment. I always gave you credit for being smarter than this." She walks over to me and pats me hard on the cheek while I close my eyes to avoid the view of her cleavage. "Now, you better get going. I'm hoping Dr. Clarke and I can have a few moments alone before we head down to the ball." She waggles her eyebrows at me and grins.

I start to wrinkle up my nose, but she says, "Don't be like that, dear. You'll be my age someday too, and, with any luck, you and William will be together to enjoy a quick shag before you head off to these dreadfully boring events."

"I'm not—"

"Yes, you are. Arthur has a car waiting out front for you, and he's asked Ben to drive you since he's really the best one at high speed car chases."

I sit, my entire body feeling numb as my mind races through everything she's just said. "Wait. Arthur?"

"Yes, total one-eighty when he found out what Will did for the family. He also may have felt bad because someone gave him a stern talking-to about interfering."

She means her.

I smile for a second, then my heart jumps to my throat at the thought of rushing to him. "But I broke it off with him. He's never going to take me back."

"You need to learn the difference between a little fight and a real reason to end things," Gran says. "What you and your young man had was called a fight. And, well done for standing your ground because that will do you well for the future, but poor show on breaking it off with him entirely and throwing the baby out with the bathwater."

"But he—"

"It was never really about him. And you know it."

"If he wanted me back, he would've tried by now, no?"

"Why should he? Because he's a man? How positively old-fashioned of you," she says. "You broke it. You fix it."

"Oh God," I say, feeling slightly nauseous. "I did break it. And if I don't fix it, I'll never be happy again, will I?"

"Nope, you won't."

I rise to my feet, feeling slightly wobbly.

She taps me in the middle of my abdomen. "This is your gut. Right here. Listen to it. What is it telling you to do right now?"

"To go," I say without thinking.

"Finally. That's the first thing you've gotten right since you came back from Vienna."

"Okay," I say, excitement and terror building in my chest. "I'll go!"

"You already said that."

I grin at her, feeling suddenly very much alive. "I'm going to rush to him and see if he's willing to give things another try."

"Yes, I know you are," she says, sounding completely irritated. "You don't have to keep saying it."

I start to hurry out of her dressing room, but then stop and turn back. "But what am I to say?"

"I don't have the first fucking clue," she says. "But you'll have exactly twelve minutes in the car to think of something."

35

Peggy the Five-Star Uber Driver

Will

"ARE YOU WILL?" the middle-aged woman in a two-door lime-green Prius asks me, pulling up to the sidewalk in front of the airport.

"I am. You're Peggy?" I ask, rushing around to the passenger side.

I open the door and am about to get in the front seat when she says, "Please get in the back. It's safer for both of us."

I pause for a moment, then flip the seat forward and do my best to fold myself into the cramped backseat. Once I'm in, I pull the seat in front of me back and start to settle myself in, only to have her say, "Are you able to reach the door handle from back there?"

Seriously? "Of course," I say, pressing myself up against the back of the front seat and straining as far as I can with my left hand. I grope around for a minute before I finally manage to get a hold of it and pull it shut.

"Nice to have someone with long arms for a change," she says. "You've no idea how exhausting it is to keep getting out of the car to shut the door. Now, before we embark on our journey together, I'd like to find out a little bit about your taste in music and preferred temperature settings."

Oh, bloody hell. "Any music is absolutely fine with me, and I don't really care about temperature. What I *do* care about is leaving right now."

"Yes, I did notice that your request for a pickup did list this as urgent, but there's always time for comfort, don't you think?"

"Not always," I say. "Sometimes you just have to rush. This, unfortunately is one of those times."

"No water for you, then?"

"No," I say, sounding impatient. I follow it up with, "Thank you, though."

"All right then, I'm just going to check my mirrors again and make sure you've got your seatbelt on," she says, turning back to me. "Very good. Now we can go."

She turns on the signal light, then shoulder checks and I do the same. Oh God, please tell me she's not waiting for that speck of a car coming in the distance.

Shit. She is.

Come on, come on, just pull out already, Peggy. You can do this.

"So, it says you want to go to Valcourt Palace. Isn't there a gala there tonight?" she asks, the signal light still ticking away while she doesn't pull out.

"Yes, there is, in fact."

"If you don't mind me saying, you don't look like you're dressed for a fancy ball."

I glance down at my outfit—white tee, army green puffy vest and navy track pants. "Well, it's a bit of a last-minute decision to go there."

"I see." She finally pulls out into the exit lane and slowly accelerates, glancing at me in the rearview mirror. "You look awfully familiar. Have I picked you up before?"

"No."

"Are you sure?"

"Absolutely positive. I'd remember you," I say, bouncing my leg with nervous energy.

Oh bollocks, she's driving ten clicks under the speed limit. I'm pretty sure I could walk faster than this. Well, obviously that's not true, but I am filled with regret for not getting in one of those yellow cabs parked out front.

"So, what brings you to the palace?"

I try to find a way to tell her I'd rather not talk about it, but instead, for some reason, I find myself launching into the entire story, telling her about the promise I made to Arabella about never going to a ball alone again, and how I'd inadvertently treated her like a child after going off with Kenneth Abernathy in search of fame and fortune. When I'm finished, I feel like a total arse and yet somehow slightly unburdened of my fears. "So, what do you think? Do you think she'll take me back?"

"She'd be a fool not to," Peggy says with a firm nod. "I'm sure as soon as she sees you, she'll change her mind and the two of you will live happily-ever-after." She pauses for a second, then yells, "Yes! I just knew if I started driving an Uber that I'd be part of something thrilling someday! You know what? Speed limits be damned. This is a time for breaking the rules!"

With that, she hits the pedal hard, causing the car to accelerate at a pace so slow, it's almost impossible to tell. She makes a whooping sound, then yells, "*Andiamo!* I've always wanted to say that."

I grin, glad that I told her everything because now that she's hit top speed, Peggy is weaving in and out of traffic like her life depends on it.

"Now, my only question is, how are we going to get past the front gates?"

"Oh, I hadn't thought of that," I say, my heart dropping into my stomach.

"I've got a few ideas for how to get us past the guards. Number one: I could put my coat under my shirt and pretend I'm about to have a baby. Men never know what to do in that situation, and they pretty much let you have whatever you want. Also, I'm a part-time doula, so I can do a pretty good imitation of a woman in advanced labour." With that, she starts breathing loudly and bending forward, screwing up her face as though she's in a great deal of pain. She stops suddenly and glances back at me with a grin. "Pretty good, right?"

"Brilliant, yes," I say, now wishing I had not told her anything. "But, perhaps we'll just keep it simple and see if I'm on the list."

"Oh, okay then," she says, looking disappointed. "But if you're not, we're totally going with the labour thing, yes?"

"By that time, they might be on to us."

"Righto…" she says, turning left onto the Langdon Bridge.

There's a long line-up of cars moving slowly down the road and it takes several minutes to get to the guard house. She rolls down the window and says in a very posh accent, "I have a Mr. William Banks here for Princess Arabella."

The guard bends down and gives me a dirty look.

I smile at him through the open window and give him a small wave. "Remember me?"

"Cheap cognac," he says. "I'll check and see if you're on tonight's list."

"I'm probably not, to be honest," I say, "But that's only because I was meant to be going out of the country tonight. But I do know Princess Arabella will want to—"

"You're on the list," he says. "But as the Princess Dowager's guest. Go on ahead."

My heart pounds in my chest and my hands feel clammy, so I wipe them on the front of my pants. They leave embarrassing wet streaks on the navy-blue nylon. Of course they do. That'll definitely add to the hiking boots and puffy vest look. As we near the palace, I see the cars ahead of us letting well-heeled couples out, one at a time, then pulling away while their passengers start up the tall stone steps dressed in gowns and tuxedos with tails.

"Well, this is quite the to-do," Peggy says. "You don't happen to have a suit in your bag, do you?"

"Unfortunately, no."

"Do you want me to stick around and wait for you in case things don't work out?" she asks as we pull up in front of the palace steps.

"No, thank you. I'll be just fine."

"Okay, suit yourself. But please make sure you leave me a five-star review and don't forget to mention that I did offer you water and your choice of music."

"Thanks, will do, but perhaps not at this exact moment," I say as I burst out of the car (which looks a lot more like a grown man struggling to climb out of a tiny green box), and take the steps two at a time, only to discover that sprinting in this situation is not the best idea I've had. Apparently, when one runs toward a palace, one finds himself surrounded by guards in short order.

"I'm on the list," I say as four of them descend upon me. "I'm a guest of the Princess Dowager. Will Banks."

"Oh, you," one of them says with a nod. "We haven't seen you around here for a while, have we?"

"Yes, well, I've been… actually it's really none of your business, is it?"

He shrugs, looking offended, then gestures for me to go inside.

I follow the crowd to the ballroom, and when I get there, I realize this is going to be much more difficult than I thought because it's packed with at least a thousand people. I stay close to the back wall and walk the width of the room, keeping my eyes peeled for her, trying to guess what she might be wearing.

Come on, Belle. Where are you?

I feel a tap on my upper arm, and I turn, my heart in my throat, hoping it's her. But no one is there.

"Down here," the Princess Dowager says.

God, she's tiny. "Your Highness," I say with a formal bow. "Thank you so much for putting me on your list. You don't happen to know where Arabella is, do you? I really need to see her."

She rolls her eyes at me. "She's probably at the airport by now. She went to find you."

My heart jumps with pure joy. "Really? She went to find me?"

"Christ, you young people are ridiculous, missing each other like this. There's this little device called a mobile phone, you know. You can place calls on it, or even send each other short written messages to indicate your whereabouts."

I laugh, then place both hands on her shoulders and give her a quick kiss on the cheek. "Thank you."

With that, I turn and hurry out of the ballroom, hoping I can somehow find a way to catch a cab from here.

A few moments later, I run down the steps of the palace—much easier, by the way—only to see Peggy's Prius almost at the gates in the lineup of vehicles. I break into a sprint, taking my phone out of my pocket and calling her number.

"Hello, Peggy here, Uber driver to the stars."

"Peggy, it's Will. Arabella's gone to the airport. Can you take me back there? I'm sprinting up behind you."

"Yes! I see you in my rearview mirror. Shall I pull off the road?"

"No! I'll catch up. You'll only have to stop for a second to let me in."

With that, I hang up so I can pump both arms and run as fast as possible, startling people in several of the cars as I go. When I get to Peggy's car, I open the door, even though she's moving very slowly along the road. She stops the car and I start to get in the front seat, only to have her say, "It's really so much safer for both of us if you get in the back."

Of course.

36

Rambling Airport Confessions and Second Chances

Arabella

WELL, that's that then. I'm too late. I got out of the limo just in time to see the plane lift into the night sky and disappear. You're probably wondering how I could possibly know which flight he was on? Easy—it said Greenland Air on the side.

Now, I'm sitting on a bench staring out at the dark runway with all its sad little blinking lights growing blurry through my tears. I blew it. He's on his way to start his new life and maybe even find someone else with whom to share it. And I'm left here to spend the rest of my days pining for a man who once loved me until I pushed him away.

I shiver, wishing I'd brought a stole, because I'm not quite ready to get back in the warm limo and go back to the life I don't want anymore, but I'm also freezing. I hear footsteps behind me, but I don't bother to turn around. It's probably Bellford carrying a jacket for me. I swallow hard, trying to force my face to suddenly look like I'm not crying.

"Is this seat taken?"

That's not Bellford's voice. My entire body reacts with a surge of joy. I look up and there he is.

"Will," I say, tears filling my eyes as I stand and turn to him. "I thought I was too late."

He stands on the opposite side of the bench, looking extra manly in his adventure man outfit. Smiling at me, he says, "I told them I'd meet them in a couple of days. I had something far more important to do here."

"I'm so sorry," I whisper. "I've been such an idiot."

He steps around the bench without taking his eyes off me. "Well then, we're perfect for each other, because I haven't exactly been a real Einstein when it comes to our relationship."

I chuckle and smile up at him while he wipes the tears off my cheeks. Taking a deep breath, I say, "I came back from Vienna all determined to chart my own course and to prove to myself I can be in charge of my own life, but then, for some stupid reason, I thought I had to do it alone, instead of trying to chart a course with the man I love. And I've spent these past weeks trying to convince myself I made the right decision, even though I knew I'd never be happy another day in my life, but then *that* thought seemed far too pathetic because I should be able to be happy without a man, shouldn't I? So I did nothing until tonight, when it hit me that you were about to leave and I would have given up the only person I'd ever want to spend my life with."

He opens his mouth to speak, but I hold up my hand. "No, please let me finish because we haven't gotten to the bit where I beg you to take me back. Except with some caveats, of course. Obviously, if this is going to work, I don't want you to keep things from me or make decisions for me. And if you do mess up from time to time, I have to stop dumping you. What happened at the beach house was really more of a fight-it-out, have-amazing-make-up-sex-and-move-on sort of thing, not a stomp-on-your-heart-break-it-off-forever thing."

I pause and get caught up staring into his beautiful brown eyes for a moment. Just the sight of him so close takes my breath away. "God, but you're gorgeous."

He grins down at me. "Belle, it's—"

"No, wait. I need to get this all out. I should have told you the truth weeks ago because the second I laid eyes on you at the studio for the finale, I knew I was never, ever, ever going to get over you. You were there looking so handsome and kind of sad even though you were pretending to be fine, and I should've just, I don't know, kissed you hard on the mouth or told you I was still in love with you and begged you to give me another chance or—"

He leans in and kisses me hard on the mouth while he pulls me to him and lifts me into the air.

Oh wow.

This is the most amazing starting-over kiss in the history of kisses. It's filled with passion and promises and complete abandon, even though, technically, we're in a public place. But it is an airport and airports tend to make people emotional.

After a few delicious moments, I pull back, feeling absolutely wild with lust. "Wow, I forgot how incredible that is."

"I didn't," he says, smiling at me. "But before we go too far and get ourselves arrested, here's what I think you need to know about me if we're going to start over. I'm going to make mistakes from time to time. That's inevitable because I've never built a life with anyone before. Once in a while, I might make a spur-of-the-moment decision and it won't be the best choice or I'll say the wrong thing, but I promise that I'm very good at learning from my mistakes. And if you don't want to go Megxit, that's okay. We'll make this work. Really, we will. And I won't let the money thing get in the way anymore because you're right. It's stupid to let something like having a bunch of money get in the way of happiness. Now, I *am* going to keep working because I love what I do, and I want you to keep doing meaningful work as well. But in between all of that, we'll be together. And I promise to always, *always* treat you like my partner in life. You're it for me, Belle. There's no one else I'm ever going to want. Just feisty, fierce, elegant, sexy, lovely you. Nothing is ever going to change that. Even if you change your mind and dump me again and never take me back, I'll still be loving you from afar. Or, if this works out, when we're old and wrinkly and sitting in a restaurant arguing over which entrée to split, it'll always be you for me."

My face screws up into an ugly cry and finally, when I feel like my heart is going to burst with happiness, I say, "God, you talk a lot. Can't we get back to snogging?"

He laughs and shakes his head, then leans in for a lingering kiss. "I'm in love with you, Arabella. And nothing will ever change that."

"Thank God, because I am so in love with you it makes me crazy and stupid and so happy." We kiss again, and I'm just about to suggest we get a hotel room for the night, when I remember the gala I'm meant to be at. "By any chance, would you be my date for this evening? It turns out my gran stood me up."

"I'd love nothing more," Will says, and I can tell by the look in his eyes, he means it.

"Then let's go."

We hold hands as we walk toward the parking lot where Bellford and Norm are waiting next to the limo. Oh, and apparently there's a woman standing next to a green Prius who seems to be waving at Will.

And for some reason, she has tears in her eyes. "I thought I'd wait around to see if you needed a ride," she says. "You know, if things didn't work out, but apparently they did because, wow, you two really made out *a lot* just now."

She glances at the limo. "Oh…you're good, then."

Will smiles at her. "Yes, thank you, Peggy. I'll make sure to give you a glowing review."

"Oh, that's not why I waited, but thank you," she says. She smiles at me. "He told me the whole story. He really loves you."

"I know. And I really love him."

"Good. Happy ending and all that." She nods, then says, "Oh, can I offer either of you a bottle of water for the road?"

37

If Cinderella Were a Super Buff, Crazy Hot Man...

Will

"So, is this as awful as you thought it would be?" Arabella asks as we hold each other. We're on the dance floor while the orchestra is playing Moonlight Serenade by Glenn Miller.

Oh, are you surprised I know that song? Well, don't be. I have pretty refined tastes for an adrenaline junkie. Just look at the woman I fell for…

"I can't remember a better night," I say, grinning down at her while we sway to the music.

"Even though you had to borrow a tux from my brother?"

"Even with that," I say, although this tux is a bit tight, to be honest. "The truth is, after spending so many nights without you, I honestly don't care where I am as long as you're there."

"Aww, you liar," she says.

I dip her, and she squeals with delight. When I lift her back up, I say, "I'm serious. My life has no meaning without you."

"You are *so* getting lucky tonight."

Pulling her close to me, I whisper into her ear, "I knew getting off that plane was a smart move."

She turns her face so our mouths line up and brushes her lips against mine. That turns into a kiss that is not exactly suitable for a gala.

I feel a tap on the shoulder and hear an "Ahem!"

I pull back quickly, only to see Arthur and Tessa dancing next to us. He's got a stern expression on his face, but his eyes are filled with amusement. "There are over five hundred bedrooms in this palace. Find one."

Arabella and I laugh while my face heats up with embarrassment.

She reaches out and pinches Arthur's cheek. "You better get used to it because Will is here to stay. Or, come and go as his career allows. Or we'll both be coming and going together. We haven't figured it all out yet, but one thing's sure, we're figuring it out together."

"Good for you," Tessa says, smiling at us.

"Yes, he is good for me," Arabella answers, grinning up at me.

"I'm just glad you finally realized it," I say, earning a mock-irritated look from Arabella.

"So am I," Arthur adds. "There are probably only a handful of men on this planet that might qualify to be good enough for my sister, but I'm glad she found you instead."

We all laugh, and Tessa slaps him on the arm. "What he meant to say is he's thrilled to welcome you to the family."

A wave of relief comes over me at her words. I want to pull her in for a massive hug, but instead, I say, "How did your photo go with those lesser British monarchs?"

She and Arthur exchange irritated looks, then she says, "The official photo released has the boys in front on tall stools and the two of us behind them so the only bits of me that are visible are my face, my shoulders, and one arm."

"Are you serious? After all that?" Arabella asks.

Tessa nods. "We drove straight to Krispy Kreme when we landed."

The four of us laugh, and I have to say, it feels amazing to share a moment like this.

Tessa points at me. "You're so lucky. You won't have to put up with that shit." She turns to Arabella and they both say, "Men," at the same time.

"Save it for man-bash Mondays," Arthur says. He glances back and forth between Arabella and me. "And you two, go find a room before you embarrass the family with all that awful PDA."

I look into Arabella's eyes. "Shall we?"

"Oh yes, we shall."

I dance her toward the doors to the terrace that have been opened to let the cool air in. Before we can get out, King Winston stops us with a very serious expression on his face. "I see you two are back together."

My heart pounds, and I'm filled with a sense of dread as I let go of Arabella and turn to face him.

He lets his face relax into a grin and holds out his hand. "Good show. You're clearly a man of integrity and solid character, William—something you more than proved in how you handled that nasty business with the show."

"Thank you, sir," I say, shaking his hand. "I want you to know, I'd do anything for Arabella."

"Thank *you*," he says with a small bow. "You saved us from a great deal of unnecessary grief. The circle of people we can trust is a small one, but I'm glad to know my daughter has picked someone who can be in that group."

"Great chat, Dad, but Will and I were just leaving," Arabella says. "Will has to be on a plane in about twenty hours, so…"

He narrows his eyes, clearly knowing why we're sneaking out early. Giving me a steely look, he says, "Just make sure you come back. Arabella is absolutely miserable without you."

I chuckle. "I promise."

Arabella tugs my arm, and we step outside together into the chilly night air. "Is this the way to your place?"

Arabella laughs. "Not really, but let's take the scenic route anyway."

Snow softly falls as we hold hands, and she leads me in the general direction of her apartment.

Soon the sound of the music fades, and the clicking of her heels on the stones fills the silence. She shivers a little, and I take off my jacket and put it on her shoulders. "Are you sure you wouldn't be more comfortable walking through the palace rather than around it?" I ask.

She stops and looks up at me. "I'm done with comfortable. From now on, I want to take the more adventurous path."

"Then that's what we'll do."

38

The Part Where the Guy Takes the Princess's (Morning) Breath Away...

Arabella

I WAKE WITH A SMILE, even though I haven't exactly spent much of the night sleeping (wink, wink). The sun is up, and I turn to face Will, only to find his side of the bed empty. Huh, that's not what I was hoping for, but I'm sure it's fine. He's probably in the loo.

I sit up in bed, trying to fix my hair with my hands, hoping I'll look sort of sexy and dishevelled, but then I notice the door to my en suite is open. And as much as I love this man, we are not going to be one of those super-relaxed, open couples who do everything together. I'm just not built that way.

"Will?" I call, but he doesn't answer. His flight doesn't leave until six this evening, and there's no way I slept *that long*. Nope, it's only eleven.

A second later, I hear the main door to my apartment open, and I hear him humming. A wave of relief washes over me as he strolls through the door with a paper bag from a bakery in town in one hand and a tray holding two coffees in his other one. "Good morning, sleepy head."

I grin at him as I watch him cross the room. "Good morning to you."

"Did you know there is the greatest Viennese bakery one block from Dwight's place?"

"I did not."

"It's true" he says, setting the bag down on my lap and taking off his puffy vest. "They have these delicious little crepes filled with apricot jelly."

"Palatschinkens?" I ask, suddenly very excited.

"I have it on good authority that you've been known to enjoy a good palatschinken from time to time."

"Gran told you that?"

"I ran into her on my way out this morning. She was just getting in," he says with wide eyes. "What would you say to breakfast in bed?"

"I'd say a resounding yes."

He leans in for a kiss, but I block him with one hand over my mouth. "Morning breath. I'll be right back."

Hurrying across the room in my bare feet, I close the door and quickly brush and rinse with mouthwash whilst running a comb through my hair, even though it's useless because it's stiff with hairspray and completely knotted up from all the sex. Whatever. He's seen me look much worse.

When I walk out, he's got our breakfast set out in their cartons. Mine is on a tray, and next to the pancakes, is the small black velvet box I should have opened the first time. Honestly, it's been killing me, wondering what the ring looked like. If it is a ring, that is. Maybe I misread that. Maybe it's a key to Dwight's place.

My heart pounds, stirring all sorts of huge, fabulous emotions in my chest as I walk across the room to him. I point to the box, and he nods.

"Since the cheesecake didn't work. I figured maybe Viennese pancakes would do the trick. But is it too quick?" he asks, looking concerned. "Should I put it back and try again in a few months?"

"No!" I shout, then I cover my mouth with both hands and laugh at myself. "I mean, now is just fine."

He picks up the box and stands, then gets down on one knee in front of me. He tilts his head and smiles at me, his face filled with love and hope and just a hint of fear. My muscles tingle with excitement, and I'm ready to say yes, but I wait, knowing he needs to do this his way. He takes my left hand in his and grips it gently.

"I thought I had it all before I met you, but I couldn't have been more wrong. You're everything I didn't know I needed. I love you with my whole heart, and not just because you're beautiful inside and out. I love you for your generous spirit and your kindness and the way your heart breaks when you hear about anyone anywhere on the planet having a rough go. I love how fun you are and how serious you can be. I love it when you get that determined look on your face, and I know you're going to manage to do whatever it is you're setting your mind to. I love the way you laugh and the way you smile and the way you speak. And…well, I could go on all day, but our breakfast'll get cold."

"We can't have that," I say, grinning through my tears. I take a deep breath, then kneel down so we're both on our knees. "I thought it only right that I meet you halfway," I whisper.

"That's because of your giant sense of justice," he says, and we both laugh.

"It's a big draw, isn't it? Men can never seem to resist my sense of justice."

Chuckling, he gives me another kiss, then tucks a lock of my wild hair behind my ear. "Well, they're going to have to because I intend to keep you to myself forever."

"Promise?"

"I do."

"Then so do I," I say, reaching for his face and holding it in both hands. "Yes, I will marry you."

I lean forward, letting our lips touch, then I stop. "That is what you were about to ask me, yes?"

"Yes, I was." He gives me a long kiss.

I pull back a little and say, "You were trying to think of my entire name, but you couldn't remember it all, could you?"

"Maybe," he says. "But I promise I'll memorize all twelve middle names before the wedding."

"It's only eight."

"Let's make it nine."

"You mean add Banks to the end?" I ask.

"If you want," he says with a shrug. "Totally your call. It's your name."

Grinning at him, I say, "I think I'd like that, but first, can I see the ring?"

"Oh that," he says, pretending he forgot about it. "Sure."

He lets go of me and opens the box. I let out a real gasp because that is one absolutely incredible, knicker-melting rock. Tears fill my eyes and when I look back up at Will, I can see his eyes are glistening too. "Will you marry me?"

"Yes," I whisper as he slides the ring on my finger and tosses the box over his shoulder.

I sob out happy tears, and we kiss some more.

Oh, and now he's pulling me onto the floor with him and I'm pretty sure our pancakes are going to get cold…

Epilogue - A.K.A. The Part When the Guy Returns After Freezing His Junk Off in Greenland for a Month...

Arabella

One Month Later

"THERE HE IS!" I shout at Bellford, who is standing close enough to me that I really needn't shout. But can you blame me? The love of my life just walked through the arrivals section of the airport, where I've been waiting for what feels like forever while Christmas tunes play over the speaker. I got here stupidly early just in case the plane landed ahead of schedule.

Will is walking next to Amanda, who notices me first. A pang of jealousy hits, but then she punches him on the arm the way I would to Arthur. She points at me and grins. Huh, I think I'm actually going to like her.

Fuck it. It's not at all regal, but I'm running. He drops his bag and rushes toward me with his arms out, and when we meet up, he lifts me in the air and spins me around while I crush his mouth with mine.

"God, I missed you," he says, squeezing me tight, then letting me slide down his body until my boots touch the floor.

"I missed you too," I answer. "*So* much."

I notice someone standing next to us, and when I look over, I see Amanda, who is carrying Will's bag as well as her own. I let go of Will and hold out my hand. "Arabella. Lovely to see you again."

"You too," she says with a grin. "I feel like I know you, on account of this guy talking about you non-stop for the last thirty days."

I chuckle, feeling more thrilled about that than I probably should. Dropping my voice, I look back and forth between them. "So, I know you're not allowed to say anything before the show airs, but you can tell me. You won, didn't you?"

They grin at each other, and I scream, then cover my mouth.

Will gives me a wide-eyed look. "We're not allowed to talk about it."

"Of course not," I say, doing my best to look very serious. "I shouldn't have asked. But you did, didn't you? Just the slightest nod. Or…wink once. You can't make me wait, Will. Honestly, I really must know."

"Sorry, rules are rules," he says with a shrug.

My shoulders drop, and I say, "Seriously? You're not going to tell me?"

Amanda and Will are doing their best to hide their smiles, then she winks at me.

"You did!" I whisper-yell and do a quick fist pump, then quickly recover. "Sorry, that wasn't at all discreet." I link arms with the two of them and start walking them to the front doors.

Bellford gives me a 'did they win?' look.

I wink at him. A slow smile spreads across his face as he leads us out.

"Come on, you two," I say as Norm opens the door. "Let's go celebrate your…" I look around, then say, "*return*," in a loud voice.

Will laughs at me. "Good thing you're not with the secret service."

"For the best, really," I answer.

Once we're all tucked in the back of the limo, they high five each other and start telling me all about their victory, both of them talking over each other. I listen and laugh with them, sharing in their happiness, knowing that this is how it's going to be with Will and me. Sometimes we'll be apart, but no matter how far, we'll always be together in our hearts. And I know that's sappy, but it's true. Because it takes a woman who is totally secure with who she is to love a man like Will Banks. And I am that woman. I'm Arabella—Princess of Avonia, Duchess of Bainbridge, UN Ambassador, and soon to be Mrs. Banks. And I've found exactly the right man who can handle a woman who wants to be all of those things. And together, we're going to have it all...

The End

Coming Soon

JUNE 2021, THE ADVENTURE CONTINUES...

Royally Tied
A Crazy Royal Love Romantic Comedy, Book 3

Don't miss the heartwarming, laugh-out-loud conclusion of the Crazy Royal Love Romantic Comedy Trilogy ...

After a whirlwind romance that has taken them all over the globe, rugged survival expert Will Banks and Princess Arabella of Avonia are getting ready to take a trip down the aisle.

Planning the perfect wedding isn't easy at the best of times, so when you include two families who couldn't be more different, tensions are bound to run high. The last thing they need is a surprise guest with a shocking secret that will rock the royals to their diamond-encrusted cores.

With one hilarious disaster after another ruining their plans, Will and Arabella must figure out how to pull it all together in time to say 'I do.'

Brimming with swoon-worthy romance, seriously funny shenanigans, and an unforgettable cast of characters, Melanie Summers is sure to make you laugh out loud and believe in love.

Afterword

A NOTE FROM MELANIE

I hope you enjoyed the beginning of Will and Arabella's adventures. I hope you laughed out loud, and the story left you feeling good. If so, please leave a review.

Reviews are a true gift to writers. They are the best way for other readers to find our work and for writers to figure out if we're on the right track, so thank you if you are one of those kind folks out there to take time out of your day to leave a review!

If you'd like to find out about my upcoming releases, sign up for my newsletter on www.melaniesummersbooks.com.

All the very best to you and yours,
Melanie

About the Author

Melanie Summers lives in Edmonton, Canada, with her husband, three kiddos, and two cuddly dogs. When she's not writing, she loves reading (obviously), snuggling up on the couch with her family for movie night (which would not be complete without lots of popcorn and milkshakes), and long walks in the woods near her house. Melanie also spends a lot more time thinking about doing yoga than actually doing yoga, which is why most of her photos are taken 'from above'. She also loves shutting down restaurants with her girlfriends. Well, not literally shutting them down, like calling the health inspector or something. More like just staying until they turn the lights off.

She's written fourteen novels (and counting), and has won one silver and two bronze medals in the Reader's Favourite Awards.

If you'd like to find out about her upcoming releases, sign up for her newsletter on www.melaniesummersbooks.com.